THE TAN

ALSO BY ROBERT WALSER
FROM NEW DIRECTIONS

The Assistant
A Little Ramble
Microscripts
Thirty Poems
The Walk

ROBERT WALSER

The Tanners

Translated from the German by Susan Bernofsky
With an introduction by W. G. Sebald
(translated by Jo Catling)

A NEW DIRECTIONS BOOK

New Directions would like to thank Jo Catling, Scott Moyers of the Andrew Wylie Agency,
and Deborah Foley of Random House for helping with the publication of W. G. Sebald's
essay, "Le Promeneur Solitaire."

Translator's note for "Le Promeneur Solitaire": All translations of Walser are taken where
possible from the published translations by Susan Bernofsky and Christopher Middleton of
his works. I should like to thank Susan Bernofsky, Curdin Ebneter, Barbara Epler, Dr. Richard
Hibbitt, Dr. Brigid Purcell, Ada Vigliani and Anthony Vivis for their assistance and advice.

New Directions gratefully acknowledges the support of Pro Helvetia, Swiss Arts Council.

swiss arts council

prohelvetia

Manufactured in the United States of America
New Directions Books are printed on acid-free paper.
First published as a New Directions clothbound in 2009
Published simultaneously in Canada by Penguin Books Canada Limited

Library of Congress Cataloging-in-Publication Data
Walser, Robert, 1878–1956.
  [Geschwister Tanner. English]
  The Tanners / Robert Walser ; translated from the German by Susan Bernofsky ; with an
introduction by W. G. Sebald (translated by Jo Catling).
    p. cm.
  ISBN 978-0-8112-1589-3 (alk. paper)
  I. Bernofsky, Susan. II. Title.
  PT2647.A64G513 2009
  833'.912—dc22   2009020788

10 9 8 7 6 5 4 3

New Directions Books are published for James Laughlin
by New Directions Publishing Corporation,
80 Eighth Avenue, New York 10011

Contents

THE TANNERS

LE PROMENEUR SOLITAIRE
A Remembrance of Robert Walser
by W. G. Sebald

THE TRACES ROBERT WALSER LEFT on his path through life were so faint as to have been almost effaced altogether. Later, after his return to Switzerland in the spring of 1913, but in truth from the very beginning, he was only ever connected with the world in the most fleeting of ways. Nowhere was he able to settle, never did he acquire the least thing by way of possessions. He had neither a house, nor any fixed abode, nor a single piece of furniture, and as far as clothes are concerned, at most one good suit and one less so. Even among the tools a writer needs to carry out his craft were almost none he could call his own. He did not, I believe, even own the books that he had written. What he read was for the most part borrowed. Even the paper he used for writing was secondhand. And just as throughout his life he was almost entirely devoid of material possessions, so too was he remote from other people. He became more and more distant from even the siblings originally closest to him—the painter Karl and the beautiful schoolteacher Lisa—until in the end, as Martin Walser said of him, he was the most unattached of all solitary poets. For him, evidently, coming to an arrangement with a woman was an impossibility. The chambermaids in the Hotel zum Blauen Kreuz, whom he used to watch through a peephole he had bored in the wall of his attic lodgings; the serving girls in Berne; Fräulein Resy Breitbach in the Rhineland, with whom he maintained a lengthy correspondence—all of them were, like the ladies he reveres so longingly in his literary fantasias, beings from a distant star. At a time when large families were still the norm—Walser's father Adolf came from a family of fifteen—strangely enough none of the eight siblings in the next generation brought a child into the world; and of all this last generation of Walsers, dying out together, as it were, none was perhaps less suited to fulfil the prerequisites for successful procreation than Robert, who, as one may say in his case with some fittingness, retained his virginal innocence all his life. The death of Robert Walser, who, inevitably rendered even more anonymous after the long years in an institution, was in the end connected to almost nothing and nobody, might easily have passed as unnoticed as, for a long time, had his life. That Walser is not today among the forgotten writers we owe primarily to the fact that Carl Seelig took up his cause. Without Seelig's accounts of the walks he took with Walser, without his preliminary work on the biography, without the selections from the work he published and the lengths he went to in securing the *Nachlass*, the writer's millions of illegible ciphers, Walser's rehabilitation could never have taken place, and his memory would in all probability have faded into oblivion. Nonetheless, the fame which has accrued around

Walser since his posthumous redemption cannot be compared with that of, say, Benjamin or Kafka. Now as then Walser remains a singular, enigmatic figure. He refused by and large to reveal himself to his readers. According to Elias Canetti, what set Walser apart from other writers was the way that in his writing he always denied his innermost anxieties, constantly omitting a part of himself. This absence, so Canetti claimed, was the source of his unique strangeness. It is odd, too, how sparsely furnished with detail is what we know of the story of his life. We know that his childhood was overshadowed by his mother's melancholia and by the decline of his father's business year after year; that he wanted to train as an actor; that he did not last long in any of his positions as a clerk; and that he spent the years from 1905 to 1913 in Berlin. But what he may have been doing there apart from writing—which at the time came easily to him—about that we have no idea at all. So little does he tell us about the German metropolis, so little, later, of the *Seeland* around Biel and his years there, and his circumstances in Berne, that one might almost speak of a chronic poverty of experience. External events, such as the outbreak of the First World War, appear to affect him hardly at all. The only certain thing is that he writes incessantly, with an ever increasing degree of effort; even when the demand for his pieces slows down, he writes on, day after day, right up to the pain threshold and often, so I imagine, a fair way beyond it. When he can no longer go on we see him in the Waldau clinic, doing a bit of work in the garden or playing a game of billiards against himself, and finally we see him in the asylum in Herisau, scrubbing vegetables in the kitchen, sorting scraps of tinfoil, reading a novel by

Friedrich Gerstäcker or Jules Verne and sometimes, as Robert Mächler relates, just standing stiffly in a corner. So far apart are the scenes of Walser's life which have come down to us that one cannot really speak of a story or of a biography at all, but rather, or so it seems to me, of a legend. The precariousness of Walser's existence — persisting even after his death — the emptiness blowing through every part of it, lends it an air of spectral insubstantiality which may deter the professional critics just as much as the indefinability of the texts. No doubt Martin Walser is correct in remarking that Robert Walser — despite the fact that his work seems positively to invite dissertation — always eludes any kind of systematic treatment. How is one to understand an author who was so beset by shadows and who, nonetheless, illumined every page with the most genial light, an author who created humorous sketches from pure despair, who almost always wrote the same thing and yet never repeated himself, to whom his own thoughts, honed on the tiniest details, became incomprehensible, who had his feet firmly on the ground yet was always getting lost in the clouds, whose prose has the tendency to dissolve upon reading, so that only a few hours later one can barely remember the ephemeral figures, events and things of which it spoke. Was it a lady called Wanda or a wandering apprentice, Fräulein Elsa or Fräulein Edith, a steward, a servant or Dostoyevsky's *Idiot*, a conflagration in the theatre or an ovation, the Battle of Sempach, a slap in the face or the return of the Prodigal, a stone urn, a suitcase, a pocket watch or a pebble? Everything written in these incomparable books has — as their author might himself have said —

4

a tendency to vanish into thin air. The very passage which a moment before seemed so significant can suddenly appear quite unremarkable. Conversely, Walser's *sottises* often conceal the profoundest depths of meaning. Despite such difficulties, however, which seem designed to foil the plans of anyone intent on categorization, much has been written about Robert Walser. Most of it, admittedly, is of a rather impressionistic or marginal nature, or can be regarded as an act of *hommage* on the part of his admirers. Nor are the remarks which follow any exception, for since my first encounter with Walser, I too have only ever been able to read him in an unsystematic fashion. Beginning now here and now there, for years I have been roaming around, now in the novels, now in the realms of the *Bleistiftgebiet* (Pencil Regions), and whenever I resume my intermittent reading of Walser's writings, so too I always look again at the photographs we have of him, seven very different faces, stations in a life which hint at the silent catastrophe which has taken place between each. The pictures I am most familiar with are those

from his time in Herisau, showing Walser on one of his long walks, for there is something in the way that the poet, long since retired from the service of the pen, stands there in the

landscape that reminds me instinctively of my grandfather Josef Egelhofer, with whom as a child I often used to go for walks for hours at a time during those very same years, in a region which is in many ways similar to that of Appenzell. When I look at these pictures of him on his walks, the cloth of Walser's

three-piece suit, the soft collar, the tie-pin, the liver-spots on the back of his hands, his neat pepper-and-salt moustache and the quiet expression in his eyes — each time I think I see my grandfather before me. Yet it was not only in their appearance that my grandfather and Walser resembled each other, but also in their general bearing, something about the way each had of holding his hat in his hand, and the way that, even in the finest weather, they would always carry an umbrella or a raincoat. For a long time I even imagined that my grandfather shared with Walser the habit of leaving the top button of his waistcoat

undone. Whether or not that was actually the case, it is a fact that both died in the same year, 1956 — Walser, as is well known, on a walk he took on the 25th of December, and my grandfather on the 14th of April, the night before Walser's last birthday, when it snowed once more even though spring was already underway. Perhaps that is the reason why now, when I think back to my grandfather's death, to which I have never been able to reconcile myself, in my mind's eye I always see him lying on the horn sledge on which Walser's body — after he had been found in the snow and photographed—was taken back to the asylum. What is the significance of these similarities, over-laps, and coincidences? Are they rebuses of memory, delusions of the self and of the senses, or rather the schemes and symp-toms of an order underlying the chaos of human relationships, and applying equally to the living and the dead, which lies beyond our comprehension? Carl Seelig relates that once, on a walk with Robert Walser, he had mentioned Paul Klee—they were just on the outskirts of the hamlet of Balgach—and scarcely had he uttered the name than he caught sight, as they entered the village, of a sign in an empty shop window bearing the words *Paul Klee—Carver of Wooden Candlesticks.* Seelig does not attempt to offer an explanation for the strange coincidence. He merely registers it, perhaps because it is precisely the most extraordinary things which are the most easily forgotten. And so I too will just set down without comment what happened to me recently while reading *The Robber,* the only one of Walser's longer works with which I was at the time still unfamiliar. Quite near the beginning of the book the narrator states that the Rob-ber crossed Lake Constance by moonlight. Exactly thus—by moonlight—is how, in one of my own stories, Aunt Fini imag-ines the young Ambros crossing the selfsame lake, although, as she makes a point of saying, this can scarcely have been the case in reality. Barely two pages further on, the same story relates how, later, Ambros, while working as a room service waiter at the Savoy in London, made the acquaintance of a lady from Shanghai, about whom, however, Aunt Fini knows only that she had a taste for brown kid gloves and that, as Ambros once noted, she marked the beginning of his *Trauerlaufbahn* (career in mourning). It is a similarly mysterious woman clad all in brown, and referred to by the narrator as the Henri Rousseau woman, whom the Robber meets, two pages on from the moonlit scene on Lake Constance, in a pale November wood — and nor is that all: a little later in the text, I know not from what depths, there appears the word *Trauerlaufbahn*, a word which I believed, when I wrote it down at the end of the Savoy episode, to be an invention entirely my own. I have always tried, in my own works, to mark my respect for those writers with whom I felt an affinity, to raise my hat to them, so to speak, by borrowing an attractive image or a few expressions, but it is one thing to set a marker in memory of a departed colleague, and quite another when one has the persistent feeling of being beckoned to from the other side.

Who and what Robert Walser really was is a question to which, despite my strangely close relationship with him, I am unable to give any reliable answer. The seven photographic portraits of him, as I have said, show very different people; a youth filled with a quiet sensuality; a young man hiding his anxieties as he prepares to make his way in bourgeois society; the heroic-looking writer of brooding aspect in Berlin; a 37-year-old with pale, watery-clear eyes; the Robber, smoking and dangerous-looking; a broken man; and finally the asylum inmate, completely destroyed and at the same time saved. What is striking about these portraits is not only how much they differ, but also the palpable incongruity inherent in each — a feature which, I conjecture, stems at least in part from the contradiction between Walser's native Swiss reserve and utter lack of conceit, and the anarchic, bohemian and dandyesque tendencies he displayed at the beginning of his career, and which he later hid, as far as possible, behind a façade of solid respectability. He himself relates how one Sunday he walked from Thun to Berne wearing a "louche pale yellow summer suit and dancing pumps" and on his head a "deliberately dissolute, daring, ridiculous hat." Sporting a cane, in Munich he promenades through the Englischer Garten to visit Wedekind, who shows a lively interest in his loud check suit — quite a compliment, considering the extravagant fashions in vogue among the Schwabinger *bohème* at the time. He describes the walking outfit he wore on the long trek to Würzburg as having a "certain southern Italian appearance. It was a sort or species of suit in which I could have been seen to advantage in Naples. In reasonable, moderate Germany however it seemed to arouse more suspicion than confidence, more repulsion than attraction. How daring and fantastical I was at twenty-three!" A fondness for conspicuous costume and the dangers of indigence often go hand in hand. Hölderlin, too, is said to have had a definite penchant for fine clothes and appearance, so that his dilapidated aspect at the beginning of his breakdown was all the more alarming to his friends. Mächler recalls how Walser once visited his brother on the island of Rügen wearing threadbare and darned trousers, even though the latter had just made him a present of a brand-new suit, and in this context cites a passage of *The Tanners* in which Simon is reproached by his sister thus: "For example, Simon, look at your trousers: all ragged at the bottom! To be sure, and I know this perfectly well myself: They're just trousers, but trousers should be kept in just as good a condition as one's soul, for when a person wears torn, ragged trousers it displays carelessness, and carelessness is an attribute of the soul. Your soul must be ragged too." This reproach may well go back to remarks Lisa was at times wont to make about her brother's appearance, but the inspired turn of phrase at the end—the reference to the ragged soul—that, I think, is an original aperçu on the part of the narrator, who is under no illusion as to how things stand with his inner life. Walser must at the time have hoped, through writing, to be able to escape the shadows which lay over his life from the beginning, and whose lengthening he anticipates at an early age, transforming them on the page from something very dense to something almost weightless. His ideal was to overcome the force of gravity. This is why he had no time for the grandiose tones in which the "dilettantes of the extreme left," as he calls them, were in those days proclaiming the revolution in art. He is no Expressionist visionary prophesying the end of the world, but rather, as he says in the introduction to *Fritz Kocher's Essays*, a clairvoyant of the small. From his earliest attempts on, his natural inclination is for the most radical minimization and brevity, in other words the possibility of setting down a story in one fell swoop, without any deviation or hesitation. Walser shares this ambition with the Jugendstil artists, and like them he is also prone to the opposite tendency of losing himself in arabesques. The playful—and sometimes obsessive—working in with a fine brush of the most abstruse details is one of the most striking characteristics of Walser's idiom. The word-eddies and turbulence created in the middle of a sentence by exaggerated participial constructions, or conglomerations of verbs such as "haben helfen dürfen zu verhindern" ("have been able to help to prevent"); neologisms, such as for example "das Man-schettelige" ("cuffishness") or "das Angstmeierliche" ("chicken-heartedness"), which scuttle away under our gaze like millipedes; the "night-bird shyness, a flying-over-the-seas-in-the-dark, a soft inner whimpering" which, in a bold flight of metaphor, the narrator of *The Robber* claims hovers above one of Dürer's female figures; deliberate curiosities such as the sofa "squeach-ing" ("gyxelnd") under the charming weight of a seductive lady; the regionalisms, redolent of things long fallen into disuse; the almost manic loquaciousness—these are all elements in the painstaking process of elaboration Walser indulges in, out of a fear of reaching the end too quickly if—as is his inclination—he were to set down nothing but a beautifully curved line with no distracting branches or blossoms. Indeed, the detour is, for Walser, a matter of survival. "These detours I'm making serve the end of filling time, for I really must pull off a book of consid-erable length, otherwise I'll be even more deeply despised than I am now." On the other hand, however, precisely these linguis-tic montages—emerging as they do from the detours and digressions of narrative and, especially, of form—are exactly what is most at odds with the demands of high culture. Their associations with nonsense poetry and the word-salad symp-tomatic of schizophasia were never likely to increase the mar-ket value of their author. And yet it is precisely his uniquely overwrought art of formulation which true readers would not be without for the world, for example in this passage from the

Bleistiftsgebiet (Pencil Regions) which, comic and heartbreaking in equal measure, condenses a whole romantic melodrama into the space of a few lines. What Walser achieves here is the complete and utter subjugation of the writer to the language, a pretense at awkwardness brought off with the utmost virtuosity, the perfect realization of that irony only ever hinted at by the German Romantics yet never achieved by any of them, with the possible exception of Hoffman, in their writings. "In vain," the passage in question tells us, regarding the beautiful Herta and her faithless Italian husband, "did she buy, in the finest first class boutiques, for her most highly respected darling rake and pleasure-seeker, a new walking cane, say, or the finest and warmest coat which she could find, procure or purchase. His heart remained indifferent beneath the carefully chosen item of clothing and the hand hard which used the cane, and while this scoundrel — oh that we might be permitted to call him thus — frivolously flitted or flirted around, there trickled from those big tragic eyes, embellished by heartache with dark rims, heavy tears like pearls, and here we must remark, too, that the rooms where such intimate misfortune was played out were fairly brimming with gloomy, fantastically be-palmleaved decoration gilded further by the height and scale of the whole." "Little sentence, little sentence" — so Walser concludes this escapade which is all but grammatically derailed by the end, "you seem to me phantastical as well, you do!" And then, coming down to earth, he adds the sober phrase, "But let us continue."

But let us continue. As the fantastical elements in Walser's prose works increase, so too their realistic content dwindles —

or, rather, reality rushes past unstoppably as in a dream, or in the cinema. Ali Baba, quite hollowed out by unrequited love and pious devotion to duty in the diligent service of the most cruel of all princesses, and in whom we may easily recognize one of Walser's alter egos — Ali Baba one evening sees a long sequence of cinematic images unfold before his eyes: naturalistic landscapes like the many-peaked Engadin, the Lac de Bienne and the Kurhaus at Magglingen. "One after another," the story continues, "there came into view a Madonna holding a child on her arm, a snowfield high in the Alps, Sunday pleasures by the lakeside, baskets of fruit and flower arrangements, all of a sudden a painting representing the kiss Judas gave Jesus in the Garden of Gethsemane, with his fat face, round as an apple, almost preventing him from carrying out his plan; then a scene from a *Schützenfest*, and, civility itself, a collection of summer hats which seemed to smile contentedly, followed by expensive crystal, porcelain, and items of jewelry. Ali Baba enjoyed watching the pictures, each quickly dissolving and being replaced by the next." Things are always quickly dissolving and being replaced by the next in Walser. His scenes only last for the blink of an eyelid, and even the human figures in his work enjoy only the briefest of lives. Hundreds of them inhabit the *Bleistiftsgebiet* alone — dancers and singers, tragedians and comedians, barmaids and private tutors, principals and procurers, Nubians and Muscovites, hired hands and millionaires, Aunts Roka and Moka and a whole host of other walk-on parts. As they make their entrance they have a marvelous presence, but as soon as one tries to look at them more closely they have already vanished. It always seems to me as if, like actors in the earliest films, they are surrounded by a trembling, shimmering aura which makes their contours unrecognizable. They flit through Walser's fragmentary stories and embryonic novels as people in dreams flit through our heads at night, never stopping to register, departing the moment they have arrived, never to be seen again. Benjamin is the only one among the commentators who tries to pin down the anonymous, evanescent quality of Walser's characters. They come, he says, "from insanity and nowhere else. They are figures who have left madness behind them, and this is why they are marked by such a consistently heartrending, inhuman superficiality. If we were to attempt to sum up in a single phrase the delightful yet also uncanny element in them, we would have to say: they have all been healed."[1] Nabokov surely had something similar in mind when he said of the fickle souls who roam Nikolai Gogol's books that here we have to do with a tribe of harmless madmen, who will not be prevented by anything in the world from ploughing their own eccentric furrow. The comparison with Gogol is by no means farfetched, for if Walser had any literary relative or predecessor, then it is Gogol. Both of them gradually lost the ability to keep their eye on the center of the plot, losing themselves instead in the almost compulsive contemplation of strangely unreal creations appearing on the periphery of their vision, and about whose previous and future fate we never learn even the slightest thing. There is a scene which Nabokov quotes in his book on Gogol, where we are told that the hero of *Dead Souls*, our Mr. Chichikov, is boring a certain young lady in a ballroom with all kinds of pleasantries which he had already uttered on numerous occasions in various places, for example "In the Government of Simbirsk, at the house of Sofron Ivanovich Bezpechnoy, where the latter's daughter, Adelaida Sofronovna, was also present with her three sisters-in-law, Maria Gavrilovna, Alexandra Gavrilovna and Adelheida Gavrilovna; at the house of Frol Vasilievich Pobedonosnoy, in the Government of Penza; and at that of the latter's brother, where the following were present: his wife's sister Katherina Mikhailovna and her cousins Rosa Feodorovna and Emilia Feodorovna; in the Government of Viatka, at the house of Pyotr Varsonophyevich, where his daughter-in-law's sister Pelagea Egorovna was present, together with a niece, Sophia Rostislavna and two stepsisters: Sophia Alexandrovna and Maclatura Alexandrovna"[2]—this scene, none of whose characters makes an appearance anywhere else in Gogol's works, since their secret (like that of human existence as a whole) resides in their utter superfluity—this scene with its digressive nature could equally well have sprung from Robert Walser's imagination. Walser himself once said that basically he was always writing the same novel, from one prose work to the next—a novel which, he says, one could describe as "a much-chopped up or dismembered Book of Myself." One should add that the main character—the *Ich*—almost never makes an appearance in this *Ich-Buch* but is left blank, or rather remains out of sight among the crowd of other passing figures. Homelessness is another thing Walser and Gogol have in common—the awful provisionality of their respective existences, the prismatic mood swings, the sense of panic, the wonderfully capricious humour steeped at the same time in blackest heartache, the endless scraps of paper and, of course, the invention of a whole populace of lost souls, a ceaseless masquerade for the purpose of autobiographical mystification. Just as, at the end of the spectral story *The Overcoat*, there is scarcely anything left of the scribe Akakiy Akakievich because, as Nabokov points out, he no longer quite knows if he is in the middle of the street or in the middle of a sentence, so too in the end it becomes almost impossible to make out Gogol and Walser among the legions of their characters, not to mention against the dark horizon of their looming illness. It is through writing that they achieved this depersonalization, through writing that they cut themselves off from the past. Their ideal state is that of pure amnesia. Benjamin noted that the point of every one of Walser's sentences is to make the reader forget the previous one, and indeed after *The Tanners*—which is still a family memoir—the stream of memory slows to a trickle and peters out in a sea of oblivion. For this reason it is particularly memorable, and touching, when once in a while, in some context or another, Walser raises his eyes from the page, looks back into the past and imparts to his reader—for example—that one evening years ago he was caught in a snowstorm on the Friedrichstrasse in Berlin and how the vividness of the memory has stayed with him ever since. Nor are Walser's emotions any less erratic than these remembered images. For the most part they are carefully concealed, or, if they do emerge, are soon turned into something slightly ridiculous or at least made light of. In the prose sketch devoted to Brentano, Walser asks: "Can a person whose feelings are so many and so lovely be at the same time so unfeeling?" The answer might have been that in life, as in fairy tales, there are those who, out of fear and poverty, cannot afford emotions and who therefore, like Walser in one of his most poignant prose pieces, have to try out their seemingly atrophied ability to love on inanimate substances and objects unheeded by anyone else — such as ash, a needle, a pencil, or a matchstick. Yet the way in which Walser then breathes life into them, in an act of complete assimilation and empathy, reveals how in the end emotions are perhaps most deeply felt when applied to the most insignificant things. "Indeed," Walser writes about ash, "if one goes into this apparently uninteresting subject in any depth there is quite a lot to be said about it which is not at all uninteresting; if, for example, one blows on ash it displays not the least reluctance to fly off instantly in all directions. Ash is submissiveness, worthlessness, irrelevance itself, and best of all, it is itself pervaded by the belief that it is fit for nothing. Is it possible to be more helpless, more impotent, and more wretched than ash? Not very easily. Could anything be more compliant and more tolerant? Hardly. Ash has no notion of character and is further from any kind of wood than dejection is from exhilaration. Where there is ash there is actually nothing at all. Tread on ash, and you will barely notice that your foot has stepped on something." The intense pathos of this passage — there is nothing which comes near it in the whole of twentieth-century German literature, not even in Kafka — lies in the fact that here, in this apparently casual treatise on ash, needle, pencil and matchstick, the author is in truth writing about his own martyrdom, for these four objects are not randomly strung together but are the writer's own instruments of torture, or at any rate that which he needs in order to stage his own personal auto-da-fé — and what remains once the fire has died down.

Indeed, in the middle of his life writing had become a wearisome business for Walser. Year by year the unremitting composition of his literary pieces becomes harder and harder for him. It is a kind of penance he is serving up there in his attic room in the Hotel zum Blauen Kreuz, where, by his own account, he spends ten to thirteen hours at a stretch at his desk every day, in winter wearing his army greatcoat and the slippers he has fashioned himself from leftover scraps of material. He talks in terms of a writer's prison, a dungeon, or an attic cell, and of the danger of losing one's reason under the relentless strain of composition. "My back is bent by it," says the Poet in the eponymous piece, "since often I sit for hours bent over a single word that has to take the long slow route from brain to paper." This work makes him neither unhappy nor happy, he adds, but he often has the feeling that it will be the death of him. There are several reasons — apart from the chains which, in the main, double-bind writers to their métier — why, despite these insights, Walser did not give up writing earlier: chief among them perhaps the fear of *déclassement* and, in the most extreme case in which he almost found himself, of being reduced to handouts, fears which haunted him all the more since his father's financial ruin had rendered his childhood and youth deeply insecure. It is not so much poverty itself Walser fears, however, as the ignominy of going down in the world. He is very well aware of the fact that "a penniless worker is much less an object of contempt than an out-of-work clerk.... A clerk, as long as he has a post, is already halfway to being a gentleman, but without a post becomes an awkward, superfluous, burdensome nonentity." And what is true of office clerks naturally applies to an even greater degree to writers, inasmuch as the latter have it in them not just to be half-way to being a gentleman but even, given the right circumstances, to rise to be figureheads of their nation. And then there is the fact that writers, in common with all those to whom a higher office is entrusted as it were by the grace of God, cannot simply retire when the mood takes them; even today they are expected to keep writing until the pen drops from their hand. Not only that: people believe they are entitled to expect that, as Walser writes to Otto Pick, "every year they will bring to the light of day some new one hundred percent proof item." To bring such pieces of "one hundred percent proof"—in the sense of a sensational major new work—to the cultural marketplace was something which Walser, at least since his return to Switzerland, was no longer in a fit state to do—if indeed he ever had been. At least part of him perceived himself, in his time in Biel or Berne, as a hired hand and as nothing more than a degraded literary haberdasher. The courage, however, with which he defended this last embattled position and came to terms with "the disappointments, reprimands in the press, the boos and hisses, the silencing even unto the grave" was almost unprecedented. That in the end he was still forced to capitulate was due not only to the exhaustion of his own inner resources, but also to the catastrophic changes—even more rapid in the second half of the 1920s—in the cultural and intellectual climate. There can be no doubt that had Walser persevered for a few more years he would, by the spring of 1933 at the latest, have found the last possible opportunities for publication in the German Reich closed off to him. To that extent, he was quite correct in the remarks he made to Carl Seelig that his world had been destroyed by the Nazis. In his 1908 critical review of *The Assistant,* Josef Hofmiller contrasts the alleged insubstantiality of the novel with the more solid earthiness of the autochthonous Swiss writers Johannes Jegerlehner, Josef Reinhart, Alfred Huggenberger, Otto von Greyerz and Ernst Zahn—whose ideological slant may, I make so bold as to claim, be readily discerned from the ingrained rootedness of their names. Of one such *Heimat* poet, a certain Hans von Mühlenstein, Walser writes in the mid-twenties to Resy Breitbach that he—like Walser himself originally from Biel—after a brief marriage to an imposing lady from Munich has now settled in Graubünden, where he is an active member of the association for the dissemination of the new spirit of the age and has married a country woman "who orders him first thing in the morning to bring in a cartload of greens from the field before breakfast. He wears blue overalls, coarse trousers of a rustic stuff and is exceedingly contented." The contempt for nationalistic and *Heimat* poets which this passage reveals is a clear indication that Walser knew exactly what ill hour had struck and why there was no longer any call for his works, either there in Germany or at home in Switzerland.

Against this background, Walser's legendary "pencil system" takes on the aspect of a preparation for a life underground. In the "microscripts," the deciphering of which by Werner Morlang and Bernhard Echte is one of the most significant literary achievements of recent decades, can be seen—as an ingenious method of continuing to write—coded messages of one forced into illegality and documents of a genuine "inner emigration." Certainly Walser was, as he explains in a letter to Max Rychner, primarily concerned with overcoming his inhibitions about writing by means of the less definitive "pencil method"; and it is equally certain that unconsciously, as Werner Morlang notes, he was seeking to hide, behind the indecipherable characters, "from both public and internalized instances of evaluation," to duck down below the level of language and to obliterate himself. But his system of pencil notes on scraps of paper is also a work of fortifications and defenses, unique in the history of literature, by means of which the smallest and most innocent things might be saved from destruction in the "great times" then looming on the horizon. Entrenched in his impenetrable earthworks, Robert Walser reminds me of Casella, the Corsican captain who, in 1768, alone in a tower on Cap Corse, deceived the French invaders into believing it was occupied by a whole battalion by running from one floor to another and shooting now out of one, now out of another firing slit. Significantly enough, after Walser entered the asylum at Waldau he felt as if he were perched outside the city on the ramparts, and it is perhaps for this reason that he writes from there to Fräulein Breitbach that, although the battle has long since been lost, now and again he "fires off" the odd small piece at "some of the journals of the Fatherland," just as if these writings were grenades or

bombs. At any rate I am unable to reassure myself with the view that the intricate texts of the *Bleistiftsgebiet* reflect, either in their appearance or their content, the history of Robert Walser's progressive mental deterioration. I recognize, of course, that their peculiar preoccupation with form, the extreme compulsion to rhyme, say, or the way that their length is determined by the exact dimensions of the space available on a scrap of paper, exhibit certain characteristics of pathological writing: an encephalogram, as it were, of someone compelled—as it says in *The Robber*—to be thinking constantly of something somehow

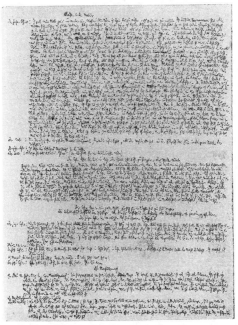

very far distant; but they do not appear to me to be evidence of a psychotic state. On the contrary, *The Robber* is Walser's most rational and most daring work, a self-portrait and self-examination of absolute integrity, in which both the compiler of the medical history and his subject occupy the position of the author. Accordingly, the narrator—who is at once friend, attorney, warden, guardian and guardian angel of the vulnerable, almost broken hero—sets out his case from a certain ironic distance, even perhaps, as he notes on one occasion, with the complacency of a critic. On the other hand he repeatedly rises to the occasion with impassioned pleas on behalf of his client, such as in the following appeal to the public: "Don't persist in reading nothing but healthy books, acquaint yourselves also with so-called pathological literature, from which you may derive considerable edification. Healthy people should always, so to speak, take certain risks. For what other reason, blast and confound it, is a person healthy? Simply in order to stop living one day at the height of one's health? A damned bleak fate ... I know now more than ever that intellectual circles are filled with philistinism. I mean moral and aesthetic chickenheartedness. Timidity, though, is unhealthy. One day, while out for a swim, the Robber very nearly met a watery end. [...] One year later, that dairy school student drowned in the very same river. So the Robber knows from experience what it's like to have water nymphs hauling one down by the legs." The passion with which the advocate Walser takes up the cause on his client's behalf draws its energy from the threat of annihilation. If ever a book was written from the outermost brink, it is this one. Faced with the imminent end, Walser works imperturbably on, often even with a kind of wry amusement, and—apart from a few eccentricities which he permits himself for the fun of it—with an unerringly steady hand. "Never before, in all my years at my desk, have I sat down to write so boldly, so intrepidly," the narrator tells us at the beginning. In fact, the unforced way in which he manages the not inconsiderable structural difficulties and the constant switches of mood between the deepest distraction and a light-heartedness which can only be properly described by the word *allegría*, testifies to a supreme degree of both aesthetic and moral assurance. It is true, too, that in this posthumous novel —already written, so to speak, from the other side—Walser accrues insights into his own particular state of mind and the nature of mental disturbance as such, the likes of which—so far as I can see—are to be found nowhere else in literature. With incomparable sangfroid he sets down an account of the probable origins of his suffering in an upbringing which consisted almost exclusively of small acts of neglect; of how, as a man of fifty, he still feels the child or little boy inside him; of the girl he would like to have been; the satisfaction he derives from wearing an apron; the fetishistic tendencies of the spoon-caresser; of paranoia, the feeling of being surrounded and hemmed in; the sense, reminiscent of Josef K. in *The Trial,* that being observed made him interesting; and of the dangers of idiocy arising, as he actually writes, from sexual atrophy. With seismographic precision, he registers the slightest tremors at the edges of his consciousness, records rejections and ripples in his thoughts and emotions about which the science of psychiatry even today scarcely allows itself to dream. The narrator does not think much of the therapies the mind doctor offers to the Robber, and still less of the universal panacea of belief, which he terms a "perfectly simple, paltry condition of the soul." "For," he says, "one achieves nothing by it, absolutely nothing, nothing at all. One just sits there and believes. Like a person mechanically knitting a sock." Walser is not interested in either the obscurantism of the medicine men or of the other curators of the soul. What matters to him, like any other writer in full possession of his faculties, is the greatest possible degree of lucidity, and I can imagine how, while writing *The Robber*, it must have occurred to him on more than one occasion that the looming threat of impending darkness enabled him at times to arrive at an acuity of observation and precision of formulation which is unattainable from a state of perfect health. He focuses this particular power of perception not just on his own *via dolorosa* but also on other outsiders, persons excluded and eliminated, with whom his alter ego the Robber is associated. His own personal fate concerns him least of all. "In most people," the narrator says, "the lights go out," and he feels for every such ravaged life. The French officers, for example, whom the Robber once saw in mufti in the resort town of Magglingen, three thousand feet above sea level. "This was shortly before the outbreak of our not yet forgotten Great War, and all these young gentlemen who sought and doubtless also found relaxation high up in the blossoming meads were obliged to follow the call of their nation." How false, then, the rolling thunder of "storms of steel" and all ideologically tainted literature sounds, by comparison with this one sentence with its discreet compassion. Walser refused the grand gesture. On the subject of the collective catastrophes of his day he remained resolutely silent. However, he was anything but politically naïve. When, in the years preceding the First World War, the old Ottoman Empire collapsed in the face of attacks by the reform party, and modern Turkey constituted itself with one eye on Germany as a potential protector, Walser was more or less alone in viewing this development with skepticism. In the prose piece "The Farewell" (*Abschied*) he has the deposed Sultan —who is under no illusions about the shortcomings of his régime—express doubts about the progress that has apparently been achieved. Of course, he says, there will now be efficient folk at work in Turkey, where chaos has always reigned, "but our gardens will wither and our mosques will soon be redundant ... (and) railways will criss-cross the desert where even hyenas quailed at the sound of my name. The Turks will put on caps and look like Germans. We will be forced to engage in commerce, and if we aren't capable of that, we will simply be shot." That is more or less how things came to pass, too, except that in the first genocide of our ill-fated century it was not the Turks who were shot and put to death by the Germans, but the Armenians by the Turks. At all events, it was not an auspicious start, and one could say that in 1909, looking through the eyes of Haroun al Rashid, Walser saw far into the future; and he will hardly have been less far-sighted as the 1920s drew to a close. The Robber, whose whole disposition was that of a liberal free-thinker and republican, *also* became soulsick on account of the looming clouds darkening the political horizon. The exact diagnosis of his illness is of little relevance. It is enough for us to understand that, in the end, Walser simply could not go on, and, like Hölderlin, had to resort to keeping people at arm's length with a sort of anarchic politeness, becoming refractory and abusive, making scenes in public and believing that the bourgeois city of Berne, of all places, was a city of ghostly gesticulators, executing rapid hand movements directly in front of his face expressly in order to discombobulate him and to dismiss him out of hand as one who simply does not count. During his years in Berne Walser was almost completely isolated.

The contempt was, as he feared, universal. Among the few who still concerned themselves with him was the schoolteacher (and poet) Emil Schibli, with whom he stayed for a few days in 1927. In a description of his meeting with Walser published in the *Seeländer Volksstimme,* Schibli claims to have recognised, in this lonely poet in the guise of a tramp and suffering from profound isolation, a king in hiding "whom posterity will call, if not one of the great, then one of rare purity." While Walser was no stranger to the evangelical desire to possess nothing and to give away everything one owns — as in *The Robber* — he made no claim to any kind of messianic calling. It was enough for him to call himself — with bitterly resigned irony — at least the ninth-best writer in the Helvetic Federation. We, though, can grant Walser the honorific title with which he endows the Robber and to which in fact he himself is entitled, namely the son of a first secretary to the canton.

The first prose work I read by Robert Walser was his piece on Kleist in Thun, where he talks of the torment of someone despairing of himself and his craft, and of the intoxicating beauty of the surrounding landscape. "Kleist sits on a churchyard wall. Everything is damp, yet also sultry. He opens his shirt, to breathe freely. Below him lies the lake, as if it had been hurled down by the great hand of a god, incandescent with shades of yellow and red [...]. The Alps have come to life and dip with fabulous gestures their foreheads into the water." Time and again I have immersed myself in the few pages of this story and, taking it as a starting point, have undertaken now shorter, now longer excursions into the rest of Walser's work. Among my early en-

counters with Walser I count the discovery I made, in an anti-
quarian bookshop in Manchester in the second half of the
1960s—inserted in a copy of Bächtold's three-volume biography of Gottfried Keller which had almost certainly belonged to
a German-Jewish refugee—of an attractive sepia photograph

depicting the house on the island in the Aare, completely surrounded by shrubs and trees, in which Kleist worked on his
drama of madness *Die Familie Ghonorez* before he, himself sick,
had to commit himself to the care of Dr. Wyttenbach in Berne.
Since then I have slowly learned to grasp how everything is
connected across space and time, the life of the Prussian writer
Kleist with that of a Swiss author who claims to have worked as
a clerk in a brewery in Thun, the echo of a pistol shot across the
Wannsee with the view from a window of the Herisau asylum,
Walser's long walks with my own travels, dates of birth with

dates of death, happiness with misfortune, natural history and the history of our industries, that of *Heimat* with that of exile. On all these paths Walser has been my constant companion. I only need to look up for a moment in my daily work to see him standing somewhere, a little apart, the unmistakable figure of the solitary walker just pausing to take in the surroundings. And sometimes I imagine that I see with his eyes the bright *See-land* and within this land of lakes the lake like a shimmering island, and in this lake-island another island, the Île Saint-Pierre "shining in the bright morning haze, floating in a sea of pale trembling light." Returning home then in the evening we look out, from the lakeside path suffused by mournful rain, at the boating enthusiasts out on the lake "in boats or skiffs with umbrellas opened above their heads," a sight which allows us to imagine that we are "in China or Japan or some other dream-like, poetical land." As Mächler reminds us, Walser really did consider for a while the possibility of traveling, or even emigrating, overseas. According to his brother, he once even had a check in his pocket from Bruno Cassirer, good for several months' travel to India. It is not difficult to imagine him hidden in a green leafy picture by Henri Rousseau, with tigers and elephants, on the veranda of a hotel by the sea while the monsoon pours down outside, or in front of a resplendent tent in the foothills of the Himalayas, which—as Walser once wrote of the Alps—resemble nothing so much as a snow-white fur boa. In fact he almost got as far as Samoa, since Walter Rathenau, whom—if we may believe *The Robber* on this point—he had met one day, quite by chance, in the midst of an incessant stream of people and traffic on the Potsdamer Platz in Berlin, apparently wanted to find him a not-too-taxing position in the colonial administration on the island known to the Germans as the "Pearl of the South Seas." We do not know why Walser turned down this in many ways tempting offer. Let us simply assume that it is because, among the first German South Sea discoverers and explorers, there was a certain gentleman called Otto von Kotzebue, against whom Walser was just as irrevocably prejudiced as he was against the playwright of the same name, whom he called a narrow-minded philistine, claiming he had a too-long nose, bulging eyes and no neck, and that his whole head was shrunk into and hidden by a grotesque and enormous collar. Kotzebue had, so Walser continues, written a large number of comedies which enjoyed runaway box-office success at a time when Kleist was in despair, and bequeathed a whole series of these massive, collected, printed volumes, coxed and boxed and bound in calfskin, to a posterity which would blench with shame were it ever to read them. The risk of being reminded, in the midst of a South Sea idyll, of this literary opportunist, one of the heroes of the German intellectual scene, as he dismissively calls him, was probably just too high. In any case, Walser didn't care much for travel and — apart from Germany — never actually went anywhere to speak of. He never saw the city of Paris, which he dreams of even from the asylum at Waldau. On the other hand, the Untergasse in Biel could seem to him like a street in Jerusalem "along which the Saviour and deliverer of the world modestly rides in." Instead he criss-crossed the country on foot, often on nocturnal marches with the moon shining a white track before him. In the autumn of 1925, for example, he journeyed on foot from Berne to Geneva, following for quite a long stretch the old pilgrim route to Santiago da Compostela. He does not tell us much about this trip, other than that in Fribourg—I can see him entering that city across the incredibly high bridge over the Sarine—he purchased some socks; paid his respects to a number of hostelries; whispered sweet nothings to a waitress from the Jura; gave a boy almonds; strolling around in the dark doffed his hat to the Rousseau monument on the island in the Rhône; and, crossing the bridges by the lake, experienced a feeling of light-heartedness. Such and similar matters are set down for us in the most economical manner on a couple of pages. Of the walk itself, we learn nothing and nothing about what he may have pondered in his mind as he walked. The only occasion on which I see the traveller Robert Walser freed from the burden of himself is during the balloon journey he undertook, during his Berlin years, from Bitterfeld—the artificial lights of whose factories were just beginning to glimmer—to the Baltic coast. "Three people, the captain, a gentleman, and a young girl, climb into the basket, the anchoring cords are loosed, and the strange house flies, slowly, as if it had first to ponder something, upward.... The beautiful moonlit night seems to gather the splendid balloon into invisible arms, gently and quietly the roundish flying body ascends, and ... hardly so that one might notice, subtle winds propel it northward." Far below can be seen church spires, village schools, farmyards, a ghostly train whistling by, the wonderfully illuminated course of the Elbe in all its colors.

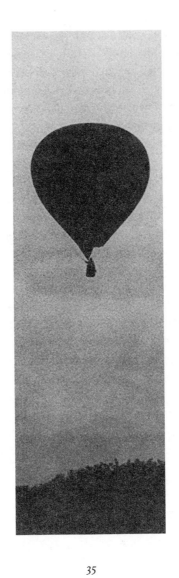

"Remarkably white, polished-looking plains alternate with gardens and small wildernesses of bush. One peers down into regions where one's feet would never, never have trod, because in certain regions, indeed in most, one has no purpose whatever. How big and unknown to us the earth is!" Robert Walser was, I think, born for just such a silent journey through the air. In all his prose works he always seeks to rise above the heaviness of earthly existence, wanting to float away softly and silently into a higher, freer realm. The sketch about the balloon journey over a sleeping nocturnal Germany is only one example, one which for me is associated with Nabokov's memory of one of his favorite books from his childhood. In this picture-book series, the black Golliwog and his friends—one of whom is a kind of dwarf or Lilliputian person—survive a number of adventures, end up far away from home and are even captured by cannibals. And then there is a scene where an airship is made of "yards and yards of yellow silk … and an additional tiny balloon […] provided for the sole use of the fortunate Midget. At the immense altitude," writes Nabokov, "to which the ship reached, the aeronauts huddled together for warmth while the lost little soloist, still the object of my intense envy notwithstanding his plight, drifted into an abyss of frost and stars—alone."[3]

—TRANSLATED BY JO CATLING

1. Walter Benjamin. "Robert Walser," in *Selected Writings: vol 2. 1927–34* (Harvard).
2. Vladimir Nabokov, *Nikolai Gogol* (New Directions).
3. Vladimir Nabokov, *Speak, Memory* (Random House).

The Tanners

One morning a young, boyish man walked into a bookshop and asked to be introduced to the proprietor. His request was granted. The bookseller, an old man of quite venerable appearance, gave a sharp glance at the one standing rather shyly before him and instructed him to speak. "I want to become a bookseller," said the youthful novice, "I yearn to become one, and I don't know what might prevent me from carrying out my intentions. I've always imagined the trade in books must be an enchanting activity, and I cannot understand why I should still be forced to pine away outside of this fine, lovely occupation. For you see, sir, standing here before you, I find myself extraordinarily well suited for selling books in your shop, and selling as many as you could possibly wish me to. I'm a born salesman: chivalrous, fleet-footed, courteous, quick, brusque, decisive, calculating, attentive, honest—and yet not so foolishly honest as I might appear. I am capable of lowering prices when a poor devil of a student is standing before me, and of elevating them as a favor to those wealthy individuals who, as I can't help noticing, sometimes don't know what to do with all their money. Although I'm still young, I believe myself in possession of a certain knowledge of human nature—besides which, I love people, of every variety, so I would never employ my insight into their characters in the service of swindling—and I am equally determined never to harm your esteemed business through any exaggerated solicitousness toward certain underfinanced poor devils. In a word: My love of humankind will be agreeably balanced with mercantile rationality on the scales of salesmanship, a rationality which in fact bears equal weight and appears to me just as necessary for life as a soul filled with love: I shall practice a most lovely moderation, please be assured of this in advance—"

The bookseller was looking at the young man attentively and with astonishment. He appeared to be having trouble deciding whether or not his interlocutor, with this pretty speech, was making a good impression on him. He wasn't quite sure how to judge and, finding this circumstance rather confusing, he gently inquired in his self-consciousness: "Is it possible, young man, to make inquiries about your person in suitable places?" The one so addressed responded: "Suitable places? I'm not sure what you mean by suitable. To me, the most appropriate thing would be if you didn't make inquiries at all! Whom would you ask, and what purpose could it serve? You'd find yourself regaled with all sorts of information regarding my person, but would any of it succeed in reassuring you? What would you know about me if, for example, someone were to tell you that I came from a very good family, that my father was a man worthy of respect, that my brothers were industrious hopeful individuals, and that I myself was quite serviceable, if a bit flighty, but certainly not without grounds for hope, in fact that it was clearly all right to trust me a little, and so forth? You still wouldn't know me at all, and most certainly wouldn't have the slightest reason to hire me now as a salesclerk in your shop with any greater peace of mind. No, sir, as a rule, inquiries aren't worth a fig, and if I might make so bold as to venture to offer you, as an esteemed older gentleman, a piece of advice, I would heartily advise against making any at all—for I know that if I were suited to deceive you and inclined to cheat the hopes you place in me on the basis of the information you'd gather, I would be doing so in even greater measure the more favorably the aforementioned inquiries turned out, inquiries that would then prove to be mendacious, if they spoke well of me. No, esteemed sir, if you think you might have a use for me, I ask that you display a bit more courage than most of the other business owners I've previously encountered and simply engage me on the basis of the impression I am making on you now. Besides, to be perfectly truthful, any inquiries concerning my person you might make will only result in your hearing bad reports."

"Indeed? And why is that?"

"I didn't last long," the young man continued, "in any of the places I've worked at thus far, for I found it disagreeable to let my young powers go stale in the narrow stuffy confines of copyists' offices, even if these offices were considered by all to be the most elegant in the world—those found in banks for example. To this day, I haven't yet been sent packing by anyone at all but rather have always left on the strength of my own desire to leave, abandoning jobs and positions that no doubt carried promises of careers and the devil knows what else, but which would have been the death of me had I remained in them. No matter where it was I'd been working, my departure was, as a rule, lamented, but nonetheless after my decision was found regrettable and a dire future was prophesied for me, my employers always had the decency to wish me luck with my future endeavors. With you, sir, in your bookshop (and here the young man's voice grew suddenly confiding), I will surely be able to last for years and years. And in any case, many things speak in favor of your giving me a try." The bookseller said: "Your candor pleases me, I shall let you work in my shop for a one-week trial period. If you perform well and seem inclined to stay, then we can discuss it further." With these words, which signaled the young man's dismissal, the old man at the same time rang an electric bell, whereupon, as if arriving on the gusts of a strong wind, a small, elderly, bespectacled man appeared.

"Give this young man something to do!"

The spectacles nodded. With this, Simon became an assistant bookseller. Simon—for that was his name.

At around this same time, Professor Klaus, a brother of Simon's who lived in a historic capital where he'd made a name for himself, had begun to worry about his younger brother's behavior. A good, quiet, dutiful person, he would dearly have loved to see his brothers find the firm respect-commanding ground beneath their feet in life that he, the eldest, had. But this was so utterly not the case, at least till now, in fact it was so very much the opposite, that Professor Klaus began to reproach himself in his heart. He told himself, for example: "I should have been a person who would long since have had every opportunity to lead my brothers to the right path. Until now I've failed to do so. How could I have neglected these duties, etc." Dr. Klaus knew thousands of duties, small and large, and sometimes it seemed as if he were longing to have even more of them. He was one of those people who feel so compelled to fulfill duties that they go plunging into great collapsing edifices constructed entirely of disagreeable duties simply out of the fear that some secret, inconspicuous duty might somehow elude them. They cause themselves to experience many a troubled hour because of these unfulfilled duties— never stopping to consider how one duty always piles a second one upon the person undertaking the first—and they believe they've already fulfilled something like a duty just by being made anxious and uneasy by any dark inkling of its presence. They meddle in many an affair that—if they'd stop to think about it in a less anxious way—hasn't a blessed thing to do with them, and they wish to see others as worry-laden as themselves. They tend to cast envious glances upon naïve unencumbered people, and then criticize them for being frivolous characters since they move through life so gracefully, their heads held so easily aloft. Dr. Klaus often forced himself to entertain a certain small modest sensation of insouciance, but always he would return again to his gray dreary duties, in the thrall of which he languished as in a dark prison. Perhaps, back when he was still young, he'd once felt a desire to stop, but he'd lacked the strength to leave undone something that resembled a nagging duty and couldn't just walk past it with a dismissive smile. Dismissive? Oh, he never dismissed anything at all! Attempting this—or so it seemed to him—would have split him in twain from bottom to top; he'd have been incapable of avoiding painful recollections of what he'd cast aside and dismissed. He never dismissed or discarded anything at all, and he was wasting his young life analyzing and examining things utterly unworthy of examination, study, attention or love. Thus he'd grown older, but since he was by no means anything like a person devoid of sensibility and imagination, he often also reproached himself bitterly for neglecting the duty of being at least a little happy. This was yet another neglect of duty, a new one, which with perfect acuity demonstrated that the dutiful never quite succeed in fulfilling all their duties, indeed, that such individuals are the most likely of all human beings to disregard their foremost duties and only later—perhaps when it's already too late—call them once more to mind. On more than one occasion Dr. Klaus felt sad about himself when he thought of the precious happiness that had faded from his view, the happiness of finding himself united with a young sweet girl, who of course would have to have been a girl from an impeccable family. At around the same time as he was contemplating his own person in a melancholy frame of mind, he wrote to his brother Simon, whom he genuinely loved and whose conduct in this world troubled him, a letter whose contents were approximately as follows:

Dear Brother,

It would appear you are refusing to tell me anything about yourself. Perhaps things aren't well with you and this is why you don't write. You are once more, as so often before, lacking a solid steady occupation—I've been sorry to hear this, and to hear it from strangers. From you, it seems, I can no longer expect any candid reports. Believe me, this pains me. So very many things now cause me displeasure, and must you too—who always seemed to me to hold such promise—contribute to the bleakness of my mood, which for many reasons is far from rosy? I shall continue to hope, but if you are still even a little bit fond of your brother, please don't make me hope in vain for too long. Go and do something that might justify a person's belief in you in some way or other. You have talent and, as I like to imagine, possess a clear head; you're clever too, and all your utterances reflect the good core I've always known your soul possesses. But why, acquainted as you are with the way this world is put together, do you now display so little perseverance? Why are you always leaping from one thing to the next? Does your own conduct not frighten you? You must possess quite a stockpile of inner strength to endure this constant change of professions, which is such a disservice to yourself in this world. In your shoes, I would have despaired long ago. I really cannot understand you at all in this, but for precisely this reason—that after experiencing all too often that nothing can be achieved in this world without patience and goodwill—I'm not abandoning my hope of one day seeing you energetically seize hold of a career. And surely you wish to achieve something. In any case, such a lack of ambition is hardly like you, in my experience. My advice to you is: Stick it out, knuckle under, pursue some difficult task for three or four short years, obey your superiors, show that you can perform, but also show that you have character, and then a career path will open before you—and it will lead you through all the known world if you desire to travel. The world and its people will show themselves to you quite differently once you yourself are truly something: when you are in a position to mean something to the world. In this way, it seems to me, you will perhaps find far more satisfaction in life than even the scholar who (though he clearly recognizes the strings from which all lives and deeds depend) remains chained to the narrow confines of his study but nonetheless, as I can report from experience, is often not so terribly comfortable. There's still time for you to become a quite splendidly serviceable businessman, and you have no idea to what an extent businessmen have the opportunity to design their existences to be the most absolutely liveliest of lives. The way you are now, you're just creeping around the corners and through the cracks of life: This should cease. Perhaps I ought to have intervened earlier, much earlier; maybe I ought to have helped you more with deeds than with mere words of warning, but I don't know, given your proud mind, with its one determination to be helped only by yourself in every way possible, perhaps I'd have done more to offend than to genuinely convince you. What are you now doing with your days? Do tell me about them. Given all the worries I've endured on your behalf, I might now perhaps deserve your being somewhat more loquacious and communicative. As for me, what sort of a person am I? Someone to be wary of approaching unreservedly and with trust? Do you consider me a person to be feared? What is it about me which makes you wish to avoid me? Perhaps our circumstance? That I am the "big brother" and possibly know a bit more than you? Well then, know that I would be glad to be young again, and impractical, and naïve. And yet I am not quite so glad, dear brother, as a person should be. I am unhappy. Perhaps it's too late for me to become happy. I've now reached an age when a man who still has no home of his own cannot think of those happy individuals who enjoy the bliss of seeing a young woman occupied with running their households without the most painful longing. To love a girl, what a lovely thing this is, brother. And it's beyond my reach. —No, you really have no need to fear me, it is I who am seeking you out once more, who am writing to you, hoping to receive a warm friendly response. Perhaps you are now in fact richer than I—perhaps you have more hopes

44

and far more reason to have them, have plans and prospects I myself cannot even dream of—the thing is: I don't fully know you anymore. How could I after all these years of separation? Let me make your acquaintance once more, force yourself to write to me. Perhaps one day I shall enjoy the good fortune of seeing all my brothers happy; you, in any case, I should like to see content. What is Kaspar up to? Do you write to one another? What about his art? I'd love to have news of him as well. Farewell, brother. Perhaps we shall speak together again soon.

Yours, Klaus.

When a week had passed, Simon entered his employer's office just as evening was arriving and made the following speech: "You have disappointed me. Don't look so astonished, there's nothing to be done about it, I shall quit your place of business this very day and ask that you pay me my wages. Please, let me finish. I know perfectly well what I want. During the past week I've come to realize that the entire book trade is nothing less than ghastly if it must entail standing at one's desk from early morning till late at night while out of doors the gentlest winter sun is gleaming, and forces one to scrunch one's back, since the desk is far too small given my stature, writing like some accursed happenstance copyist and performing work unsuitable for a mind such as my own. I am capable of performing quite different tasks, esteemed sir, than the ones entrusted to me here. I'd expected to be able to sell books in your shop, wait on elegant individuals, bow and bid adieu to the customers when they're ready to depart. What's more, I'd imagined I might be allowed to peer into the mysterious universe of the book trade and glimpse the world's features in the visage and operation of your enterprise. But I experienced nothing of the sort. Do you imagine my young years in such a sorry state that I need to crumple up and suffocate in a lousy bookshop? You are equally mistaken if you suppose, for example, that a young man's back exists in order to be hunched. Why didn't you allocate for my use a good proper desk so I could comfortably sit or stand? Are not splendid American-sized desks available for purchase? If one wishes to have an employee, I believe, one should know how to accommodate him. This is a knack which, apparently, you don't have. Lord knows, all sorts of things are demanded of a young beginner: industry, loyalty, punctuality, tact, sobriety, modesty, moderation, purpose, and who knows what else. But to whom would it ever occur to start demanding virtues from a business owner such as yourself? Should my strength, my desire for activity, the pleasure I take in my own person, and the talent for being so gloriously capable of all these things be squandered on an old, meager, narrow bookshop? No, before I do any such squandering, I might join the army and sell my freedom altogether, if only for the sake of getting rid of it. It does not please me, respected sir, to own a half-measure, I would prefer to number among those who are utterly without possessions, for then at least my soul will still belong to me. You may be thinking it's inappropriate for me to speak with such vehemence, and that this is not a fitting place for a speech: So be it, I shall hold my tongue, pay me what I am owed and you will never set eyes on me again."

The old bookseller was quite astonished now to hear this

young, quiet, shy individual—who had worked so conscientiously during the past week—speaking in such a way. From the adjoining work rooms, some five heads belonging to clerks and shop assistants pressed together, watching and witnessing this scene. The old gentleman said: "If I had suspected you of such inclinations, Mr. Simon, I would have thought twice before offering you employment in my shop. You appear to be quite peculiarly fickle. Since a desk isn't to your liking, the entire enterprise displeases you. From what region of the world do you come, and are all the young people there cut from the same cloth? Just look how you are now standing before me—the old man. No doubt you don't yourself know what, in that callow head of yours, you actually want. Well, I have no intention of preventing you from leaving—here is your money, but in all honesty I must say this gives me no pleasure." The bookseller paid him his money, and Simon pocketed it.

When he arrived at home, he saw his brother's letter lying on the table, he read it and then thought to himself: "He's a good person, but I'm not going to write to him. I don't know how to describe my circumstances, and they aren't worth describing anyhow. I've no cause for complaint, and just as little reason to jump for joy, but grounds aplenty to keep silent. It's quite true, the things he writes, but for just that reason I shall be satisfied with the truth—let's leave it at that. That he is unhappy is something he himself must come to terms with, but I don't believe he is really so terribly unhappy. Letters often come out sounding that way. Writing a letter, you get carried away and make incautious remarks. In letters, the soul always wishes to do the talking,

and generally it makes a fool of itself. So it's best I don't write."
—And with this, the matter was settled. Simon was filled with
thoughts, with beautiful thoughts. Whenever he was thinking,
beautiful thoughts flooded his mind quite involuntarily. The
next morning—the sun was blindingly bright—he reported to
the Employment Referral Office. The man who sat there writing got to his feet. This man knew Simon quite well and was in
the habit of addressing him with a sort of mocking agreeable
familiarity. "Ah, Mr. Simon! Back again? What brings you to us
today?"

"I'm looking for a job."

"You've certainly stopped by here often enough while seeking
employment, a person might be tempted to think you uncannily
swift when it comes to job-seeking." The man laughed, but his
laugh was gentle; he was incapable of harsh laughter. "What was
your last place of employment, if I'm allowed to ask?"

Simon replied: "I was a nurse. I proved to be in possession of
all those qualities needed for tending the infirm. Why does your
jaw drop at my admission? Is it so terribly strange for a man my
age to try out various professions and attempt to make himself
useful to all different sorts of people? I find this quite a nice trait
in myself, for it requires a certain courage. My dignity is in no
way injured—on the contrary, I pride myself on being able to
solve all manner of life problems without trembling in the face of
difficulties that might scare most people off. I am useful, and this
certainty is enough to satisfy my pride. I wish to be of service."

"And so why did you not continue in the nursing profession?"
the man asked.

48

"I don't have time to stick to a single profession," Simon replied, "and it would never occur to me to repose, as many do, upon one type of profession as if it were a mattress with springs. No, I wouldn't succeed at that even if I lived to be a thousand. I'd rather go and join the army."

"Be careful that's not what happens."

"There are other escape routes as well. The army remark is just a casual expression I've gotten in the habit of using to conclude my speeches. There are so many ways out for a young man like myself. In the summertime, I can go find a farmer and work in the fields to help bring in the harvest on time: He'll welcome me and be grateful for my strength. He'll feed me and feed me well, they really cook out in the country, and when I leave him again, he'll press a few banknotes into my hand, and his young daughter, a fresh-faced lovely girl, will smile at me in parting in such a way that she will occupy my thoughts for a long time as I continue on my road. What harm is there in being on the road, even if it's raining or snowing, as long you have healthy limbs and remain free from cares? You, squeezed into your corner there, cannot even imagine how glorious it is to ramble down country roads. If they're dusty, then dusty is just how they are, no need to trouble your head about it. Afterwards you find yourself a cozy cool spot at the edge of the forest and as you lie there your eyes enjoy the most splendid view, and your senses repose in the most natural way, and your thoughts wander as taste and pleasure fancy. You'll no doubt counter that another person can do just the same thing—you yourself, for example, when you're on vacation. But vacations, what are they? The thought of them makes me laugh. I wish to have nothing to do with vacations. One might even say I hate them. Whatever you do, just don't set me up with a position involving vacations. This wouldn't appeal to me at all—in fact I think I'd die if I were given vacations. As far as I'm concerned I wish to do battle with life, fighting until I keel over: I wish to taste neither freedom nor comfort, I hate freedom if it's hurled at my feet the way you throw a dog a bone. That's vacation for you. If you might happen to think you see standing before you a man with a hankering for a vacation, you are very much mistaken, but I have every reason to suspect this is just what you think of me, alas."

"Here's a temporary post at a lawyer's office that needs filling for approximately one month. Would that suit you?"

"Most certainly, sir."

With this, Simon landed in the lawyer's office. He earned a pretty penny there and was perfectly content. Never had the world appeared lovelier to him than during this lawyer episode. He made some pleasant acquaintances, spent the day writing in an easy, effortless manner, checked over calculations, took dictation—at which he was particularly skillful—and to his own surprise behaved in such a charming way that his superior took a lively interest in him; he drank his daily cup of tea in the afternoon, and while he was writing, daydreamed out the breezy bright window. Daydreaming without neglecting his duties—he was supremely skilled at this. "I am earning so much money," he thought to himself, "that I could have a young woman." The moon often shone in the window as he worked, and this enchanted him.

In conversation with his little ladyfriend Rosa, Simon expressed himself in the following manner: "My lawyer has a long red nose and is a tyrant, but I get along with him quite well. I take his grumpy dictatorial nature as humorous and am myself surprised at how well I submit to all his commandments, many of which are unfair. I love it when things get a bit caustic, that suits me well, launching me to certain warm heights and whetting my appetite for work. He has a beautiful slender wife whom I should like to paint if I were a painter. She has, take my word for it, wonderful large eyes and splendid arms. Often she busies herself with something or other in the office; how she must look down on me, poor devil of a copy clerk. When I look upon such women I tremble and yet I'm happy. Are you laughing? Unfortunately I am accustomed to show myself before you without inhibitions, and I can only hope this pleases you."

Indeed Rosa did love it when people were open with her. She was a peculiar girl. Her eyes had a marvelous gleam, and her lips were downright lovely.

Simon went on: "When I'm on my way to work at eight in the morning, I feel so beautifully connected to all the others who must also report to work at eight. What a great barracks modern life is! And yet how beautiful and contemplative all this uniformity. Constantly you long for something that might be approaching, something you ought to encounter. You're so utterly bereft of possessions, so very much the poor devil, and you find yourself utterly at sea amid all this erudite, orderly precision. I ascend the four flights of stairs, go in, say "Good morning" and begin my work. Good God, how little is being asked of me, how little knowledge they expect. How little those around me seem to suspect I might be capable of quite different things. But this charming lack of demandingness on the part of my employers suits me perfectly. I can think while I am working—I have great prospects of becoming a thinker. I often think of you!"

Rosa laughed. "What a scoundrel you are. But do go on, it's quite interesting, what you're saying."

"The world is in point of fact marvelous," Simon continued, "I can be sitting here with you and no one can stop us from chatting for hours. I know you like listening to me. It's your opinion that my way of speaking is not without grace, though now I find myself compelled to laugh horribly inside because I've said this. But it's my habit to say anything and everything that comes to my mind, even if it should happen to be, for example, self-praise. I can also criticize myself with just the same lightness—I'm even pleased when I have occasion to do so. Why shouldn't we say whatever's on our minds? How much is lost if you insist on first examining everything at length. I don't like to spend too long considering before I speak, and whether the words are suitable or not, out they come! If I am vain, my vanity will inevitably come to light; if I were miserly, there would be miserliness speaking in my words; if I am decent, then doubtless my respectability will peal out from my lips; and if God had made an honest man of me, stalwartness would emanate from me regardless of what I was saying. In this respect I find myself free of worries, because I know myself and us a little and because I would be ashamed to display timidity while speaking. If, for example, I insult, wound, injure or annoy someone with words, can't I make this bad impression disappear again with the next few words? I never start thinking about how I am speaking until I notice disagreeable wrinkles on the face of my listener, such as those I now see on your face, Rosa."

"It's something else—"

"Are you tired?"

"Go home now, why don't you, Simon. It's quite true I'm feeling tired. You're sweet when you talk. I'm very fond of you."

Rosa held out her little hand to her young friend, who kissed it, said good night and departed. When he was gone, little Rosa sat there for a long time crying quietly to herself. She was weeping over her beloved, a young man with curls on his head, an elegant gait, an aristocratic mouth, but a dissolute lifestyle. "And so you love the one who doesn't deserve it," she said to herself, "and yet should I love out of reason, out of wishing to assign value? How laughable. What do I care about what is valuable—all I want is what I love." Then she went to bed.

2

One day Simon rang the bell rather shyly—it was noon—before an elegant house standing off on its own in a garden. The bell sounded to him as if a beggar had rung it. If he himself were sitting inside the house just now, as its owner for instance who was perhaps eating lunch, he would have turned indolently to his wife and asked: Who could be ringing the bell just now, surely a beggar! "When you think of elegant people," he thought as he waited, "you always picture them at the dinner table, or in a carriage, or getting dressed with the help of male or female servants, while you always imagine a poor man standing outside in the cold with his coat collar drawn up, as mine is now, waiting before a garden gate with a pounding heart. Poor people have, as a rule, rapid, pounding, ardent hearts, while those of the rich are cold, roomy, upholstered, well-heated, and nailed shut! Oh, if only someone would rush fleet-footed to the door, what a relief that would be. There's something constricting about standing and waiting at a wealthy portal. Despite my little bit of worldly experience what weak legs I am standing on." —And indeed he was trembling when a girl came hurrying up to open the door for the one standing outside. Simon always had to smile when someone opened the door and invited him in, and now, too, this smile was in evidence, a smile that resembled a timid appeal and perhaps could be seen on many other faces as well.

"I'm looking for a room."

Simon removed his hat before a beautiful lady who appeared and looked the newcomer up and down with great attentiveness. This pleased Simon, for he believed it was her right to do so, and because her air of friendliness was unabated.

"Would you like to come with me? There, up the stairs."

Simon invited the lady to precede him. To do so, he gestured with his hand, actually employing his hand for this purpose for the first time in his whole life. The woman, opening a door, showed the young man the room.

"What a beautiful room," cried Simon, who was truly astonished, "far too beautiful for me, unfortunately, far too elegant for me. I am, you should know, so very poorly suited to such an elegant room. And yet I would dearly love to inhabit it—all too dearly, far far too dearly. In fact, it wasn't right to show me this chamber. It would have been better had you shown me the door at once. How do I come to be casting my gaze into such a gay, beautiful space—it's as if it were made for a god to dwell in. What beautiful dwellings are inhabited by the well-to-do, the ones who possess something. I have never possessed anything, have never been anything, and despite the hopes of my parents will never amount to anything at all. What a lovely view from the windows, and such pretty, shiny furniture, and such charming curtains—they give the room a girlish look. I would perhaps become a good, tender person here, if it's true, as people say, that surroundings can change a person. Might

I gaze at it for a little while longer, remain standing here one more minute?"

"Of course you may."

"I thank you."

"What sort of people are your parents, and, if I may ask, in what sense are you 'nothing,' as you expressed yourself a moment ago?"

"I'm unemployed."

"That wouldn't matter to me. It all depends!"

"No, I have little hope. Though admittedly I shouldn't be saying such things if I am to speak with perfect truthfulness. I'm overflowing with hope. Never, ever does it abandon me. —My father is a poor but joyful individual who would never dream of comparing his currently bleak circumstances with his glory days. He lives like a lad of twenty-five and can't be bothered to ponder his condition. I admire him and seek to emulate him. If he can still be cheerful in his snowy old age, it must be his young son's duty, thirty times—indeed one hundred times—over, to hold his head high and meet people's gazes with eyes that flash like lightning. But the gift of thought was given to me—and to my brothers even more than me—by our mother. My mother is dead."

A dismayed "ah" came from the mouth of the lady, who was still standing there kindly.

"She was a good-hearted woman. We children always, constantly still speak of her whenever and wherever we're reunited. We live scattered all across this round, wide world, and this is excellent, for we all have such heads on us, you see, that they shouldn't come together for very long. There's a ponderousness to each of us that would be burdensome if we appeared together in human society. But this is something that, thank goodness, we avoid, and each of us knows perfectly well why that's imperative. And yet we love one another with appropriate fraternal love. One of my brothers is a fairly prominent scholar, another a stock market specialist, and yet another nothing more than just my brother, for I love him more than a brother—and thinking of him, it never occurs to me to emphasize any of his qualities except simply the fact that he is my brother: mine, someone who looks just like me, and nothing more. I would like to live here in your home together with this brother of mine. The room is large enough for both of us. But no doubt this isn't possible. What does the room cost?"

"What does your brother do?"

"He's a landscape painter! How much would you charge for the room?— — Oh, that much? This is assuredly not too expensive for this room, but for us it's far too much. Besides which, come to think of it, now that I am peering at you more keenly: The two of us would hardly be suitable, strolling in and out of this house as though we belonged here. We are still so coarse, you'd be disappointed in us. What's more, our habits are a bit rough on duvet covers, furniture, linens, window curtains, doorknobs and stair landings—you'd be horrified and would lose your temper with us, or perhaps you would forgive us and strive to turn the other cheek, which would be even more humiliating. I don't wish to be the cause of your having trouble with us at some later point. Surely you would! Do hear me out. I can see it all perfectly clearly. Basically, the two of us have, in the long run, little respect for anything fine and delicate. People such as ourselves should be left standing before wealthy garden gates—free to make derisive remarks about all the splendor and attention to detail. We are great deriders! Adieu!"

The eyes of the beautiful woman had begun to gleam intensely, and now all at once she said: "I should like to take in you and your brother after all. As for the price, I am certain we can reach some agreement."

"No, it's best that we don't."

Simon was already heading downstairs. Then the lady's voice called out after him: "Please stay a little longer." And she hurried after him. At the bottom she caught up with Simon and forced him to stand still and listen to her: "What could you be thinking of, leaving again so soon. Can't you see that I want, that I would like to keep the two of you? Even if you don't pay a thing. What does it matter? Not at all, not at all, just come with me, come. Come into this room with me. Marie! Where are you? Bring in the coffee at once."

Inside she said to Simon: "I wish to get to know you and your brother. How could you go running off like that? I am so often all alone in this isolated house that I feel frightened. My husband is always gone, off on some distant journey, he is an explorer and goes sailing off on seas the very existence of which his poor wife hasn't even an inkling. Am I not a poor woman? What is your name? What's the name of the other one, your brother? My name is Klara. Just call me Miss Klara. It pleases me to hear this simple name. Are you feeling a bit more trusting now? This would make me so, so very happy. Don't you think we'll be able to live together and get along? Certainly we'll be able to—I think you must be quite gentle. I'm not afraid to have you in my home. You have honest eyes. Is your brother older than you?"

"Yes, he is older and a much better person than I am."

"You are an honest man to say such a thing."

"My name is Simon, and my brother is Kaspar."

"My husband's name is Agappaia."

She turned pale as she spoke these words, but quickly pulled herself together and smiled.

Simon wrote to his brother Kaspar:

What odd fish we are, the two of us. The way we drift about this earth, it's as if only you and I were alive, and no one else. What a crazy sort of friendship the two of us have forged, it's as though among all mankind no one else could be found who might be worthy of the designation "friend." We're not really brothers at all, we're just friends, two people who find themselves companions in this world. I'm not truly made for friendship, and can't understand what it is about you I find so splendid that I'm forced constantly to imagine myself at your side, pressed against your back as it were. I'll soon be thinking your head is my own, for you're so very often in my head already; and if things go on like this, perhaps I'll soon be seizing things with your hands, walking with your legs and eating with your mouth. Truly there is something mysterious about our friendship when I say to you I consider it quite possible that our hearts have been trying to draw apart from one another, but they're incapable of separating. I'm overjoyed I have to admit that you still can't quite manage this, for your letters sound so nice and for the time being I also wish to remain under this mystery's spell. For us this is good, but how can I be speaking in such a horribly dry tone: I find it simply, not to tell a lie, enchanting. And why shouldn't two brothers overdo things a little? We fit together quite well—and we did even back in the days of still hating one another when we nearly beat each other to a pulp. Do you remember? This appeal, with a dash of healthy laughter, is all that's needed to stir up within you, to glue together, paste, and draw pictures that are truly more than worth remembering. We had become, for reasons I can no longer recall, mortal enemies. Oh, how accomplished we were at hating—our hatred was decidedly resourceful in inventing torments and humiliations to inflict on one another. Once at the dinner table, just to provide a single example of this lamentable and childish state of affairs, you threw a platter of sauerkraut at me, because you couldn't resist, saying: "Here, catch!" I have to tell you, at the time I was trembling with fury even if only for the fact that here was this lovely opportunity for you to insult me so cruelly, and there was nothing I could do about it. I caught the platter, but was stupid enough to savor the pain of this mortification all up and down my gullet. And do you remember how, one noon—it was a quiet, a deathly quiet summer-hot Sunday afternoon mad with this deathly silence—someone came creeping up to you in the kitchen and asked you to be friends with me again. It was an incredible feat of self-control, let me tell you, to overcome those feelings of shame and defiance to reach out to you, the very figure of an enemy inclined to scornfully reject me. I did this and to this day am grateful to myself for doing so. Whether you're grateful as well is a matter of the most joyous and fragrant indifference. I can only guess. Go away, I hear you trying to get a word in. Sorry, not possible. Desist! —How many delightful hours I thereafter enjoyed in your company. All at once I found you tender, loving, considerate. I think blissful feelings of joy burned on our cheeks. We wandered, you as painter and I as observer and commentator, through the meadows on the broad mountain slopes, wading in the scent of the grass, in the wetness of cool mornings, under the heat of midday and with the damp, infatuated setting of the sun. The trees watched what we were doing there, and the clouds balled themselves up, no doubt in anger at possessing no power to break our newly forged love. In the evenings we would come home horribly broken, dusty, starved and exhausted, and then suddenly you went off one day. The devil knows I helped you leave, as though I'd bound myself to do so for some sort of retainer, or as though I were in a hurry to see you depart. Certainly it was an unheard-of pleasure for me to see you setting off, for you were traveling out into the wide world. How far from wide this world is, brother.

Come visit me soon. I can give you shelter just as I would shelter a bride whom I assume to be in the habit of reposing on silk while servants wait on her. Admittedly I have no servants, but I do have a room fit for a born lord. The two of us, you and I, have just been offered a splendid chambre as a gift, it's been laid at our feet. You can paint pictures here just as well as in your luscious fat landscapes, after all you have your imagination. It ought by rights to be summer now so that I might throw a garden party on the lawn in your honor, with Chinese lanterns and garlands of flowers, so as to receive you in a manner approaching what you deserve. Come all the same, but see to it your coming is quick, otherwise I'll have to come get you. My lady and landlady is pressing your hand in hers. She is convinced that she knows you already just from my descriptions. Once she meets you, she'll never want to meet anyone else again. Do you have a decent suit? Are your trousers not sagging too terribly about your knees, and does your head covering still merit the designation hat? Otherwise you may not appear before me. Just a joke, what silliness. Let your little Simon embrace you. Farewell, brother. I hope you'll come soon—

Several weeks had passed, spring was beginning to return, the air was damper and softer, uncertain fragrances and sounds began to assert themselves, coming seemingly from beneath the earth. The earth was soft, one walked on it as on thick supple rugs. You thought you must be hearing birds singing. "Spring is on its way," people on the street said to one another, awash in sensations. Even the stark buildings were taking on a certain fragrance, a richer hue. Such a peculiar state of affairs, and yet it was such an old, familiar phenomenon—but everyone perceived it as utterly novel, it inspired strange, turbulent thoughts, a person's limbs, senses, heads, thoughts, everything was stirring as if all these things wished to start growing anew. The water of the lake gleamed so warmly, and the bridges snaking across the river appeared to arch more boldly. Flags were flapping in the wind, and it gave people pleasure to see them flap. And then the sunshine drove everyone out into the beautiful, white, clean streets in clusters and groups, where they remained standing, greedily luxuriating in the warm air's kisses. Many coats of many people were cast aside. You could see the men moving more freely again, and the women had such strange expressions in their eyes, as though something blissful were emerging from their hearts. At night one heard the sound of vagabond guitars for the first time, and men and women stood amid a whirl of gaily frolicking children. The lights of the lanterns flickered like candles in quiet rooms, and when you went walking across the night-dark meadows, you could feel the blooming and stirring of the flowers. The grass would soon grow again, the trees soon begin again to pour their green over the low roofs of the houses and block the view from the windows. The forest would be luxuriant, voluptuous, heavy, oh the forest.— — Simon was working once more at a large commercial firm.

This firm was a bank that enjoyed international significance, a large building with a palatial look to it in which hundreds of young and old, male and female people were employed. They all wrote with diligent fingers, made calculations using calculating machines and also sometimes their memories, thought using their thoughts and made themselves useful with their knowledge. There were any number of young, elegant letter-writing clerks who could speak four to seven languages. These clerks stood out from the rest of the calculating pack by virtue of their refined foreign airs. They had traveled on ocean liners, attended the theater in Paris and New York, visited tea houses in Yokohama and knew how to amuse themselves in Cairo. Now they were handling the bank's correspondence and waited for their salaries to increase while casting aspersions on their homeland, which they found tiny and dingy. The calculating pack consisted for the most part of older individuals who clung to their posts large and small as if to beams and stakes. All of them had long noses from years of calculations and went about in threadbare, shabby, abraded, creased and crumpled garments. But among them were a number of intelligent individuals who perhaps secretly pursued strange exotic hobbies and thus led lives that, while quiet and isolated, were nonetheless dignified. Many of the younger clerks, however, were incapable of spending their free time in refined ways; mostly they were the offspring of rural landowners, innkeepers, farmers and craftsmen, who, the moment they arrived in the city, did all they could to cultivate a refined urban air, though they never quite succeeded, and so they failed to advance beyond a certain clodhopperish coarseness. Meanwhile there were also quiet characters with delicate manners who stood out oddly amid the louts. The bank's director was an old quiet man whom no one ever saw. It seemed that the threads and roots of the entire monstrous enterprise lay in a tangle inside his head. As a painter thinks in colors, a musician in notes, a sculptor in stone, a baker in flour, a poet in words, and a farmer in patches of land, this man appeared to think in money. One good thought of his, thought at just the right moment, could bring in half a million in the space of half an hour. Possibly! Possibly more, possibly less, possibly nothing at all, and to be sure, this man must secretly have lost money now and then without his subordinates being any the wiser: They went off to lunch when the church-bell rang at noon, returned at two, worked another four hours, went away, slept, awoke, got up for breakfast, went back into the building just like before, resumed their labors, and no one knew a thing, for no one had time to learn anything at all about these mysterious goings-on. And the morose quiet old man went on thinking in his private office. For matters pertaining to his employees he had only a weak half-smile. This smile had something poetic, exalted, plan-hatching and legislative about it. Simon often tried to imagine himself in the director's shoes. But this image generally vanished before his eyes, and every last concept receded from him when he thought about this: "There is something proud and exalted about him, but also something incomprehensible and almost inhuman. Why in the world do all these people, copyists and calculators, indeed even girls in the bloom of youth, go through the selfsame entryway into the selfsame building just in order to scribble away, try out pens, calculate and wave their arms about, study and blow their noses, sharpen pencils and carry papers about in their hands? Do they do so out of pleasure or under duress, and are they conscious of performing some sensible fruitful activity? All of them come from quite different directions, some even arrive by train from distant regions, pricking up their ears to see whether they still have time to run a private errand before work: They are as patient as a herd of lambs, and when evening arrives they scatter, each on his own particular trajectory, and tomorrow they'll all be back again at the same time. They see one another, recognize each other by gait, voice and way of opening a door, but they have very little to do with one another. They are all alike and yet are strangers to each other, and when one of them dies or embezzles something, they puzzle about it for the space of a morning, and then things go on as before. It's been known to happen that in the middle of his copy-work one of them has a stroke. Does it help him that he was employed at this firm for a good fifty years? For fifty years on end he went in and out the selfsame door, employed the selfsame turns of phrase in business letters a thousand times over, went through several new suits and often felt surprised how long each pair of boots lasted. And now? Can one say this man has lived? And don't thousands of people live just like this? Were perhaps his children the thing that mattered most to him in life, was his wife the joy of his existence? Yes, that could be. I don't want to pretend to be an expert in these matters, for this would appear quite appropriate to me, given my youth. Outside it is spring, and I could spring right out the window, that's how painful I find this long, long not-being-allowed-to-move-one's-limbs. A bank is a foolish thing in springtime. How would a banking establishment look standing, say, upon a lush green meadow? Perhaps my pen would look to me like a young flower freshly sprouted from the earth. But no, I've no desire to make fun. Perhaps this is all exactly as it has to be, perhaps everything has a purpose. I just can't make out the big picture because the view itself I see too intensely. This view is somewhat discouraging: this sky outside the windows, and in my ear this sweet singing. The white clouds are out walking in the sky, and I have to sit here writing. Why do I have an eye for the clouds? If I were a cobbler, at least I'd be making shoes for children, men and ladies, and then all these people could go walking in the streets on spring days wearing my shoes. I would experience spring when I saw my shoes on their feet. Here I cannot feel the springtime—the springtime is disturbing me."

Simon hung his head, furious to be having such tender feelings.

One evening as he was on his way home across the bridge all lit up for the night, Simon noticed a man walking ahead of him in long strides. This figure in its greatcoated slimness filled him with sweet alarm. He thought he recognized this walk, these trousers, this odd cauldron of a hat, the fluttering hair. The stranger was carrying a flimsy portfolio beneath one arm. Simon hastened his steps, overcome with tremulous forebodings, and suddenly he threw his arms about the walker's neck, crying out "Brother!" Kaspar embraced him. Loudly conversing, they went home, that is: They had a rather steep ascent to make up the mountainside whose slope the city had covered with gardens and villas. At the top, they were welcomed by the small run-down cottages of the outskirts. The setting sun blazed in their windows, turning them into radiant eyes gazing fixedly, beautifully into the distance. Down below lay the city, spread out broad and luxuriant upon the plain like a glittering twinkling carpet, the evening bells, which are always different from morning bells, were ringing far below, the lake lay, its outlines indistinct, in its delicate ineffable form at the foot of the city, the mountain and all the gardens. Not many lights were sparkling yet, but those whose glow could be seen were burning with a splendid unfamiliar keenness. People were now walking and hastening down below in all the crooked hidden streets, you couldn't see them, but you knew they were there. "It would be splendid to stroll down elegant *Bahnhofstrasse* just now," Simon said. Kaspar walked in silence. He had become a magnificent fellow. "How he strides along," Simon thought. Finally they were standing before their house. "Really?" Kaspar laughed: "You live at the edge of the forest?" Both of them went inside.

When Klara Agappaia beheld the new arrival, a strange flame began to flicker in her large weary eyes. She closed her eyes and tilted her lovely head to one side. She didn't appear to be feeling such great pleasure at the sight of this young man, it looked like something quite different. She tried not to be self-conscious, tried to smile the way a person smiles when welcoming a guest. But she didn't quite manage it. "Go upstairs," she said, "I'm just so tired today. How odd. I really don't know what's wrong with me." The two young men went to their room: It was filled with moonlight. "Let's not light the lamp," Simon said, "we can go to bed just like this." —Then there was a knock at the door, it was Klara, who said, standing outside: "Have you two got everything you need, is nothing missing?" —"No, we've already gone to bed, what could be missing?" —"Good night, my friends," she said and opened the door a little, shut it again and went away. "She seems to be a peculiar woman," Kaspar remarked. Then they both fell asleep.

3

The next morning the painter unpacked his landscapes from their portfolio, and first an entire autumn fell out of it, then a winter, all the moods of Nature came to life again. "How little this is of what I saw. Swift as a painter's eye is, his hand is so sluggish, so slow. There are still so many things I have to paint! Often I think I'll go mad." All three of them, Klara, Simon and the painter, were standing around the pictures. Few words were spoken, and these were just exclamations of delight. Suddenly Simon leapt over to his hat, which lay on the floor of the room, thrust it savagely, furiously upon his head and dashed out the door, shouting, "I'm late!"

"An hour late! This is something a young man should not allow himself," he was told at the bank.

"And if he nonetheless does allow it?" the one being scolded replied defiantly.

"What, insolence on top of everything else? Well, go right ahead! Suit yourself!"

Simon's conduct was reported to the director, who decided to dismiss the young man; he called him to his office and gave him this news in a quite soft, even kindly voice. Simon replied:

"I'm perfectly happy things have come to an end. Do you

perhaps suppose you're striking me a blow by sending me away—robbing me of courage, destroying me or anything of the sort? On the contrary, I'm being raised up and flattered, at long last I'm being infused with new hope. I was never made to be a writing and calculating machine. I like to write, I like doing calculations and find it desirable to behave in a decorous manner towards my fellow men, I enjoy being industrious, and as long as it does my heart no injury, I passionately love to obey. I'd also be perfectly capable of submitting to certain laws if this were important, but it's been some time now since such things had any importance for me here. When I found myself running late today, I merely felt angry and annoyed, I was by no means filled with honest conscientious concern, nor did I reproach myself, or if I did so, it was only for still being such a cowardly fool that I leap to my feet at the stroke of eight and start running like a wind-up clock that runs whenever it's wound. I thank you for having the energy to dismiss me and request that you think of me however you please. You are surely an admirable, commendable, great man, but, you see, I too wish to be one, and that's why it's good you're sending me away, why it was so advantageous for me to comport myself today in a manner one might call unseemly. In your offices, which are so highly touted and where anyone at all would be delighted to find employment, there can be no question of a young man developing and growing. I don't care a whit about enjoying the benefits associated with receiving a fixed monthly income. While receiving it, I degenerate, becoming addlepated and lily-livered, I ossify. You may be surprised to hear me making use of such expressions, but you must admit I am speaking the complete truth. Only one person can be a man here: you! —Doesn't it ever occur to you that among your poor subordinates there might be some who feel the urge to be men themselves: effective, productive, respect-inspiring men. I can't possibly find it agreeable to stand off to one side in this world just to avoid acquiring a reputation as a malcontent and therefore a scarcely employable person. How great is the temptation here to feel afraid—and how faint the appeal of extricating oneself from this miserable fear. My having set in motion this all but impossible development on this day is something I cannot help appreciating in myself, let people say what they will. You, Herr Direktor, have barricaded yourself in here, you're never visible, no one knows whose orders they are following, and in fact one isn't following orders at all but rather merely stagnating according to one's own bad habits, which turn out to be perfectly appropriate. What a trap for young people with a tendency to be indolent and sluggish. Here nothing is demanded of all the strength that might animate a young man's spirit, nothing is required that might distinguish a man and human being. Neither courage nor wit, neither loyalty nor industry, neither creative drive nor the desire for challenges can help a person to advance himself here: Indeed, displaying strength and capabilities is even looked down upon. Naturally, how could it not be looked down upon in such a slow, sluggish, dry, miserable system? Farewell, sir, I leave in order to work myself back to health, even if this means shoveling dirt or carrying endless sacks of coal on my back. I love all sorts of work, excepting the sort whose performance does not require the exertion of all one's faculties."

"Shall I write you out a letter of reference, even though you don't really deserve one?"

"A letter of reference? No, please don't. If I have earned no other reference than at most a bad one, I'd rather have none at all. From now on I shall write my own references. I shall no longer call upon anyone other than myself when someone asks me for references, and this will make the best possible impression on sensible clear-minded people. I am glad to be leaving you without a letter in hand, for a reference from you would only remind me of my own cowardice and fear, a condition of sluggishness and relinquished strength, of days spent in idleness, afternoons filled with furious attempts at escape, evenings dedicated to sweet but pointless longings. I thank you for having had the intention of letting me go with an amicable gesture—that shows me I've been standing before a man who possibly grasps at least some of what I say."

"Young man, you are far too hot-headed!" the director said. "You are undermining your own future—"

"I don't want a future, I want a present. To me this appears of greater value. You have a future only when you have no present, and when you have a present, you forget to even think about the future."

"I wish you well but I fear that something unfortunate will befall you. You interest me, that's why I've been listening—otherwise I wouldn't have wasted so much time on you. Perhaps you haven't found your calling, perhaps you'll amount to something yet. In any case, I hope things will go well for you."

With a nod of the director's head Simon was dismissed and

soon found himself on the street outside. He observed a man pacing up and down in front of a pastry shop, probably he was waiting for someone, perhaps a woman, who could say? But the man aroused his interest. He was, at first glance, horrifically ugly, with a quite unusually large curved skull, a full beard and a rather weary, even animal, expression in his eyes. He had a mincing walk that was nonetheless noble, and his clothes were of good quality and tasteful. In his hand he held a yellow walking stick; he appeared to be a scholar, but one who was still young. There was something gentle, even heart-stirring about this man and his bearing. It seemed as though one might venture to address him freely—and Simon did:

"Forgive me, sir, for speaking to you in this way. The moment I set eyes on you something about you appealed to me. I would like to make your acquaintance. Shouldn't such a heartfelt wish be sufficient grounds for addressing a few words to a person like yourself in the middle of the street? You seem as if you're searching for someone, as if you suspect there might be someone waiting for you here on this square. But with this crowd of people milling about it will be difficult for you alone to discover the individual in question. I'll help you look if you are willing to confide a few details of the person you hope to meet. Is it a lady?"

"Yes, most assuredly a lady," the gentleman replied, smiling.

"What does she look like?"

"Dressed in black from head to foot. A tall slender creature. Large eyes that, when you see them, will follow you for a long, long time, even if they aren't still gazing at you at all. About her neck she wears a necklace of large white pearls, and on her ears long dangling earrings. Her joints are circled by simple gold hoops—I mean her wrist joints, of course. Her face has something full, oval, voluptuous about it. You'll see. About her mouth, though this is deceptive, there is a trace of something cagey and crafty, it's a rather shut-tight mouth. By the way, she likes to wear a broad-brimmed hat with drooping feathers: The hat appears to have just flown up and landed on her head and hair. If this description isn't yet sufficient, let me also draw your attention to the fact that she is accompanied by a greyhound on a thin black leash. She never goes out without him. I shall remain standing here at my post and await your report. I am grateful for your offer, quite aside from the fact that, based on the words you've addressed to me, I find you quite interesting: And indeed the crowd of people swarming about keeps increasing in size. There appears to be some sort of festival in progress."

"Yes—something of that sort. I don't generally pay much attention to these things."

"Why not?"

"Oh, you know, each person has his own path to follow. Goodbye for now!"

And with this, Simon went off as quickly as possible through the thick crowd of people. From all sides he was pressed and shoved, almost lifted into the air. But he pushed back as well, finding it highly amusing to pass slowly through the mass of bodies and faces in this way. Finally he reached a sort of island, that is, a small empty space, and, glancing about, he suddenly caught sight of Frau Klara. She really did have a dog with her. Since moving into her house, he hadn't paid her much attention, and so didn't know she was in the habit of going out with her dog at her side.

"There's a man looking for you," he said when she noticed him.

"My husband, no doubt," she replied. "Come with me, we'll go together. He's suddenly returned from his journey without writing me so much as a line. It's always like this. How did you make his acquaintance, and how do you come to be tracking down ladies on his behalf? You are certainly a strange person, Simon. What's that? You've given up your job? So what are you planning to do now? Come with me, this way. We can get through more easily over here. I'll introduce you to my husband."

It was decided they would spend the evening at the theater. They sent word to Kaspar, who showed up at the appointed hour at the theater, a white splendid building towering up beside the shore of the lake. When the curtain rose, it revealed a gray empty space. But this space soon came to life, when a dancer with bare legs and arms came on stage and began dancing to a soft music. Her body was veiled in a transparent, fluttering, flowing garment which appeared to mirror the lines of the dance in the floating air. You could sense the complete innocence and gracefulness of this dance, and it wouldn't have occurred to anyone present to find her immodest or to ascribe impure intentions to the girl's nakedness. Her dance often resolved into a simple striding, but this too remained a dance, and at some points the dancer appeared to be borne aloft upon her own waves. When, for example, she raised one leg and curled her lovely foot, she did so in such a novel unperturbed manner that everyone thought: I have seen this before, but where? Or did I just dream it? There was something weighty about the girl's dance, it seemed a part of nature. To be sure, measured strictly by the laws of ballet, her art was perhaps somewhat lacking, her abilities might seem paltry compared with the abilities and achievements of ballerinas. But by means of her girlishly bashful gracefulness alone she possessed the art of filling people with delight. When she sailed to the ground, with such sweet heft, and when she flew up to attain greater momentum, the wildness and innocence of her motions bewitched all the souls witnessing it. And as she moved, she too was exhilarated by her fleeting motions, and her arousal devised ever new flourishes to accompany the notes. Her hands resembled two beautiful white fluttering doves. The girl smiled as she danced, clearly this made her happy. Her artlessness was felt to be the highest art. At one point she flew in huge soft leaps, like a stag being pursued, from one beat to another. Like waves splashing up to crash down on a low shoreline, she'd seem to be dancing to scatter into spray, but next she went flowing off like a wide, sunny, powerful wave, like a wave in the middle of a lake, and now it was like a flurry of flakes and little stones, constantly changing and always poignant. The sensibilities of all who saw her danced along with her, filled with pleasure and pain. Some had tears in their eyes from watching this dance, pure tears of vicarious delight, vicarious dancing. How beautiful it was, when the girl had completed her dance, to see aged imposing women shoot passionately to their feet, waving their handkerchiefs and throwing flowers into the abyss of the stage to honor the girl. "Be our sister," everyone's smiles seemed to be asking. "What a joy it would be to call you my daughter if you so wished," these ladies appeared to be exulting. Gazing at the young girl upon the stage, the hundred-headed audience forgot the boundary, the wall separating them from her. Innumerable arms arced through the air as though in imagined caresses; hands were trembling as they waved. Words shouted down to the stage were the inventions of pure joy. Even the cold golden statues adorning the stage appeared to wish to come to life and for once crown a head with the laurel wreaths they held in their gold hands. Simon had never before found the theater so beautiful. Klara was utterly delighted, who could have been otherwise on such an evening. Only Herr Agappaia remained silent and said not a word. Kaspar said: "I'm going to paint an ovation like this, what a splendid picture it would make." "But difficult to paint," Simon said, "this perfume and gleam of joy—this shimmer of delight, the coldness and warmth, the definite and blurry, the colors and shapes in this perfume, the gold and the heavy red, drowning like this in all the colors—and the stage, the tiny focal point and the small blissful girl standing upon it, the clothing of the women, the faces of the men, the boxes and all the rest—really, Kaspar, it would be quite difficult indeed."

Klara said: "Think of a silent landscape, the way all of it is just lying there, the forests and hills and the wide meadows, and here we are in this glittery theater. How strange. But perhaps it's all just nature—not only the vastness and silence out there, but also the small agile things that are the work of man. A theater is also part of nature: What nature instructs us to create must itself belong to nature, though perhaps that's just a natural anomaly. Let

77

culture become ever so refined, it will nonetheless remain a part of nature, for culture is only a long drawn-out process of inventing, spread over the ages, and performed by creatures who must always cling to nature. If you paint a picture, Kaspar, that will be nature, for you paint using your senses and fingers, which nature has given you. No, we do well to love nature and remain mindful of it—even, if I may be permitted to say so, to worship nature—for human beings must do their praying somewhere, otherwise they turn bad. If only we can love what is nearest at hand! That's a blessing that makes us roll thoughtfully along with the earth, driving our centuries tempestuously on, a blessing that makes us feel our lives more intensely and with greater bliss—and so we must seize and grab hold of it a thousand times over, in a thousand moments—oh, what do I know!"

She had become inflamed as she spoke. "Does that make any sense, what I just said?" she asked Kaspar.

Kaspar did not reply. They had long since left the theater behind and were on their way home. Simon had walked on a bit ahead with Herr Agappaia.

"Tell me something," Klara asked her companion.

"I have a colleague, Erwin by name," Kaspar began, walking beside the woman. "He doesn't have much talent, or perhaps he was once talented, in his early youth. Nonetheless, despite the fact that his painting offers him no prospect of success, he is fanatically in love with his art. He declares all his pictures lousy, and lousy is what they are, but he works on them for years. He keeps scraping off the paint to try again. To love nature as he does must be a torment—and it's also disgraceful: No sensible man allows himself to be made a fool of by any one thing, tormented and tricked for so long, even by nature itself. Of course, it isn't art that torments him: He himself is doing the tormenting with his pathetic notions of art and the world. This Erwin loves me. When both of us were just starting out, we would paint together. We would romp about the open meadows and beneath the trees, which I always see only in the fullest, most opulent blossom when I think back on that 'godful' time. This word 'godful' is one that Erwin himself coined in his blind enthusiasm when he stood before landscapes whose beauty surpassed his powers of apprehension. *Kaspar, just look at this godful landscape,* is something he said to me I don't know how many hundreds of times. Even back then, although he was turning out attractive little pictures that were made with talent, he was a harsh unsparing critic of his own work. He destroyed pictures of his that were successful, and preserved only the botched ones, because only they appeared to him to have value. His talent suffered terribly beneath this constant distrust, until finally the bad treatment caused it to shrivel up and run dry like a spring that's been scorched by the sun and parched. I often advised him to sell his finished pictures at a modest price, but because of my importunity he almost declared our friendship null and void. Day after day he became more and more puzzled at how I could go on lightheartedly, even frivolously painting, but he admired my talent, which he had to acknowledge. But he wished I would pursue my art with more seriousness of purpose, and I replied that in the practice of art all that was required to accomplish something were diligence, a joyful zeal, and the observation of nature, and I drew his attention to the harm that could and must come about when one approached a matter with exaggerated holy solemnity. He did in fact believe me, but he was too weak to tear himself away from this bullheaded seriousness he'd sunk his teeth into. Then I left on a journey and received the most poignant letters from him, full of sadness over my departure. He said I was the only one who'd been able to keep his spirits up, such as they were. He asked me to return or, failing that, to allow him to join me. Indeed, he did join me. He was always right behind me like my very own shadow, no matter how often I treated him with coldness, scorn or even condescension. He steered clear of women, indeed he hated them, for he was afraid they might distract him from the holiness of his life's work. I made fun of him for this, and it may be that I treated him rather contemptuously. His paintings became ever more clumsy, and he went on sketching ever more obsessively. I advised him to make fewer studies and instead get his hand used to the brush. He tried it, and wept at the sight of my own offhanded productivity. Then the two of us undertook a shared journey to my homeland—you can imagine! The paths there led one across broad high mountains, then steeply down into deep valleys and at once back up again. To me it was an easily grasped pleasure, something to savor, a slight quickening of the breath, a greater demand on the legs, and nothing further. Erwin could barely move forward: In truth, his strength had been sapped by the excesses of his artistic longings. One day the two of us—it was nearly evening, and we stood high up on a mountain meadow—glimpsed between the fir branches the three lakes of my native region. Edwin cried out at the sight. It was indeed unforgettably beautiful. Down below, the noise of the railway could be heard, and the sound of bells rang up to where we stood. The city had not yet come into view, but I stretched out my hand to show Edwin the spot where it must lie. Like the raiment of princesses, the lakes lay spread out all sparkly and gently gleaming, ringed in by noble processions of mountains, with enchantingly delicate shorelines, so far off in the distance and yet so near. That very evening the two of us reached home, dust-covered and ravenous. My sister was happy I'd brought this reticent guest with me. This was perhaps three years ago now. Little by little she drew closer to him, and I believe I am correct in thinking that a secret love for him was kindled within her. It pained her to see how I treated her chosen ward. She asked me to speak of him in a more friendly and respectful way when I made jocular remarks at his expense. The poor fellow didn't last long. One day he took his leave. He was prevailed upon to write a few lines in my sister's journal—it's all so comical, and yet somehow profound. Perhaps while he was writing in her book he rested his hand thoughtfully and imagined a future for himself together with my sister. What was art offering him? I felt a bit worried my sister might make something like a scene. But she just looked at him warmly and kindly as they said goodbye. He couldn't bring himself to look at her, he didn't dare. Did he appear to himself a miserable wretch? Probably. Perhaps because he had a birthmark that covered half his face he was incapable of believing that a girl might love him and want him for a husband. But in my eyes it only made him look more noble. I very much liked looking at him. We were traveling, and once he asked my permission to write to my sister. 'What's it got to do with me,' I exclaimed. 'Write to her if you feel like it!' He went home again, back to the utterly dead, dismal surroundings of his academy professors. I pitied him, but parted from him coldly, or at least I displayed coldness toward him: For me it's unpleasant to show warmth to someone I find so pitiable. He wrote a few letters which I never answered, and even today he still writes to me and I don't respond. He's clinging to me in desperation. Under such circumstances, is it necessary to respond? He's lost, he's made no progress whatsoever. His recent pictures are horrible. And yet no other person has ever had so close a bond with me as he did. . . . And when I think of those days when the two of us were so captivated by nature! So many things in this world pass. All you can do is work, make things, create, that's what we're here for, not for inspiring pity."

"The poor thing," Klara said, "I do pity him. I wish he were here, and if he were ill, how gladly I would care for him. An unhappy artist is like an unhappy king. What pain he must feel deep in his soul to know he's so lacking in talent. I can imagine that so well. The poor fellow. I would like to be his friend, since you have no time to take pity on him. I could make time for him. What unfortunate people there are in this world!"

Kaspar said in a low voice, seizing her hand for the first time: "How kind you are!"—

The forest was inky black, everything was dark, the house was a dark patch in the darkness. Simon and Agappaia were waiting for the two others at the door.

"They aren't coming. Come, let's go inside."

"I'm going to go to bed this minute," Simon said.

When he was already lying in bed, about to shut his eyes, he suddenly heard a shot ring out. In sheer terror, he leapt out of bed, tore open the window and looked outside. "What was that?" he shouted down into the darkness. But only his own voice echoed back at him from the forest. The forest was eerily cloaked in a deathly silence. Suddenly he heard a man's voice speaking just below him: "It's nothing, go to sleep. Forgive me for alarming you. I often go shooting in the woods at night, it gives me pleasure to hear the shots resound and echo. Some people whistle a melody to amuse themselves when everything all around them is so quiet. Me, I shoot. Take care not to catch cold there at the open window—the nights are still cold. In a minute you'll hear me shooting again, and this time you won't be frightened. I'm still waiting for my wife to return. Good night. Sleep well." Simon lay back down. Nonetheless he couldn't fall asleep. The man's voice had sounded so peculiar to him, so calm, that's precisely what was so odd. So icy—actually the voice had an ordinary friendliness about it, and that's just what was so icy. Surely something lay behind it. But perhaps it was just that he didn't yet know this man's habits. "Lord knows," he thought to himself, "there are plenty of odd fish swimming about. Life is so tedious, and this encourages the development of oddities. You can turn odd before you know it. And so Agappaia too might not see anything queer about this queer habit of his. He can just call it sporting and so lay to rest any other thoughts that might suggest themselves. All the same, I'm going to try to get some sleep now." —But other thoughts now came to him, all having to do with nighttime: He thought of small children afraid to enter dark rooms and who cannot fall asleep in the dark. Parents instill in their children the most dreadful fear of the dark and then, as punishment, lock recalcitrant ones up in silent dark rooms. Then the child clutches at the darkness in this deep dense dark and finds only darkness and nothing more. The child's fear and this darkness are soon the best of friends, but the child is not managing to befriend its fear. The child has such talents for feeling fear that the fear just grows and grows. It soon overpowers the little child, being such a large, dense, heavily-breathing entity; the child might wish for example to cry out, but doesn't dare. This not daring increases the fear even further; for there must be something utterly terrifying there if the child is too frightened even to utter cries of fear. The child believes someone is listening in the dark. How melancholy it is, thinking of such an unfortunate child. How the poor little ears strain to hear something: even the thousandth part of some faint little sound. Not to hear anything at all is more frightening by far than hearing something, when a person stands in the dark listening. Even this alone: The child cannot help listening and almost hearing its own listening—sometimes it merely listens and sometimes it hearkens, for the child is capable of such distinctions in its nameless fear. When we speak of listening, this presupposes something to be heard, but hearkening is often done in vain, it is a waiting to hear, a hoping. Hearkening is the activity performed by a child locked away in a dark room as punishment for disobedience. And now let us imagine someone approaching—approaching softly, so dreadfully softly. No, it's better not to imagine this. Better not imagine it at all. A person who imagines such a thing will die of terror along with the child. Children have such sensitive souls, how could one be thinking up terrors for such souls! Parents, parents, never shut your recalcitrant children in dark rooms if you have first taught them to fear the dark, which is otherwise so dear, so sweet—

Now Simon was no longer afraid of anything else occurring that night. He fell asleep, and when he woke up the next morning he saw his brother sleeping peacefully beside him in his bed. He could have kissed him. He got dressed as carefully as possible so as not to wake the sleeper, quietly opened the door and went downstairs. On the stairs he met Klara, who seemed to have been waiting there for some time. But Simon had scarcely said good morning before the woman, who appeared to be filled with violent emotion, threw her arms about his neck, drew him to her and kissed him lovingly. "I want to kiss you too, you're his brother," she said in a soft, urgent, rapturous voice.

"He's still asleep," Simon said. He was in the habit of gently brushing aside acts of tenderness not meant for him, but his equanimity only redoubled her agitation. She wouldn't let him go on down the stairs, instead she held him even closer, seizing his head in her two hands and pressing kisses on his forehead and cheeks. "I love you like a brother. Now you are my brother. I have so little and yet so much, do you understand? I have nothing left, I have given it all. Will you shun me? No, you won't, will you. Your heart is mine, I know it is—and having such a confidant makes me rich. You love your brother as no one does. With such strength and will. He told me about you. How beautiful you appear to me. You are so different from him. It's impossible to describe you. He said this too, that one cannot quite grasp you. Yet how trustingly one throws oneself at you. Kiss me. I am yours in any way your heart desires. Your heart is what's beautiful about you. Don't say anything. I understand that one doesn't understand you. You understand everything. You are fond of me, say yes, do. No, don't say yes. It isn't necessary, isn't necessary at all. Your eyes have already said yes—I always knew it. I always knew there were people like you, don't ever force yourself to behave coldly. He's asleep? Oh, no, don't leave yet! I must quarrel a bit more with you first. I am a foolish, foolish, foolish woman, don't you agree?"

She would have gone on speaking in this tone, but Simon fended her off, quite gently, as was his wont. He told her he was going for a walk. She watched him walk away, but he paid not the least attention to her gaze. "I shall help her if she requires my services; of course I shall!" he said to himself. "Probably I would lay down my life for her, if her well-being required her to demand this; quite probably! Yes, it is fairly certain, considering that it would be for a woman like that. She's got something about her. In a word: She holds sway over me, of course, but what's the point of pondering this further? I have other things to think about. For example, I feel happy this morning—my limbs feel like fine flexible wires. When I feel my limbs, I am happy, and then I'm not thinking of any other person on earth, not a woman, not a man, I'm quite simply thinking nothing at all. Ah, how beautiful it is here in the forest on a sunny morning. How lovely it is to be free. Perhaps a soul is thinking of me at this moment, perhaps not—in any case, my soul isn't thinking of anything at all. Such a morning always awakens a certain brutality in me, but this does no harm, on the contrary, it's the basis for my selfless enjoyment of nature. Splendid, splendid. How the grass flashes in the sunlight. How the white sky burns all about the earth. This softening might come to me today. When I think about someone, I do so with abandon. But it's more delicious to be as I am now. Lovely morning. Shall I sing you a song. It's true, you yourself are a song. I'd much rather shout and run about like the devil, or fire off shots like that foolish devil Agappaia—"

He threw himself down upon the meadow and began to dream.

—4—

That same morning Kaspar and Klara took a small brightly colored boat out on the lake. The lake was utterly placid, a gleaming motionless mirror. Now and then a steamer crossed before them, creating for a brief while broad gentle waves, and they sliced through these waves. Klara was clad in a snow-white dress; wide sleeves hung languidly from her beautiful arms and hands. She'd removed her hat: Absentmindedly, with a lovely gesture, she'd let her hair down. Her mouth was smiling across to the mouth of the young man. She didn't know what to say, had no wish to say anything. "How beautiful the water is, it looks like a sky," she said. Her forehead was as serene as their surroundings—lake, shore and cloudless sky. The blue of the sky had streaks of fragrant shimmering white in it. The white sullied the blue a little, seasoned it, made it more yearning and faltering and milder. The sun was half shining through, like sunshine in dreams. There was a certain hesitancy to everything, the air fluttered about their hair and faces—Kaspar's face was solemn but serene. For a while he rowed with powerful strokes, then let the oars sink, and the boat bobbed on unguided. He turned around to look at the receding city, saw its towers and rooftops glittering faintly in the half-sun, saw industrious people hurrying across the bridges. Carts and wagons followed, the electrical tram jolted past making its peculiar sound. Wires were humming, whips were cracking, one could hear whistles and great resounding dins from somewhere or other. All at once the eleven o'clock bells rang out amid all the silence and distant trembling sounds. Both of them were feeling indescribable joy at this day, this morning, the sounds and colors. Everything was dissolving into perception and sound. Being lovers, they heard all things melded as a single sound. A simple bouquet lay in Klara's lap. Kaspar had taken off his jacket and was now rowing again. Then came the stroke of noon, and all these working and professional people dispersed like a trampled anthill into all the streets and directions. The white bridge was swarming with nimble black dots. And when you considered that each dot had a mouth with which it was now planning to eat lunch, you couldn't help bursting into laughter. What a singular image of life, the two of them felt, laughing. They now turned back as well; after all, they too were human and beginning to get hungry; and the closer they drew to shore, the larger the ants became; and then they disembarked and were dots themselves, just like the others. But they kept strolling blissfully up and down beneath the light-green trees. Many curious people turned to look at this strange pair: the woman in her long white gown whose train swept the ground and the churl of a lad who didn't even have on clean trousers, who stood in such insolent contrast to the lady he accompanied. Thus do people wax indignant and form false judgments about their fellow man. All at once someone came striding quickly up to Kaspar. Indeed, it was someone who had every reason to greet him in this fashion, namely Klaus, who hadn't seen his brother in years. Behind him came their sister and another gentleman, and now there was a general exchange of greetings. The stranger's name was Sebastian.

Simon was meanwhile sitting scarcely a thousand paces away in a dining establishment, a small room stuffed full of eating people. All sorts of folks came to eat here who had to eat cheaply and quickly. Simon was quite fond of the place, though it was utterly devoid of elegance and comfort. After all, he did have to watch his expenses. This dining hall had been established by a group of women who, taken all together, called themselves the Association for Moderation and the Public Good. Indeed, anyone who went there had to be satisfied with a perfectly moderate and scanty meal. And all were satisfied for the most part, aside from occasional petty, narrow-minded dissatisfactions. Everyone who frequented the place appeared content with the food, which consisted of a plate of soup, a piece of bread, a portion of meat, ditto vegetables and a miniscule, dainty dessert. The service left nothing to be desired beyond a bit more alacrity, and in fact all in all the waitresses were swift enough considering the large number of hungry eaters. Each received his meal promptly enough, though each felt some slight impatience for even prompter distribution. There was a constant stream of meals being served up, doled out and devoured. Some whose meals had already been put away may well have wished they hadn't yet finished and cast envious glances at the ones still awaiting what was in fact quite agreeable to devour. Why did they eat so quickly? An absurd habit, gulping down one's meals so fast. The service staff was made up of charming, delightful girls from the rural areas surrounding the city. At first these creatures made quite a few blunders, but soon they learned to hold their own and, by fending off what they must, give themselves time to fulfill the most urgent burning desires. Where so many desires are present, it's necessary to differentiate and select among them. Now and then one of the originators of this establishment would come in, a benefactress, and observe the common folk at table. One such lady held a lorgnette to her eye to peer at the food and those devouring it.

Simon was partial to these ladies and always felt happy when they came in, for it seemed to him as if these dear kind women were visiting a room filled with small poor children to watch them enjoying a feast. "Are not the masses like a big poor little child that must be given a guardian to watch over it?" something in him cried out, "and is it not better for it to be watched over by women, who after all are elegant ladies and have kindly hearts, than by tyrants in the old if admittedly more heroic sense?" —So many different sorts of people were eating in this dining hall, all united as a single harmonious family! Female students predominated. Did students have the time and money to lunch at the Hotel Continental? And then there were serving men in thin blue smocks with boots on their legs, large bristly moustaches and rather rectangular mouths on their faces. Could they help it if their mouths were rectangular? No doubt many a guest at the Hotel Royal displayed rectangular proclivities in the moustache region. To be sure, the angularity in that case was whitewashed with roundness, but what significance did this have? Maidservants without posts were represented as well, down-at-the-heels copyists, and outcasts in general: the penniless, stateless, even some who had not so much as an address to their names. Here one also encountered women of easy virtue: females with oddly coiffed hair, blue faces, chubby hands and expressions simultaneously shameless and demure. All these people—especially, of course, the holy rollers, a contingent of whom was present—displayed, as a rule, shy courteous behavior. Each gazed into the faces of the others while eating; not a word was spoken, except, now and then, a quiet, polite one. This was the visible blessing of the public good and moderation. Something comical, artless, subdued and yet also liberated rested upon these squalid individuals, in their manners, which were as colorful as the wings of a summer bird. Others comported themselves with more delicacy here than the most refined guest at the finest establishment. No telling who they were, what they had been in earlier days, before winding up at this public dining hall. After all, wasn't life in the habit of jumbling together human fates as if shaking them in a dice cup? Simon was sitting in a little corner niche, a sort of window bay, eating butter with honey spread together on a slice of bread, and drinking a cup of coffee: "What need have I to eat more on such a beautiful day. Is not the blue sky of early summer peering sweetly through the window at my golden meal? Yes, this meal is most certainly golden. Just look at the honey: Hasn't it a bright-yellow, sweet-golden appearance? Upon the little white plate this gold flows about so appealingly, and scraping off a bit with my knife point, I imagine I am digging for gold and have just discovered a treasure. The white of the butter lies delightfully beside it, and then comes the brown hue of the tasty bread, and most beautiful of all is the dark brown of the coffee in the delicate clean cup. Is there any meal on earth that could look more beautiful and appetizing? And I am sating my hunger quite excellently with it, and need I do more than sate my hunger to be able to say: I have eaten? There are people, I hear, who make a culture, an art out of eating; well, can I not say just the same of myself? Most certainly! It's just that my art is a humble one and my culture more delicate, for I enjoy this modest fare more rapturously and voluptuously than others enjoy endless cornucopias of plenty. Besides, I don't like it when meals drag on and on—I lose my appetite. What pleases me best is feeling the desire to eat again and again, and for this reason I eat sparingly and with delicacy. Which incidentally brings me another benefit as well: delectable conversations with ever new people."

Simon had scarcely murmured or thought these words when an old man with white hair sat down in the empty seat beside him. The old man's face displayed a gray, haggard pallor, his nose was dripping, or rather, a large drop hung from his nose, unable to fall and yet heavy enough to fall. One was constantly expecting it to fall at any moment. But the drop clung on. The man ordered a dish of boiled potatoes and nothing more, and then he ate his potatoes, carefully sprinkling them with salt from the tip of his knife, with elaborate pleasure. But beforehand he folded his hands together and said a prayer to his Lord God. Simon allowed himself the following little prank: He secretly ordered a slice of roast meat from the serving girl and, when it arrived, he had a good laugh at the man's astonishment when the plate was set down before none other than himself.

"Why do you pray before you eat," Simon asked simply.

"I pray because I need to," the old man replied.

"Then I'm glad I saw you praying—I was just curious what sort of sentiment prompted you."

"One has many sentiments when one prays, young man! You, for example, surely do not pray at all. Young people today have no time for it, nor the desire. I can understand this. When I pray, I am merely continuing my habit, for I have grown used to prayers, and they give me comfort."

"Were you always poor?"

"Always." —

As the old man spoke this word, the clean yet nonetheless musty and squalid dining room was suddenly graced by the appearance of beautiful Frau Klara. Every hand holding a fork, a spoon or a knife, or the handle of a cup hesitated for a moment before going on with its work. Every mouth popped open, and all eyes were riveted at the sight of a figure so unlikely to have any business in such a place. She was the consummate lady, never more so than at this moment. It was exactly—even for Simon's eyes and senses—as though from an open fluttering sky an angel had emerged and was now floating down to earth and visiting some dark hole in order to bring happiness to those who lived there simply with her heavenly appearance. This is just how Simon had always imagined a benefactress visiting the poor and wretched, people who possessed nothing more than the questionable privilege of being constantly flogged with worries as if with birch canes. In this charitable establishment it appeared to come quite naturally to Klara to comport herself like a regal remote creature that had just flown here from distant borderlands, from a different world and walk of life. Precisely this splendor and radiance compelled all these timid persons to gape, struggle for breath and use their free hands to steady the hands holding their knives for fear they might drop them, they were trembling so. Klara's beauty suddenly, painfully, gave them something to consider. All at once it occurred to every one what other things existed in this world besides harsh labor and the fear of not making ends meet. Health like this—this luxuriant, voluptuous, smiling charm—had nearly vanished from their imaginations; life in all its bleak unsavory ordinariness was slipping through their fingers, ground down in worry and squalid graspings. All these things now occurred to them—though perhaps not in each case with such great clarity—occurred tormentingly, for a torment it is to behold beauty whose very scent intoxicates but which can kill a person whose thoughts take the liberty of smiling along with beauty's smile. All of them therefore frowned involuntarily, showing grimacing faces to the woman towering over them, for they were seated on low chairs, squeezed into narrow spaces, while she in her loftiness stood erect above them. She seemed to be looking for someone. Simon kept quiet in his corner, steadily smiling at the woman as she peered about. And it was a long time before she noticed him, although the room was relatively small; it must have been strenuous to accustom her eyes to this jumbled dark hodge-podge and pick out individual figures such as she wasn't in the habit of noticing at all. She was about to withdraw again, having grown somewhat impatient, when her eyes swept over Simon and recognized him. "So here's where you're sitting, all tucked away in a corner?" she said, and with the greatest joy sat down beside him, on the chair between her young friend and the old man, whose nose still bore the large glistening drop. The old man was asleep. It was not permitted to sleep in such establishments, but it was a quite common occurrence for old people to fall asleep here after eating, out of sheer exhaustion they could no longer control. Perhaps this old man had a long fruitless peregrination through all the city's streets behind him. Quite possibly he'd asked for work everywhere his thoughts could even faintly suggest he try. Growing ever more weary, he had perhaps nonetheless tried to achieve something this day, might have expended his last resources scaling a mountain, for the city extended up the mountainside, and at the mountain's summit he was rejected just as swiftly as down below; and so he went back down again, his heart filled with death, his strength shattered, until he came to this place. The very thought that this old man might, as one could suppose, have gone out looking for work, that he still had the will to work, old as he was—there was something piteous and horrifying about the very idea. But this was a thought that lay quite near at hand. This old man had no other home than this dining establishment, but even here only during certain hours, for afterward the restaurant was closed. Perhaps this was why he prayed: to give the awful seriousness of his situation a soft soothing melody. This was why he said: "I need to pray." So it wasn't at all sanctimoniousness but just the utterly plaintive need to sense the presence of a hand that wished to caress him, the hand of a child or daughter softly, consolingly stroking his old creased forehead. Perhaps the old man had begotten daughters—and what about him now? It was easy to give in to such thoughts, sitting there beside the old man watching him sleep like this, his head strangely immobile, hands propping his chin. Klara said: "Your brother has come, Simon, in his officer's uniform, and your sister too, and one other gentleman named Sebastian." Hearing these words, Simon paid what he owed, and the two of them left together. When they were gone, one of the serving girls noticed the sleeping man, gave him a shake and declared with mock severity: "No sleeping! You there! Can't you hear? You mustn't sleep!" At this, the old man woke up.

This day was followed by a splendid evening. All the world was strolling along the lake's lovely shore beneath broad, large-leaved trees. Walking here among all these many lighthearted, quietly conversing people, one felt transported to a fairy tale. The city was ablaze with the setting sun's flames; later it smoldered, black and dark, in the glowing ashes of the sun that had set. There's something delightful and enchanting about a summer sun. The lake glittered in the dark, and all the lights shimmered in the depths of the still water. The bridges were looking splendid, and when you walked over them you could see small dark boats shooting past in the water below; in these rowboats sat girls in light-colored dresses, and often when one of the larger flat-bottomed boats slowly, ceremoniously floated past, you could hear the warm crepuscular sounds of an accordion. The notes vanished in the black and then sonorously reemerged, clear and warm, heartbreakingly dark. How far it carried, the sound of this simple instrument played by some boatman! The sound seemed to be making the night even larger and deeper. From the far distant shoreline the lights of rural settlements shimmered, their reddish glint like gemstones in the dark heavy raiment of a queen. The entire earth was fragrant, lying there as still as a sleeping girl. The huge shadowy dome of the night sky arched above all eyes, all the mountains and lights. A sense of space-lessness hovered about the lake, and the sky now had something enclosing, encompassing, overarching about it. Whole groups of people were collecting. The young folk appeared to be wax-ing rhapsodic, and upon all the benches silent, still people sat pressed close together. There was no lack of flighty, pridefully coquettish women, nor of men who had eyes for these women alone, who kept walking behind them, constantly hesitating be-fore rushing forward again until at last they found their pluck or the words to address these ladies. Many were given a proper dressing-down, as the expression goes.

Simon was walking beside Klaus, happy that his felicitous simple answers to all the many questions his brother kept ask-ing were successfully instilling in the latter the conviction that he was definitely by no means a lost soul yet. With both a certain pride and humility in his voice he addressed his more seasoned brother, who all the same was like an unschooled child when asking about certain things, though he always displayed a lov-ing concern. Without even trying, they spoke in beautiful, long, circuitous sentences, and it delighted Klaus to see how compre-hending Simon was regarding various things he'd at first as-sumed his brother, given his circumstances, would simply make fun of and laugh at. "I didn't think you half so serious as you are proving to be!" Simon replied: "I don't make a habit of displaying my reverence for a great many things. I tend to keep matters like this to myself, for I believe: What's the point of wearing a serious expression if one's been earmarked by fate—I mean, if a person has perhaps been chosen—to play the fool. Fates aplenty exist, and to them I shall submit without complaint. Is there any other choice? Besides, I'd like to see someone just try to accuse me of hanging my head, dumbfounded, despondent. I've already made it clear to various people how things stand with my innermost being." —When Simon spoke like this, he did so in fluent sentences and with proper intonation, and with such perfect calm affability that Klaus didn't view these declarations as chips on his younger brother's shoulder but rather as a certain searching on his soul's part to clarify its own status vis-à-vis the world. Klaus was managing to convince himself that Simon possessed some serviceable qualities, but he was nonetheless still somewhat afraid that these qualities might merely be floating, cavorting, beckoning and dancing superficially about the person of his brother rather than rooted firmly within him. After all, it was simple enough for such a soul to grow ardent in speech, conjuring up an entire world of obedience and sweet serviceability that might intoxicate it for hours on end, particularly on such an occasion as a reunion after many years. And yet Klaus was delighting in his brother's presence and said all sorts of sweet comforting things to him with visible pleasure. Behind them, at a certain remove, pressed tightly together, walked Klara and Kaspar. The painter was intoxicated by the beauty and music of the night. He was dreaming of horses galloping through nocturnal gardens bearing lovely slender riders on their backs whose skirts played on the ground with the horses' hooves. Then he laughed at it all—impudent, irrepressible laughter—laughed at all the people, the landscape and every last thing that came before his eyes. Klara didn't even try to quiet him, on the contrary, she was delighting in the beauty of this unshackled spirit. How she loved the youth, the impudence, even the presumptuousness of this boyish creature laboring to reach manhood. He might be jabbering away ridiculously, saying things that, coming from another's mouth, she'd have found inane and idiotic—but on his lips she loved them. What was it about this person that compelled her to find him so unconditionally fetching in every situation and gesture—his behavior, all he did and left undone, his speaking and his silence? In her eyes he was a match for all mankind, superior to other men, and yet he was scarcely a man at all. His gait, how should she put it, had something awkward about it and yet also commanding. This entire young person displayed not a trace of agitation, and yet there was something shy, foolish, profoundly childish about him. So calm and yet so swift to catch fire! She could see his hair, luminous in the darkness, youthful and undulant. Add to that his gait and the way he held his head aloft with such modest, questioning, contemplative pride. How this youth must daydream when he was thinking of someone. Kaspar had grown quieter. Always she gazed at him, always! On this night filled with wandering strollers, it was lovely to gaze at him, so lovely one might swoon. She found looking at him even lovelier than kissing him. She saw his lips part as if in pain;

surely he wasn't thinking anything in particular, no, most certainly not; it was just the way he held his lips that made her think of pain. His eyes were coolly, calmly gazing into the distance, as though they knew of better things to be observed there. His eyes seemed to be speaking: "We, we are looking upon beauty; do not torment yourselves, all you other human eyes, for you shall never see what we do!" His eyebrows curved with enchanting lightness, as if in worry, like angels bending over children—the eyes—which looked, as they gazed about, as though they might be injured at any moment. "To be sure, any human eye can easily be injured, but gazing at his eyes instantly fills me with pain, as though I can see them already pierced by splinters. So large and prominent and yet apparently so unconcerned, they are always heedlessly wide open; how easily they might be injured!" she lamented. She didn't even know if he loved her, but what did it matter, after all she loved him, and that was enough, indeed it could not be otherwise; she was on the verge of tears. Then Simon and Klaus came back to join the others. Klara pulled herself together as best she could, took Simon's arm and walked on with him before the others. "Let me look into your eyes," she said to him. "You have such lovely eyes, Simon—looking at them is like lying in bed when all is calm, and saying a prayer."

Klaus and Kaspar walked in silence. They hadn't been on such good terms for the past year or two; a minor dispute had broken out between them, and they'd stopped seeing one another or even exchanging letters. Klaus took this very much to heart, while Kaspar simply accepted it as somehow inevitable. He said to himself that it lay in the very nature of things to find oneself misunderstood at times, even by a brother. He didn't want to keep looking over his shoulder at things in the past; they were over and done with—unworthy of further thought. He preferred to keep marching straight ahead and considered it harmful to gaze back at former ties. Now, finding it unbearable to remain silent at Kaspar's side, Klaus began to speak of his brother's art, encouraging him to take a trip to Italy some time so as to come into his own there as a mature artist.

Kaspar cried out: "I'd rather the devil came for me right this minute! Italy! Why Italy? Am I suffering from an illness, must I be sent to recover in the land of oranges and pine trees? Why should I go to Italy when I can be here, a place I like? Would I have anything better to do in Italy than paint, and am I not able to paint right here? Or do you mean I should go to Italy because it's so beautiful there? Isn't it beautiful enough here? Can it possibly be more beautiful there than here, where I live and work, where I behold a thousand beautiful things that will remain when I myself have long since rotted away? Is it possible to go to Italy when one wishes to be productive? Are the beautiful things more beautiful in Italy than here? Maybe they're just more sophisticated, and for this reason I prefer not to see them in the first place. When sixty years from now I've reached the point of being able to paint a wave or a cloud, a tree or a field, then we'll see whether or not it was clever of me not to go to Italy. Can I be missing out if I haven't seen those temples with their columns, those humdrum town halls, those fountains and arches, those pine and laurel trees, those Italian folk costumes and splendid edifices? Must one wish to devour everything with one's eyes?

I find it infuriating when people accuse me of harboring plans to become a better artist in Italy. Italy is just a trap we bumble into if we're stupendously dumb. Do the Italians come visit us when they wish to paint or write? What use is it to me to go into raptures over bygone cultures? Shall I—if I am honest with myself—have enriched my spirit by these means? No, I'll just have spoiled it, made it cowardly. Let an ancient, vanished culture be as magnificent as it likes, let it trump us in vibrancy and splendor, there's still no cause for me to go snuffing about in it like a mole; I prefer to observe it, as long as this is feasible and amuses me, in books, which are constantly at my beck and call. In truth, lost, bygone things are never so utterly worthy of our estimation; for when I gaze about me in the present, which is so often disparaged as lacking beauty and grace, I find no dearth of images that delight me and beautiful sights enough to fill both eyes to overflowing. This mania for all things Italian that has strangely, shamefully beset us makes my blood boil. Perhaps I am mistaken, but even twenty bristly devils stinking up the air and waving their horrific pitchforks around wouldn't manage to drag me off to Italy."

Klaus was shocked and saddened by the vehemence with which Kaspar was gauging matters. He'd always been like this, and, as things stood, it couldn't be anticipated how a person might succeed in establishing fruitful relations with him. Klaus said nothing, merely offered his brother his hand in parting, for they had reached the place where he was staying.

Back in his monotonous room, he said to himself: "So now I've lost him all over again, and all because of a perfectly innocent, well-meaning but in fact somewhat incautious remark. I just don't know him well enough, that's all, and maybe I never shall. Our lives are too different. But perhaps the future, which we never quite fathom, will bring us together some other time. It's best to wait and endure as one slowly becomes a more seasoned better person." Feeling terribly lonely, he resolved to depart again soon and return to his own province.

–5–

Sebastian was a young poet who recited his poems from a small stage to the audience seated below. Thanks to the impetuousness of his performance, he tended to wind up looking a bit ridiculous. He'd run away from home at an early age, living in Paris at sixteen and returning home at twenty. His father was music director in the small town where Hedwig, the sister of the three brothers, also resided. There Sebastian lived out his odd ne'er-do-well existence, sitting or lying for days at a time in a dusty attic room, stretched out on a narrow bed in which he slept at night without taking the trouble to tidy it before going to sleep. His parents considered him a lost cause and let him do as he pleased. They gave him no money, for they considered it inappropriate to support the dissolute lifestyle to which they knew he was prone with financial contributions. Sebastian could no longer be persuaded to undertake serious university studies; with some book or other tucked beneath his arm, he would wander about in the mountains and forests, often not returning home for days and passing the night, when the weather even halfway permitted, in tumbledown huts no longer used by human beings, not even rough, savage shepherds, in meadows whose altitude made them closer to the heavens than to any human civilization. He always wore the same threadbare suit of light yellow cloth and let his beard grow, but otherwise made a point of looking attractive and clean. He tended his fingernails more carefully than his mind, which he allowed to go to seed. He was handsome, and since it was known he wrote poems, his person was soon surrounded by a half-ridiculous, half-melancholy aura of enchantment, and plenty of serious-minded people in town honestly pitied the young man and warmly took his part every chance they got. As he was excellent company, he was often invited to social gatherings, which was some small compensation for the fact that the world was setting him no tasks that might satisfy his urge to achieve something. Sebastian possessed this urge to a considerable degree, but he'd strayed too far from the tracks of generally accepted and prescribed strivings. When he now strove, it was perhaps too fiercely, and, since he realized his strivings did him no good, he no longer felt much desire to pursue them. He also played songs of his own composition on the lute, singing along in his pleasant soft voice. The only injustice—a large one, to be sure—that had been done him was that he'd been coddled as a schoolboy, thereby helping him arrive at the notion that he was something like a child prodigy. How this proud fantasy insinuated itself into the boy's receptive heart! Grown women favored the company of this lad, who was old beyond his years and understood such a great many things, and he inspired them with an incomparable attraction at the expense of his own human development. Sebastian was in the habit of saying: "My days of glory lie far behind me now." It was horrifying to hear so young a man speak in such a way. Indeed, no matter what he did, aspired to, set about and performed, he managed to do this so wearily, coldly, and half-heartedly that he didn't truly do anything, he was just toying with himself. Hedwig once said to him: "Sebastian, listen to me, I think you often cry over yourself." He nodded his head, confirming this. Hedwig felt pity for him and sometimes slipped him a little money or something of the sort to make his life somewhat more bearable. Now, for example, she'd taken him along on this little trip to visit her brothers. This same evening when Klara was so blissful, Klaus sad and lonely, Simon in good spirits, and Kaspar irritable and overbearing, the two of them, Hedwig and her bard, went strolling silently, slowly along the shore of the lake. What was there to say; and so they kept silent. Kaspar approached them, saying:

"I hear you've been working on a poem that's to mirror the events of your life. How can you mean to portray a life when you've scarcely yet experienced one? Just look at yourself: How strong and young you are, and to think that youth and strength like this plans to cower behind a desk singing its life in verse. Save it for when you're fifty. Besides, how shameful, a young man crafting poetic lines. That's not work, it's just a hiding-place for the idle. I wouldn't be saying any of this if your life were completed and had been crowned by some great, extenuating experience that would justify a person letting his flaws, virtues and meanderings pass in review. You, however, appear never to have failed, nor to have carried out a good deed either. Start writing poems when you've established yourself either as a sinner or an angel. Or better yet, don't write poems at all."

Kaspar had a low opinion of Sebastian; that's why he was

mocking him. He had no understanding whatever for tragic individuals, or rather, he understood them all too easily, all too well, and therefore had no respect for them. Moreover, he was in a diabolical mood this evening.

Hedwig leapt to defend the poor insulted fellow who was unable to stand up for himself: "How awful of you to speak in such a way, Kaspar," she cried to her brother with an ardor that sprang from her eagerness to defend the lad, "and certainly not clever either. You enjoy hurting a person who should be spared and respected by all for the sake of his unhappiness. Mock all you like. I know you regret your words. If I didn't know you so well, I'd have to consider you a ruffian, a tormenter. It's so easy to torment an unfortunate, defenseless person, one might as well torture some poor animal. The defenseless all too easily fill the strong with a desire to inflict pain. If you can feel strong, be happy, and leave the weaker ones in peace. You show your strength in a bad light, misusing it to torment the weak. Why isn't it enough for you to stand on a firm footing, do you have to place your foot upon the necks of others, the hesitant seekers, making them doubt themselves even more and sending them plummeting down, down into the waters of despair? Must self-confidence, courage, strength and determination always commit the sin of pitilessly, tactlessly riding roughshod over others, even though these others aren't in their way at all, they're just standing there covetously listening to the peals of fame, respect and success ringing out? Is it noble and good to insult a soul filled with longing? Poets are so easily hurt; oh, one should never hurt poets. By the way, I'm not even speaking about you now, my little Kaspar; for have you

yourself amounted to much of anything in this world? You yourself perhaps still amount to nothing and have no cause to scoff
at others who amount to nothing as well. When you wrestle
with fate, let others do the same as best they can. Both of you
are already wrestling, so why battle one another? How foolish,
how unwise. Both of you will find pain enough in the perils and
meanderings and promises and failures in your art; must you
insist on causing one another even more pain? In all truth, I'd
be a poet's brother if I were a painter. And never be so swift to
look in scorn upon someone who is failing or appears lethargic
or inactive. How quickly his sunshine, his poems can arise from
these long, dull dreams! And where does that leave the ones who
were so hasty with their scorn? Sebastian is struggling honestly
with life, that in itself should be a reason to respect and love him.
How can one mock him for his soft heart? Shame on you, Kaspar, and may you never again give me cause—if you have even
a trace of love for your sister—to get worked up like this over
you. I'd rather not. I revere Sebastian because I know he has the
courage to admit his many failings. As for the rest, it's all just idle
chatter—feel free to leave if you prefer not to walk with us. What
a face you're making, Kaspar! Just because a girl who enjoys the
privilege of being your sister happens to give you a lecture, is
this grounds for anger? No, don't be angry. Please. And of course
you're allowed to make fun of poetry. Why ever not. I was taking
things too seriously a moment ago. Forgive me."

A delicate, shy but tender smile was playing in the dark about
Sebastian's lips. Hedwig devoted herself to flattering her brother
until his mood improved. He then gave an imitation of her im-

passioned speech, causing all three of them to break out in resounding laughter. Sebastian in particular laughed himself silly. Gradually all had grown still and empty beneath the trees; people had returned to their homes, the lights were dreaming, but many lights had been extinguished as well, and the distance no longer glittered. There in rural parts, it seemed, lights were snuffed out earlier; the distant mountains now lay like dead black bodies, but still isolated human couples remained who weren't making for home, but rather looked as if they meant to spend the entire night conversing wide-awake beneath the sky.

Simon and Klara were sitting, immersed in long hushed conversation, upon a bench. They had so many things to say to one another, they could have talked on and on forever without stopping. Klara would have gone on speaking about Kaspar, and Simon of the woman seated beside him. He had a strange, free, open way of speaking about people who were his immediate companions, who sat or stood beside him listening to what he said. This came about of its own accord, he always felt most strongly about whoever was occasioning his speech, and so he spoke of them and not of others who were absent. "Doesn't it torment you," she asked, "that we speak only of him?" "No," Simon replied, "his love is my love. I always asked myself whether either of us would ever fall in love. I always saw this as a marvelous thing for which neither of us was good enough. I've read a great deal about lovers in books, I've always loved lovers. Even as a schoolboy I spent hours bent over books of this sort, trembling and shaking and fearing along with my lovers. It was almost always a proud woman and a man of an even more unbending nature, a laborer in a work shirt or a lowly soldier. The woman was always a fine lady. A common pair of lovers wouldn't have piqued my interest in those days. All my senses grew up with these books, perishing again and again when I closed their covers. Then I stepped into life and forgot all these things. I became obsessed with questions of freedom, but I dreamt of experiencing love. What good would it do me to be angry that love has now arrived but not for me? How childish. I am almost even happy that this love desires not me but another, I would like to witness this first and only later experience it. But I shall never experience love. I think life has other plans for me, other intentions. It forces me to love everything it throws my way, every being. I am allowed to love you, too, Klara, if only in a different, perhaps a foolish way. Isn't it silly that I know perfectly well that, if you should wish it, I could die for you, would willingly do so. May I not die for you? I'd find this so perfectly natural. I place no value on my life, I value only the lives of others, and nonetheless I love life, but I love it only because I hope it will give me the opportunity to throw it away in some respectable fashion. Isn't it idiotic to speak in this way? Let me kiss your two hands so you'll feel how I belong to you. Of course I am not yours and you will never demand anything at all of me, for what could it possibly occur to you to ask of me? But I love women of your sort, and it is agreeable to give gifts to a woman one loves, and so I am giving you myself, since I don't know what would make a better present. Perhaps I can be useful to you, I can jump about for you with these legs of mine, I can hold my tongue when you want someone to keep silent for you, I can lie if you happen to find yourself in the position of requiring a shameless liar. There are quite noble instances of this sort. I can carry you in my arms, if you should happen to fall down, and I can lift you over puddles to keep your feet from getting dirty. Take a look at my arms. Don't they look as though they were already lifting and carrying you? How you would smile if I were to carry you, and I would smile as well, for one smile, as long as it is not indelicate, always calls forth another. This gift that I am giving you is a portable, eternal one; for man, even the simplest of men, is eternal. I shall belong to you even when you have long since ceased to be anything at all, not even a grain of dust; because a gift always outlives its recipient so that it can mourn its lost owner. I was born to be a gift, I've always belonged to someone or other, and it's always filled me with chagrin to spend a day wandering about without finding anyone to whom I could offer myself. Now I belong to you, though I know how little I mean to you. You have no choice but to not value me highly. It often happens that one scorns a gift. My soul, for example, is filled with scorn when I think of presents. I virtually abhor receiving gifts. This is why fate has willed me to be loved by no one; for fate is good and all-seeing. I would be unable to endure being loved, but I find the absence of love endurable. One mustn't love a person who insists on loving, one would only be disturbing him in his devotions. I wouldn't want you to love me. What's more, the fact that you love another makes me so happy; for now, please understand me, you are clearing the way for me to love you. I adore faces that turn away from me, toward some other object. The soul, which is a painter, loves this sort of allure. A smile is so lovely when it crosses lips one surmises rather than sees. This is how you'll please me—do you suppose there's no need to? But no, now I remember: you don't have to please me, you've no need to at all; for I am incapable of judging you, at most I might manage a plea; but I no longer know what I am saying."

Klara was in tears over his declaration. She had long since drawn him close to her and with her beautiful hands, which had grown cool in the night air, was touching his burning cheeks. "What you just said to me, there was no need for you to say it, I knew these things already, already knew them, already—knew." —Her voice took on that tenderness we employ when we wish to convince animals we've hurt a little to feel love and trust for us again. She was happy, her soft voice resonating with long high notes of joy. Her entire body appeared to be speaking when she said: "You do well to love me now that I'm compelled to love. Now my love will be twice as joyful. Perhaps I shall be unhappy some day, but how blissful I'll be in my unhappiness. Only once in our lives do we women feel joyous at being made unhappy, but we know how to savor this unhappiness. But how can I be speaking to you of pain? Just look how indignant I am at having spoken like this—how can I dare to have you at my side and not believe in my own happiness? You make a person believe, you make belief possible. Remain my friend always. You are my sweet boy. Your hair glides through my hands, and your head, full of such unfathomable thoughts of friendship, rests in my lap. How beautiful this makes me feel; you're making me feel like this—you must kiss me. Kiss me, kiss me on the mouth. I wish to compare your kisses, Kaspar's and yours. I want to imagine it is him kissing me when you kiss me. A kiss is such a wonderful thing. If you kiss me now, it will be a soul kissing me, not a mouth. Did Kaspar tell you how I kissed him and how I asked him to kiss me too? He should kiss differently, he must learn to kiss like you, but no, why should he kiss like you? The way he kisses, I must kiss him back at once, but you kiss in such a way that a person has to let you kiss her again, just like now. Remain fond of me, remain as dear as you are, and kiss me one more time so that, as you said before, I'll feel that you belong to me. A kiss makes this so comprehensible. This is how women like to be instructed. You have quite a good understanding of women, Simon. One shouldn't be able to tell this just by looking at you. Now come, let us go."

They got to their feet, and when they had walked a little way they met the three others. Hedwig took her leave of her brothers and Frau Klara. Sebastian accompanied the girl. When the two had walked some distance away, Klara quietly asked Kaspar: "Can you trust your sister to the company of this gentleman?" Kaspar replied: "Would I be allowing this if it weren't all right?"

When they got home, they heard a shot ring out in the forest. "He's shooting again," Klara said quietly. "What's the point of these shots?" Kaspar asked, and Simon, laughing, interjected the swift reply: "He's shooting because things still seem odd to him. There's still a sort of idea behind it, and when that ceases to interest him, he'll soon give it up, you'll see." Once more they heard a shot. Klara furrowed her brow with a sigh, then attempted to suffocate her apprehension with laughter. But this laughter sounded harsh, and for a moment both brothers flinched.

"You're acting strange," Aggapaia said to his wife, suddenly appearing at the front door just as they were about to go in. She remained silent as though she hadn't heard him. Then all of them went to bed.

This same night Klara, being unable to sleep, wrote a letter to Hedwig:

My dear girl, sister of my Kaspar, I must write to you. I cannot sleep, cannot find rest. I am sitting here half-clothed at my desk, involuntarily thrust to and fro by dreams. I feel as though I could write letters to all the world, to any random stranger, any heart; for to me all human hearts tremble with warmth. Today when you pressed my hand you looked at me for such a long time, questioningly and with a certain severity, as though you already knew how things stood with me, that I was in a bad way. Could it be that I appear bad in your eyes? No, I feel certain you won't condemn me when you know everything. You're the sort of girl one doesn't wish to keep secrets from, but the sort one wishes to tell everything, and I do wish to tell you everything so that you'll know everything, so that you'll be able to love me; for you will love me once you know me, and I so long to be loved by you. I dream of having all beautiful, intelligent girls gathered around me, as friends and advisors, but also as my pupils. Kaspar tells me you want to be a teacher and sacrifice yourself to the education of young children. I too wish to be a teacher, for women are born educators. You wish to become something, be something: This suits you well, and corresponds to my image of you. It also corresponds to this age we live in, and the world, which is a child of this time. This is lovely of you, and if I had a child, I would send it to study with you, I would entrust it to you completely so that it would become accustomed to revering and loving you as a mother. How the children will look up to you, look to see whether there is severity or benevolence in your eyes. How they will lament in their small, blossoming hearts when they see you arrive for class with a worried expression; for your soul is comprehensible to children. You will not have to spend long with poorly behaved children; for I imagine that even the most poorly behaved, poorly brought-up among them will quickly come to feel ashamed of their misbehavior and will regret having caused you pain. To obey you, Hedwig, how sweet that must be. I should like to obey you, to become a child and feel the pleasure of being allowed to be obedient to you. And you intend to move to a small, quiet village? All the lovelier! Then you will have village children to teach, and they are even better to educate than children from the cities. But even in the city you would be successful. You long for the countryside, the cottages and the little gardens before them, the human faces one sees there, the river that goes rushing past, the lonely, enchanting shore of the lake, the plants one searches for and finds in the silent forest, the animals in the countryside and the entire country world. You will find all these things; for this is where you belong. One belongs in the place one longs for. Surely you will one day find there the answer to the question of what one must do to be happy. You are already happy now, and I can feel quite well how dearly I would love to possess your good cheer. When one sees you, one would like to imagine one has known you a long time and that one even knows what your mother looks like. Other girls one might find pretty, even beautiful, but just looking at you is enough to make a person wish to be known and loved by you. There is something enticing, something almost grandmotherly in your bright young face; perhaps it's the country air you have about you. Your mother grew up on a farm? What a beautiful, dear farmwife she must have been. She suffered a great deal in the city, Kaspar once told me; I can believe it; for I see her as if she were standing here before

116

me, this mother of yours. I understand she behaved haughtily and suffered on this account. Of course; because in the city one isn't allowed to display such pride as in the country, where a woman can easily imagine herself the mistress of all she surveys. I'm hoping to please you a little by speaking of your mother, whom you tended and cared for when the poor thing was broken and ill. I've seen a picture of your mother too, and I shall honor and love her if you'll allow me. If you give your permission, I'll do so even more warmly. If only I could see her, could throw myself at her feet, take her hand and press my lips to it. How much good this would do me. It would be like a provisional, paltry, incomplete payment of a debt; for I am her debtor, and yours as well, Hedwig. Your brother Kaspar was no doubt often unkind and treated you harshly; for young men must often be hard on those who love them best if they are to clear themselves a path out into the world. It makes sense to me that artists must often shake off love as a hindrance. You saw him when he was very young, a mere schoolboy going to school, you reproached him for his poor conduct, argued with him, you both pitied and envied him, protected and warned him, scolded and praised, you shared with him his first, awakening sentiments and told him it was good to feel things; you withdrew from him when you realized his aspirations were different from yours; you gave him leave to do as he pleased, hoping he would prosper and not fall. When he was gone, you longed for him and ran to throw your arms about his neck on the day of his return, and at once you went back to taking him under your wing; for he is the sort of person who seems constantly in need of a wing to rest under, constantly. Thank you for this. I haven't breath enough, heart enough, words enough to thank you. I don't even know if I'm allowed to. Perhaps you want nothing to do with me. I am a sinner, but perhaps sinners deserve to be permitted to learn what a person must do to appear humble. I am humble, not defeated, certainly

not broken, but rather filled with flaming, suppliant, imploring humility. I
wish to make good again with humility what I have done wrong out of love.
If you place any value on having a sister who is happy to be your sister, I
am at your service. Do you know what your brother Simon has given me?
He has given me himself, as a gift, he has thrown himself away on me, and
I should like to throw myself away on you. But, Hedwig, one cannot throw
oneself away on you. After all, this would mean wanting to give you little.
But I am a great deal happier ever since Kaspar embraced me. Now I'm
starting to boast and speak pridefully, let me stop. I'm going to see if I can
fall asleep. The forest is sleeping too, why should people be unable to sleep.
But I know I'll be able to sleep now.

—While the woman was writing this letter, Simon and Kaspar
were sitting beside the lamp they'd lit. They had no desire to go
to bed yet and were still conversing. Kaspar said: "For the past
few days I've painted nothing at all, and if things go on like this,
I'm going to give up on art and become a farmer. Why not? Must
it be art or nothing? Isn't it possible to live in other ways as well?
Perhaps it's only a habit that makes us think we must devote
ourselves to art at all costs. Why not set it aside and return to
it ten years from now! That would make us look at everything
differently, much more simply, much less fantastically, and this
couldn't hurt. All that's needed is the courage and the trust. Life
is short when you're distrustful, but long when you're capable
of trust. What would we be losing? I feel myself becoming more
and more sluggish from day to day. Should I be pulling myself
together and forcing myself like some schoolboy to do my duty?
Do I have duties to perform with regard to art? One can turn

the question this way and that, twisting it about however one pleases. Painting pictures! How utterly stultifying this now appears to me, how utterly meaningless. You've got to be able to let yourself go. Whether I paint one hundred landscapes or just two of them, what difference does it make? A person who paints constantly can still remain a bungler because he'd never think to imbue his pictures with even a trace of his experiences, for he's experienced nothing all the days of his life. When I have more experiences under my belt, I'll use my brush more wisely, more introspectively, and I believe this will make a great difference. What does the quantity matter. But nonetheless: Somewhere inside me a feeling is telling me it isn't good to get out of practice for even a single day. It's just laziness talking, accursed laziness!—"

He said no more, for a long horrifying scream pierced the walls at just this moment. Simon seized the lamp and both of them hurled themselves down the stairs to the room where they knew she slept. It was Klara who had screamed. Agappaia had come running as well, and they found the woman lying stretched out upon the floor. It appeared she'd been about to undress for bed when she'd been overcome by a violent seizure and had fallen to the ground. Her hair had come loose, and her magnificent arms were twitching feverishly where they lay. As her chest rose and fell spasmodically, a confused smile flew about her lips, which were open wide. All three men knelt down beside her, holding her arms still until the twitching gradually subsided. It seemed she hadn't hurt herself in the fall, as she easily might have. They picked up the unconscious woman and laid her, half clothed as she was, upon her bed, which was neatly turned down. She grew calmer when her corset was opened. She gave a sigh of relief and now appeared to be sleeping. And she smiled more and more beautifully, delirious now, speaking in whispered notes that sounded like bells ringing far off in the distance, acute and yet scarcely perceptible. They listened breathlessly, discussing whether or not there was any point to bringing a doctor from the city. "Wait a while," Agappaia said calmly to Simon, who had wanted to set out for the doctor right away, "it will pass. This isn't the first time." They continued to sit there listening, exchanging meaningful glances. From Klara's mouth came not much that was comprehensible, just brief, fragmentary sentences, half sung and half spoken: "In the water, no, just look, deep, deep. It took a long time, long, so long. And you do not weep. If you knew, it's so black and so muddy all around me. But look. A violet is growing from my mouth. It's singing. Do you hear? Can you hear it? You might think I'd drowned. How lovely, so very lovely. Isn't there a ditty about it? That Klara! Where is she now? Go looking for her, go look. But you'll have to go into the water. That'll make your skin crawl, won't it? My skin no longer crawls. A violet. I can see the fish swimming. I am perfectly still, I no longer do anything at all. Be sweet, be kind. You look displeased. That's where Klara is lying, right there. Do you see her, do you? I'd wanted to say something else to you, but I am content. What did I want to say? Can't remember. Can you hear me ringing? It's my violet ringing. A little bell. I always knew. But don't say so. I can't hear anything any more. Please, please—"

"Go on, go to bed. If it gets worse, I'll come wake you," Agappaia said.

It didn't get worse. The next morning Klara was in good spirits and had no memory of what had occurred. She had a touch of headache, that's all.

Klara felt divine. Dressed in a dark-blue morning coat that flowed loosely about her body in opulent folds, she sat upon the balcony, which provided a view of fir trees whose tips bobbed gently to and fro in the light morning breeze. How glorious the forest is, she thought, leaning out toward it over the delicately worked railing to have its fragrance closer. "How it lies there, the forest, as though already slumbering its way closer to night. When you walk into a forest during the daytime, in broad sunlight, it's as if you're walking into an evening where the sounds are piercing and fainter, the scents moist and more tender, where a person can rest and pray. In the forest you pray involuntarily, and it's also the only place in the world where God is near; God seems to have created forests so we can pray in them as if in sacred temples; one person prays in one way, another in another, but everyone prays. When you lie beneath a fir tree reading a book, you are praying, if praying is the same as being lost in thought. Let God be where He will, in the forest you can sense Him, and you offer up your little bit of belief with silent rapture. God doesn't want us to believe in Him so terribly much, He wants us to forget Him, it even makes Him happy to be scorned, for He is benevolent and great beyond all measure; God is the most pliant thing in the universe. He insists on nothing, wants nothing, requires nothing. Wanting things might be something for us humans, but not for Him. Nothing is for Him. He is happy when people pray to Him. Oh, this God is enraptured and cannot contain His bliss when I go and thank Him, thank Him only just a little. Even if my thanks are superficial, God is so grateful. I'd like to know who could be more grateful than He. He has given us everything, He's so incautious and kind, and the way things are with Him, He cannot help being happy when the beings He's created think of him a little. This is the unique thing about our God, that He wants to be God only when it pleases us to elevate Him as our God. Who teaches humility better than He does? Who is more prescient and still? Perhaps God merely has inklings of us, as we do of Him, and all I'm doing, just now for instance, is giving voice to my own inklings. Does He also sense that I'm sitting here on the balcony, admiring His splendid forest? If only He knew how beautiful His forest is. But I think God has forgotten His Creation, not out of bitterness—how could He be capable of bitterness—no, He's simply forgotten, or at least it looks as if He's forgotten us. You can feel many different things about God—He permits all sorts of thoughts. But when you think of Him, you can easily lose Him: that's why we pray. Great God, lead us not into temptation: That's how I prayed as a child, lying in my little bed, and I always felt pleased with myself when I prayed. How happy I feel today, how glad; my entire being is a smile, a blissful smile. My whole heart is smiling, the air is so fresh, I think it must be Sunday, people will come from the city to go walking in the forest, and I shall pick out some child, ask the parents to entrust it to me for a little while and then we'll play. How I can just sit here like this, feeling joy at my very existence, at my sitting here and leaning over the railing! How beautiful I find myself—I could almost forget Kaspar, forget everything. How could I possibly ever have cried over anything, felt perturbed over anything? How imperturbable the forest is, and yet also so flexible, warm, alive and sweet. What a respiration comes from the fir trees, what rustling! The rustling of the trees makes all music superfluous. Indeed, I like to hear music only at night, never in the morning, the morning is too sacred. How strangely refreshed I feel. How mysterious it is to lie down to sleep, no, first to be tired and then lie down, and then wake up again and feel newborn. Every day is our birthday. It's like getting into the bath when one climbs out of the veils of nighttime into the waves of the blue day. Now the blaze of noon will soon come, until the sun longingly sinks down again. What longing, what a miracle from eve to morn, from noon to eve, from night to morn again. We'd find everything miraculous if we were sensible of it all, for how could one thing be miraculous and another not? I think I must have been ill yesterday and no one's telling me. How beautiful and innocent my hands look still. If they had eyes, I'd hold up a mirror to show them how beautiful they are. How fortunate any man is whom I caress with my hands. What peculiar thoughts I'm having. If Kaspar were to come now, I'd have to weep at letting him see me like this. I haven't been thinking about him, and he'd sense I hadn't given him a thought. All at once I feel so wretched—the thought that I've neglected him. But am I his slave? What is he to me?"

She began to cry. Then Kaspar came up to her: "What's the matter, Klara?"

"Nothing! What could be the matter? After all, here you are. I missed you. I'm happy, but I can't stand being happy all alone, without you. That's why I was crying. Come here, come," and she pressed him to her, hard.

−6−

Simon was beginning to find his torpid, wastrel's life unbearable. He felt he'd soon have to return to the world of work and day-labor: "After all, there's something appealing about living like most people. It's starting to annoy me to be so idle, such an oddity. Food has stopped tasting good to me, going for walks just makes me tired, and what's so uplifting and grand about letting yourself be stung all over by wasps and gadflies on hot country roads, striding through villages, jumping down steep walls, perching atop erratic blocks, propping your head in your hands, starting to read a book and being unable to finish it, then taking a dip in a lake that is lovely but remote, getting dressed again and setting off for home and then at home finding Kaspar so lethargic he no longer knows what leg to stand on or what nose to think with or what finger to lay beside which of his noses. With such a lifestyle, it's easy to acquire a large number of noses and the desire to spend all day long laying all ten fingers beside all ten noses to reflect. Meanwhile all your noses are laughing and thumbing their noses at you. Well, and what's so divine about watching your ten or more noses thumb their noses at you? By this I mean only to illustrate the fact that all this lying-about makes you a dunce. No, I'm starting to feel something like pricks of conscience and believe that merely feeling such pricks is not enough: I must undertake something. Running about in the sunshine cannot, in the long term, be viewed as an activity, and only a simpleton sits around reading books, for a simpleton is what you are if all you ever do is read. Labor in the company of others is, in the end, the single thing that educates us. So what should I do? Write some poems perhaps? To wish to try something of the sort on such a hot summer day, I'd have to be named Sebastian, and then maybe I would want to. That's what he's doing, I'm convinced of it. Sebastian's the kind of person who first goes on an outing—studying lakes, forests, mountains, streams, puddles and sunshine, possibly taking some notes—and then goes home and writes an essay about his outing that gets printed in newspapers of world-historical significance. Perhaps this sort of thing could be suitable for me? Probably, if I could manage it, but I'm such a dilettante. I'd best go back to scraping out letters, erasing calculations, squandering ink—yes, that's what I must do, though there isn't much honor in starting all over from scratch in a field I quit. But it must be done. In such a case it doesn't do to think of honor but of what is necessary and irremediable. I'm twenty years old now. How could it be that I am twenty already? How discouraged some other person might be—twenty years old and having to start again from scratch, from where you stood just leaving school. But, since it can't be helped, I'll display as much good humor as possible, and in any case, I have no wish to get ahead in life, I just want to live in a way that counts for something. Nothing more. And really, all I want is to make it till winter comes again, and then, when it's snowing and wintertime,

I'll know how to go on, it'll come to me how I should best go on living. It gives me great pleasure, dividing my life into small, simple, easily solvable equations like this—sums there's no need to rack my brains over, they solve themselves. During the winter, by the way, I'm always more clever and enterprising than in the summer. With all that warmth, all that blossoming and fragrance, there's no getting anything done, but cold and frost spur you on. So before winter comes, let me put myself in funds, and then enjoy the lovely wintertime spending the money sensibly. I wouldn't insist on studying languages all winter long for days on end in unheated rooms until my fingers froze off, but all the same summer is for the sort of people who are given vacations, the ones who spend time at summer resorts and find enjoyment in leaping barefoot if not naked though warm meadows, sometimes with a leather apron bound about their loins like John the Baptist, who incidentally is said to have eaten grasshoppers. So now upon the bed of daily toil let me lie down to sleep and not wake up again until snow is flying across the earth and the mountains turn white and howling northern storms come up to freeze your ears and melt them in the flames of frost and ice. The cold is like a blaze to me, awe-inspiring, beyond description! So it shall be or my name is not Simon. In the winter, Klara will be wrapped up in thick soft furs, and I shall accompany her in the streets and it will snow upon us, so quietly, secretly, soundless and warm. Oh, when it is snowing in the black streets, going out to do the shopping, and the shops all lit up with lamps. To walk into a shop beside Klara or a few steps behind her person and say: My lady wishes to purchase this or that. Klara, fragrant in her furs, and her face—how beautiful it will be when we then go back out into the street. Perhaps when it is winter she'll be working in some elegant establishment, just like me, and I will be able to come collect her every night—unless she should one day instruct me not to collect her. Perhaps Agappaia will send his wife packing, and then she will be forced to take up some employment or other, which will be easy for her, given what an imposing person she is. That's as far ahead as I wish to think. Thinking further than that is something done perhaps by Herr Spielhagen of the Corporation for Electrical Illumination but not by me, for, occupying no such position, I don't accrue so many obligations in this world that I am compelled to think any further ahead. Ah, wintertime! If only it would come soon—"

The very next day found him working at a large machine-producing factory that employed a number of young people to take inventory. He spent his evenings reading by the window, or else supplemented his trip home from the factory to Klara's house with a lengthy detour around the entire mountain, passing through the dark verdant forested ravines that cut into the broad mountain. He would always stop at a spring he passed to quench his prodigious thirst, then would lie down in a secluded forest meadow until night arrived, reminding him to go home. He loved watching the summer evening give way to summer night, this slow rosy subsiding of the forest's hues into the blackness of deep night. He was in the habit then of dreaming without words or thought, setting aside all self-reproach and surrendering to a delicious exhaustion. Often it seemed to him that a large fiery-red ball went whistling up into the air from the dark bushes beside him, from the sleeping earth, and when he looked, it was the moon dancing up into the sky, floating ponderously against its backdrop, the universe. How his eye then clung to the pale weightless shape of this loveliest of heavenly bodies. That this far-distant world appeared to be tucked away just behind the bushes seemed so strange to him, close enough to be fingered and grasped. Everything appeared to him near at hand. What was the concept of distance in the face of such withdrawal and drawing near. The infinite suddenly appeared to him infinitely close. When he returned, passing amid all the heavy, singing, fragrant nocturnal verdure, Simon perceived it as a mysterious, dear gesture when Klara walked to meet him, as she did every evening, and welcomed him home. Her eyes always appeared to have been weeping when she walked toward him like this or waited. Then the two of them would sit together until deep into the night on the small balcony, which had been transformed into a little mid-air summer-house, playing a game with tiny cards, or else she would sing some melody or have him tell her a story. When at last she bid him goodnight, he would sleep so soundly it might have been a magic spell, this "good night" of hers, giving her the power to shackle him to an exceptionally beautiful, deep slumber. In the morning, silver dew would glitter in the bushes, on the blades of grass and leaves as he walked to his place of employment to get to work writing and helping with the inventory. One Sunday he returned from a walk to find Klara sleeping on the divan in his bedroom. From outdoors the sound of an accordion could be heard coming from one of the squalid huts built into the foothills, where poor workers lived, at the edge of town. The shutters had been drawn and the room held a hot green light. He sat down at the foot of the divan beside the sleeper, and she touched him lightly with her feet. Overjoyed at the sensation of her feet pressing against him, he gazed intently at the face of the slumbering woman. How beautiful she was when she slept. She was one of those women who are most beautiful when their faces are immobile, at rest. Klara was breathing in peaceful waves; her chest, half-exposed, rose and sank gently; a book had fallen from the hands now dangling at her side. The idea arose in Simon that he might kneel beside her and quietly kiss these lovely hands, but he refrained. He might have done so had she been lying there awake, but sleeping? No. Secret, surreptitious, furtive expressions of tenderness are not for me, he thought. Her mouth was smiling, as though she were just casually sleeping, fully aware she was asleep. This smile upon the sleeper's lips barred all uninnocent thoughts, but it forced one to gaze at this mouth, this face, this hair and these elongated cheeks. Still sleeping, Klara suddenly pressed her feet more urgently against Simon, then she woke up and looked about her questioningly, and for a long time remained looking into Simon's eyes as though there were something she failed to grasp. Then she said: "Simon! I have something to tell you."

"What is it?"

"We aren't going to live in this house much longer. Agappaia has gambled and lost everything. He's fallen into the hands of swindlers. The house has already been sold, it's been bought by your Ladies' Association for the Public Good and Moderation.

The ladies are going to create a woodland health spa for the working class. Agappaia has thrown in his lot with a group of Asian explorers and will be traveling far away with them soon to discover a sunken Greek city somewhere in India. I no longer figure in his plans. How strange, this doesn't even distress me. My husband was never capable of causing me distress. Enough! I shall keep house in a simple room down in the city, and Kaspar and you will visit me. I shall take a job, some employment or other, just like you. We're moving out this autumn, and the house is to be renovated straight away. What do you say to all this?"

"The news is very much to my liking. I'd already been thinking it was time for a 'change.' Now the change has come of its own accord. I look forward to visiting you in your new home."

And the two of them laughed as they imagined the future.

Kaspar was living in a small rural town, where he'd been commissioned to decorate a ballroom, that is, to paint its walls from top to bottom. Autumn had meanwhile arrived, and one day Simon—this was on a Saturday—set out after work with the intention of walking all night to cover the distance separating him from Kaspar. Why shouldn't he be able to keep going all night long? He'd taken a map and with a compass carefully measured out the hours he would require to reach this town, and indeed it seemed he would be able to get there in exactly one night if he used his time well. His journey first led him through the suburban district where Rosa lived, his old friend, and he did not fail to pay her a brief visit on his way. She was delighted to see him again after such a long time, but called him wicked and disloyal for having abandoned her like that, saying these things more in a pouting than an aggrieved tone of voice, and she would not be dissuaded from giving Simon a glass of red wine to drink, saying it would strengthen him for his nocturnal journey. She also quickly fried a sausage for him on her gas stove, and as she cooked teased the one who stood there with words that, while not unkind, were nonetheless pointed; she said he must be well provided with women, and laughingly drew his attention to the fact that he didn't really deserve this sausage but should have it all the same if he would visit her more diligently in future. Eating his sausage, Simon promised he would, and soon thereafter set out upon his journey, feeling a bit apprehensive at the labors that lay before him. But he really had no desire to turn back now like a coward and take the train instead. So he kept on walking, stopping often to ask for directions to avoid making a false turn. When he reached a signpost where two paths diverged, he would light a match and hold it up at the necessary height to see in which direction a path continued. He walked with frenzied speed, as if the path might slip from beneath his feet and run away. Rosa's red wine was burning in his veins, and he only wished the mountains would come soon, feeling with what pleasure and ease he would conquer them, and so he arrived in the first village but had some difficulty finding his way among all the different roads, which crisscrossed in all possible directions. Calling out to a blacksmith who was still hammering away, however, he learned that he was on the right road, and next came a landscape that was all blurry, consisting of nothing but bushes;

the path was leading uphill; and then came a sort of plateau that was somehow frightening. It was pitch black, not a star in the entire sky; now and then the moon came out, but the clouds would conceal its light again. Walking next through a dark fir forest, Simon began to gasp for breath and paid more attention to where he set his feet; for he kept tripping over stones in the path, and this he found rather irksome. The fir forest came to an end, and Simon breathed more freely—walking in dark woods all alone like that is not without its dangers. A large farmhouse suddenly stood before him as if it had sprung up from beneath the earth, blocking his view, and a large dog came shooting out and lunged at the walker but didn't attack. Simon calmly and quietly stopped in his tracks, staring at the dog, and so the dog didn't dare bite him. Onward! Bridges came that rang out thunderously beneath his rapid steps, for they were made of wood, old wooden bridges with roofs and pictures of saints at either end. Simon began to walk with mincing steps to entertain himself. As he passed through the open but gloomy fields, a heavy-set man suddenly stood before him, shouting and glaring at him ferociously. Simon shouted in turn, "What do you want?" but then dodged around the man and ran off without waiting to hear what the man wanted. His heart was pounding—it was the suddenness of his appearance, not the man himself, that was so startling. Then he marched through a sleeping, endlessly long village. A long white monastery building looked at Simon expectantly and then vanished behind him. Once more, the path led uphill. Simon ceased to think about anything at all, the growing exertion lamed his thoughts; silent walls gave way to isolated groups of trees, forests to clouds, stones to springs: Everything seemed to be walking alongside and then sinking down behind him. The night was damp, dismal and cold, but his cheeks burned, and his hair was wet with perspiration. All at once he glimpsed something lying stretched out at his feet, something broad, shimmering and glinting—a lake; Simon stopped short. From then on he was walking downhill on an appallingly poorly-maintained path. For the first time his feet ached, but he paid no attention and kept on going. He heard apples falling with soft thuds in the meadow. How mysteriously beautiful the meadows were: unfathomable and dark. The village that next followed awoke his interest thanks to the elegant buildings it had to show for itself. But now Simon no longer knew which direction to take. Search as he might, he couldn't find the right path. This infuriated him, so he chose the main road without giving it much thought. He must have walked nearly an hour before a distinct feeling told him he had picked the wrong direction, and he turned around again, practically weeping with rage and slamming his shoes against the road as though his feet were at fault. He came back to the village: Two hours wasted—what ignominy! This time he quickly found the right road, since he was looking more carefully, and trotted away, beneath trees that were relinquishing their foliage, on a narrow side road completely covered with rustling leaves. He reached a forest, a mountain forest ascending precipitously before him, and since Simon could no longer see any path, he simply kept walking straight ahead, finding his way though thick fir branches as he climbed higher and higher, scratching his face and scraping his hands, but at least he was still ascending, until at last the forest he had been wrestling his way through with groans and curses came to an end, and an open pasture lay before his eyes. He rested for a moment: "Good Lord, if I arrive too late, how embarrassing!" Onward! He was no longer walking so much as leaping along, heedlessly thrusting his feet into the soft earth of the fields. A pale shy morning light grazed his eyes from somewhere or other. He leapt over hedges that seemed to be mocking him. He was no longer even looking for a path. A proper broad road—this remained suspended in his fantasy as an exquisite treasure for which he longed with all his heart. Again he was walking downhill, through narrow small ravines with houses stuck to their slopes like little toys. He smelled the nut trees beneath which he was walking; down in the valley there appeared to be something like a town, but this was just an eagerly grasped-at hunch. Finally he found the road. His legs themselves appeared jubilant at the find, and he walked more calmly now until he found a fountain and threw himself like a madman on its water pipe. Down below he reached a small town, passing a gleaming-white, diminutive, apparently ecclesiastical palace whose ruinous state moved him deeply, and once more the road led him out into the open countryside. Here the first gray glimpses of daylight appeared. The night seemed to be growing pale; the long silent night showed signs of motion. Simon was now thrusting the road aside in his haste. How comfortable such a smooth road seemed to him, leading now uphill in wide meanderings, then guiding him down again in a splendid straightaway. Banks of mist sank down upon meadows and certain day sounds began to reach his ear. How long a night was.

During this night he'd spent walking upon the earth, perhaps a scholar had sat up at his desk by lamplight—perhaps even his brother Klaus, spending just as sour and laborious a wakeful night. Surely the awakening day must appear just as wondrous to a sedentary figure as it did to him, the walker of country roads. Already the first early-morning lamps were being lit in the small houses. A second, larger town appeared, at first its outskirts, then alleyways, then large gates and a wide main street where Simon noticed a splendid edifice with sandstone statues. This was an old city castle now serving as a post office. Already out walking on the street there were people of whom he could ask his way, just as the evening before. And again he marched out into the flat, open countryside. The mist was dissipating, colors appeared, enchanted colors, enchanting colors—morning colors! It seemed it was going to be a splendid, blue autumn Sunday. Now Simon encountered people, women above all, in their Sunday best, women who had perhaps already walked a long way in order to go to church in town. The day was becoming ever more colorful. Now you could see the red, glowing fruit lying in the meadows beside the road, and ripe fruit was constantly falling from the trees. It was real orchard country Simon was walking through. He passed journeymen ambling along at their leisure; they didn't see walking as such a serious matter. An entire company of these lads lay stretched out on the edge of a meadow in the sun's first rays: the very image of ease! A cow was led down the road, and the women said "good morning" so prettily. Simon ate apples as he walked; he too was now strolling peacefully through the unfamiliar, beautiful, opulent land. The houses beside the road were so inviting, but even more beautiful and dainty were the houses situated deeper in the landscape, surrounded by trees, in the midst of all that green. The hills rose gracefully, softly into the air, the sky above was beckoning, everything was blue, shot through with a magnificent, fiery blue, groups of people were riding about on carts, and finally Simon beheld a tiny little house beside the road, with a town beyond it, and his brother was just sticking his head out the window. He had arrived punctually, barely a quarter of an hour later than the two had agreed. Joyfully he went into the house.

Inside, in his brother's room, he gazed at everything with wondering eyes, though there wasn't much to observe. In one corner stood the bed, an interesting bed—after all, it was where Kaspar slept; and the window was a marvelous window—though made of simple wood and with plain curtains—since Kaspar had just stuck his head out this very window. The floor, table, bedspread and chairs were covered with drawings and pictures. Each separate sheet now slid through the visitor's fingers, every one beautiful and so perfectly executed. Simon found it all but inconceivable what a worker this painter was, so many things lay before his eyes that he could scarcely manage to look at them all. "Why, it's nature herself you've painted," he exclaimed. "I find it so bittersweet to look at new pictures of yours. Each one is so beautiful, they gleam with sentiment and seem to strike nature in her heart, and yet you are always painting new things, always striving for something even better—possibly you also destroy many things that have turned out poorly in your eyes. I'm incapable of finding any of your pictures weak, each one moves me and bewitches my soul. Even just a brushstroke of yours, or a color, gives me a firm and unshakeable conviction of your talent—it's simply wonderful. And when I look at your landscapes, painted so expansively and so warmly by your brush, I always see you, and along with you I feel a sort of pain which tells me there is never an end to art. I understand art so well—the urgency human beings feel for its sake, that longing to vie for Nature's love and good graces in this way. Why do we wish to see a charming landscape reproduced in a picture? Is it just for the sake of pleasure? No, we are hoping this image will explain *something*—but this is a something that will surely always remain inexplicable. It cuts so deeply into us when we, lying at a window, dreamily watch the setting sun; but that's nothing at all compared to a street when it's raining and the women are daintily raising their skirts, or to the sight of a garden or lake beneath the weightless morning sky or to a simple fir tree in winter or to a boat ride at night, or a view of the Alps. Fog and snow enchant us no less than sunshine and colors: Fog refines the colors, and snow is, after all, and particularly beneath the blue of the warm early spring sky, a profound, marvelous, almost incomprehensible thing. How beautiful that you paint, Kaspar, and paint so beautifully. I'd like to be a little bit of nature and be loved by you the way you love every bit of nature. A painter must love nature so ardently and achingly, even more tempestuously and tremblingly and openly than a poet, such as Sebastian, for example— and people are saying he's built himself a hut up in the high pastures so he can worship nature undisturbed, like a Japanese hermit. But poets, no doubt, are less faithfully attached to nature than you painters; for as a rule they approach nature with their heads over-educated, over-stuffed. But perhaps I'm mistaken, and in this case I would gladly be mistaken. How you must have worked, Kaspar. Surely you have no cause to reproach yourself. I wouldn't do so. Not even I reproach myself, and truly, I have ample cause. But I don't, because this makes a person nervous, and nervousness is an ugly state unworthy of human beings—"

"I couldn't agree more," Kaspar replied.

The two of them then strolled through the little town, looking at everything, which didn't take long, and yet, considering the seriousness with which they regarded it all, did in fact take quite some time. They passed the mailman, who handed Kaspar a letter, making a face as he did so. The letter was from Klara. The church was admired, as was the majesty of the town's towers and the defiant protective walls, which however had often been breached, the vintners' huts and gazebos set into the mountainside, places where life had died out long ago. The fir trees gazed down solemnly at the small old town, and at the same time the sky was so sweet above the houses which appeared defiant and sullen in their thickness and breadth. The meadows were shimmering and the hills with their golden beech forests beckoned the viewer up to their distant heights. In the afternoon the young men went into the forest. They were no longer speaking much. Kaspar had fallen silent, his brother sensed what he was thinking of and preferred not to rouse him, for it seemed to him more important for things to be thought over than spoken about. They sat down on a bench. "She won't let go of me," Kaspar said, "she's unhappy." Simon said nothing, but he felt a certain joy on his brother's behalf, that the woman was unhappy over him. He thought: "How lovely I find it that she is unhappy." This love enchanted him. Soon, however, the two took leave of one another; it was time for Simon to return, by train this time.

—7—

Winter arrived. Simon, left up to his own devices, sat dressed in a coat, writing at the table in his small room. He didn't know what to do with all the time on his hands, and since his profession had accustomed him to writing, he now sat and wrote offhandedly, without forethought, on small strips of paper he'd cut to size with scissors. Outside the weather was damp, and the coat Simon had wrapped himself in was serving the function of a heating stove. This sitting at home in his room seemed so cozy to him, while out of doors violent winds were raging, promising snow. He felt so comfortable sitting like that, engaged in his activity and embracing the notion that he'd been utterly forgotten. He thought back on his childhood, which wasn't yet so terribly far behind him but nonetheless appeared as distant as a dream, and wrote:

I wish to recall to my mind my childhood, as my current circumstances make this a fascinating and instructive task. I was a boy who liked to lean back against warm heating stoves. Doing this made me fancy myself both important and sad, and I would wear a simultaneously self-satisfied and melancholy expression. What's more, I donned felt slippers whenever possible for indoor wear—changing shoes, exchanging wet ones for dry, gave me the greatest pleasure. A warm room always struck me as ravishing. I was never ill, and always envied people who could fall ill, as they were then cared for and had somewhat more delicate words addressed to them. For this reason I often imagined myself falling ill and was touched when I heard, in my fantasy, my parents speaking tender words to me. I had a need to be treated with affection, but this never happened. My mother frightened me because she uttered affectionate words so infrequently. I had a reputation for being a scallywag—not without cause, as I recall—but it was nonetheless sometimes hurtful always to be reminded of that. I would so have loved to be coddled; but when I saw it was out of the question that attentions of this sort would be shown me, I became a ruffian and made a point of provoking the children who enjoyed the advantage of being well-mannered and loved—my sister Hedwig and my brother Klaus. Nothing gave me greater pleasure than when they boxed my ears, for this demonstrated that I'd been skillful enough to arouse their ire. I don't have many memories of school, but I know I found it a sort of compensation for the minor affronts I suffered in my parents' home: I was able to excel. I took great satisfaction in bringing home good grades. School frightened me, and so I always behaved well there; whenever I was at school my conduct was diffident and restrained. The teachers' weaknesses didn't remain hidden from me for long, but I found them more terrifying than ridiculous. One of the teachers, a cloddish, monstrous person, had a real drunkard's face; it nonetheless never occurred to me to suspect him of drinking, and yet a mysterious rumor was circulating in the world of the school about another teacher, saying drink had been his downfall. The expression of suffering on this man's face is something I shall never forget. I considered Jews more refined than Christians, for there were several enchantingly beautiful Jewish girls who set me trembling when I met them on the street. Often *my father would send me on errands to one of the elegant Jewish homes; it always smelled of milk in this house, and the lady who would open the door to me there would have on wide white dresses and would bring with her a warm spicy scent that at first I found distasteful, but later I came to love. I think I can't have worn such nice clothes as a child, in any case I would gaze with malicious admiration at a few of the other boys who wore beautiful high-topped shoes, smooth stockings and well-tailored suits. One boy in particular made a deep impression on me because of how delicate his face and hands were, and the softness of his movements and the voice that came from his lips. He was exactly like a girl, dressed always in soft fabrics, and with the teachers he enjoyed a respect that bewildered me. I felt a pathological longing to have him deign to speak to me, and was overjoyed when one day he suddenly addressed me before the window of a stationery store. He flattered me, saying I wrote so beautifully, and that he wished his own handwriting were that beautiful. How it delighted me to be superior in at least this one respect to this young god of a boy, and I fended off his compliments blissfully blushing. That smile! I can still remember how he smiled. For a long time his mother was my dream. I overvalued her to the detriment of my own mother. How unjust! This boy was attacked by several pranksters in our class who put their heads together and declared him to be a girl, a real one just dressed up in boy's clothes. Naturally this was pure nonsense, but the claim struck me like a thunderbolt, and for a long time I imagined I ought to be worshiping this boy as a girl in disguise. His overripe figure provided ample fodder for my high-strung romantic sentiments. Naturally I was too shy and proud to declare how fond I was of him, and so he considered me one of his enemies. What elegant aloofness he could convey. How curious to be thinking of this just now!—In religion class I once delighted one of my teachers by finding just the right word for a certain feel-*

ing; this too I shall never forget. In various subjects I was indeed quite good, but it always felt shameful to me to stand out as a model pupil, and I often practically made an effort to get bad marks. My instincts told me that the students I surpassed might hate me, and I liked being popular. I found the thought that my schoolmates might hate me rather frightening—a calamity. It had become fashionable in our class to detest all swots, and therefore it often happened that clever, intelligent pupils would try to look stupid as a precaution. This conduct, when it was recognized, counted among us as exemplary behavior, and indeed, there was no doubt something heroic about it, even if only in a misunderstood sense. To be singled out for praise by teachers therefore carried with it the danger of being held in low regard. What a curious world: school. One of my earliest years at school, I had a classmate, a little squirt of a thing with blotches on his pointy face, whose father was a basket weaver and swillpot known to all and sundry. The little fellow was constantly being made to pronounce the word "schnapps" before the entire mocking classroom, which he couldn't do—he always said "snaps" instead of "schnapps" because of some miserable speech impediment. How we howled with laughter. And when I now think back on it: How crude this was. Another boy, a certain Bill, a jovial little fellow, was always late for school because his parents lived in a remote, rugged mountain region far from town. The latecomer would always be forced to hold out his hand as punishment for his tardiness, whereupon he would receive a biting, sharply painful blow of the cane. Every time, the pain would force tears from the lad's eyes. How intently we witnessed this castigation. Let me emphasize, by the way, that I have no wish to make accusations about anyone—the teacher in question, say—as one might easily suspect, but am simply reporting what I recall from those days.—Up on the mountain, in the forest above the town, all sorts of rough unemployed derelicts—then

144

even more than now, I would assume—were in the habit of gathering to drink from schnapps bottles in the thickets, play cards or court the women-folk who were present, recognizable as women by the scraps of clothes they wore, their faces home to misery and affliction. These people were known as vagrants. One Sunday evening we—Hedwig, Kaspar and I—were out walking with a girl we called Anna, who was fond of us all, on a narrow path that led over this mountain, and as we stepped out into a forest clearing full of rocks, we saw a man seize one of these rocks in his fist and smash it audibly into the face of another man, his opponent, so that blood came spurting out and the man who had been struck fell at once to the ground. This fight, whose end we didn't witness, as we immediately fled, appeared to have started because of a woman; at any rate I can still see clearly before me the dusky tall figure of a woman who at the time was standing by, nonchalant, observing the fight with a wicked expression. This encounter filled me with a profound distress and terror that kept me from eating and made me avoid that part of the forest for a long time. There was something horrifyingly primitive, even primeval about the sight of those men doing battle—

Kaspar and I had a friend in common, the son of a member of the Cantonal parliament and respected merchant, whom we dearly loved on account of his submissiveness and his willingness to take part in any plan we hatched. We often went to visit him in his parental, parliamentary home where we were always given a friendly welcome by an exquisite lady, his mother. We would play for hours with our friend's building blocks and tin soldiers and amuse ourselves splendidly. Kaspar excelled at building fortresses and palaces and sketching out battle plans. Our friend was very attached to us; to Kaspar, I thought, even more than me; and he often visited us at home as well, though things at our house were admittedly less refined. Hedwig was very fond of him. His mother was completely different from ours, the rooms gleamed more than at our house, and the tone was different; I mean, the tone of the conversations; but at our house, all in all, things were more lively. At the time, there was a wealthy lady in our town living all alone in a magnificent garden, in a house of course, but the house was invisible thanks to all the ivy and trees and fountains that concealed it. This lady had three daughters, beautiful, pale girls who were said to have a new dress to put on every two weeks. They didn't keep these dresses in their cupboards, but rather sent special messengers to sell them to the townsfolk. At one point Hedwig owned a silk dress and pair of shoes that had belonged to one of these girls, and these second-hand items inspired in me, when I looked at and touched them, a secret repulsion combined with the greatest interest and a concern that often made me the butt of jokes. The lady was always sitting at home; at most she might put in an appearance at the theater, where she looked alarmingly white in her dark red box. The middle girl was probably the most beautiful of the three. I always imagined her seated on horseback; she had a face that looked as if made to gaze down from the back of a prancing horse upon a gaping crowd of people, causing them all to cast down their eyes. All three girls have no doubt long since married.—Once we had a conflagration, not in the town itself, but in a neighboring village. The entire sky all around was reddened by the flames, it was an icy winter night. People ran upon the frozen, crunching snow, including Kaspar and me; for our mother had sent us to find out where the fire was. We reached the flames, but it bored us to spend so long gazing into the burning beams, besides which we were freezing, and so we soon ran back home again, where Mother received us with all the severity of one who's been made to worry. My mother was already unwell in those days. Not long afterward, Kaspar left school, where he was no longer prospering.

I still had one more year ahead of me, but a certain melancholy took hold of me and bid me look with bitterness upon all things scholastic. I saw the end approaching and the imminent start of something new. What it would be—on this subject I could muster only the most foolish thoughts. I saw my brother often, laden down with packages, in his life of employment, and thought about why he looked so downcast as he worked, with his face drooping toward the ground: It couldn't be so nice after all, this new thing, if you weren't allowed to raise your eyes. But Kaspar had already begun to plan his career, he always seemed to be dreaming, and had such a curious calmness about him, which didn't please our father at all. We were now living on the edge of town in humble lodgings the sight of which was enough to chill you through. This dwelling did not suit Mother. In general she had a most peculiar illness: She always felt wounded by her surroundings. She liked to go on about elegant little houses set in gardens. What do I know. She was a very unhappy woman. When for example we were all sitting at the dinner table, keeping fairly silent as was our custom, she would suddenly seize a fork or knife and hurl it away from her, right off the table, making all of us turn our heads to one side; if you tried to calm her, she would feel insulted, and if you reproached her, she would feel even more insulted. Father had his hands full with her. We children recalled with melancholy and pain the days when she'd been a woman who was received everywhere with an admixture of affection and esteem, when if she called you to her with her ringing voice, you happily rushed to her side. All the ladies in town paid her compliments which she brushed aside with grace and modesty; this bygone time appeared to me even then like a magical fairy tale filled with wonderful fragrances and images. And so I learned quite early to devote myself passionately to beautiful memories. Once more I saw the tall building where my parents ran a delightful costume jewelry *shop, where people were always coming in to buy things, where we children had a bright, large nursery which the sun seemed particularly to enjoy filling up with light. Right beside our tall building crouched a short, crooked, squashed, ancient one beneath a pointed gable roof; a widow lived there. She had a hat shop, a son and a female relative, along with a dog, I believe, if memory serves. When you walked into her shop, she would greet you in such a friendly way that merely to stand in front of this woman would be a goodly pleasure. She would then press various hats upon your head and lead you to the mirror with a smile. Her hats all smelled so wonderful that you couldn't help standing there transfixed. She was a good friend of my mother. Right next door, that is, right next door to the hat shop, a snow-white pastry shop glittered temptingly, a confectionery. The confectioner's wife appeared to us to be an angel, not a woman. She had the most delicate oval face you could imagine; kindness and purity appeared to have given this face its shape. A smile that turned anyone it touched into an enchanted pious child sweetened her already sweet features. The entire woman appeared to have been made to sell sweets, delicacies and dainties that could only be touched by the very tips of one's fingers, to preserve their exquisite flavors. She too was a friend of my mother. Mother had many friends—*

Simon stopped writing. He went over to a photograph of his mother that hung on the dirty wall of his room, and, rising up on tiptoe, pressed a kiss upon it. Then he tore up what he'd written, neither out of pique nor with much premeditation; simply because it no longer held any value for him. Then he went to visit Rosa out in the suburbs and said to her: "Soon I shall find employment, perhaps in a small rural town, which at the moment I'd find the most beautiful thing imaginable. After all, small towns are delightful. In such a place, you have your old comfortable room, for which you pay curiously little rent. Returning to this room from your place of work is easily accomplished with just a few steps. All the people say hello to you on the street, wondering who this young gentleman might be. The women with daughters are already, in thought, granting you their daughter's hand—the youngest daughter, no doubt, the one with curly ringlets and dangling, heavy earrings on her tiny ears. At work you'll soon have made yourself indispensable, and the boss would be happy to have made such an acquisition. After returning home in the evening, you'd sit in a heated room, and the pictures on the walls would be gazed at, one of which might perhaps represent lovely Empress Eugenie and the other a revolution. The daughter of the house would perhaps come in and bring me flowers, why ever not? Are all these things not possible in a small town where people welcome one another so affectionately? One day, however, during my warm bright lunch break, this very same girl would knock shyly at my door—a door dating, by the way, from the Rococo period—would open it, come into the room and say to me, tilting her head to one side in an infinitely delicate gesture, 'How quiet you always are, Simon. You are so modest and make no demands at all. You never say: I need this or that. You take everything as it comes. I fear you are dissatisfied.' I would laugh and reassure her. Then suddenly, as if the oddest feelings had come over her, it might occur to her to say: 'How quiet and beautiful the flowers are on the table there. They look as if they have eyes, and it seems to me as if they're smiling.' I would be astonished to hear words of this sort on the lips of a small-town girl.

Then I would suddenly find it quite natural to go walking with slow steps toward the one standing there hesitantly, place my arm about her figure and kiss her. She would permit this, but not in such a way that one might be tempted to indulge in unlovely thoughts. She would cast her eyes down before her, and I would hear the pounding of her heart, the rising and falling of her beautiful, round breast. I would ask her to show me her eyes, and she would open them, allowing me to gaze into the heaven of her open, questioning eyes. A long asking and gazing would follow. First there would be an imploring look from her, then I would be moved to look at her in just the same way, and then of course I would be unable to suppress a laugh, and she would nonetheless trust me. How wonderful that can be, in a small town where people say so much with their glances alone. I would once more kiss her oddly curved and bowed mouth and flatter her in such a way that she would have no choice but to believe all my compliments and then it wouldn't be flattery at all, and I would tell her I considered her my wife, whereupon she, once more tilting her head to one side in that marvelous way, would say yes. After all, how else could she respond with me pressing her mouth shut as one does a child's, if I covered her with kisses, this magnificent girl now incapable of suppressing a smile of high spirits and victorious pride? Indeed, the victor would be she and I her victim, this would be apparent quite soon, for I would become her husband and thus would sacrifice and present to her my entire life, my freedom and all my desires to see the world. Now I would always be observing her, finding her ever more beautiful. Until the nuptials, I would be like a rogue chasing after all the charms she might let drop behind her. I would watch to see her kneel down on the floor in the evening to make a fire in the stove. I would laugh a great deal, like a lunatic, to avoid always resorting to overly delicate expressions of affection, and perhaps I would often treat her roughly as well just to catch a glimpse of pain in her face. After behavior like this, I wouldn't hesitate to kneel down beside her bed, secretly, in her absence, and to pray to her with a flaming heart. I might even go so far as to take her shoe, even if it were covered with blacking, and press it to my lips; for an object in which she has placed her little white foot would easily suffice to produce in me a feeling of worship; after all, it doesn't take much to pray. I would often climb the high, rocky mountains that lay nearby, casually hoisting myself up by the little saplings, passing along precipices, and when I reached the top, just above a rockfall, I would lie down in a yellow pasture and reflect on where I was and ask myself whether in fact a life like this, sharing close quarters with a wife who was dear to me but nonetheless really quite demanding would satisfy me. I would merely shake my head over such questions and with splendidly healthy senses go on sending daydreams down into the valley where this little town lay spread. Perhaps I would weep for half an hour, why not, in order to appease my longings and then would lie there peaceful and happy again until the sun sank, whereupon I would go back down and squeeze my maiden's hand. Everything would be decided on and bolted shut behind me—but my heart would rejoice in this firm, commanding conclusiveness. Then I would celebrate my marriage and in this way give my life new life. My old life would sink like a beautiful sun, and I wouldn't cast so much as a glance after it, for I would consider that dangerous and weak. Time would pass and now we would be bending—to give an illustration for our affection—not over flowers but over children and would feel delight at their smiles and countless questions. Our love for our children and the thousand cares they would demand of us would make our own love gentler and all the greater but also quieter. It would never occur to me to wonder whether my wife still pleased me, nor would it cross my mind to tell myself I was living a small paltry life. I would have experienced everything life has to offer by way of experiences, and willingly would renounce all thoughts holding out and dangling before me all the elegant adventures I was missing out on. 'What can still be called missing out here?' I would ask myself calmly, with a superior air. I would have become a solid individual, this would be all and would remain all until the death of my wife, who might possibly have been fated to die before me. But I don't wish to think any further, for all these things lie too far distant in the darkness of the beautiful future. What do you say to all this? I'm always such a dreamer, but you must at least admit my dreams these days possess a certain uprightness and reflect my desire to become a better person than I am at present."

Rosa was smiling. For a while she said nothing, merely observed Simon attentively, and then asked: "How is your brother, the painter?"

"He's planning to go to Paris soon."

Rosa turned pale and shut her eyes, breathing with difficulty. Simon thought: So she loves him too.

"You love him," he said softly.

*   *   *

The next morning Simon stepped out of the house wearing a short, dark blue coat, with a delicate, useless little stick in his hand. A thick heavy fog received him, and it was still blackest night. An hour later, though, the sky began to lighten as he stood on a hilltop gazing back at the metropolis beneath him. It was cold, but the sun rising fiery-red above the snowy bushes and fields promised a glorious day. He remained transfixed by the sight of this red ball that kept soaring higher and higher and said to himself that the sun in winter was three times again as beautiful as a midsummer sun. The snow was soon blazing with this peculiarly bright-red warm hue, and this warming sight and the actual frostiness of the air all around had an invigorating, stimulating effect on the wanderer, who, not allowing himself to be delayed any longer, went striding stalwartly on. The path was the same one Simon had taken that night in autumn; he practically could have found it in his sleep by now. In this way he walked all day long. At midday, the sun poured beautiful warmth down on the region, the snow was on the verge of melting again, and there were bits of green peeping out damply in several spots. The trickling streams reinforced the impression of warmth, but toward evening, as the sky showed itself resplendently dark blue and the sun's red rays were vanishing over the mountain ridge, it at once turned bitter cold again. Simon was once more ascending the mountain he'd climbed before, that autumn night, though in more frantic haste; the snow crunched beneath his footsteps. Heavily laden with snow, the fir trees' thick branches arched down splendidly to the earth. When he was approximately halfway to the top, Simon suddenly saw a young man lying in the snow in the middle of the path. There was still enough last light in the forest that he could observe the sleeper well. What had possessed this man to lie down here in the bitter cold, in such a secluded part of the forest? The man's broad hat lay across his face, just as one often sees on a hot, shadeless summer day, when a person lying down to rest will shield himself from the sun's rays to be able to fall asleep. There was something unsettling about this covered face in the middle of winter, a season when it could hardly be considered pleasurable to settle down for a rest in the snow. The man lay there motionless, and already it was beginning to get darker in the forest. Simon studied the man's legs, shoes, clothes. His outfit was pale yellow, it was a summer suit, a quite thin, threadbare one. Simon took the hat from the man's face, it was rigid and looked terrifying, and now all at once he recognized this face, it was Sebastian's face, no two ways about it—these were Sebastian's features, this was his mouth, his beard, his rather broad flat nose, his eyes and eyebrows, his forehead and hair. And he'd frozen to death here, without a doubt, and he must have been lying here on the path for a while. The snow displayed no footprints; it was conceivable he'd been here for a considerable length of time. His face and hands had long since turned rigid, and the clothes were stuck to his frozen torso. Sebastian must have sunk to the ground here with an immense, no longer endurable weariness. He'd never been particularly robust. He always stooped over, as though he couldn't bear to walk upright, as though it caused him pain to hold his back and head straight. Looking at him, one couldn't help feeling he hadn't been strong enough for life and its cold demands. Simon cut some branches from a fir tree and covered the body with them, but first he drew a small, thin notebook from the dead man's jacket pocket where it had been sticking out. It appeared to contain poems, though Simon could no longer make out the letters. Night had fallen. Stars were sparkling through the gaps between the fir trees, and the moon, a fine delicate hoop, observed the scene: "I don't have time," Simon said silently to himself, "I've got to hurry to reach the next town, otherwise it wouldn't frighten me at all to spend a bit more time with this poor devil of a dead man, a poet and dreamer. How noble a grave he chose for himself. His resting place lies amid splendid green snow-covered firs. I shall not report this to anyone. Nature gazes down upon her dead man, the stars are quietly singing at his head, and the night birds are squawking—this is the best music for a person who no longer feels or hears. Your poems, dear Sebastian, I shall bring to a publisher, where they will perhaps be read and consigned to print, so that at least your poor, sparkling, melodious name will remain to the world. What splendid peace: reposing and growing stiff beneath fir branches in the snow. You couldn't have chosen anything better. People tend to inflict harm on the eccentric—and this is what you were—and then laugh at their pain. Give my greetings to the dear, silent dead beneath the earth and don't get too badly scorched in the eternal fires of nonexistence. You are elsewhere. Surely you're somewhere splendid, you're a rich fellow now, and publishing the poems of a rich elegant fellow is certainly worthwhile. Farewell. If I had flowers, I'd strew them over you. For a poet one never has flowers enough. You had too few. You were expecting some, but you never heard the flutter of their petals above you, nor did they alight upon your shoulders as you dreamed they might. I too am a dreamer, you see, as are many, many people you'd never suspect, but you believed dreaming to be your prerogative, whereas the rest of us dream only when we fancy ourselves utterly miserable, and are happy to be able to stop at will. You despised your fellow creatures, Sebastian! But this, my dear man, is something only a strong individual may allow himself, and you were weak! But now that I have found your hallowed grave, let me not heap scorn upon it. I cannot know what you have suffered. Your death beneath the open stars is beautiful, I shall not soon forget it. I shall tell Hedwig of your grave beneath these noble firs and make her weep with my description. At least people will still be able to read your poems, even if they didn't have much use for you before." —Simon strode away from the dead man, casting one last glance back at the little pile of fir branches beneath which the poet now slept, then turning away from this image with a rapid twist of his supple body, he hastened further up the mountain, moving as fast as he could in the snow. And so he was having to ascend this mountain at night for a second time, but this time life and death were shooting through his entire body in feverish shudderings. In this icy, star-resplendent night he felt like crying out exultantly. The fire of life bore him tempestuously away from that gentle, pale image of death. He no longer felt any legs, just veins and tendons, and these pliantly obeyed his forward-striding will. High up on the open mountain meadow he had his first full, sublime view of the glorious night and laughed out loud, like a boy who's never seen a dead man before. What was a dead man? What else but a reminder to live. This and nothing more. A delightful memory calling one back, and at the same time a being-driven-on into the uncertain, lovely future. If he was able to face the dead so calmly, Simon felt that his future must still be spread out broad and wide before him. He was overjoyed that he'd been able to see this poor, unhappy person one last time and that he'd found him in so mysterious a guise, so silent, so eloquent, so dark and peaceful and so graciously at an end. Now, praise God, there was nothing remaining about this poet that you could smile or turn up your nose at, just something you could feel.—Simon slept splendidly in his bed at an inn, the very same inn whose ballroom had been painted by his brother. He used the following day for more walking on grueling roads full of snow. He beheld always a blue sky above him, houses to either side of the road—beautiful large homes that led one to assume the rural population here was prosperous and proud, hills covered with black, bedraggled trees into which the blue sky was creeping, and people who walked past him and others who were walking in his direction but who were soon overtaken, for he was striding along while the others were comfortably strolling. When night fell, he was walking through a silent, narrow, strange valley entirely encircled by forest and filled with twists and turns and odd glimpses of high-up villages where the evening lights were burning and very few people could be seen out-of-doors. But as he was now starting to be tormented by serious exhaustion, he stopped at the next inn. The pub downstairs was filled with people, and the innkeeper's wife looked more like an elegant lady of good lineage than a waitress with the duty of serving patrons. He shyly made his wishes known, whereupon the beautiful woman looked him up and down strangely. But he was so weary, so worn-out that he felt only pleasure when, a short while later, he was led to his room, where he blissfully lay down in an ice-cold bed and at once fell asleep. The third day brought him to a vast, beautiful city where he had only one piece of business: finding an editor to whom he could entrust Sebastian's poems. When he'd reached the building that had been described to him, he realized it would be incautious to go in himself and present the poems of a man who'd been found dead. And so he inscribed the cover of the blue notebook with the title: "The Poems of a Young Man Found Frozen to Death in the Fir Forest, for Publication If Possible," and he dropped the notebook into the big, stocky mailbox with a loud clunk. Having accomplished this, Simon took himself off again. The weather had grown milder, snow was spiraling in large wet flakes down upon the roads now drawing him on. The people in this city, which he didn't know at all, looked at him with such odd expressions of surprise that he almost couldn't help imagining they knew him, a perfect stranger. Soon he'd left the actual city behind and was walking through an elegant villa district, then he abandoned this too and passed through a forest, a field, another field, then a smaller forest, then a village, then a second and a third, until night fell.

−8−

It was snowing in the small village that morning. The children arriving at school had wet snowy shoes, trousers, skirts and heads and caps. They brought the scent of snow into the schoolroom with them, along with all sorts of debris from the muddy, sodden roads. Because of the snowfall, this horde of little ones was distracted, pleasurably agitated and not terribly inclined to attentiveness, which made the teacher a bit impatient. She was just about to start the religion lesson when she became aware of a dark, slender, mobile, ambulatory spot before the window, a spot that couldn't have been made by any peasant, for it was too delicate and agile. It went flying right past the row of windows, and all at once the children saw their teacher race from the room, the lesson forgotten. Hedwig now went out the door of the schoolhouse to throw herself into the arms of her brother, who was standing right before her. She wept and kissed Simon and led him into one of the two rooms she had at her disposal. "You come unannounced, but it's good you've come," she said, "take off your things and put them here. I have to go teach some more, but I'll send the children home an hour early today. It won't make any difference. They're so completely inattentive today that I have ample cause to be annoyed and send them off earlier than usual." —She arranged her hair, which had gotten rather out of joint during their impetuous greeting, said goodbye to her brother and went back to work.

Simon began to make himself at home in the country. His suitcases were delivered by mail, whereupon he unpacked all his things. He no longer had many possessions: a few old books he hadn't wanted to sell or give away, linens, a black suit and a bundle of small items like twine, scraps of silk, neckties, shoelaces, candle stumps, buttons and bits of thread. The teacher at the next school over agreed to loan out an old iron bedframe and a straw mattress to go along with it: This was sufficient for sleeping in the country. The bedstead was transported from the neighboring village on a wide sled in the middle of the night. Hedwig and Simon sat down upon this strange vehicle; the son of the teacher who was Hedwig's friend, a strapping lad who'd just finished his military service, guided the sled downhill into the hollow in which the schoolhouse was located. There was much laughter. The bed was set up in the second room and furnished with the necessary bedding and thus made ready for a sleeper who had no exaggerated demands to make of a bed, which of course Simon did not. At first Hedwig thought for a while: "Well, he's coming to me now because he doesn't have anywhere else to live in all the wide world. That's what I'm good for. If he'd had somewhere else to sleep and eat, he wouldn't have remembered his sister." But she quickly dismissed this thought, which had arisen in a moment of defiant pride and had been pursued only because of the manner of its arrival, not because it was agreeable. Simon in his turn felt a little ashamed to be making claims on his sister's kindness in such a way, but this feeling didn't last long either; for habit soon swallowed it up, he quite simply grew used to all of this! He really didn't have any money left, but right away, just a day or two after his arrival, he sent around a letter to all the notary publics in the region asking them to send him work, as he was a skilled copyist with a lovely hand. And why did one need money in the country! Not much was needed. Gradually all the fragile walls separating the two schoolhouse inhabitants fell away, and they lived as if they'd always lived together, joyfully sharing both deprivations and amusements.

It was early spring. Already you could leave windows standing open with less hesitation, and the stoves scarcely needed stoking. The children brought Hedwig entire bouquets of snowdrops, so that soon they were at a loss what to do with them all, as there weren't enough small containers in the schoolroom. The air in the village was heady with the first fragrant hints of spring. People were already taking walks in the sunshine. Imperceptibly, as if in passing, Simon had become known among these simple folk, no one asked many questions about who he was, people said he was one of the teacher's brothers, and this was enough here to gain him respect. He'd be staying a little while, as a visitor, they thought. Simon walked around looking fairly tattered, but with a certain offhand elegance that became him and attractively concealed the squalor of the fabrics he wore. His torn shoes didn't attract much notice. Simon found it enchanting to walk about the countryside in faulty shoes; he felt this to be one of the greatest advantages of country living. If he were to get some money, he might begin to consider whether to have his footwear set to rights, but these would be only the faintest, most unhurried deliberations. Perhaps he'd hesitate for a fortnight first; for what is a fortnight in the country? Back in the city you always had to do everything right away, but here you had the lovely obligation to defer everything from one day to the next, indeed, things deferred themselves of their own accord; for the days arrived so softly, and before you could even think about it, it would be evening already, followed by a fervent night, a veritable slumber of a night, which was then quietly woken again by the day, woken gently and with tenderness. Simon also loved the more often than not muddy village roads, the narrow ones that led you over hillocks of debris, and the wide ones where you sank into the muck if you didn't watch your step. But that was what he liked about it! Walking on these roads gave you the opportunity to watch your step, you could show off as a city slicker who was accustomed to picking his way with great attentiveness and a slightly trumped-up look of horror when presented with mud. The old farmwives could then think to themselves what a tidy, cautious young man he was, and the girls could laugh at the great leaps Simon executed to avoid the moats and puddles. The sky was frequently encircled with clouds, dark puffy fat clouds, and delightful storms were often blowing, agitating the forest and hurtling across the moss where people were at work cutting sod, their horses patiently standing by. Oftentimes too the sky would be smiling so that all who saw it were instantly compelled to smile as well. Hedwig's face would take on a joyous expression, and the teacher who lived on the upper floor would poke his glasses inquisitively out the window, in his way enjoying the exquisite treat of this balmy sky. Simon had gone into a little shop to buy himself an inexpensive pipe and some tobacco. It appeared to him beautiful and fitting to smoke only pipes in the country, for a pipe could be filled, and filling the pipe was a gesture that accorded well with the open fields and the forest where he spent almost the entire livelong day. In the warm midday sun, he would lie in the pale yellow grass beneath the splendidly gentle sky, stretched out on the riverbank, and was not merely allowed to dream, he was compelled to. But he didn't dream of far-off, distant, beauteous things but rather contented himself with contemplations and daydreams pertaining to his immediate surroundings; for he knew nothing more beautiful. Hedwig, the one closest to him, was the object of his dreams. He had forgotten the entire rest of the world, and the pipe tobacco he was smoking only served to bring him back to the village, the schoolhouse, Hedwig. Of her he imagined:

"She is sitting in a boat with a man who's abducted her. The lake is no larger than a pond in a park. She keeps peering into the large black brooding eyes of the man sitting utterly motionless in the boat beside her and thinks: 'How his eyes gaze into the water. At me he does not look. But the entire huge surface of the water is gazing at me with his eyes!' The man has a shaggy beard of the sort robbers are in the habit of wearing. He can be gallant like none other. He is capable of taking gallantry to the point of losing his life without blinking an eyelash and most certainly without placing his hand on his heart to boast of his deeds. This man is no boaster. He has a warm, wonderfully masculine voice, but he never uses it to pay a compliment. Never does flattery of any sort cross his proud lips, and he ruins his voice intentionally to make it sound harsh and heartless. But the girl knows he has a boundlessly good heart: Nonetheless she doesn't dare appeal to his heart with a request. A string resounds across the water in long sound waves. Hedwig thinks she might die in this resounding air. The sky above the water looks exactly like this weightless, water-hued sky currently floating above me: a floating hovering lake high above me, that fits perfectly and the trees in the picture correspond to the region's tall, swaying trees—there is something manorial, park-like about them. But in the picture everything is cramped and condensed, and now I am strolling through this scene once more, giving no more thought to its correlation with myself and this region: The man now seizes the oar and gives the boat a cavalier thrust. Hedwig senses he might be doing this to offset his own warmth and love—to him, feeling love and tenderness is an affront, and he punishes himself mercilessly for having allowed himself to harbor such affectionate sentiments in his breast. He's so unnaturally proud; not a man at all, just a cross between a boy and a giant. It doesn't hurt a man to find himself overwhelmed by sentiment, but it hurts a boy who wants to be more than a man with honest feelings, a boy who wants to be a giant, wants to be only strong and not at times also weak. A boy has chivalric virtues that a man whose thoughts are sensible and mature will always thrust aside, seeing them as superfluous in the festival of love. A boy is less cowardly than a man since he is less mature, for maturity can easily make one dastardly and selfish. You need only observe the hard, cruel lips of a boy: this outspoken defiance and the exemplified insistence on a promise he's secretly given himself. A boy keeps his word, a man might find it more appropriate to break it. The boy finds beauty in the severity of this word-keeping (as in the Middle Ages) and the man finds beauty in replacing one promise he's uttered with another, which he promises like a man to keep. He is the promiser, and the boy is the enforcer of the promised word. Curls dance about his youthful forehead, a defiance unto death upon his curved lips. Eyes like daggers. Hedwig trembles. The park's trees are so soft, they are dissolving in the light blue air. There beneath the trees sits the man she despises. This man who sits beside her, loveless—him she must love, though he promises nothing. He hasn't yet opened his mouth to make a promise, he's had the gall to abduct her without, in compensation, whispering even a single sweet nothing in her ear. Whispering is the business of that other one; this man doesn't know the first thing about it. Even if he did, he wouldn't do so, or he'd do so on some occasion where others wouldn't dream of uttering anything at all. But she is giving herself to him, without knowing why. She has nothing to gain from this, has nothing to hope for, as women are so fond of doing, she has only inconsiderate treatment in store for her, the violent moods a master freely inflicts upon his property. But she feels happy when he speaks to her in a curt, heedless voice, as though she were already his. And she is his, after all, and the man knows this. He pays no more heed to what is his already. Her hair has come undone, splendid hair that plunges down her narrow, red cheeks like liquid cloth. 'Tie it back,' he commands, and she struggles to obey. She is in raptures as she obeys, and of course he'd see this even with his eyes shut; for then he would hear a moan cross her lips such as only those who are happy can give voice to, those hastily performing a task that is perhaps burdensome to their hands but a joy to their hearts. They get out of the boat and go ashore. The earth is soft and gives way slightly beneath their steps, like a carpet, or like several carpets placed one atop the other. The grass is the sparse yellowed grass from the year before, just like the grass here where I am smoking my pipe. Then suddenly a girl appears on the scene, a quite small, pale, gloomy-eyed girl. She appears to be a princess; for her garments are magnificent and puff out at the sides in a heavy arc from which her breast protrudes like a small burgeoning bud. The garments are a deep red, the hue of dried-out blood. Her face has a transparent pallor, it's the shade of a wintry evening sky in the mountains. 'You know me!' With these words she addresses herself to the dumbfounded man, who stands there paralyzed. 'You still dare to look upon me? Go, kill yourself. I command you!' This is how she speaks to him. The man looks as though he means to obey her. How does he look? Well, the way one looks when there is something irrevocable to be done. In such cases a grimace is customary. The face trembles, and one must bite and knead it into submission with the full force of one's will. It wants to break apart. A piece of nose is about to fall off. At any rate, this is the sort of thing to expect on such occasions. But I don't wish to go on sharing this madman's intentions to kill myself; for this must be done with a long knife, and I believe I have only a tobacco pipe, not a knife. I was liking my dream at the beginning, but now I see it's starting to degenerate, and this doesn't suit Hedwig at all; for Hedwig is gentle, and when she suffers, she suffers in a more beautiful, silent way. She'd no doubt just laugh at my man there in his shaggy beard if he attempted such insolence. The landscape I sketched out was quite nice all the same, but only because it was mostly borrowed from the countryside that surrounds me. One should never lose the natural ground beneath one's feet while dreaming, especially about people, for otherwise one soon arrives at the point of making one's characters utter words like: 'Go, kill yourself.' And then one of them will have to wear a facial expression that is ridiculous and well-suited to spoil even the loveliest dream!—"

Simon went home. He'd made it his habit to amble homeward each day at a certain hour when evening was approaching, usually with his gaze lowered to the brown dark earth, to make the tea at home, in the preparation of which he'd developed a skill that always struck the right balance, for it was a matter of using not too little and not too much of this noble fragrant plant, keeping the crockery meticulously clean and placing it in an appetizing, graceful way upon the table, preventing the water from boiling away on its spirit burner, and then combining it with the tea in the prescribed manner. For Hedwig it provided some modicum of relief that all she had to do to have tea was pop out of the classroom for a moment before rushing back to work. In the morning when he got up, Simon would put his bed to rights, then go to the kitchen to make the cocoa, which, to Hedwig's pleasure, came out quite tasty; for with this task, too, he was always in hot pursuit of the best way to give an undertaking, modest as it might be, the required perfection. He also took it upon himself as a matter of course, without previous study or particular exertion, to light the fire in the heating stove and keep it burning, and to clean Hedwig's room, whereby his skill in manipulating the long broom very much came in handy. He would open the windows to allow fresh air to enter the room, but he closed them again promptly when he thought it was time, in order to achieve a room that was both warm and nice-smelling. Everywhere in the room, in little pots, flowers that had been snatched from their natural environment went on blooming, distributing their fragrance between these four narrow walls. The windows had simple but charming curtains, which added considerably to the brightness and friendliness of the room. On the floor lay warm rugs that Hedwig had had made from gathered-up scraps of cloth by unfortunates serving prison terms, who carried out tasks of this sort exceptionally well. A bed stood in one corner, in the other a piano, and between them was an old sofa with a flowered cloth slipcover, an adequately large table before it, chairs on either side; and then there was a washstand in the room, a small writing table with a blotting pad and a bookshelf filled with books; and a small inverted crate on the floor that, covered with a soft cloth, served for sitting and reading, as reading sometimes made one feel the need to be close to the floor and fancy oneself an Oriental; further, a little sewing table with a sewing basket containing all those fantastical items indispensable to a girl who sets any store in housekeeping; a round, odd stone bearing a postmark and stamp, a bird, a stack of letters and postcards; and on the wall a horn for blowing into, a cup to drink from, a walking stick with a large crook, a backpack with a canteen, and the tail-feather of a falcon. Also hanging on the walls were Kaspar's paintings—a crepuscular landscape with a forest; a rooftop seen from a window; a foggy gray city (to Hedwig particularly lovely); a bit of river in voluptuous evening hues; a field in summer; a Don Quixote; and a house nestled against a hill in such a way that one could borrow the words of a poet to declare: "O'er yonder stands a house." Upon the piano, whose top was covered with a silken scarf, stood a bust of Beethoven in a greenish shade of bronze, several photographs and a small, dainty empty jewelry box, a keepsake from their mother. A curtain that looked like a theater curtain separated the two rooms and the two sleepers. In the evening, the teacher's room appeared particularly cozy when the lamp was lit and the shutters closed; and in the morning, the sunlight would awaken a sleeper who was anything but eager to emerge from her bed but in the end had no choice.

The notaries left Simon in the lurch, not a single one contacted him. As a result, he found himself compelled to earn money in other ways, since he hoped to demonstrate to his sister his good intentions when it came to sharing household expenses. He took up a sheet of paper and wrote:

COUNTRY LIFE

I arrived here in a house in the country along with the snow, and although I am not the master of this house, nor harbor any ambition to become master, I can nonetheless feel myself to be at home here and am perhaps in this way happier than the owner of the stateliest dwelling. Not even the room I'm living in belongs to me; it belongs to a gentle, dear teacher who has taken me in and feeds me when I am hungry. It pleases me to be the sort of fellow who depends on the kind mercy of others, for in general I like depending on someone so I can love this person and keep a close watch to see whether I haven't forfeited his kindness. One might well associate a quite particular sort of conduct with this sweetest of all unfreedoms: conduct that lies halfway between insolence and tender, soft, natural attentiveness, and at this I excel. Above all one must never allow one's host to perceive one's gratitude; this would be displaying a faint-heartedness and cowardice that can only insult the giver. In your heart you worship the kind person who has summoned you under his roof, but it would bespeak a lack of sensitivity to press your thanks insistently upon him—he doesn't want such thanks, as his generosity wasn't and isn't motivated by the wish to receive something beggarly in return. Under certain circumstances, giving thanks is only a form of begging, nothing more. Then there's another thing: In the country, thanks are more silent and still than loquacious. The person obliged to feel gratitude acts in a certain way because he sees his counterpart doing so as well. Refined givers are almost even more diffident than takers, and they prefer for takers to take unselfconsciously, since this allows them, the givers, to give decorously, without fuss. The teacher, by the way, is my sister, but this circumstance wouldn't prevent her from driving me, as a ne'er-do-well, from her doorstep if the desire happened to seize her. She is courageous and sincere. She received me with a mix of loving-kindness and distrust, as was quite natural, for how could she help but assume that if this good-for-nothing brother of hers came sailing and sauntering up to see her, his comfortably-settled sister, it had to be because in all God's world he hadn't the slightest notion where else to go. Certainly there was something disturbing and hurtful about this, for if truth be told I hadn't written her a single letter for months, indeed years. She must have thought I was coming only out of concern for my own body, which at times might truly profit from a good whipping, rather than because I was worried about my sister and wished to see her. Things have changed meanwhile, these sensitivities have been put to rest, and now we live side by side not merely as blood relatives but as comrades who get along splendidly. Ah, in the countryside it's simple enough for two people to get along. It's customary here to thrust aside distrust and secrecy more quickly, and to love more cheerfully and brightly than in the thronging city with its hordes of people and constant woes. In the country, even the poorest man has fewer worries than a far less impoverished city-dweller—for in the city everything is measured by human words and human deeds—while worries here go on worrying as quietly as they may, and pain provides pain's own natural surcease. In the city, everyone races about pell-mell trying to get rich (for which reason so many think themselves bitterly poor), while in the country, at least to a large extent, the poor are spared the insult of constantly being compared with the rich. They can peacefully go on breathing despite their poverty, for they have a whole sky above them to breathe! What is the sky in the city? —I myself have only a single small silver coin left by way of money, and this must cover the laundry. My sister, who has no secrets from me except those that are utterly unspeakable, has even confessed to me that her money has run out. Not that we're starting to worry. We have the most luscious bread here, and fresh eggs and fragrant cakes, as much as we could wish for. The children bring us all of this, for their parents send it to school for Teacher. In the country, people know how to give in such a way that it does honor to the taker. In the city you practically have to be afraid to give because it's begun to defile the taker, I truly cannot say for what reason, perhaps because in the city takers display insolence toward the kind givers. So then people take care not to display noble sympathies toward those suffering privation and give only furtively, or as a form of personal aggrandizement. What atrocious weakness, fearing the poor, and for this reason consuming one's own riches alone rather than allowing oneself the glory attained, say, by a queen when she reaches out her hand to a lowly beggar-woman. I consider it a great misfortune to be poor in the city because a person isn't allowed to ask for things, it being quite clear that benevolence is not the order of the day. One thing at least holds true: Better not to give nor feel pity at all than to do so unwillingly, conscious of having succumbed to a weakness. In the country, giving doesn't make a person weak; people wish to give and sometimes give themselves entirely to the pastime of giving. If a person is wary of giving, he will surely himself—should he one day find himself trampled by destinies of various sorts and forced to ask for help—ask badly and accept what he is given gracelessly and with embarrassment, that is, in a beggarly fashion. How reprehensible it is when those blessed with commodities insist on ignoring the poor. Better to torment them, force them into indentured servitude, inflict compulsion and blows—this at least produces a connection, fury and a pounding heart, and these too constitute a form of relationship. But to cower in elegant homes behind golden garden gates, fearful lest the breath of warm humankind touch you, unable to indulge in extravagances for fear they might be glimpsed by the embittered oppressed, to oppress and yet lack the courage to show yourself as an oppressor, even to fear the ones you are oppressing, feeling ill at ease in your own wealth and begrudging others their ease, to resort to disagreeable weapons that require neither true audacity nor manly courage, to have money, but only money, without splendor: That's what things look like in our cities at present, and I find the picture disagreeable, it needs bettering. In the countryside, matters are still quite different. Here, a poor devil knows better where he stands;

172

he can gaze up at the wealthy and well-off with a salubrious envy, and this is permitted, as it only serves to increase the grandeur of the object of these glances. In the country, the wish to possess a house of one's own is a deeply rooted longing that reaches all the way up to God. For here, beneath the vast open sky, possessing a beautiful roomy house is heavenly. In the city, things are different. There an arriviste can dwell right beside a count of ancient lineage; indeed, money can raze houses and sacred old edifices at will. Who would wish to own a building in the city? There, owning a home is nothing more than a business, not a matter of pride and pleasure. City buildings are filled from top to bottom with the most different sorts of people, all of whom cross paths without knowing one another or expressing the desire to be allowed to make each other's acquaintance. Is this a dwelling in the true sense? And long, long streets are filled with just such buildings, which certainly don't deserve to be referred to as homes. In the countryside more happens, properly speaking, than in town; for while city-dwellers coldly, jadedly read of recent occurrences in the newspaper, news in the country passes feverishly, breathlessly from mouth to mouth. Something happens in the country perhaps once a year, but then it is an experience shared by all. A village with all its nooks and crannies is certainly almost always livelier and richer in intelligence than city folk generally assume. Many an old woman with facial features that would perhaps suit any fellow's grandmother sits here behind white window-curtains with her store of enchantingly heartfelt tales, and many a village child is far more advanced in the education of her heart and mind than one might like to suppose. Often it's happened that a village child like this, having been transferred to a school in town, has astounded her new classmates with her well-developed intellect. But let me not disdain the city and praise the country beyond its due. It's just that the days here are so beautiful that one quickly learns to forget the city. They awaken a silent longing that draws one off into the distance—and yet one has no wish to go any farther. There is a going in all things and a coming in all. As the day takes its leave, it gives us in exchange the wonderful twilight when you can go strolling about on paths the evening appears to have discovered—paths you discover for the evening. The houses become more prominent, and their windows gleam. Even when it's raining, it's still beautiful; for then one thinks how good it is it's raining. Since my coming here, spring has almost arrived, and it's arriving more and more, you can leave your doors and windows standing open, and we're starting to turn over the earth in the garden, everyone else has already done so. We're the late bloomers, as befits us. An entire cartload of black, moist, expensive soil has been delivered, and this must be mixed with the dirt already in the garden. This will be a job which— implausible as it may sound when I say so—I'm looking forward to. I'm not a born lazybones, really not; I'm a ne'er-do-well only because various offices and notaries public are refusing me employment since they don't have any idea how useful I could be to them. Every Saturday I shake out the rugs, which is work of a sort, and I'm industriously learning to cook, also a form of ambition. After the meal I dry the plates and chat with the teacher; for there is much to be said and discussed, and I love chatting with a sister. In the morning I sweep the room and carry packages to the post office, then return home and set to pondering what else there is to do. Ordinarily there's nothing, and so then I go down into the forest and sit beneath the beech trees until the time has come, or I believe the time has come, for me to re- turn home. When I see people at work, I involuntarily feel ashamed that I have no occupation, but it seems to me that beyond feeling this shame there's nothing I can do. To me it's as if the day has been tossed into my lap by a benevolent god who likes to give things to good-for-nothings. I demand of myself nothing more than the willingness to work, and the resolve to seize hold of any job I should espy before me—and that way things go well. This outlook, you see, accords quite splendidly with country living. You mustn't overdo it all too much here, otherwise you lose your view of the lovely whole, along with your perspective as an observer—for even a looker-on must, in the end, exist in the world. The only pain I feel is occasioned by my sister, as I am incapable of repaying the debt I owe her and must watch her laboriously fulfilling her sour duties while I lie about daydreaming. Later ages will punish me for my malingering if intervening earlier ones haven't done so already, but I believe I am pleasing to my God just as I am; God loves the happy and hates the sad. My sister is never sad for long; for I am constantly cheering her up and giving her something to laugh about by behaving ludicrously, for which I have a talent. But it is only my sister laughing at me, only she who finds me appealingly comical—with others, I comport myself in a dignified manner, though not stiffly. If one doesn't wish to be taken for a scoundrel, it's one's duty to justify one's existence to the outside world through serious behavior. Country people are quite sensitive about the comportment of young people, whom they wish to see courteous, staid, and modest. I shall conclude here and hope I've earned some money with this essay; if not, I nonetheless found it most interesting to write, and my doing so has caused several hours to pass. Several hours? Indeed! For in the country a person writes slowly—you're constantly being interrupted, your fingers have become less nimble, and even your thoughts wish to think in a country manner. Farewell, cosmopolitans!

−9−

Simon brought his letter to the post office. The following Sunday, Klaus came to visit, the older brother. It was drizzling, and the sight of the cold raindrops slapping the already wide-awake blossoms was enough to give you the shivers. Klaus looked not a little astonished to discover Simon living with his sister—he'd assumed he was abroad somewhere—but he remained as amicable as he was able, not wishing to spoil their Sunday. All three of them remained rather quiet, often standing there before one another without speaking; they appeared to be hunting for words. Klaus brought a certain contemplative alienation to Hedwig's home. Upon closer examination, all sorts of things here proved, in fact, to be out of place. The main object, of course, being Simon's presence. Klaus was determined not to utter any reproaches today, though in truth he felt sorely tempted; but he avoided all divisive remarks. He gazed at his brother questioningly and significantly, as though to say: "I am astonished at your behavior. How can you be considered an adult? Is it honorable to take advantage of your sister's position to live in idleness? It's truly dishonorable! I'd be saying this to you quite openly, but I wish to spare Hedwig, who would be hurt by such remarks. Far be it from me to spoil our Sunday!" Simon understood nonetheless. He knew quite well what was meant by this expression, this stiff unnatural warmth as they greeted one another, this silence and discomfiture. He was just glad Klaus held his tongue; for otherwise he'd have to respond with something he was already finding abhorrent as a justification. Certainly, certainly! His position was deplorable for a young man like him, there was no excuse for his behavior. But it was so lovely to be here—lovely, lovely! Gripped suddenly by emotion, he said to Klaus: "I know perfectly well what you think of me, but I swear to you this will end soon. I think you know me a little. Do you believe me?" Klaus pressed his hand, and their Sunday was saved. Soon it was time for lunch, and Hedwig no doubt noted with a secret smile the changed situation between the brothers. "He's a good man, Klaus. Klaus is good," she thought, and with even greater pleasure served the delicious meal. There was a splendid soup, in whose exquisite preparation Hedwig was highly skilled, followed by pork with sauerkraut and finally a roast rich with fat. Simon chatted unrestrainedly about heaven and earth, drawing his brother into all sorts of conversations and then returning again and again to praise the splendid meal with such comical enthusiasm that each time Hedwig burst out laughing until she was filled with good cheer and forgot everything that might have been considered worrisome. In the afternoon, the dismal weather notwithstanding, they took a short walk. The field through which they trudged was so wet they soon turned back again. All of them that evening were quiet once more. Simon tried to read a newspaper, Klaus spoke as if intentionally about the most trivial matters, with Hedwig replying distractedly. Before he took his leave, Klaus said a few words to the girl, whom he'd summoned to the kitchen, words on which the one standing in the other room preferred not to eavesdrop. What could it be. Let it be whatever it was. Then Klaus departed. When they both—having accompanied their guest on the first leg of his return journey—were back at home again, just the two of them, their hearts involuntarily felt gayer, like schoolchildren after the stern inspector has left. They breathed more freely, feeling they could be themselves again. Hedwig now began to speak, and the apprehensiveness inspired by what she was about to say made her voice sound more intimate and raised its pitch: "Klaus is just the same as ever. There's always a tiny bit of fear to contend with in his presence. Being with him involuntarily turns a person into a guilty schoolgirl awaiting her scolding for having been imprudent. In his eyes, you've always been imprudent, even when you think you've been acting in a serious way. His eyes see things so differently—they look at the world in such a strangely alarming manner, as if there's always something to fear. He's constantly worrying both himself and others. That tone issuing from his mouth is assembled out of a thousand well-intentioned misgivings—he has so little trust in the world and the threads that bind us to it of their own accord. He looks as if he wants to lecture you like a schoolmaster and at the same time sees perfectly clearly that he is lecturing unawares—he doesn't wish to lecture, but that's just what he does, despite his best intentions, because of his innermost nature, for which we can't hold him responsible. He is so unquestionably kind and affectionate, but he cannot stop questioning whether it's appropriate to be gentle and kind.

Severity ill becomes him, and yet he believes he can accomplish with severity what he's failed to achieve by means of kindness. He thinks of kindness as incautious, and yet he's so very kind! He forbids himself to be artless and kind, which is what he'd most dearly love to be, because he's so afraid of spoiling something in this way, and then appearing imprudent in the eyes of the world. He sees only eyes observing him, never eyes wishing to gaze peacefully into his. You can't gaze peacefully into his eyes, since it's quite palpable how nervous this makes him. He always thinks people are thinking something about him and he needs to get to the bottom of those thoughts. If he can't find anything wrong with you to carp about, he seems ill at ease. And yet he *is* kind! Happy he is not. If he were, he'd start speaking differently in a instant, I know he would. And it isn't that he begrudges others their happiness, but he's constantly inclined to criticize the happiness and carefree spirits of those around him, which I'm sure must cause him pain. He doesn't like to hear talk of happiness, and I can understand why. It's quite obvious, any child can understand it: Yourself joyless, you hate the joy of others. How often this must pain him, for he's noble enough to feel what injustices he's committing. He is absolutely noble, but—how shall I say this—also a bit corrupted on the inside, just a tiny bit, because of having been neglected and then always struggling to shrug off this neglect. Yes, fate has most certainly given him the cold shoulder—he's far too worthy for its frostiness and whims. That's how I'd like to put it; for I feel pain on his account! You, for instance, Simon. My God. For you one feels quite different things, my eternally jolly brother! Do you know, thinking of you, one always says to oneself: He ought to get a beating, a really sound beating, that's what he deserves! You make a person feel astonished with wonder—why haven't you yet plunged into an abyss? It would never occur to anyone to feel pity for you. Generally people consider you a carefree, impudent, happy fellow. Is it true?"

Simon burst into laughter and this set the tone for the next hour. Then there was a knock at the door. The two of them got up, and Simon went to see who was there. It was the teacher from the next school. Her husband, a rough and ruthless individual, had beaten her yet again. They did what they could to comfort her, and in this they succeeded.

The weather was growing ever warmer and the earth more resplendent, it was covered with a thick, blossoming carpet of meadows, the fields and pastures were steaming, the forests offered an enchanting sight with their beautiful, fresh, rich green. All of nature was presenting itself, expansive, stretching, curving, rearing up, whizzing and rustling and buzzing, fragrant and motionless as a bright beautiful dream. The land had become perfectly fat, lush, opaque and glutted. It was lolling, as it were, in voluptuous surfeit. It was green and dark brown and flecked with black, white, yellow and red, blossoming with hot breath, almost perishing beneath its profusion of blossoms. It lay there like a luxuriating, veiled woman, immobile, shifting her limbs, perfumed with scents. The gardens spread their fragrance into the streets and out over the fields, where men and women were working; the fruit trees were a bright, twittering singing, and the nearby, round, vaulted forest was a choral song of young men; the bright paths scarcely penetrated the green. In forest clearings, one would see a white, dreamy, indolent sky that one could imagine sinking down and rejoicing as birds rejoice, tiny birds that one has never before seen but that are so natural a part of nature. Memories arrived that a person didn't wish to analyze and dissect, you weren't capable of this, it caused such sweet pain, and you were too indolent to feel a pain through to the end. Thus you walked and thus stopped in your tracks, turning in all directions, gazing off into the distance, gazing up, away, down, across and to the ground, feeling deeply affected by all the languor of this blossoming. The buzzing in the forest was not the buzzing in the barer clearing, it was different and required in turn a staking out of new positions for new daydreams. Always you were having to tussle, resist, gently thrust aside, reflect and waver. It was all one great wavering, a struggle, a finding yourself weak. But this was sweet, quite simply sweet: a bit difficult, and then a bit parsimonious, then hypocritical, then crafty, then nothing at all, then perfectly stupid; and finally it became rather difficult to find anything else beautiful any longer, this just didn't seem called for, and so you sat, strolled, loitered, drifted, trotted and tarried in such a way that you yourself became a bit of spring. Could all this buzzing feel delight at its own buzzing and cooing and singing? Was it given to the grass to observe its own beautiful variability? Might it have been possible for the beech to fall in love with its own appearance? Without growing weary or blunted, you let things be as they were, let them go, let them waver this way and that. All of nature, the way it was looking, was just a loiterer, a lingering and dangling! Scents hung in the air, and all the earth lingered and waited. Colors were the blissful expression of this. You could discern something prematurely weary and portentous in the bush with its blossoms. It was a sort of no-longer-wishing-to-go-on, but all one great smile. The blue, hazy wooded mountains sounded like far-off, distant horns, you felt the landscape to be a bit English, it was like a luxuriant English garden, the luxuriant growth and the interweaving and wafting of voices drew your senses to this affinity. You thought: In such and such a place things might look just now as they do right here, the region conjured up all other regions in your heart. It was comical and far-reaching, a carrying-off and bringing-hither: A bringing, as things are brought by young lads, an offering up, such as children might offer, an obeying and harkening. You could say and think whatever you pleased, yet it was always just the same unspoken, unthought thing—light and heavy, blissful and painful, poetic and natural. You understood the poets, or rather you didn't actually understand them, for, walking along like this, you would have been far too indolent to imagine understanding them. You had no need to understand anything at all, there was no understanding, and yet understanding arrived of its own accord, dissolving in the effort of listening for a sound or gazing into the distance or remembering that in point of fact it was now time to return home and discharge some admittedly rather minor duty, for even in springtime there are duties to discharge.

The nights were becoming splendid. The moon fell in love with the white of the blossoming bushes and trees and the long windings of the roads, and made them gleam. Moonlight shone in the fountains and the flowing river water. The churchyard with its silent graves was transformed into a white fairy place, making you forget the dead who lay buried there. The moon inserted itself among the tangle of thin, hanging, hair-like branches, providing light enough to make out the inscriptions on the headstones. Simon walked around the edge of the churchyard several times, then struck out on a further path that led him through the flat raised field, thrust himself between low, illuminated bushes, came upon a small, sloping meadow between them, and sat down there upon a stone to ponder the question of how much longer he was likely to continue this life of mere observation and contemplation. Soon it must surely come to an end, for things could not go on in this way. He was a man, and to him pertained the rigorous discharge of duty. Soon he would have to take action once more, this was becoming clear to him. When he got home, he said as much to his sister in fitting words. He shouldn't be thinking about such things, at least not yet, she said. All right, he replied, I won't think about it yet. What's more, the thought of remaining here further was so enticing. What was it he wanted, what was driving him? He could hardly have travel money to make a trip somewhere, and as for the place he might to be going, what awaited him there? No, he would gladly remain where he was for an indeterminate brief time. Probably he'd drive himself mad with longing for the place once he left it, and what good would that do him? No, he'd have to make short work of it, this longing; for it would ill befit him. But didn't people often engage in unbefitting pastimes? What's more, he would be staying on, and had no intention of surrendering any further to these trains of thought, which he found vexing.

Thus a few more days arrived and vanished. Time arrived so soundlessly and then withdrew without one's noticing. In this way it actually moved fairly quickly, although before leaving it hesitated for a long while. The two of them, Simon and Hedwig, now became even more powerfully attached to one another. They spent their evenings chatting by lamplight and never wearied of speaking. They talked of food over their meals, whose simplicity and delicacy they praised with carefully chosen words, and as they worked they spoke of work; every activity they accompanied with words, and then they discussed the joys and pleasures of walking while out on their walks. They had long since forgotten they were only brother and sister, they felt conjoined more by fate than shared blood, interacting with one another more or less like two locked-up prisoners who are making an effort to forget their lives with the help of their friendship. They idled away a great deal of time, but they wished to see it wasted in this fashion, for each of them felt what gravity lay concealed behind these exchanges, and both believed themselves perfectly capable of speaking and acting in full earnestness if they only wished. Hedwig sensed she was revealing herself to her brother more and more and was fully conscious of the feeling of consolation this gave her. She found it flattering that he was living with her not only because it was of practical advantage and in accordance with her condition, but also because he found it interesting, and she thanked him for this by becoming even more truly fond of him than before. To both it appeared that each found the other valuable enough to feel pride at spending a bit of their lives together. They spoke and thought a great deal about memories, promising to serve up everything they could recall from that early, bygone age when both were children. Do you remember? This was the way so many of their conversations began. And so they immersed themselves in the precious images of the past and were always at pains to let these remembrances, regardless of their object, instruct their hearts and minds, careful always to whet their laughter on them, or—when the memories were sorrowful—maintain still their high spirits, as was only fitting. The past, in turn, made the present appear sharper and more tender, and then this very present moment they were perceiving took on a more vivid and richer aspect, as if doubled or trebled in a mirror, and it more visibly, more clearly pointed the way to the future they often imagined together, an activity that filled them with a mild intoxication. What future could be lovelier than the one glimpsed in a daydream; and the thoughts they thought were always light and gay.

10

One evening Hedwig said: "I almost have the impression there's something like a thin but opaque wall cutting me off from life. I can't even manage to feel sad about it, just pensive. Perhaps other girls feel something similar, I don't know. Perhaps I missed out on my life's true profession when I set out to find a career for life. Studying to learn a profession is something we girls do half-heartedly anyhow, for us it isn't the main thing. How strange it now seems to me that I became a teacher. Why not a dressmaker, or something completely different? I can no longer even imagine the feelings that drove me to take up such a profession. What sense of wonder and promise held me in its thrall? Did I think I would become a benefactress, did I feel I had no choice but to see this as my duty, my calling? You believe all kinds of things when you lack experience, and later you experience things that make you see the world quite differently. How very strange. Taking life as seriously as I did involves a certain severity in the way one treats oneself. I must tell you, Simon: I took life too seriously, too sacredly; I didn't stop to consider that I was a girl when I under-took a task fit only for men. No one told me I was a girl. No one flattered me with such an observation. No one thought of me so thoughtfully as would have been necessary to observe so simple a thing, which I'd have heeded even if my first response was indignation. If these words had come from a heart, I'd have heeded them. But all the words I heard were superficial, offhanded: 'Do this, do that. It's good you want to take up a profession. It does you honor.' And so on. What an honor it is to be a miserable girl filled with emptiness and longings, as practicing this honorable profession has made me. A profession is a burden to be borne through life by a man with strong shoulders and a powerful will: A girl like me is crushed by it. Does my profession bring me joy? None at all. Please don't be too shocked by this confession; I'm only making it because you're the sort of person one almost longs to confess to. You understand me, I know you do. Others would perhaps understand me just as well, but only out of a sense of obligation. You understand willingly, as you have no reason to feel shocked by simple, honest confessions. On the inside, you're living my entire life along with me, your sister. In fact you're far too good to be only my brother. What a pity you can't be more to me: This too you'd do willingly; for I see you nodding your head. Let me continue. When a person has you as a listener, it's a pleasure to speak. And so hear this: I've decided to give up my school career, and soon; for I lack the strength to withstand this life much longer. I thought it would be so lovely: introducing children to the world, teaching them, opening their souls to virtue, watching over them and guiding them. And indeed the task is lovely, but it's also far too strenuous for a weak woman like me; I'm no match for it, not by far. I thought I was, but now I realize the opposite is true: I find myself buckling beneath my responsibilities. I thought it would be a daily source of refreshment to me, but I only experience it as an excessive and unjust burden. Something that oppresses you can't help but seem unjust. Do you think it's unfair of me to feel this way? Don't my feelings themselves set the standard for measuring injustices against my person? And can I help it if this injustice is, in its way, guileless and sweet: the children? The children! I can no longer endure them. At the beginning I rejoiced at all their faces, their little gestures, their eagerness, even their mistakes. I rejoiced at the thought of devoting myself to this young, shy, helpless little band of humans. But can a single thought belie the life one is experiencing, can one think away a life with an idea? Beware the day when your idea and your sacrifice no longer mean much to you—when you can no longer manage to think the thought that's supposed to compensate for all the rest with the heartfelt passion needed to justify this exchange within your soul. Woe betide you if you even notice an exchange was made. For then you'll begin to brood, making distinctions, weighing one thing against another, gloomily and balefully comparing; you'll feel unhappy at having become so fickle and unfaithful, and you'll rejoice when each day finally draws to a close so you can hide yourself away somewhere and weep. Having just once tasted unfaithfulness, you're ready to abandon your life's guiding principle, which demands utter devotion, and yet you declare: I'll do my duty and think of nothing else! The children are still dear to me, they've always been dear to me. Who can help being fond of children? But when I'm teaching, I think of other things, things more distant and greater than their little souls, and this constitutes a betrayal I can no longer endure. A schoolteacher must lose herself in little things with all her heart, otherwise she cannot exercise power, and without power she is worthless. Perhaps I'm expressing myself in an exaggerated way, and I'm also quite aware that all or most people to whom I might say these things would find them exaggerated. But my way of speaking accords with my view of life; surely it's out of the question I might speak some other way. I haven't yet learned to feign contentment, satisfaction or a sense of well-being I don't feel, and anyone who thinks I might learn this is mistaken. I'm too weak to pretend and deceive, and ponder this as I may, I cannot see any grounds that would justify this dissimulation. If I speak to you now in this way, it's because I'm taking advantage of a moment—whose arrival I've long been awaiting—to unburden myself of my weaknesses once and for all. It's such a relief to be permitted to confess one's weaknesses after months of nerve-racking restraint, which have demanded more strength than I possess. Since I cannot possibly go on indefinitely performing duties that bring out the worst in me, I'm now looking for work that will appeal both to my pride and to my weakness. Shall I succeed in finding it? I truly cannot say, but one thing I do know for certain is that I must search until I've succeeded in convincing myself that happiness and duty can coincide. I wish to become a private tutor and have already written to a wealthy Italian lady offering my services in a perhaps somewhat overly long letter in which I inform her that I am in a position to instruct two children, a girl and a boy, in all the subjects she might desire. I don't now remember everything I wrote, just that I am eager to exchange the schoolroom for a nursery, that I love and respect children, that I can play the piano and embroider pretty things and that I'm the sort of girl who flourishes under a firm hand. I expressed myself with rather proud words, saying I was adept at loving-kindness and obedience but incapable of flattery, that I could flatter only if I myself were to demand it of me; that I would rather imagine my future employer as proud and strict than lenient, that it would cause me pain and disappointment if I were to discover that one might, if one had such intentions, easily, insolently deceive her; that I wasn't planning to enter her employment for the purpose of resting, but rather that I hoped to be given work for both my heart and hands. I confessed to her that I was already, anticipatorily, feeling heartfelt love for her two children, that I in no way lack the respect for children a person needs to be able to educate them both strictly and with devotion, that I expected to be given free rein to serve her, my lady, that I possessed a simultaneously strict and easy-going notion of service, and that it would be impossible to convince me to deviate from it. I wrote that it would be pointless to expect from me slick or lickspittle slavishness, and that I lacked all talent for performing courtesies in a crude, indecorous way, but that I would gladly forgo gentle treatment and instead be governed coldly and strictly as long as it was not in an insulting manner, that I knew my own station and would at all times distinguish it from hers, that I would not insist on justice but only on a pride that would forbid her from treating me unjustly, that it would fill my heart with joy if she would occasionally, even just once a year, be so kind as to give me some sign of her satisfaction, which I would treasure far more than familiar treatment, which I'd find humiliating rather than a kindness, that

I was hoping to find a lady I could look up to in order to learn how a person should behave in all circumstances, and that she had no cause to fear that by engaging me she would be taking a gossip into her service who would enjoy blurting out her secrets. I told her I was incapable of saying how dearly I wished to admire and obey her and to show her how very adept I would be at never being a burden to her. I then gave voice to the fear and at the same time the hope that, while I don't yet speak the language of her country, I should soon master it if they would only show me how to go about this. Otherwise I couldn't think of anything that would not give me the right to join her household, I said by way of conclusion, except perhaps the shyness that still adhered to my person, but which I hoped to overcome, as clumsiness and awkwardness were otherwise not in my nature—"

"Have you sent off the letter already?" Simon asked.

"Yes," Hedwig went on, "what could have stopped me? Perhaps I shall soon be going away from here, and this departure worries me; for I am leaving behind a great deal and shall perhaps not receive anything in exchange that would allow me to forget what I've discarded and abandoned. Nevertheless I have firmly made up my mind to leave; I don't wish to be alone with my dreams any longer. You too will be leaving soon, and then what would I be doing here? You'll leave me behind like some leftover scrap, like an object that's gone bad, or rather it'll be like this: The entire place, this village, everything here will be the scrap, the abandoned, discarded, disregarded object—and I'll still be sitting right in the middle? No, I've become far too accustomed to seeing the life we lead here with the help of your eyes, finding it beautiful as long as you did; and you did find it beautiful, and so I found it beautiful as well. But I wouldn't go on finding it beautiful and large enough for me, I'd despise it for being limited and dull, and it would in fact become limited and dull because of my indifference and contempt. I cannot live and at the same time despise my life. I must find myself a life, a new life, even if all of life consists only of an endless search for life. What is respect compared to this other thing: being happy and having satisfied the heart's pride. Even being unhappy is better than being respected. I am unhappy, despite the respect I enjoy; and so in my own eyes I don't deserve this respect; for I consider only happiness worthy of respect. Therefore I must try whether it is possible to be happy without insisting on respect. Perhaps there is a happiness of this sort for me, and a respect accorded to love and longing rather than cleverness. I don't want to be unhappy just because I lacked the courage to admit to myself that a person can be unhappy on account of trying to be happy. Unhappiness of this sort is worthy of respect; the other isn't; it isn't possible to respect a lack of courage. How can I sit by any longer as I condemn myself to a life that brings only respect, and brings respect only from people who always want you to be just the way it suits them best? Why should it suit them at all? And why must a person go through the experience of learning that what you derive from all of this is worth nothing at all? So now you've worried and waited and provided, and in the end you've been made a fool of. It's bitterly foolish to insist on waiting for things; nothing ever comes to us if we don't go and get it ourselves. To be sure, we're given a scare by cowards who make such a show of being worried on our account. I almost hate them now, the ones who start shaking their heads the minute you say anything even the least bit bold. I'd like to see how they behave when they hear that the act requiring courage has been successfully carried out. How these advice-givers will scatter before the mighty heart of a freely performed deed! And how they enslave you with their saccharine love if you fail to find this courage and instead submit to them. People here will be so sorry to see me move away and will be unable to understand how I can be leaving behind such a pleasant and beneficial place; and I too shall be leaving the country with a sentiment that still wishes to persuade me to remain. I dreamt of becoming a farmwife, of belonging to a man, a simple and tender human being, of owning a home with a bit of land and bit of garden, with a bit of sky to go along with them, of planting and tilling and demanding no other love than respect and experiencing the delight of watching my children grow up, which I'd have found perfectly adequate compensation for the loss of a deeper love. The sky would have touched the earth, each day would have rolled the one before it down into time and times, and with all my cares I'd soon have become an old woman standing on sunny Sundays at the door of my house, already almost uncomprehendingly watching the people walk past. Then I'd never again have striven for happiness and would have forgotten all more ardent sentiments, I'd have obeyed my husband and his commands, along with what I'd have envisioned as my duty. And I'd have known what duties were expected of a farmer's wife. My dreams would have gone to sleep with the days like evenings, they would never again have made demands. I'd have been contented and gay—content because I didn't know any better and gay because it wouldn't have been right to show my husband an ill-tempered, worry-darkened brow. My husband would perhaps have been tactful enough to go easy on me at first, when many things would still be surging and thrashing ardently within me, and to educate me gently for the tasks that lay ahead, which I would have gratefully accepted; and then things would have been all right, and one day I'd have observed with astonishment that I no longer enjoyed the company of women whose dispositions were characterized by impetuousness and longing, that is, those whose nature was as mine once had been, for I considered them dangerous and harmful. In a word: I would have become just like all the others and would have understood life just as all the rest understood it. But all these things remained a mere dream. I would be wary of saying something like this to anyone but you. Dreamers aren't ridiculous in your eyes, nor do you despise anyone for dreaming, since you despise no one at all. And it's not as if I were usually so high-strung. How could I be? It's just that I've gone on a bit too long just now, and when I speak in such a way, it's easy for me to say too much. A person can't help wishing to elucidate all her feelings, and yet this isn't possible, all you do is talk yourself into a frenzy. Come, let's go to bed—"

In a gentle, calm voice she said good night.

"I'm glad to be here all the same," she said the next morning. "How can one go wishing oneself away from a position so tempestuously. As if this were so important! I could almost laugh to think of it, and I'm a bit ashamed to have been so forthcoming yesterday. And yet I'm glad; for you do have to speak your mind sometimes. How patiently you were able to listen to me, Simon! Almost reverentially! And yet this too makes me glad. In the evening one isn't the same as in the morning, no, one is so utterly different, so dissimilar in the way one expresses oneself and in one's feelings. Merely having slept soundly for a single night, I've heard, can utterly change a person. I can certainly believe it. Having spoken in such a way yesterday appears to me now, on this bright morning, like an anxious, exaggerated, sad dream. What can have been the matter? Should one take things so irritably, so hard? Think no more about it! I must have been tired yesterday—I'm always tired in the evenings—but now I feel so light, so healthy, so fresh, as if new-born. I have such a feeling of suppleness, as if someone were lifting me up and bearing me along the way a person is carried on a litter. Open the window while I'm still lying here in bed. It's so lovely to lie in bed while the windows are being opened. Where can I have found all the joyousness that envelops me as I lie here. Out of doors, the beautiful landscape appears to me to be dancing, the air is slipping indoors to me. Is it Sunday today? If not, it's a day that seems made to be a Sunday. Do you see the geraniums? They stand so prettily before the window. What did I want yesterday? Happiness? Don't I already have happiness? Should one have to go off searching for it at unknown distances among people who surely have no time to be thinking about such things? It's good when you don't have time for too many things, quite good in fact, for if we had time enough, we'd surely die of presumptuousness. What a brightness there is in my head. Now there's not a single thought in my head that isn't lying there like its mistress—me—feeling glad and light, exactly like me. Would you bring me breakfast in bed, Simon? I'd enjoy having you serve me as if I were a Portuguese noblewoman and you a young Moor who comprehends my every gesture. Of course you'll bring me what I ask. Why shouldn't you be attentive? How long have you been here with me? Wait, it was winter when you arrived, snow was falling, I can still remember it quite clearly—how many fair and rainy days have since gone by. Now you'll be leaving soon; but you mustn't rob me of the pleasure of having you here with me a few days more. And three days from now I'll say to you: "Stay another three," and you won't be any better able to resist me then than you are now, bringing the breakfast to my bedside. You're a curiously unresisting and unscrupulous person. Ask anything of you, and you'll do it. You want everything anyone wants. I think a person might ask all sorts of improper things of you before you'd start to think ill of him. One can't avoid feeling a certain touch of contempt with regard to you. I do despise you a tiny bit, Simon! But I know it doesn't matter to you if one speaks to you like this. I consider you, by the way, quite capable of performing a heroic deed at a pinch: You see, I do think quite well of you. With you, people allow themselves all sorts of things. Your behavior liberates our behavior from every sort of restraint. Years ago, I used to box your ears, I was always tattling on you to Mother and having you punished when you'd committed some misdeed, and now I'm asking you: Come give me a kiss, or rather: Let me give you one, a nice cautious kiss on the forehead. There! Compared with last night I'm like a saint this morning. I feel a presentiment of the times that are coming—let them come! But don't laugh at me. Though if you laughed I'd also be pleased; for laughter is the most fitting sound for an early blue morning. And now please leave the room so I'll be at liberty to get dressed—"

Simon left her alone.

"I was always in the habit," Hedwig said to Simon in the course of the day, "of treating you somehow as my subordinate. In their dealings with you, perhaps others do, too—you hardly give an impression of intelligence—what people are more likely to see in you is love, and you know pretty well how that's received. I don't think you'll ever have much success in society the way you are and the way you act, but I'm also confident you'll never trouble your head about this—that wouldn't be like you, in my experience. Only those who know you will think you capable of heartfelt sentiment and incisive thought—others not. And that's the rub, the main point, the underlying cause why you'll probably be unsuccessful in life: A person must get to know you to find you credible, and this takes time. Success depends on first impressions, which will always fail you, but at least this won't make you lose your composure. Not many will love you, but the ones who do will promise themselves everything from you, and with their liking for you they'll be simple, good human beings—your foolishness can take you far. There's something idiotic about you, something unstable, something . . . how should I put it, lackadaisically foolish—and that's what will offend many people: They'll call you impertinent—and having made many harsh, hastily judgmental enemies, you'll find they might very well succeed in making you hot under the collar. But this will never frighten you. Some people will always seem unkind to you, and to them you'll look insolent; there will be frictions, you must be prepared for this! And in larger groups of people where it's important to show oneself to advantage and to stand out by virtue of one's eloquence, you'll always keep silent because it won't appeal to you to open your mouth when everyone's already jabbering away. As a result, you'll be overlooked: And then you'll start to feel defiant and behave inappropriately. Yet some, on the other hand, those who've gotten to know you, will consider it a gift to engage in heartfelt conversation with you; you're skilled at listening, and in conversation this is perhaps more important than speaking. People will happily entrust their secrets and private affairs to a close-mouthed person like you, and in general you're a master when it comes to discretion in silence and speech—unconsciously, I mean, it's not as if you need to go to particular trouble on this account. You speak a bit awkwardly, and your mouth, a little ungainly, first pops open and then remains that way until you start to speak, as if you were expecting the words to come flying up from somewhere or other and land there. In the eyes of most, you'll cut an uninteresting figure: Girls will find you dreary, women irrelevant, and men utterly untrustworthy and ineffectual. See if you can't change a little in that department, if you're able. Pay a bit more attention to yourself and be more vain; for being completely free of vanity is something even you will soon have to realize is an error. For example, Simon, look at your trousers: all ragged at the bottom! To be sure, and I know this perfectly well myself: They're just trousers, but trousers should be kept in just as good a condition as one's soul, for when a person wears torn, ragged trousers it displays carelessness, and carelessness is an attribute of the soul. Your soul must be ragged too. The other thing I wanted to say to you—You don't think I'm saying all these things to you in jest, do you? Now he's laughing. Don't you consider me just a little bit more experienced than you are? Not at all! You're more experienced? But if I say that many more experiences still lie before you, isn't that demonstrating experience? Surely it is—"

For a moment she reflected, then went on:

"When you've left me behind, as must happen soon, don't write to me. I don't want you to. I don't want you to feel obliged to inform me about your further adventures. Neglect me, just as you used to neglect me. What good can writing do us? I shall go on living here and find it a pleasure to think often about the three months you spent with me. The countryside will buoy me up and show me your image. I shall go to visit all the places we admired together, and I shall find them even more beautiful; for a defect, a loss, makes things more beautiful. I and the entire region shall be missing something, but this absence, and yes even this defect, will introduce even more tender sentiments to my life. I'm not inclined to feel pressured just because something's lacking. Why would I! On the contrary, there's something liberating, relief-bringing about this. And after all—Gaps exist to be filled with something new. When I'm about to get up in the morning, I shall imagine I hear your footsteps, see your face and hear your voice—and then I'll laugh at this illusion. Do you know: I'm fond of illusions, and you are too, I can tell. It's peculiar how much I've been chattering these days. These days! I think by now the days themselves ought to feel how precious they are to me, ought to do me the kindness of coming and departing more slowly, in a more protracted, leisurely, loitering way, and more quietly too! And in fact that's what they're doing. When they approach, it feels like a kiss, and when they darkly withdraw it's like someone pressing my hand or waving to me, sweetly, familiarly. The nights! How many nights you slept here beside me, slept beautifully, for you're an accomplished sleeper and slept so well in that little room there, on the straw bed that soon will be ownerless and sleepless. The nights that will be arriving now will creep up to me shyly the way little children with guilty consciences approach their father or mother, with their eyes cast down. The nights will be less silent, Simon, when you're gone, and I'll tell you why: You were so quiet at night, your sleep increased the silence. We were two silent, peaceful human beings during all these nights; now I'll have to be silent alone, of necessity, and it will be less silent; for I'll often sit upright in bed in the dark, listening for something. Then I shall feel how much less silent it now is. Perhaps I'll weep then—but not at all because of you, so don't give yourself airs on my account. Just look, he's already puffing himself up! No, Simon, no—no one is going to weep for you. When you're gone, you're gone. That's all. Do you think a person would weep for you? It's out of the question. You must never imagine that. One can feel that you're gone, one takes note of it, but then? Might one feel longing or something of the sort? No one feels longing for a person like you. You simply don't inspire it. No heart will go trembling off in search of you. Might one devote a thought to you? What a notion! Well, yes, carelessly, the way one drops a needle, one might occasionally call you to mind. That's all you'll merit, even if you live to be a hundred. You haven't the slightest talent for leaving behind memories. You don't leave behind anything at all. I can't imagine what you might leave behind in any case, as you have no possessions. There's no call for you to laugh in such an impudent way, I'm speaking seriously. Out of my sight this minute! March!"

For the next few days the weather was foul and rainy, and this too was a reason to stay on. How could Simon begin his journey in such weather? Certainly he might have been able to, but was there any point leaving when the weather was poor? And so he stayed. Another day or two, he thought, that's all. He spent practically the entire time sitting in the large empty classroom, reading a novel he wished to finish before he left. Sometimes he walked up and down between the rows of school benches, always holding this book: Its contents so gripped him he couldn't tear his mind away. But he didn't make much progress in his reading; he kept getting mired in thoughts. I'll keep reading as long as it keeps raining, he thought; when the weather turns fair, I'll go on—not with my reading, though: in the real sense.

On the last day, Hedwig said to him:

"No doubt you'll be leaving now, it's what we agreed. Farewell. Come here to me, come close, and take my hand. Quite possibly I shall soon throw myself at a man who doesn't deserve me. I'll have wasted my life. I'll enjoy a great deal of respect. People will say: What a capable woman she is. In all truth, I have no desire ever to hear from you again. Try to be a good man. Get involved in public matters, give people cause to talk about you, it would give me pleasure to hear of you from others. Or just go on living as best you're able, remain in the dark, struggle on in the darkness with the many days left to come. I shall never suspect you of frailty. What else should I say to wish you luck on your journey? Go on, thank me. Yes, you! Do you really have no intention of thanking me for your time here, which I made possible for you? But no, don't thank me, it wouldn't suit you. You're incapable of bowing and saying you can't even begin to express your thanks. Your behavior's your gratitude. You and I chased and drove the hours before us at such a clip they got winded. Do you really not own any more things than fit in that tiny suitcase? You are truly poor. A single suitcase is the entire household you inhabit in this world. There's something enchanting about this, but also something wretched. Go now. I shall watch from the window as you walk away. When you reach the edge of the hill up there, turn around and look back at me one last time. Why should any further words of tenderness be exchanged? Between you, the brother, and me, the sister? Does it matter if a sister never sees her brother again? I am sending you away somewhat coldly because I know you and know you hate affectionate farewells. Between us this means nothing. Now bid me adieu and then be on your way—"

11

It was about two in the afternoon when Simon arrived by train in the metropolis he'd left behind around three months before. The station was full of people and completely black, filled with that train station odor that's absent only from small, rural stations. Simon was trembling as he got off; he was hungry, stiff, exhausted, sad and sapped of all courage, besides which he couldn't shake off a certain trepidation, though he kept telling himself his trepidation was utterly foolish. Like most travelers, he checked his luggage at the luggage window and lost himself in the crowd. As soon as he was able to move freely again, he immediately felt better and once more was conscious of his effortless good health—now in top form owing to his time in the country. He ate something at one of those odd public establishments. So here he was eating again, without much appetite; for the food was meager and poor, good enough for a down-at-the-heels city-dweller, but not for a spoiled denizen of the country-side. The people looked at him attentively, as if they could tell he'd just arrived from the country. Simon thought: "These people must surely sense that I'm used to better food; something of the sort can be discerned in my approach to this meal." In fact he left half of it behind on his plate, paid his bill and couldn't help remarking airily to the waitress how far from tasty he'd found it. The waitress gazed at the scornful customer contemptuously, amicably contemptuously, just ever so slightly, as if she had no need to feel indignant at the affront, seeing it was a person of this sort who'd complained and not another. If it had been someone else, well then, certainly, but on account of such a one!— Simon walked out. He was feeling happy, the second-rate meal and the girl's insulting glance notwithstanding. The sky was a pale blue. Simon gazed at it: Yes, here too he had a sky. In this respect it was perfectly silly to be so partial to the countryside at the city's expense. He resolved to stop thinking back on the countryside now and to acclimatize himself to this new world. He saw how people went walking on before him, going much faster than he did; for in the country he'd grown accustomed to an ambling, deliberate gait, as though he were afraid of advancing too quickly. Well, for today he decided to permit himself to go on walking like a peasant, but from tomorrow on he'd stride forward in a different manner. He observed people affectionately, however, with no trace of shyness, he met their eyes and looked at their legs to see how they were moving them, at their hats to observe the progress of fashion, and at their clothes to be able to judge his own outfit still good enough compared with the many unlovely garments he was now industriously scrutinizing. How hurriedly they walked, these people. He would have liked to stop one of them and address to him the words: What's the rush? But then he seemed to lack the courage for such a foolish undertaking. He felt fine, though he was also a bit weary and tense. A tiny, undeniable mournfulness held him in its grasp, but that harmonized well with the light, happy, somewhat overcast sky. It also harmonized with the city, where to wear too sunny an expression was all but unseemly. Simon had to confess to himself that he was walking there looking for nothing, but he nonetheless found it expedient to assume the bearing of a seeker, someone pressing rapidly forward like all the others, for he had no wish to play the role of the idle newcomer. He preferred not to call attention to himself, and it did him good to see his behavior wasn't attracting notice. From this he concluded that he was still capable of city life, and so he carried himself a bit more upright than before and acted as though he were carrying around with him a small, elegant intention, one that he was imperturbably pursuing, but which elicited from him no worry, only interest, and would not dirty his shoes or tire his hands. He was just now walking through a beautiful affluent street planted on both sides with blossoming trees, a street in which, given how broad it was, you had the sky more freely before your eyes. It was truly a splendid bright street, just the sort to conjure up the most pleasant existences and inspire dreams. Simon now completely forgot his plan of walking through this street with a deliberate air. He let himself go, allowed himself to drift, looking now at the ground, now up above, now to the side into one of the many shop windows, before one of which he finally remained standing, without actually looking at anything. He found it agreeable to have the noise of the beautiful lively street at his back and yet also in his ears. His perceptions distinguished the footsteps of individual passers-by, all of whom no doubt could only assume he was standing there taking a good look at something on display in the shop window.

Suddenly he heard someone addressing him. He turned around and beheld a lady demanding that he carry a package she was holding out to him all the way to her home. This lady was not particularly beautiful, but at this moment Simon's task was not to lose himself in reflections concerning the degree of her beauty but rather, as an inner voice cried out to him, to step lively and do as she instructed. He took the package, which wasn't at all heavy, and carried it, following behind the lady as she cut across the street with small, measured steps without turning even once to look back at the young man. Having arrived before an, as it appeared, distinguished building the woman commanded him to come upstairs with her, and so he did. He saw no reason why he should refuse to comply. Accompanying this lady into her home felt perfectly natural, and obeying her voice was quite appropriate for his situation, which was so undefined. He would perhaps still have been standing before the shop window gaping, he thought as he climbed the stairs. When they reached the top, the woman invited him inside. She went on ahead and gestured him into a room whose door she opened. To Simon the room appeared quite splendid. The woman came in, sat down on one of the chairs, cleared her throat a little, looked at the one standing before her and asked whether he might make up his mind to enter her service. The impression she had of him, she went on, was that of an individual standing idly about in the world, a person one would be doing a favor by offering him work. As for the rest, she found him quite passable, and would he please tell her whether he was inclined to accept her offer?

"Why not," Simon replied.

She said: "It seems I wasn't mistaken when I concluded, immediately on first seeing you, that you were a young man who'd be happy to find a foothold somewhere. So tell me, what's your name, and what have you done in the world until now?"

"My name is Simon, and as of yet I've done nothing at all!"

"How can that be?"

Simon said: "I received a small inheritance from my parents which I've just now consumed down to the last cent. I didn't consider it necessary to find a job. The thought of learning a profession had no appeal for me at all. I found the days so beautiful I'd have considered it impertinent to desecrate them with work. You know how much is lost by daily work. I was incapable of acquiring a body of knowledge if it meant renouncing the sight of the sun and the evening moon. It took me hours to contemplate an evening landscape, and I'd spend nights on end sitting not at a desk or in a laboratory but in the grass with a river flowing past my feet and the moon peering at me through the branches of the trees. No doubt you'll look down at such a statement, disconcerted, but should I be telling you a lie? I've lived in both countryside and city, but to this day I have shown no person on earth any service worthy of particular note. I do wish to do so now that an opportunity seems to have presented itself."

"How could you have lived so wantonly?"

"I never had much respect for money, madam! Given the appropriate circumstances, on the other hand, it might well occur to me—or even strike me as a matter of some urgency—to value money belonging to others. It would seem to appear that you harbor a desire to take me into your service: Well, in this case I should naturally keep a sharp eye on your interests; for in such a case, I should have no other interests than yours, which should be mine as well. My own interests! When could I ever have gotten so far as to have interests of my own? When could I have had serious matters to pursue? I've frittered away my life up till now—intentionally, since it always struck me as utterly worthless. Devoting myself to the interests of others would suit me well; after all, a person with no goals of his own lives only for others' purposes, interests and plans—"

"But surely you wish to imagine some sort of future for yourself!" —

"I've never once given it a moment's thought! You're looking at me with a rather worried, unfriendly expression. You distrust me and think me incapable of serious intentions. And in fact I must confess that to this day I've never once carried intentions of any sort around with me, as I've never before been asked by anyone to entertain an intention. This is the first time I've ever found myself standing before a person who wishes to avail herself of my services; this flattering circumstance compels me to be bold and tell you the truth. If I've been a dissolute person until now, what does it matter as long as I'm now set on becoming a better one? Are you capable of doubting my wish to show you gratitude for having scooped me up on the street and brought me to your room with the intention of giving me a human destiny? I have no future plans in mind—just the intention of pleasing you. And I know how pleasant it is when a person does his duty. So now here's the future I'm imagining: performing my duties, which are the tasks you'll set me. I've no desire to go thinking ahead to a future much more distant than the immediate one. The path my life will follow is of no interest to me, let it meander as it likes, just so people are pleased with me—"

Hereupon the lady said: "Although it is strictly speaking incautious to offer employment to a person who is nothing and can do nothing, I am willing to do so, for I believe you have the desire to work. You will be my servant and do everything I demand. You can consider yourself particularly fortunate to enjoy such benevolence, and I hope you'll make an effort to deserve it. You surely have no credentials, otherwise this would be the moment when I'd ask for your credentials. How old are you?—"

"Twenty and a bit!"

The lady nodded. "That's an age when a person must think of setting himself a task for life. Well, for the moment I'm prepared to overlook many aspects of your person that don't entirely suit me, and shall give you the opportunity to become a reliable man. We shall see!—"

With these words the conversation was ended.

The lady led Simon through a suite of elegant rooms—noting, as she strode on ahead of her young companion, that one of his tasks would be to keep these rooms clean—and asked whether he was capable of scrubbing a wooden floor with steel wool, but didn't wait to hear his reply, as though she already knew the answer and had asked for the sole purpose of asking something or other to keep the questions whizzing arrogantly and interrogatively about his ears; then she opened a door and ushered him into a smaller room, warmly lined with tapestries of all sorts, where she introduced him to a little boy lying in the bed with these brief words: He would be serving this young master, who was ill, and how he was to do this would be explained to him later. The boy was a pale attractive lad, though disfigured by his sickness, who coldly met Simon's gaze without saying anything. You had the impression he was unable to speak or do more than just babble when you examined his mouth, which lay helplessly in his face as though it didn't belong there, as if it were merely pasted on and hadn't always been his. The boy's hands, though, were very beautiful, they looked as if they bore all the pain and dishonor of his illness, as though they'd taken it upon themselves to bear this enormity, the entire beautiful burden of weeping sorrow. Simon couldn't help gazing lovingly at these hands for a moment longer than was permitted; for at once he was commanded to follow the lady, who led him down a corridor to the kitchen, where she said that when there were no more important tasks for him, he was to make himself useful to the cook. Most gladly, Simon replied, looking at the girl who appeared to be mistress of the kitchen. Thereupon—the next morning to be precise—he took up his service, that is, this service strode up to him and demanded this and that of him and no longer left him a minute to think about whether or not such service pleased him. He'd spent the night in the room with the boy, his young master, sleeping and constantly waking up again; for he'd been instructed to sleep only lightly, softly and superficially, that is, intentionally poorly, so that he'd get accustomed to leaping quickly out of bed when the sick lad called in even the faintest whisper, to receive his orders. Simon believed he was the man for such sleep; for when he swiftly thought it over, he despised sleep and was glad to avail himself of an opportunity that compelled him to disdain all solid, deep sleep. The next morning, he didn't feel in the least as if he'd slept badly—though he also couldn't have said how many times he'd leapt out of bed—and went to work in good spirits. His first task was to run down to the street with a fat white pot in his hands and have a woman there fill it with fresh milk. While performing this duty, he was able to spend a moment observing the awakening, damply gleaming day, letting this spectacle intoxicate and ignite both his eyes before he ran back upstairs. He made the observation that his limbs obeyed him supplely and well as he hurried up and down. Then, even before the woman had arisen from her slumber, he and the girl had to tidy the rooms assigned to him: the dining room, the parlor and the study. The floor was to be swept clean with a broom, the carpets given a brushing, table and chairs dusted, windows breathed on and polished and all the objects located in the room touched, picked up, cleaned and returned to their places. All of this was to be performed with lightning speed, but it seemed to Simon that when he'd done it three times, he'd be able to do it with his eyes closed. After this work was completed, the girl indicated to him that he might now clean a pair of shoes. Simon picked up the shoes—indeed, these were truly the lady's shoes. They were beautiful shoes, delicate shoes with fur trim and made of a leather as soft as silk. Simon had always adored shoes, not just any shoes, not stout sturdy ones, just delicate shoes like these—and now he was holding just such a shoe in his hand, and it was his duty to clean it although he didn't actually see anything that required cleaning. Women's feet had always appeared holy to him, and to his eyes and senses shoes were like children, happy favored children who knew the happiness of clothing and enclosing the delicately mobile, sensitive foot. What a lovely human invention a shoe is, he thought as he wiped the shoe with a cloth to pretend he was cleaning it. He was caught red-handed by the woman herself, who now came into the kitchen and looked him over sternly; Simon lost no time wishing her a good morning, to which she responded with a mere nod. Simon found this utterly charming, indeed ravishing—to be bid good morning and reply only with a nod of the head, as if to say: That's right, dear boy, yes, thanks so much, I did hear what you said, you said it nicely, I'm pleased with you!

"You must clean my shoes better, Simon," the woman said.

Simon was delighted to have been reprimanded. Back in the days when he'd gone wandering through hot, scorched, abandoned streets without direction, how often his heart had yearned for a cruel harsh reprimand, a curse, even words of disparagement or abuse, just to have the certainty that he wasn't utterly alone, that his existence wasn't going entirely unheeded, even if the heed paid it was a rude negative sort. "How sweet this reprimand sounds coming from her womanly mouth," he thought, "and how this binds me to her, how tightly it binds and knots and shackles me, a reprimand like that feels like a tiny, scarcely at all painful box on the ears prompted by a mistake one has made"; and Simon secretly resolved to go on making mistakes, that is, no, perhaps not exclusively, as that would mark him as a dunce, but regularly to have minor slip-ups, nice intentional ones, so as to have the pleasure of seeing this sensitive female, who was used to having things just so, filled with indignation. Indignation? Well, maybe not exactly indignation, but at least a sort of questioning, an astonishment at his, Simon's clumsiness. Then a person would be given the opportunity to shine in other ways, and so one would be allowed the pleasure of watching a stern, vexed face turn into a more friendly, satisfied one. How delightful to be able to transform another's mood from displeasure to contentment when this person had been aggrieved just a moment before. "I've already acquired one adorable reprimand today," Simon thought, and further: "How pleasant it is to be the one being reprimanded—this is, in a matter of speaking, a more mature, superior state. I was made to be reprimanded, for I'm always grateful to receive reprimands; the only people who deserve the favor of being reprimanded are those who know how to express their thanks by assuming an appropriate bearing."

Simon was in fact standing there appropriately, and he felt: "Now I've really become this woman's servant; her reprimanding me shows she feels within her right to rebuke me without much forethought, and from me in return she expects a decorous silence. When a superior castigates a subordinate official, this causes him pain, and it's always secretly one's intention to hurt a subordinate by drawing his attention to one's own higher standing. One reprimands a servant only with the intention of instructing and training him to be as one wishes; for a servant belongs to one, whereas one's relationship with a subordinate official ends along with the workday. I, for example, have now been chastised with heartfelt warmth, and in addition one must consider that this reprimand came from a woman who belongs to those women who are always lovely when they set about something of the sort. Indeed, one need only hear ladies giving voice to reprimands to realize how much better they are than men at rebuking those at fault while avoiding petty slights. But perhaps this is wrong, and it's just that I consider words that would wound me coming from a man to be far from insulting—encouraging even—on a woman's lips. Standing before a man, I'm always conscious of a proud equality, but with a woman: never, since after all I'm a man or at least preparing to become one. With a woman, one must always feel either superior or sub-ordinate! —To obey a child if it has a charming way of giving orders is easy for me, but to obey a man: Fie! Only cowardice and financial interests might cause one man to cower before another: such base motives! So I'm glad it's my duty to obey a woman; this comes quite naturally, as it can never be injurious to one's honor. A woman can never injure a man's honor except by adultery, but in these cases the man is most likely behaving like a dunce and a weakling who cannot be dishonored even by the betrayal itself, as the very possibility of its occurring has long since dishonored him in the eyes of all who know him. Women can make you un-happy, but they can never dishonor you; for true unhappiness is no disgrace and can appear comical only to coarse people and sensibilities, individuals who, let us note, dishonor only them-selves with their derision."

"Come here!"

With these words the lady plucked the servant from his pre-sumptuous train of thought and commanded him to go dress the sickly lad. He obeyed and did as she asked. He carried a basin of fresh water to the bedside and with a sponge carefully washed the boy's face, gave him a glass half filled with clean water and had him rinse his mouth, which the boy lying in bed did very prettily with his beautiful hands, applied brush and comb to his hair, and finally served him his breakfast on a silver tray, watching as it was methodically consumed—with a great deal of picking up and putting down—without growing weary or even impatient; for how ugly and unfitting impatience would have been here; then he carried the dishes back out again and returned to dress the invalid, who was unable to dress himself. He lifted the light thin body somewhat gingerly from the bed, having first pulled the stockings over the feet and legs, placed little house slippers on the feet, picked up the trousers to put them on, buckled the belt, tossed the suspenders properly from back to front—all of this quickly, soundlessly and with economy of gesture—then placed the collar around the boy's neck, a wide, folded boy's collar, skillfully attached necktie to shirt button, the shirt of course having already been put on; and now he presented the vest, had the boy slip his arms through the armholes, and then the same with the jacket and the few objects the boy was in the habit of carrying around, such as watch, watch fob, pocketknife, handkerchief and notebook, and the opus was finished. Now Simon had to straighten the bed of his young master, as well as tidying the entire bedroom just as the lady had showed him, opening the windows, distributing the pillows, comforters and sheet on the windowsills and doing all these things just as they ought—and as it appeared to him they ought—to be done. The lady watched his every move the way a fencing instructor observes the movements of his pupil, and found that he devoted himself to these tasks with talent. Not that she uttered even a single word of approval. This would never have occurred to her. Besides which, the servant ought to realize from her silence that she condoned his manner of working. She was glad to see how tender he was with her son, for she had noted how Simon's each gesture as he dressed the invalid expressed his respect for him. She couldn't help smiling as she saw how hesitantly he'd touched the boy at first, and then later, as he overcame this hesitation, his gestures had become more firm, steady and calm. She was quite pleased with the young man so far, she had to confess to herself. "If he continues in this way, I'll have to love him for not deceiving me in the feeling I had about him right from the start," she thought. "He's very quiet and respectable and appears to be talented at familiarizing himself quickly with any situation. And since he, as I believe I am allowed to conclude from his manners, comes from a good background, I shall insist on intelligent, attractive behavior on his part, for the sake of his mother, who is perhaps still alive, and that of his siblings, who perhaps hold positions of some respect and are concerned about his fate, and it will delight me when I see him getting the hang of things and behaving as is expected of him. Perhaps I shall soon be permitted to treat him in a more confidential manner than one is usually forced to adopt with one's servants. But I shall take care all the same not to give him an excuse to get fresh with me by overhasty friendly accommodations. His character contains a faint smack of impertinence and audacity, and these must not be encouraged. I shall always have to suppress the pleasure I take in him if I wish him always to have the desire to please me. I think he is much taken with my stern face; I guessed something of the sort when he smiled a moment ago as I was giving him what was after all a rather unfriendly dressing-down. One must guess about people if one wishes to see them at their best. He has soul, this young man, and so one must approach him in a soulful, soul-conscious way to get anywhere with him. One must be considerate while at the same time acting as if one isn't showing any particular consideration, since after all that's certainly not necessary. But it's better and wiser to be considerate if it can be done without a fuss." —She resolved to see Simon in this adventurous light, and now sent him out to do the shopping.

What a novelty it was for Simon to go hurrying through the streets with a basket or leather tote bag in his hand, to purchase meat and vegetables, to walk into shops and then run back home again. In the streets he saw people going about their various sorts of business, each animated by an intention, as he was himself. It seemed that people were surprised at his figure. Might his way of walking fail to accord with the full basket he was easily carrying? Were his gestures too unrestrained to correspond to his commission, that is, to running errands? But these were friendly glances he was receiving; for people saw he was hurrying and busy, and he must have given the impression of a dutiful man. "How beautiful it is," Simon thought, "to rush through the streets like this with a duty in one's head alongside all the swarms of people, being overtaken by a few who have longer legs, while flying past others who walk more indolently, as though they have lead in their shoes. How agreeable it is to be seen by these spick-and-span maidservants as one of their own, to observe what a sharp eye these simple creatures have, to note that they might be tempted to stop for a bit and chat with you for ten minutes. How the dogs go tearing along the street as if they were chasing the wind, and how busily the graybeards are still rushing about with their hunched necks and backs! Can you look at this and still wish merely to stroll? How charming women are whom you're allowed to race past without attracting their notice. How could you expect them to notice you? That would certainly be something! It's enough to have observant eyes yourself. Does a person have senses only to be kindled by others and not to kindle oneself? The eyes of women on a morning street like this are so utterly splendid when they gaze off into the distance. Eyes looking past you are more beautiful than eyes that gaze directly at you. It's as if they lost something. How quickly you think and feel when you're walking so briskly. Just don't start looking at the sky! No, it's best just to sense that somewhere up there, above your head and all the buildings, something beautiful and broad is hovering, a hovering something that is perhaps also blue and most certainly fragrant. You have duties—and this too is a hovering, flying, enthralling something. You are carrying on your person something that must be counted out and handed over if you wish to be seen as reliable, and given my present circumstances, I consider it infinitely agreeable to be reliable. Nature? Let it conceal itself for the moment. Yes, it seems to me as if it were in hiding there, behind the long rows of buildings. The forest has, for the time being, lost its appeal for me, and I don't wish to be tempted by it. All the same, there's something beautiful about thinking that everything's still there while I fleetingly, busily rush through the blinding streets, paying no heed to anything that's not simple enough to be understood by my nose."—Once more he counted the money in his vest pocket with sentient fingers, not taking it out, and then went home.

Now he had the table to set.

He had to spread a clean white tablecloth over the table with the creases facing up, then lay out the plates in such a way that their rims didn't protrude over the edge of the table, then distribute forks, knives and spoons, set glasses in their places along with a carafe of fresh water, lay napkins upon the plates and set the salt-cellar on the table. Setting and laying, placing and touching and arranging, touching daintily, then more firmly, touching cloth only with fingertips and plates with great care, distributing and adjusting, the silverware for instance, being noiseless in the process, swift and yet also cautious, both careful and bold, stiff and smooth, calm yet vigorous, not letting the glasses clink together or the plates clack, but also showing no astonishment should a clinking or clacking be heard, instead finding this comprehensible, and then announcing to one's masters that the table was set before bringing out the dishes and withdrawing through the door, only to go back in again when the bell was rung, watching the food being eaten and taking pleasure in this, telling oneself it was more agreeable to watch others eat than to eat, then clearing the table again, carrying out the dishes, putting a leftover scrap of roast meat in one's mouth and making an exultant face, as though this were an action that required an exultant look, then eating oneself and finding that one really did deserve to eat now: All these things Simon had to do. He didn't have to do all of it, for instance he wasn't required to look exultant when he stole, but it was his first tender theft, and for this reason he had to be exultant; for it reminded him vividly of childhood, when one steals something or other from the pantry and exults.

After the meal, he had to help the girl clean the dishes, wash and dry them, and the girl was not a little surprised to see how nimble he was at this task. Where had he learned how? "I used to live in the country," Simon responded, "and in the country one does such things. I have a sister there who's a teacher, I always helped her dry the dishes."

"That was nice of you."

12

To Simon it appeared quite marvelous to be laboring in this quiet kitchen in the middle of the big city. Who'd ever have thought it? No, human beings never quite managed to envision their futures. He who in earlier days had gone wandering freely across mountain meadows, sleeping like a hunter beneath the stars and gasping for breath when he discovered vistas that gave new expanse and depth to the earth below, who wished the sun were even hotter, the wind stormier, the nights darker and the cold more bitter when he ran around out of doors in all seasons and weather, searching, rubbing his hands together and puffing— now he was cooped up in a tiny kitchen drying a dripping plate while it was still warm. He was glad. "How glad I am to be so hemmed in, so confined, so enclosed," he thought. "Why should a person always be hankering for wide open spaces, and isn't longing so restrictive a sentiment? Here I am tightly squeezed in between four kitchen walls, but my heart is wide open and filled with the pleasure I take in my modest duty."

He did find it a bit humiliating to be in a kitchen, occupied with a task ordinarily performed only by girls. It was a bit humiliating and a bit ridiculous, but nonetheless most certainly mysterious and odd. No one could possibly dream of finding him here.

This thought had something gratifying and proud about it. Having such a thought could make one smile. The girl asked what he'd been in his former life, and he replied: "A copy clerk!" She couldn't comprehend how a person could possess so little ambition as to leave behind his desk in order to creep into domestic service. Simon replied that his case, first of all, involved nothing that might be described as creeping, as she so charmingly expressed herself, and secondly it was still an open question which was preferable: sitting behind a desk or leading a plate wiper's existence. He by far preferred the open, airy, warm, steamy, interesting kitchen to the dry-as-dust office where the air was usually stale and the general mood embittered. How could one feel bitter in a kitchen where a roast was stewing in the pan, vegetables cooking, soup steaming, the copper shining down so sweetly from the rack and the plates making such a friendly sound when one knocked them together. But being a servant, the spirited maiden rejoined—it wasn't much, it didn't amount to anything. He didn't want to amount to anything, Simon said softly. She let that be the end of it, but she found he was a curious, difficult to understand person. But she also thought: "He's decent," and felt he might be "allowed some liberties." Simon had just finished his drying when the lady walked into the kitchen and bid him come into the other room, she had a task for him. "What lovely task might she have for me," Simon wondered, and he followed the woman striding on ahead. "During the afternoon, there's nothing further for you to do, so you might as well read to my son and me. Do you know how to read aloud out of a book?" Simon said he did.

And then he read to them for a full hour. His breath was somewhat strained, but he read with accurate, clear, good enunciation, in a warm voice that demonstrated the reader was moved by what he read. The lady appeared pleased, and the boy was all ears to the very end, whereupon he thanked Simon graciously for the treat. Simon, whose cheeks were glowing bright red with emotion, found it lovely to be thanked. He betook himself, since for the moment he didn't know what else to do, into the domestics' quarters, which were lit up red by the evening sun, and began to smoke out the window.

"I disapprove of your smoking here," said the woman, entering the room.

He, however, went on smoking, and she left again, rather miffed. "Certainly I can understand her disapproval, but must she really approve of everything about me? I'm not about to give up smoking. No, I won't, devil take it! Even if twenty ladies were to come one after the other and forbid me to smoke." He was furious, but at once his mood lightened again, and he said to himself: "I ought to have tossed the cigarette away; that was impertinent!"

At just this moment when he was preparing to launch into a monologue, a scream rang out in the corridor, followed immediately by the loud crash of crockery falling to the ground. Simon opened the door and saw the woman gazing with a mournful, silent, crestfallen face at the floor, where lay the shards of a porcelain platter she had no doubt been fond of. She had wished to carry the platter with a piece of cake on it from the icebox to her room and had managed to drop it, she herself couldn't say how.

All it had taken was the most fleeting misperception, or something of the sort, and the misfortune had occurred. When the woman beheld Simon, who was standing behind her, her expression instantly changed from crestfallen to enraged and accusatory, and she said to him in a tone that clearly signified what she was feeling: "Pick this up!" Simon squatted down and gathered up the shards. As he did so, his cheek brushed against the skirt of his employer, and he thought: "Forgive me for having stood by and witnessed your maladroitness. I understand your anger. It is I who bear the guilt for breaking the platter you dropped. I broke it. How this must pain you. Such a beautiful platter. Surely you were fond of it. I feel sorry for you. My cheeks are brushing against your dress. Every shard I gather up says to me: 'You wretched creature,' and the hem of your dress says to me: 'O happy one!' I'm intentionally taking my time about gathering up the shards. Does it now fill you with fresh rage to be forced to notice? I'm finding it amusing to have been the miscreant. I like you when you're angry with me. Do you know why your anger so pleases me? Your way of being angry is so tender! You're only angry because I witnessed your clumsiness. You must have a fair bit of respect for me if it so mortifies you to have made a fool of yourself in my presence. You the grand lady in the presence of ignoble me. With what enchanting rancor you bade me gather up the shards. And I'm not even hurrying as I do so; for I wish you to become utterly furious and incensed over my taking so long with the shards that cannot help telling me the story of your clumsiness, and telling it to you as well. Are you still standing here? The strangest sentiments must now be intermingling within you: shame, pain, fury, vexation, equanimity, irritability, tranquility, surprise and majestic dignity, with so many trivial, unmentionable accompaniments slinking alongside, snatched away again each moment before a person can properly grasp them; that one there was like a pinprick or a whiff of perfume or a pair of twinkling eyes.—Your silk dress is beautiful when one considers that it contains a female body capable of trembling with excitement and weakness. Your hands are beautiful hanging down toward me in all their length. I hope you'll box my ears with them some day. Now you're leaving already, without having scolded me. When you walk, your dress giggles and whispers on the floor. A moment ago you forbade me to smoke. But I shall have the impudence to smoke when I walk behind you on the way to market to help with the shopping. There you will see me smoking: gleaming white cigarettes, and I certainly hope you'll then have the presence of mind to slap the cigarette from my lips. Just now I had to employ all the gestures at my disposal to beg your forgiveness for your having broken a platter. I wish I might have the opportunity to perform some misdeed that would give you cause to send me packing. Oh no, no! What am I thinking. I must be mad. Truly, this shard incident has made me mad. Now it's no doubt evening out on the street. The lanterns will be burning pale yellow in the waning daylight. I'd like to be out there on the street now. There's no help for it, I must go downstairs—"

"I'd like to go out for a brief while," he said, walking into her room. "May I?"

"Yes! But see you don't stay out too long!"

Simon raced outside and down the stairs, where a veiled

female figure stared after him in astonishment, then out of the building to the street, into the air, into mobile damp glittering evening freedom. How strange it was, he thought, this belonging to a household where you lived just like a prisoner. How strange to be a grown man and as a grown man be compelled to seek out a woman, to enter a dark room where you only half see the woman sitting there in the dark, and ask her permission to be allowed to go out. As if you were a piece of furniture in her possession, an object, a purchase, something, a thing, a something or other, and as if this something were nothing or were something only insofar as it was suited to be a thing of this particular sort, something of hers! Strange, too, that you might nonetheless experience this state of affairs as a sort of refuge, a home. That you might feel you were now walking about the streets ten times more exaltedly for having received permission to do so from a person you were obliged to ask. Requesting permission, to be sure, had something schoolboyish about it, he thought; but even graybeards were often enough required to seek permission, sometimes under humiliating circumstances. And so all of life was marvelous, and you had no choice but to enter into this marvel, even if it often looked to you rather strange.

He walked down the street, falling in love with its sweet tableau of rising stars, of dense trees that stretched in long straight rows, and the peacefully ambulating people, the evening's splendor, the deep, restless inklings of night. He too was walking peacefully, almost dreamily. In the evening it was no disgrace to put on a dreamy appearance when all were involuntarily compelled to dream in this atmosphere filled with the scent of the early summer twilight. Many women were strolling about with small elegant little bags in their gloved hands, with eyes in which the evening light went on glowing, in narrow dresses cut in the English style or voluminous dragging skirts and robes that filled the streets with their marvelous breadth. Woman, Simon mused, how she glorifies the image of the city street. A woman is made to promenade. You can feel her parading, enjoying her own swaying, beautiful gait. At sunset, women determine the tone of the evening, their figures being well suited to this with these arms full of melancholy and ampleness and these breasts full of breathing mobility. Their hands in gloves look like children wearing masks, hands with which they beckon, and in which they are invariably holding something. Their entire bearing translates the evening world into sonorous music. If you now, as I am just doing, go walking along behind women, you already belong to them in your thoughts, in sentient oscillations, in breaking waves that crash against your heart. They do not beckon, and yet they do beckon you. Though they carry no fans, you can see fans in their hands, flashing and glinting like embossed silver in the fading, blurred evening light. Mature, voluptuous women go particularly well with such an evening, just as gray-haired old women go with winter, and blossoming girls with the newly arisen day, as children go with dawn and young wives with the heat of midday when the sun shows itself to the world at its most glowing.

It was nine o'clock when Simon returned home. He had stayed away too long, and had to listen to reproaches like this one: If this were to happen again, even one single time more, then— —. He wasn't actually listening, he took in only the sound of the reproach, inwardly he was laughing, outwardly he appeared dejected, that is, he put on an imbecilic expression and decided it was superfluous to open his mouth to say anything in reply. He undressed the boy, put him to bed, and lit a nightlight.

"Might I ask for a lamp of my own?" he asked the lady.

"What do you want the lamp for?"

"To write a letter."

"Come sit here with me, you can write here!" the lady said.

And he was permitted to sit down at her desk. She gave him a sheet of letter paper, an envelope for the address, a stamp, a pen, and allowed him to use her stationery case to write on. She sat close beside him in an armchair, reading a newspaper as he wrote:

Dear Kaspar, I am back in the city so well known to you and am sitting at a beautiful, dark-hued writing desk in a brightly lit room while down below in the street, in the summer night, beneath the trees with all their dangling leaves, people are out strolling. Unfortunately I cannot promenade along with them, for I am chained to a household, not exactly by my hands and feet, but by the sense of duty I am gradually developing, which does, after all, need to be established sooner or later. I have become the servant of a woman who has a sick little boy whom I look after, not much differently than a mother looks after her son, for his mother, my mistress, observes my every move as if her eye were guiding my actions and she were instilling in me her own solicitousness when I care for the boy. As I write this, she is now seated beside me in an armchair, for this is her own room; I'm sitting here with her permission. Matters now stand as follows: Every time some personal errand sends me out of doors, I must first ask "May I go out?" like an apprentice asking permission of his master. All the same, at least it's a lady I'm having to ask, which sweetens the indignity of it. Being a servant, you should know, if you do not already, involves waiting attentively for orders, anticipating desires in advance, skillful swiftness and swift skillfulness in setting the table and brushing out carpets. I have already attained a certain perfection at the task of cleaning the shoes of my lady, whom I call simply my lady. This is only a small minor task, and yet it requires one to strive for perfection just like the greatest endeavor. With the small young gentleman I shall have to go for walks in the future when the weather is fair. There is a little brown carriage in which I can push the boy about—which, come to think of it, I'm not particularly looking forward to, since it will be tedious. Good Lord, do it I shall. My mistress is the sort of woman whose most striking and distinctive feature is her bourgeois sensibility. She's a housewife through and through, but in such a strict and straightforward sense that one can see this characteristic as genteel. She's quite a master at losing her temper, and I in turn have mastered the art of giving her cause for this. Today, for example, she broke a fancy porcelain bowl out of thoughtlessness and was furious with me for not having been the one to break it. She unleashed her fury at me because I was the disagreeable witness to her clumsiness, and made the sort of face one often sees caricatured in Fliegende Blätter. A real Fliegende Blätter face. I picked up the shards as daintily and slowly as possible in order to vex the woman, for I must admit it gives me pleasure to vex her. She is charming when vexed. Beautiful she isn't, but severe women like this radiate a profound magic when they get worked up. The entire demure past of such a woman trembles in her fits of excitement, which are delectable to witness, as they've been ignited by such delicate causes. For me, this is just how it is: I can't help adoring such women, for I admire and pity them at one and the same time. Such women can be haughty in their speech and bearing—so much that their cheeks nearly explode and their mouths get all pointy with the most painful scorn. I love scorn of this sort, for it makes me tremble, and I love being filled with shame and fury: This drives me on to higher things, spurs me on to deeds. But my lady there, the scornful one, is after all just a good gentle woman, this I know, and that's what's so scoundrelly about this whole business: my knowing this. When I obey her, responding to the commanding tone of her voice, I can't help laughing all the while, for it clearly gives her pleasure to see how willingly and swiftly I obey. And now when I ask her for something, she snaps at me but then does kindly give in, perhaps feeling a bit of vexation at the fact that I have petitioned her in such a way that it isn't possible to deny me. I am always hurting her just a little, thinking: It serves her right! Go on! Keep hurting her, just a little. It amuses her. It's what she wants. She isn't expecting anything different! It's so easy to recognize women, yet so much about them is unrecognizable. Isn't that strange, dear brother? In any case women are the most instructive thing a man can find anywhere on earth.—If she only knew, the one sitting here beside me, what I've been writing! One of my most ardent desires is to have my ears boxed by her as soon as possible, but I doubt, painful as this is to realize, that she's capable of it. A good resounding box on the ears: If I could experience this, I'd gladly give up all kisses I might hope to expect. This ear-boxing business, I admit, is damnable on my part, but it's also a genuinely bourgeois sentiment: It brings one back to childhood, and isn't it quite ordinary to feel longing for what lies far behind you? There's some-thing far-in-the-past about my mistress; glimpsing that element sends your thoughts far, far back in time, to a place possibly even more distant than childhood. I'll no doubt kiss her hand one of these days, and then

230

she'll give me the boot or chuck me out, as they say. May I do so, and may she. What would be so awful about that?—Oh, I'm going to the dogs here, let me tell you, it already shows. My mind is occupied with folding napkins and polishing knives, and what's queer is that I like it. Can you imagine a greater idiocy? How are you? I spent three months in the country, but now it feels to me as if that time's already far in the past. I have every intention of becoming a person who devotes himself fully to each day without considering his ties to more nebulous things. Sometimes I'm too lazy even to think of you, and this strikes me as enormously indolent. I hope to see Klara again soon. Perhaps you've forgotten her already, and then I shouldn't be bringing up the matter to begin with. And so I shan't. Adieu, dear brother.

"Whom did you write to?" the woman asked, worn out by her newspaper reading, when she saw Simon had finished his letter.

"A friend of mine who now lives in Paris."

"What does he do?"

"At first he was a bookbinder, but since he didn't have much success with this profession, he's become a waiter in a restaurant. I love him very much, we went to school together, and that's when I got attached to him, because he was unhappy already as a boy. Once I saw him being taunted by his classmates, who then threw him down a flight of stone steps, and I caught a glimpse of his beautiful, terrified, sorrowful eyes. Since that day I've been his closest friend, and if pity truly binds people together, I shall have to feel bound to him forever without even thinking about it. He's one year older than I am, but in his manners and lifestyle he's years ahead of me, for he's always made his home in great cities where a person matures more quickly. In the old days he was always going on about painting, and during the time he was pursuing a bookbinder's career, he often tried to paint pictures, but—painful as this was to him—he never got terribly far with his paintings and one day he confessed to me shamefacedly that he'd resolved to throw himself into the maelstrom of life and forget about art and his dreams, and so he became a waiter. What a washout, but at the same time: What an admirable leap forward! I told him how I admired and loved him for his decision, hoping to console him for those quiet, lonely hours when he might find himself surrendering to pangs of memory. Clearly he would often long for that better world while all around him life was raging. But you see, madam, my friend is a proud and worthy man. Too proud to mourn a life that's slipped through his fingers, and too worthy to be able to just lay it to one side. Each of his sentiments is known to me. Once he wrote me that he was about to die of monotony and boredom. That was his soul. And another time, he wrote: 'All these stupid daydreams! Life is what's sweet. I'm drinking absinthe and am filled with bliss!' That was his masculine pride. Let me tell you: Women are mad for him, there's something heart-beckoning about him, but also something icy-cold. Everything about his appearance, the waiter's tailcoat notwithstanding, radiates love and tact."

"What is the name of this unhappy wretch?" the woman asked.

"Kaspar Tanner."

"What? Tanner? That's your name. So he's your brother, even though you called him your friend just now."

"Of course he's my brother, but much more than this he's my friend! A brother like that has to be called a friend if you want to use the right terminology. We're brothers only coincidentally; but our friendship is quite intentional, and this makes it far more valuable. What is brotherly love? Once back when we were still brothers, we grabbed one another by the throat and tried to do each other in. What charming love! Among brothers, envy and hatred are perfectly ordinary phenomena. When friends hate one another, they part ways; when brothers hate—brothers whom fate has ordained to live beneath a single roof—the outcome is not so tranquil. But this is an old story and not the nicest one."

"Why haven't you sealed your letter?"

"I'd like you to look over what I've written."

The woman smiled:

"No, this I will not do."

"I speak of you inappropriately in this letter."

"I'm sure it's not so bad," she remarked, rising to her feet: "Go to bed."

Simon did as she commanded, thinking as he left:

"I'm getting cheekier and cheekier. One of these days she'll send me packing for good!"—

Three weeks later, liberated from all obligations, Simon stood in a narrow, steep, hot alleyway before a building, deliberating whether or not to go in. The noonday sun was blazing down, making the walls release their unsavory odors. Not the slightest breeze was stirring. Where in this alley could a breeze have slipped in? Out in the modern streets there might be breezes wafting, but in here it felt as if centuries had passed since a breath of air last breezed and blew. Simon had a small sum of money in his pocket. Should he board a train and travel to the mountains? Everyone was traveling to the mountains these days. Strange unfamiliar people, men and women, moved singly, in pairs, or little groups through the white bright streets. From the hats of the ladies, amusing veils fluttered down, and the men were going about in knee-length trousers and light-colored summer shoes. Oughtn't he decide to follow these strangers to the mountains? Surely it would be cooler up there, and in a hotel perched high up on a peak he would surely find work. He might even play the role of tour guide, he was rugged enough for this, and also clever enough to say at the appropriate time: "Observe, ladies and gentlemen, this waterfall, or this scree, or this village, or this cliff face, or this blue shimmering river." He'd have what it takes to depict a landscape in words for his traveling guests. He could also, should the circumstance arise, carry a fatigued and fearful Englishwoman in his arms when it came time to cross a pass just three shoe-lengths wide. Certainly he had a desire to do so. Oh yes, those American girls and Englishwomen: He'd learn to speak English, which to his mind was a sweet language that sounded like whispers and sighing, both gruff and soft.

But he didn't go to the mountains, instead he went into this old, tall, thick, dark building in the alleyway, knocked at a door and asked a woman who came out to see who was knocking whether she had a room to let.

Indeed, she did.

He asked if he could have a look at it, and if it was a room— not too large, not too dear—suitable for a person without much money.

After she had showed him the room, the woman asked:

"What do you do?"

"Oh, nothing at all. I'm unemployed. But I'm going to look for work. Don't be concerned. I'll pay you this sum here in advance so you won't have to worry too much. Here, take it."

And he placed a rather large coin in her hand as prepayment. This was a plump female hand, and the woman, who was satisfied, said:

"Unfortunately the room isn't sunny, it faces the alley."

"All the better," Simon replied, "I love shade. I'd hate to have the sun shining into my room just now in this warm season. The room is very nice, and, let me add, very cheap. It's perfect for me. The bed appears to be good. Oh yes. Please. Let's not poke about too much. Here is also a wardrobe that can hold more clothes than I possess, and here to my delighted astonishment I espy an armchair for comfortable sitting. Indeed, if a room has such an armchair to show for itself, it is, in my eyes, most opulently furnished. There's even a picture hanging on the wall: I love when there's only a single picture hanging in a room, you can observe it all the more closely. I see as well a mirror for examining my face. It's a good one, it reflects my features clearly. Lots of mirrors distort the features they reflect when you look into them. This one is quite excellent. Here at this table I shall write my letters of application which I shall send off to various commercial firms in order to obtain a post. I hope I shall succeed in this. I can't see why I shouldn't, as I've had success so many times already. For your information, I've changed jobs many times now. This is an error that I hope I shall be able to correct. You are smiling! Yes, but it's quite serious. With this room you've become, as it were, my benefactress, for it's a room in which a person like me can feel happy. I shall always make an effort to observe my obligations toward you promptly."

"I believe you will," the woman said.

"At first," Simon said, "I wanted to go to the mountains. But this shady room is more beautiful than even the whitest mountains. I'm feeling a bit tired and would like to lie down for an hour, may I?"

"Why, of course! It's your room now!"

"Oh, surely not!"

And then he lay down for a nap.

He had a strange dream that pursued him for a long time after:

236

It was in Paris, but why Paris he no longer remembered. At first he was walking down a street completely covered with succulent green foliage so that the trains of the ladies' dresses dragged the leaves behind them with a rustling sound. Meanwhile a soft green rain of tiny whispering leaves was falling, and an inexpressibly gentle wind was blowing, like the breath of clouds. The buildings were wonderfully tall, some gray, some yellowish, some snowy white. The men walking along on the street wore their hair long, hanging down so that their curls tumbled past their shoulders, and there were also dwarfs dressed in black tailcoats and red hats walking there who were able to slip right through the others' crossing legs. The ladies in their long-trained dresses cut splendid figures: tall, far taller than the men, who themselves appeared quite slender. Upon the slender busts of the women, lorgnettes hung down below their waists, and arches of heavy opulent hair spanned their lovely heads. Up on top sat tiny little hats with even tinier little feathers, but a few of them were wearing large, broad, splendidly pendulous feathers that appeared to be bending their whole heads back. The hands and arms of these women were a wondrous sight, covered to above their delicate elbows with long black gloves. In fact everything looked wondrous as far as the eye could see. The large buildings insisted on constantly rocking up and down like strange naturalistic stage sets in a theater. The light belonged half to the daytime and half to the already quite advanced night. The scene was now a building completely enshrouded in wild vegetation. "This is where the most beautiful women in Paris live," is what you'd be told if you asked. All at once a fragrant white cloud bowed down into the street. The astonished question: "What's that?" was met with the answer: "As you see, monsieur, it's a cloud. A cloud is by no means a rare sight in the Parisian streets. You must be a foreigner, since this can still surprise you." The cloud remained lying there on the street as white foam, resembling a large swan. Many ladies ran up to it and plucked off little bits, which they placed, moving their arms with wondrous grace, upon their hats, or else they threw the bits at one another in jest, which stuck to their dresses. A person thought: "Just look, these Parisians! They're quick to chuckle at the foreigner and his astonishment. But aren't the Parisians themselves astonished each day anew at their city's beauty?" Then the wicked street urchins of Paris arrived to tickle the cloud with burning matches, and so it flew back up into the sky again, light and majestic, until it vanished above the buildings. Again one could observe the street. In the beautiful restaurants that extended out onto the sidewalks, waiters were serving in light green tail coats, and ladies were drinking coffee and chatting in delightful voices. Poets stood upon raised platforms, singing the songs they'd written at home. They were clad in noble brown velvet—by no means ridiculous figures, far from it. The works they presented were deemed amusing, but without anyone paying particular attention to them, which in Paris would have been impossible. Beautiful slender dogs trotted along behind human beings and comported themselves as if they knew that in Paris one must behave well. Each and every figure and individual seemed to be more floating than walking, more dancing than striding, more flying than running. And yet all of them were running, walking, leaping, strid-

238

ing and marching in a quite natural way. Nature appeared to have taken up residence in this street. Entire flocks of sheep passed through the street amid a constant "ding ding," as if the street were a valley at dusk, the dark-clad shepherd marching at their head. Then came cows with larger bells: "ding dong" and "dang dong"! And yet this was a street and not some mountain pasture, it was the middle of Paris, the heart of European elegance. Though to be sure the street was as broad as a large wide river. Now all at once the lamps were being lit by small, fleet-footed boys carrying long lighting sticks. They used these sticks to open the valves at the top of the lanterns to let the gas come flowing out of its pipes, and these they lit. They sprang from one lantern to the next until all of them were burning. Now lights were glimmering on all sides and seemed to be perambulating along with the wandering people. What sort of magical white light was this—and these devilish boys lighting it, where had they come leaping out from—and to where, away from what, with what aim? Where were they at home, did they too have parents, brothers, sisters, did they too go to school, could they too grow up, get married, father children, grow old and die? Dressed in short blue jackets, all of them seemed to be wearing rubber shoes, for one could barely hear them, flitting by rather than walking. Now they were gone. And as evening fell you could see marvelously odd female figures in the promenading street. They wore their hair in oversized splendor, bright yellow and deep black. Their eyes gleamed and shimmered so brightly it hurt to look at them. The most splendid thing about them were their legs, which were not covered by trains or skirts but instead could be seen to the knee, at which point they were encased in trousers rustling with lace. Their feet were clad almost all the way up to their pliant knees in tall boots crafted of the finest leather. The boots themselves were the daintiest things that could possibly have been appropriate to sheathe a supple female foot. You needed only observe this to laugh with all your heart. The gait of these women displayed a heart-thrilling buoyancy, then a gravity, then a dance-like lightness. Their way of walking was worthy of being sketched and experienced, raising you up and drawing you along after it, and made your eyes start dreaming of sweetness, made your soul awaken so as to ponder how it came about that God made women so beautiful. One felt quite vividly: "If the gods could somehow be at home somewhere on earth, which admittedly isn't conceivable, their place would have to be Paris." All at once without seeing it coming, Simon found himself standing upon a staircase carved and carpentered of dark wood that led him up into a room where a girl lay sleeping upon a day-bed. When he looked more closely, it was Klara. A small cat was slumbering beside her, and the sleeping woman cradled it in one arm. A Negro servant brought in supper, and Simon sat down at the table while from the ceiling of the room rippled a soft, muted music, like the plashing of a precious, inventive fountain, murmuring now in the distance and now just beside his ear. "In Paris, meals are served strangely," Simon thought as he tucked in just like in a fairy tale by the Brothers Grimm. Then the sleeping woman awoke. "Come here, I want to show you something," she whispered to him. He got up, and using a magic wand, or so it appeared, she opened a double door—at least she didn't seem to be employing her hands. "I've become a sorceress," she said, smiling at Simon's astonishment, "do not doubt me, but don't by any means let this terrify you either. I shall show you nothing repugnant." He went with her into the next room, she breathed on him with her fragrant warm breath, and all at once he saw his brother Klaus sitting there writing at his desk. "He is industriously writing his life's work," Klara said in a low, expressive voice. "Look what a thoughtful face he's making. He is immersed in his contemplations of the course of rivers, the history and age of mountains, the twists and turns of the valleys and the earth's strata. But in between he is thinking of his brother, he's thinking of you now! Just look at the folds in his brow. You appear to be causing him worry, you wicked boy! Unfortunately he cannot speak, otherwise we'd both hear what he's thinking about you and what he has to say about your worrisome conduct. He loves you, just look at him! A person like that loves his brother and wants to see him established in the world as a good, respected man. But the picture, I see, is already dissolving. Come. Now I'll show you something different."—As she said this, she opened a second, somewhat smaller door with her little wand, which she really was carrying in her hand, and Simon glimpsed his sister Hedwig stretched out upon a cot draped in white linen. There was a wonderful scent of herbs and flowers in this room. "Look at her," Klara said, and a trembling made her clear, quiet voice unsteady, "she is dead. Life caused her too much pain. Do you know what it means to be a girl and suffer? I wrote her a letter, you know, back in those days: a lengthy, ardent letter filled with longing, and she will never again lift her hand to answer it. She is departing without having answered the world's question: 'Why don't you come?' How wordlessly she parts from us: so girlishly, like a blossom! How dear she was. You as a brother cannot feel this nearly as acutely as I do, her friend. Do you see how she is smiling! If she were still able to talk, she would surely speak friendly words. She spoke severely. She bit her own lips in misery. But you can't see this now looking at her mouth. Death must have kissed her if she can still be smiling even in death! She was a courageous girl. Like a flower she died, like a flower that dies when it withers. Let us go on. In my magical realm, gaping is forbidden. Have I hurt your feelings? Well? Surely not: What can be painful about such a beautiful death? The rest of you left her to suffer, that's what was painful. . . . I don't wish to hurt you. Come, now you shall see something else." And with these words she caused a third door to spring open, and Simon gazed into a roomy studio and smelled the odor of oil paint. On the walls he saw his brother's paintings hanging, and he himself, Kaspar, was working with his back turned at an easel, utterly immersed, it appeared, in his work. "Shh, don't disturb him, he's working," Klara said, "one mustn't disturb people when they're creating something. I always knew he lived only for his art, even then, when I still thought I'd be following him, thought I'd be able to. No, it's better this way. I'd only have held him back and impeded him. He must forget everything around him, even what is dearest to him, if he wants to create. Such creation demands the killing off of everything dear and heartfelt so that all this love and true feeling can be transferred to the work itself. You won't understand this—only Kaspar understands. When you see me looking at him like this, don't you think I feel the urge to throw myself into his arms? To hear what he says to me when I ask in a whisper, trembling with apprehension: 'Do you love me, Kaspar?' He would surely caress me then, but I'd be filled with premonitions and on his beautiful forehead I would discover a faint trace of displeasure. And this discovery would hurl me, like a woman damned unto all eternity, down a thousand depths into a foul ignoble abyss. No—this Klara shall not do—I value her too highly, and he is too precious and dear to me just as he is. And so I stand behind him, free to imagine how he is creating things, how he is rolling the huge, fiery, steaming orb of art before him, like a splendid wrestler sacrificing his last breath to achieve victory over his opponent. Look how entranced he is, plying his brush—ringing the thousand-toned bell of his colors and working to make every line more linear, every color more colorful, every emphasis more deliberate and every longing more poignant. His gaze (which I so loved) was always lost in forms, and here in Paris he requires only a simple room to capture the world in images. He has seized Nature in his arms like a voluptuous mistress and is now pressing kiss after kiss upon her lips until both of them—Kaspar and Nature—are out of breath. It almost seems to me as if Nature were powerless and impotent before true artists and overcome with devotion just like the sort of mistress who denies you nothing. In any case, as you can see, Kaspar has plenty to do, his head, feelings and both hands are all fully occupied; like a wild, untamed horse he thrusts and labors, and when he sleeps at night, he keeps working on and on in wild dreams; for art is rigorous and seems to me the most difficult task an honorable, upright man can set himself. Never disturb him at his holy task; he is creating works for the pleasure of generations to come. If I were wishing now to impose on him my weak poor love, what an unlovely contemptible thing that would be. What's more, a woman has no desire to kiss when she cannot help feeling that injured thoughts lie twitching between her kisses, dying: The kisses are strangling them. What a heedless murderess she would be! Like this, though, everything is lovely; to be sure, it hurts a bit to have to stand behind a turned back, behind his shoulders and curls, but in exchange for this you hear bells ringing in your soul and feel the sweet justification and the peerlessness of your position in the world. At some point our other feelings must be moderated and put in order, they must be kept in their place. Even a weak woman knows perfectly well what she must do. To watch an artist, observing each of his movements thoughtfully, is more beautiful than wishing to influence him, greedily wishing to get something for yourself, to mean something to him and to the world. Every position has its significance, but unwarranted meddling and interference will never have any meaning! There are many things I still should say to you. But now come." —Again as Simon was being led away by Klara, a wondrous, incomprehensible music could be heard emanating from all the rooms, from all the ceilings and walls, like a distant thousand-voiced twittering of birds from a little forest. They returned to the first room and saw the little black cat insert its paw into a narrow-mouthed milk jug. But when it saw the two people, the cat leapt away and crouched behind a chair from whence it peered forth attentively with its burning yellow eyes.

Klara opened a window and: What a wonderful sight! It was snowing in the summery, green street, snowing so thickly, so very flake-upon-flake, that it was impossible to see between them. "This is no rarity here in Paris," Klara said, "it snows at the hottest times of the year, there are no particular seasons here, just as there are no particular ways of speaking. In Paris one must be prepared for anything. If you live here for a while, you too will learn this and will get quickly over your astonishment, which is uncalled for. Everything here is swift, graceful, modest comprehension. And respect for the world is considered the highest, finest thing. You'll learn soon enough. This snow, for example: Do you think you can imagine it piling up higher than these tall buildings? But it's true, and in all probability we shall now lie buried beneath the snow for a full month. What does it matter: We have light and a warm room. I'll be asleep, for the most part, for sorceresses need a great deal of sleep; you'll play with the little cat or read a book, I have the most beautiful Parisian novels here in my library. The Parisian poets write delightfully, you'll see. And then after a month—oh, by the way, we also have music, don't we—and then, as I said, after a month spring will arrive in the Parisian streets. Then you'll see how after their long confinement people will embrace out on the street, weeping tears of joy at seeing each other again. Everything will be a great hugging and embracing. Desires long suppressed will erupt from gleaming eyes, lips and voices—there will be much kissing in May, but you'll experience this yourself. Just imagine, then the air will settle into the streets all blue and warm-moist—the sky will be taking a walk in Paris, intermingling with the rapturous passers-by. The trees will all blossom on a single day and share their wonderful perfume, birds will be singing, clouds will dance and flowers will flit through the air like a rain shower. And money will appear in every pocket, even the poorest, most tattered one. But now I want to sleep. Can you see how sleepy I'm becoming already? Meanwhile, put the time to good use and study one of the works you'll find that is capable of absorbing you for an entire month. Such books exist. Good night!" —And with that she fell asleep. But the cat wanted to lie down beside her, Simon lunged after it, the cat slipped away, he gave chase, and again and again it slipped through his hands when he was already grasping it. All this lunging about made him dreadfully short of breath, and his gasping woke him up.

"What a melancholy dream I've just had," he thought as he rose from the bed. Meanwhile evening had come. He went to the window and for the first time looked down into the alleyway that lay far beneath him. Two men were just walking by, there was just barely room for the two of them to walk comfortably side by side between the high walls. They were speaking, and the sound of their words rose to his ears with a strange clarity up the walls which then carried the sound even further. The sky was a golden, deeply saturated blue that awoke an indeterminate longing. Directly opposite Simon in the house across the way, two female figures appeared and prodded him with their rather impertinent, laughing glances. He felt as if he were being touched with unclean hands. One of the figures addressed him across the alleyway without even raising her voice—it was as if the three of them were sitting together in a single room that just happened to contain a narrow band of sky: "You must be very lonely!"

"Oh, yes! But it's lovely to be lonely!"

And he closed the window as the two women burst into laughter. What could he have discussed with them that would not have been unseemly? Today he wasn't in the mood. The changes once again affecting his life had put him in a somber frame of mind. He drew the white curtains, lit the lamp, and went on reading the Stendhal novel that he hadn't managed to finish reading in the countryside with Hedwig.

—14—

After he'd read for an hour, he extinguished the lamp, opened the window, and went out of his room and then out the building's front door to the steeply inclined street. A heavy, warm darkness received him. The old part of town was full of tiny drinking establishments, so many that a person walking along might find it difficult to choose. He took a few more steps in the lively, bustling street, then went into a bar. A small, jolly company was assembled at a round table, their focal point apparently a humorous little fellow in their midst, for everyone started laughing whenever he opened his mouth. He must have been one of those people who, whatever he happens to say, always has a comical, laugh-muscle-stimulating effect. Simon sat down at a table occupied by two young men and involuntarily listened to what they were saying. They were conversing earnestly, using many quite intelligent expressions. The subject of their discussion seemed to be a young, unhappy man whom both had apparently known quite well. But now one of them was listening without interruption as the other told his story, and Simon heard the following:

"Yes, a splendid fellow! Even as a boy, when his hair was still long and his trousers short and he went out for walks on the streets of our small town holding his nursemaid's hand, already people would turn to look at him, saying: 'What a stunning little fellow!' He completed his assignments with a great deal of talent—his school assignments, I mean. His teachers loved him, he was docile and easy to teach. His cleverness made it easy for him to fulfill his responsibilities at school. He was a splendid gymnast, and skilled at drawing and sums. I know at least that the teachers held him up as a role model to later generations of pupils, and even to some of his older schoolmates. His soft features and those magnificent eyes filled with masculine presentiment bewitched all who came into contact with the lad. He enjoyed a certain celebrity by the time his parents sent him away to continue his studies. Coddled by his mother, which everyone could understand, and admired by all, his spirit must have acquired early on that softness that comes with privilege and recognition, that lassitude, that lovely insouciance that permits a young person to easily master the pleasures of life. When school holidays arrived, he'd come home with glorious grade reports and a horde of young schoolfellows who thrilled his mother's ear with tales of his various successes. Naturally he concealed from his mother the successes that even then he'd begun to have with girls of easy virtue, who found him handsome and kind. He spent his holidays hiking through the lowlands; and in the vast high mountains that beckoned to him because they reached so high up and so far off into the indeterminate distance, he would spend not just hours but days in the gay company of rapturous dreamers like himself. He bewitched and beguiled them all.—In his good health and his mental and physical suppleness he resembled a god who seemed only to be spending a short time at

249

a classical gymnasium for his own amusement. When he was out walking, girls turned to look after him as though the glances he'd cast back in their direction were drawing them on. Upon his blond, handsome head he wore a blue student cap at a rakish angle. He was enchantingly frivolous. Once—the county fair was on, and the large square where usually herds of animals were rounded up was now covered with stands, huts, carousels, slides, pony rides—he substituted a bird rifle loaded with real shot for the ordinary harmless pop-gun at a shooting gallery where he could often be seen, since the girl who worked handing out the guns there had caught his fancy. The tiny bullet pierced the canvas wall of the booth and continued on into the wagon parked right behind it and missed injuring a small sleeping child by a hair's breadth. This was the wagon that served these itinerant folk as their family home. Naturally this prank came to light, several others were added to it as well, and the next time holidays came around, the report of the young pupil's grades contained an acrimonious comment from the school principal, who wrote the parents a generous letter simultaneously filled with ceremonious sentiments and the warm recommendation that they voluntarily take their child out of school, since his expulsion would otherwise be an imminent necessity. The reasons: senseless behavior, inciting others, being a bad influence, and irresponsibility. The letter went on about the principal's great responsibility, the duties to be fulfilled while also taking into consideration—in short, all those things that are always invoked in such cases: morality under siege, the need to protect those not yet corrupted, and so on—"

The man telling the story paused for a little while.

Simon took advantage of this opportunity to draw attention to his presence and said:

"Your story interests me from several points of view. Please, permit me to continue listening to you. I am a young man who has just turned his back on a career opportunity and could perhaps learn something from what you are relating; for it seems to me you always gain something by listening to a true story—"

The two men took a good look at Simon, but he seemed not to make too bad an impression on them, as the one who had been speaking invited him to go on listening if this gave him pleasure, and then he continued:

"The youth's parents were naturally filled with great consternation and even greater worry by his expulsion; for where might one find parents so indifferent that they might behave in their usual way under such distressing circumstances. At first they were of the opinion that it would be best to remove the rogue entirely from his scholarly course of study and have him apprenticed to learn a solid profession like machinist or metalworker. Even the word and land America entered their thoughts; given their son's predicament, it must have occurred to them of its own accord. But things came to pass quite differently. Once more the mother's tender heart prevailed as it had so often before when the father was determined to take drastic steps; she had her way. The young man was sent to study at a far-off, isolated institute where he was to prepare for the profession of schoolmaster. This was a French institute where the boy would have no choice but to behave in a fitting manner. At any rate by the time he'd served his sentence and left the place behind, he'd become a practical-minded, youthful teacher. He found a temporary post near his native town. He taught the children as best he could, and at home, when time allowed, read the French and English classics in their original tongues; for he had a truly wonderful talent for languages, and, secretly thinking of another career, he wrote letters to America seeking a post as a private tutor, an endeavor that bore no fruit, and lived a life divided between duty and a reserved unrestrainedness. Since it was summer, he often went with his pupils to bathe in the deep, swift-running canal. He'd join his pupils in the water to show them how to go about learning to swim. But one day the current caught hold of him and whisked him away so fast it looked as if he would surely drown. The pupils were already running back to town, shouting: 'Our teacher has drowned!' But the strong young man was able to fight his way free of the treacherous whirlpools and came home again. Some time later, though, he found himself in a different place: surrounded by mountains in a small but affluent village filled with companionable people who respected him less as teacher than as a human being. He was an accomplished pianist in addition to being a generally quite likeable fellow who, when in company with several others, was expert at twining the magical thread of conversation entirely about himself. A perfectly dear but no longer very young maiden fell so terribly in love with the teacher that she arranged for him to enjoy all manner of comforts and conveniences and introduced him to all the most influential people in the village. She came from an old family of officers whose ancestors had once performed military service in foreign lands. One day, as a memento, she gave him a charming little ornamental dagger that was surely by no means innocuous as a weapon and in its day may well have dripped blood occasionally. It was a splendid piece, and the good, dear woman presented this trinket with downcast eyes, perhaps suppressing a deep sigh. When with a romantically noble bearing he sat at the piano and played, she would listen, unable to take her eyes off him. Often she went ice-skating with him, since it was winter, upon the high-up small mountain lake, and both of them delighted in this pleasurable activity. Soon the young man wished to depart again, however, and all the more so as he felt all too vividly the warm, tempting bond that would so dearly have liked to fetter him to this village forever, but from which he must escape if he was still to possess the wish to aspire to some form of greatness in the world. So he went traveling, using the money of this woman, who was rich and found it gave her a melancholy and lugubrious joy to give him money without any restrictions on its use. And he traveled to Munich, where he lived the high life in the manner of the students there, then came home again, started looking for a post, and found one at a private institute that lay at the foot of a mountain range embellished with fir forests. There he was required to instruct young boys from all over the globe, the offspring of the wealthy, which he did for a time with great love and much interest, but then he got into trouble with his superior—the proprietor of the institute—and left. Then it was the turn of Italy, to which he journeyed as a private tutor, followed by England, where he was given two half-grown girls to instruct but only got up to mischief with them. He returned home again, his head haunted by wild notions and his heart, now empty, burning with helpless fantasies that had no claim on reality. His mother, into whose lap he longed to throw himself, died around this time. He was empty and inconsolable. He imagined immersing himself in politics, but for this he possessed neither sufficient general knowledge and cool-headedness nor the necessary polish and tact. He also wrote stock market reports, but senseless ones; for they were written poetically, products of an already destroyed mind. He authored poems, plays and musical compositions, painted and drew, but childishly, like a dilettante. Meanwhile he'd taken up a post again, though admittedly only for a brief time, and then a new post, and then a new one! He drifted around between a dozen different places, believing and finding himself betrayed and hurt everywhere he went, he lost his sense of propriety vis-à-vis his pupils and borrowed money from them, for he was always out of cash. He was still a slender, handsome man, gentle and elegant in appearance and still noble in his bearing as long as he had his wits about him. But this was now rarely the case. Nowhere on earth could he hold a job for long—he'd be sent away as soon as people got wind of his true nature, or else leave of his own accord, giving the most peculiar, cobbled-together explanations. This, of course, led to utter fatigue and enervation. From Italy he'd still been writing his brother enthused, idealistic letters. In London, where he suffered deprivations, he once walked into the business office of a prosperous silk merchant, an uncle of his, petitioning for support in his miserable circumstances; he was asking for money, perhaps not explicitly, but it was clear what he meant, and they sent him away, shrugging their shoulders, without giving him anything. How his beautiful, gentle human pride must have suffered when he found the courage to go beg alms from ignoble people. But what was he not forced to do, seeing the deprivations he suffered! One may speak of pride, but one must also remember all of life's happenstance, all the circumstances that can make it inhuman to keep demanding pride from a human being. And the one asking for help was soft. He'd always possessed a childishly soft heart, and it was a simple matter for the pain and regret over his lost chances to destroy this heart. One day, after all his wanderings, he turned up at home again: pale, fatigued and exhausted, with his clothes in tatters. His father no doubt received him heartlessly, and his sister as kindly as she dared before the eyes of their incensed father. It was his idea to find a little editorial job somewhere, and he meanwhile loitered about the city, where he gave all the girls rings and said he wanted to marry them. It was quite clear he was already becoming infantile. There were rumors, of course, and people laughed. Then he went away again, to take up a teaching post, but there it was demonstrated that for this world he was no longer suitable. One day he came into the schoolroom with one bare foot; one of his feet was missing its shoe and stocking. He no longer knew what he was doing, or else he was simply doing what his other, mad mind commanded him. During this same period he erased a demerit that had been recorded in his military service record, one he'd received years before on account of a serious failing on his part. As a result—since this bold crime came to light—he was locked up in prison. From there, since his mental state was soon apparent, he was transferred to a madhouse, where he still lives today. I know all these things because I was often his companion, over many years, both in civilian life and in the military, and I also helped bring him to the place where he is now, where he had to be brought unfortunately."

"How sad!" the other man said.

"Let's drink up and go," said the one who'd been telling this story, adding: "Some insist on claiming that the girls of ill repute he'd been involved with had destroyed him, but I don't believe this; I think people tend to exaggerate the bad influence these wenches can exert on a man. These things aren't quite so serious, and perhaps madness just ran in the family."

Simon leapt to his feet, violently agitated, his cheeks flushed with indignation:

"What's that you're saying? In the family? You're quite mistaken, my noble storyteller. Take a good look at me, if you will. Do you perhaps see in me as well something that might run in the family? Must I too be sent to the madhouse? This would indubitably occur if it ran in the family, for I too come from this family. That young man is my brother. I'm not at all ashamed to identify as my brother this merely unfortunate and by no means insidious individual. Is his name not Emil, Emil Tanner? Could I know this if he were not my own dear natural brother? Is his father, who is also mine, not a flour merchant by any chance, who also does a flourishing business in wine from the Burgundy region and oil from Provence?"

"Indeed, all that is true," said the man who'd been telling the story.

Simon went on: "No, it cannot possibly run in the family. I shall deny this as long as I live. It's simply misfortune. It can't have been the women. You're quite right when you say it wasn't them. Must these poor women always be at fault when men succumb to misfortune? Why don't we think a bit more simply about it? Can it not lie in a person's character, in a particle of the soul? Like this, and always like this, and therefore in the soul? Look, if you will, how I am moving my hand just now: Like this, and in the soul! That's where it lies. A human being feels something, and then he acts in such-and-such a way, and then collides with various walls and uneven spots, just like that. People are always so quick to think of horrific genetic inheritances and the like. To me that seems ridiculous. And what cowardice and lack of reverence to insist on holding his parents and his parents' parents responsible for his misfortune. This shows a lack of both propriety and courage, not to mention the most unseemly soft-heartedness! When misfortune crashes down upon your head, it's just that you've provided all that was needed for fate to produce a misfortune. Do you know what my brother was to me, to me and Kaspar, my other brother, to us younger ones? He taught us on our shared walks to have a sense for the beautiful and noble, at a time when we were still the most wretched rascals whose only interest was getting up to tricks. From his eyes we imbibed the fire that filled them when he spoke to us of art. Can you imagine what a splendid time that was, how ambitious—in the boldest, most beautiful sense of the word—our quest for understanding? Let's drink one more bottle together, I'm buying, yes that's right, even though I'm just an unemployed ne'er-do-well. Hey there!

Innkeeper, a bottle of *Waadtländer*, your finest. —I'm a person who knows no pity. I forgot all about my poor brother Emil long ago. I can't even manage to think of him, for you see, I'm the sort whose standing in the world is so precarious that he must struggle with all his might to keep on his feet. I don't want to fall down until such time as I'll no longer harbor thoughts of getting up again. Yes, that's when I might perhaps have time to think of these unfortunates and feel pity: when I myself have become pitiable. But this isn't yet the case, and for the moment when it comes to my own death I intend to go on laughing and jesting. In me you behold a fairly indestructible individual able to endure all sorts of adversity. Life need not be so sparkly to enchant my eyes—to me it's already sparkling. I generally find it quite beautiful and can't understand the ones who carp and call it ugly. Here comes the wine. Drinking wine always makes me feel so elegant. My poor brother is still alive! I thank you, sir, for having forced my memory to encounter this unhappy man today. And now, leaving all soft-heartedness behind: Let us raise our glasses, gentlemen: Long live misfortune!—"

"Why, if I might ask?"

"You go too far!"

"Misfortune is educational, that's why I'm asking you to raise your glasses with this glittering wine to drink a toast to it. And again! There. I thank you. Let me tell you, I'm a friend of misfortune, a very intimate friend, for misfortune merits feelings of closeness and friendship. It makes us better—that's doing us quite a good turn. Indeed, such an act of friendship must be reciprocated if a person wishes to behave respectably. Misfortune is our lives' cantankerous but nonetheless honest friend. It would be quite insolent and dishonorable of us to overlook this fact. At first glance we never quite understand misfortune, and for this reason we hate it the moment it arrives. Misfortune is a refined, quiet, unannounced fellow who always surprises us as if we were mere galoots and easily surprised. Anyone who has a talent for surprising others must certainly, regardless of who he is and where he comes from, be something quite extraordinarily refined. Not letting any forebodings come to light and then suddenly standing there; having about one not the faintest inquisitive, anticipatory taste or odor, and then all at once clapping a person chummily on the shoulder, addressing him in a familiar tone while smiling and showing him a pale, mild, all-knowing, beautiful face: This takes more skill than eating bread, requires other devices than those flying contraptions mankind has already started boasting about with grandiose, bombastic words even though they're still just half invented. No, it's destiny—misfortune—that's beautiful. It's also good, for it contains fortune, its opposite. It appears to be armed with weapons of both sorts. It has an angry crushing voice, but also a gentle mellifluous one. It awakens new life when it has destroyed old life that failed to please it. It spurs one on to live better. All beauty, if we still harbor hopes of experiencing beautiful things, is due to it. Misfortune allows us to grow tired of beautiful things and shows us new ones with its outstretched fingers. Isn't unhappy love the most emotional sort and thus the most delicate, refined and beautiful? Does not abandonment ring out in soft, flattering, soothing notes? Are these things I am saying all new to you, gentlemen? Well, they surely are new when someone says them aloud; for they rarely get said. Most people lack the courage to welcome misfortune as something in which you can bathe your soul just as you bathe your limbs in water. Just take a look at yourself when you've undressed and are standing there naked: What splendor: a naked healthy human being! What good fortune: being clothed no longer and standing there naked! It's already a stroke of fortune to have come into this world, and having no other good fortune than your health is still fortune that outsparkles and outshines all the finest gemstones, all the beautiful tapestries and flowers, the palaces and miracles. The most marvelous thing of all is health, this is a fortune to which nothing comparable can be added, unless a person in the course of time has become savage enough to wish he might become ill in exchange for a money-purse filled with cash. This plenitude of splendor and good fortune—if we are indeed inclined to see the naked, firm, pliant, warm members that have been given us for our journey through life as such a plenitude—must be counter-balanced, and thus we have misfortune! It can prevent us from bubbling over, it provides us with a soul. Misfortune educates our ears to perceive the beautiful sound that rings out when soul and body, intermingled and conjoined, respire as one. It turns our body into something bodily-soulful and gives our soul a firm existence at our center so that if we choose, we can feel our entire body as a soul, the leg as leaping soul, the arm as carrying soul, the ear as a hearing one, the foot as a nobly walking soul, the eye as the seeing one and the mouth as the kissing one. It makes us truly love, for where can we have loved if no misfortune was present? In dreams it's even more beautiful than in reality, for when we dream we suddenly understand the sensuality of misfortune, its enchanting kindness. Otherwise it's usually a hindrance, particularly when it arrives in the form of financial loss. But can this be a misfortune? Say we lose a banknote—what are we losing? Admittedly, this circumstance is highly disagreeable, but it's no cause to feel inconsolable for any longer than it takes to realize that this is hardly true misfortune. And so on! One could speak a great deal about this; and eventually grow weary of the topic—"

"You speak like a poet, sir," one of the men remarked with a smile.

"That may be. Wine always makes me speak poetically," Simon replied, "as little a poet as I am otherwise. I tend to lay down rules for myself and in general am hardly disposed to get carried away by fantasies and ideals, since I consider doing so ill-advised and presumptuous in the extreme. Take my word for it, I can be quite dry. It's also far from permissible to assume any person you happen to hear speaking of beauty is a poet with his head in the clouds, as seems to be your habit; for I do believe it can occur even to an in general coldly calculating pawn-shop broker or bank cashier to think of matters not pertaining to his money-grubbing profession. As a rule, we reckon too few individuals capable of sentimental reflection, for people haven't learned to look at each other. I've taken it upon myself to engage in bold, heartfelt conversation with every single person so that I'll quickly see what sort he is. You often make a fool of yourself using a rule like this in life, and occasionally you might even get your ears boxed—by a delicate lady, for example—but what harm does that do? I find it enjoyable to disgrace myself and maintain the conviction that the respect of individuals in whose eyes you lose face the moment you begin to speak openly isn't so terribly valuable that losing it is any reason to feel glum. Human respect must always suffer beneath human love. That's what I wanted to say in response to the somewhat derisive remark you made at my expense."

"I had no intention of hurting your feelings."

"In that case, how nice of you," Simon said and gave a laugh. Then he added abruptly after a moment's pause: "As for your story about my brother, by the way, it did in fact affect me. He's still alive, my brother, and scarcely anyone still thinks of him; for when a person steals away, above all to such a dismal place, he's soon stricken from people's memories. The unfortunate! You know, I could argue that it would only have taken the tiniest alteration in his heart, perhaps a single teeny jot more in his soul, and he'd have been a productive artist whose work would have enraptured humankind. It takes so very little to make a person strong—and so very little, on the other hand, to thrust him into utter misfortune. What use is there talking about it. He's ill, and he's standing now on the side where there's no longer any sunshine. I shall think of him more often now, for his misfortune is just too cruel. It is a misery even ten criminals wouldn't deserve, much less him, who had such a heart. Yes, misfortune is sometimes far from lovely, I now freely confess this. I should warn you, sir: I'm a defiant person and like to go about making wild claims, which is no way to act. My heart is at times quite hard—particularly when I see that others are filled with pity. I feel such an impulse then to start raging and laughing in the middle of that nice warm pity. Very bad of me, very very bad! As for the rest, I am by no means a good man, far from it, but I hope one day I will be. It was a pleasure for me to be permitted to speak with you. The happenstance is always the most valuable. I would appear to have drunk rather a lot, and it's so warm here in the barroom, that I feel an urge to go outside. Farewell, gentlemen! No, not *au revoir*. Absolutely not. I wouldn't dream of it. I feel no urge at all to see you again. There are still so many people I have yet to meet, I can't go about frivolously saying *au revoir*. That would only be a lie; for I have no desire to see you again unless it's by chance, and then it will be a pleasure for me, though only to a certain extent. I don't like to make a fuss and prefer to be truthful, this is perhaps my distinguishing characteristic. I hope it also distinguishes me in your eyes, though you are now gaping at me in a rather astonished and foolish way, as if you were insulted. Well, then, be insulted! Devil take it, what can I have said to insult you? Well?"

The innkeeper walked over and asked that Simon keep his voice down:

"It's best you leave now, it's time."

And Simon allowed himself to be steered gently out into the dark alleyway.

It was a deep, black, humid night. It was as if the night were some creeping entity making its way along the walls. From time to time a tall building would be standing there, a dark shape, and then another one would glow yellow and white as though

263

it possessed some magic power that made it luminous in the dark night. The walls of the buildings smelled so strange. Something moist and close emanated from them. Isolated lights now and then lit up a patch of street. Up above, the bold rooftops jutted out over the smooth high walls of buildings. The entire wide night seemed to have laid itself into this little tangle of alleyways in order to sleep here or dream. There were still isolated late-night individuals walking about. Here someone was staggering and singing as he went, another one was cursing loud enough to cleave the heavens in two, a third was already collapsed on the ground while a policeman's helmet came glinting from behind the corner of a building. When you walked, your steps resounded beneath your feet. Simon encountered an old, inebriated man who was reeling from side to side the full width of the street. It was a wretched and at the same time jolly sight: the way the dark, awkward figure was being thrust back and forth as though shoved by an nimble, invisible hand. Then the old, white-bearded man dropped his walking stick and wanted to pick it up from the ground—no doubt a daunting task for this drunkard, who appeared about to fall down himself. But Simon, seized by a smiling merciful sentiment, hurried over to the man and his stick, picking up the latter and pressing it into the man's hand, who murmured his thanks in the mysterious language of drunkenness, in a tone of voice that suggested he had cause to be still insulted. This sight immediately had a sobering effect on Simon, and he turned out of the old part of town into the newer, more elegant district. As he was crossing a bridge over the river that separated the two halves of the city from one another, he inhaled the strange perfume of the flowing water. He strode down the street in which he'd been addressed three weeks previous by that lady before the shop window, saw a light still burning in the home of his former mistress, reflected that she'd still been his mistress only yesterday, and then went on walking beneath the trees until he came to the broad dark lake lying there before him, appearing to be asleep across its entire splendid expanse. Such sleep! If an entire lake could sleep like that with all its bottomless depths—that was an impressive sight. Yes, it was certainly a strange thing, barely comprehensible. Simon went on gazing out at it for a while until he began to long to sleep himself. Oh, he would sleep excellently now. It would come over him so peacefully, and tomorrow he would remain lying in bed a long time, tomorrow was Sunday after all. Simon went home.

The next morning he didn't wake up until the bells were ringing. From his bed, he noted that out of doors it must be a splendid blue day. The light flashing in the windowpanes suggested a glorious morning sky high up over the alleyway. Gazing at the wall of the building opposite, one was conscious of bright-golden intimations. It was difficult to think how dark and dismal this blotchy wall must look under a sky thick with clouds. One gazed at it for a long time, imagining what the lake must look like now with all the sails upon it in the golden blue morning weather. Certain mountain meadows, certain views and certain benches beneath the lush green trees, the forest, the streets, the promenades, the meadows upon the back of the broad mountain with its full complement of trees, the rampant green slopes and forest ravines, the spring and woodland brook with its large stones and water singing softly when you sat down beside it to be lulled to sleep. All these things could be seen quite clearly when Simon gazed over at the wall that after all was just a wall, but today was reflecting an entire vision of a blissful human Sunday, just because something like a breath of blue sky was bobbing up and down above it. And of course the bells were ringing all this time with their familiar notes, and bells, yes, they know how to awaken images.

Still lying there in bed, he resolved to be more industrious from now on, to study something, a language for example, and in general to start living a more regulated existence. He'd let so much slip through his fingers! Learning surely brought a person great pleasure. It was so lovely to engage in these heartfelt, vivid imaginings of how it would be to keep studying and studying assiduously, never once emerging from one's studies. He sensed a certain human maturity within him: And how much lovelier all this studying would be if approached with the sum of this already attained maturity. Yes, that's what he would do now: study, set himself tasks, and take pleasure in uniting both teacher and pupil within his own person. What about, for example, taking up a melodious language such as French? "I would learn words and imprint them firmly on my memory. My constantly active imagination would come to my aid. Tree: l'arbre. With all my feelings I would see this tree. Klara would come to mind. I'd see her in a white dress with wide folds beneath a broad, shady, dark green tree. In this way many things, things I had almost already forgotten, would return to me. My mind would grow stronger and more active in grasping. It blunts you if you never study anything. How sweet this smallness is, this beginner's stage! I'm now finding this prospect vastly appealing and don't understand how I could have been defiant and sluggish so very long. Oh, all sluggishness is just defiance, an insisting on one's own knowledge and the putative superiority of this knowledge to that of other people. If only we knew how little we knew, things might still turn out well. Hearing the sound of the foreign word, I would think of the German one more warmly and spread its meaning out more fully before me in my thoughts, and so even my own language would become a new, richer sound filled with unfamiliar images. Le jardin: garden. Here I would think of Hedwig's country garden that I helped plant when spring arrived. Hedwig! In a flash it would all come back to me, the things she said, did, suffered and thought during all the days I spent with her. I have no cause to forget people and things so quickly, above all my sister. After we'd already planted the garden it snowed again one night, and we were terribly worried that nothing would grow. That would have been quite a blow, for we were hoping to harvest a great many splendid vegetables from our garden. How lovely it is to be able to share one's worries with another person. Just imagine how it must be to suffer the pains and fight the battles of an entire people! Yes, all these things would come to me if I were studying a language—and many others as well, so many that I can't even imagine them yet! Just to study, to study, who cares what! I'll also immerse myself in natural history, all on my own, without a teacher, using some inexpensive book that I can go and buy right away tomorrow, since today is Sunday, so of course all the shops are closed. All of this is quite feasible, clearly. Why else is one alive? Could it be I've stopped thinking I owe myself anything at all? I've got to pull myself together—it's certainly high time."

And he leapt out of bed as though he felt the need to get started with his new plans right this minute. Quickly he got dressed. The mirror told him that he looked quite nice indeed, which satisfied him.

As he was about to go downstairs, he came upon Frau Weiss,

his landlady and room-letter. She was dressed all in black and held a small prayer book in her hand, having just returned from church. She gave a cheerful laugh as she beheld Simon and asked whether he hadn't wanted to go to church himself.

He responded that he hadn't been to church in many years.

The entire kindly face of the woman flinched as she heard these words, which she found unsuitable coming out of a young man's mouth. She wasn't angry, for she was by no means an intolerant holy roller, but she couldn't restrain herself from telling Simon he wasn't really doing what he should. Besides which, she added, she didn't believe him; he didn't have that look. But if it were in fact true, she hoped he'd keep in mind that it wasn't right never to go to church.

Wishing to keep her in a good mood, Simon promised he'd go to church soon, whereupon she gave him a quite friendly look. Meanwhile he was on his way downstairs, not letting her delay him any longer. "A nice woman," he thought, "and she likes me, I can always tell when women like me. How amusingly she pouted because of church. The sort of pout that covers the entire face always looks good on women. I like to see such a thing. Besides which she respects me. I shall make a point of preserving her respect. But I shan't speak with her too much or often. This will make her wish to engage me in conversation, and she'll be happy whenever I do say something to her. I like women of her sort. She looks wonderful in black. How sweet the little prayer book looked held in her voluptuous hand. A woman who prays actually becomes even more sensually appealing. How beautifully this pale hand stood out against the black of her sleeve. And her face! Well, that's enough now. In any case it's most agreeable to have something sweet in reserve, an auxiliary supply, as it were. This gives you a sort of home, a place of refuge with another person, a recourse, a magic spell—for I cannot live without there being a certain magic present. She still had a desire to go on speaking with me, back there on the stairs. But I broke off our conversation; for it pleases me to leave unfulfilled wishes behind with women. This allows one to inflate one's value rather than decreasing it. The women themselves, incidentally, wish for you to act in such a way."

The street was swarming with people in their Sunday best. The women were all wearing light-colored, white dresses, the girls wore colorful broad ribbons on their white skirts, the men were simply dressed in lighter-colored summer fabrics, boys wore sailor suits, dogs were trotting along behind a couple of people; in the water, confined in a wire enclosure, swans swam about, and a few young people leaned over the railing of the bridge, observing them attentively; other men were walking rather solemnly to their polling places to cast their votes in the election, bells were ringing for the second or third time, the lake shimmered blue and swallows flew high above in the air, over rooftops all agleam in the sunlight; the sun was first of all a Sunday-morning sun, then a sun pure and simple, and then a special sun for a pair of artist's eyes that were no doubt present somewhere in the crowd; here and there, the trees of the municipal parks burgeoned with green, spreading their crowns; in the darker world beneath the shade trees, still more women and men were strolling about; sailing vessels flew before the wind upon blue distant water, and lethargic boats tied to barrels were rocking near the shore; still more birds were flying here, and people were standing still, gazing at the blue, whitish distance and the mountain peaks in that distant sky were like precious, white, all but invisible lace, and the whole sky like a light-blue dressing gown. Everyone was busy watching, chatting, feeling, showing, pointing, noticing and smiling. From a pavilion the sounds of a band came darting like fluttering, twittering birds from amid the foliage. Simon too was walking there in all the green. The sun cast bright spots upon the path through the awning of leaves, as well as on the grass, on the bench where nursemaids were rocking perambulators back and forth, on the hats of the ladies and the shoulders of the men. Everyone was chatting, gazing, glancing, calling out greetings and promenading back and forth. Elegant carriages rolled along the street, now and then an electric streetcar whizzed past, and the steamboats were whistling, you could see their smoke flying away, heavy and thick, between the trees. Out in the lake young people were bathing. Admittedly you couldn't see them as you strolled up and down beneath the foliage, but you knew there were bare bodies swimming about, luminous in the liquid blue. What wasn't luminous today? What wasn't flickering? Everything scintillated, flashed, shone and swam in colors and dissolved into sounds before your eyes. Simon said to himself several times in a row: "How beautiful a Sunday is!" He looked into the eyes of the children and all the people, he gazed at everything blissfully and, bewildered, now he glimpsed a beautiful isolated gesture, and now the picture as a whole appeared before his eyes. He sat down beside an apparently still-young man upon a bench and looked the man in the eyes. A conversation began to unfold between the two of them, for it was so easy to begin talking when everyone was so happy.

The other man said to Simon:

"I'm a nurse, but at present I'm nothing but a loafer. I come from Naples, where I cared for the sick at the International Hospital. It's quite possible that ten days from now I'll be somewhere in the American interior, or else in Russia; they send us wherever nurses are needed, even to the South Sea Islands. It's one way to see the world, quite true, but your own homeland becomes so unfamiliar, I can't express this clearly enough. You for example no doubt have always lived in your own native land, it constantly surrounds you, you feel encircled by familiar sights, you do your work here, you're happy here and surely experience adversity here as well, never mind, but at least you're allowed to feel connected to a soil, a land, a sky, if I may say it thus. It's lovely to be bound to something. You feel at ease, you have the right to feel at ease, and every reason to expect the understanding and love of your fellow men. But me? Nothing of the sort! You see, I've grown too wicked for my own narrowly circumscribed homeland—perhaps also too good, too all-comprehending. I can no longer share the sentiments of my countrymen. I now understand their preferences just as little as I do their anger and dislikes. In any case, I'm a stranger there, and when you've become a stranger, people do hold it against you. And certainly they're right—for it was wrong of me to become estranged. Even if my views about so many things are now more worldly and intelligent, what use is this if they serve only to offend my countrymen's sensibilities?

They must be wicked views if they cause offense. You have to hold a country's customs and values sacred if you don't wish to become a stranger there one day, as has happened now with me. In any case, I'll soon be traveling far from home again, to wherever my patients are—"

He smiled and asked Simon: "What do you do?"

"I'm an outlandish figure in my own homeland," Simon replied. "Actually I'm a copy clerk, and you can no doubt imagine how great a role I therefore play in my fatherland, where the copyist is pretty much at the very bottom of the social hierarchy. Other young people intent on pursuing commercial trades go off traveling to distant lands for educational purposes and then return home with a sack full of knowledge to find that honorable positions have been reserved for them. I however—take my word for it—shall always remain in this country. It's as if I were afraid that in other countries no sun would shine, or an inferior one. I'm bound fast to this place and am always seeing new things amid the old, perhaps this is why I'm so unwilling to leave. I'm going to the dogs here, I can see that perfectly well, and nonetheless I must, or so it seems to me, go on breathing beneath the sky of my homeland if I wish to live at all. Naturally I don't enjoy much respect, I'm generally seen as a wastrel, but this doesn't matter at all to me, not one bit. Here I am and shall no doubt remain. It's so sweet to remain. Does nature go abroad? Do trees wander off to procure for themselves greener leaves in other places so they can come home and flaunt their new splendor? Rivers and clouds are always leaving, but this is a different, more profound sort of leave-taking, without any returning. It's

273

not really a departure anyhow, just a flying, flowing way of being at rest. Such a depature—how beautiful it is, if I may say so! I'm always looking at the trees and telling myself: They aren't leaving either, so why shouldn't I be permitted to remain? When I find myself in a city in winter, I feel tempted to see it in spring: Seeing a tree in winter, I wish to see it resplendent in the springtime, sending out its first enchanting leaves. After spring, the summer always comes, inexplicably beautiful and quiet, like a glowing huge green wave arising from the unfathomable depths of the world, and of course I wish to enjoy the summer here, do you understand me, sir, here, where I saw the spring blossoming. Take, for example, this little strip of meadow or lawn. How sweet it looks in early spring when the snow upon it has just melted beneath the sun's rays. It's this tree and this lawn and this world that matter: In other places, I don't think I'd even notice summer. What it comes down to is that I have a truly devilish desire to remain right where I am, along with all sorts of not terribly amusing reasons that preclude my undertaking a journey abroad. For example: Would I have any money for travel? As you surely know, a person needs money to travel by rail or boat. I have money enough for perhaps twenty more meals; but I don't have the money to travel. And I'm glad not to have any. Let other folks go traveling and come home more clever. I'm clever enough to be able to die here with dignity one day, in the land of my birth."

After a brief moment of silence, during which the nurse gazed at him intently, he went on:

"What's more, I haven't the least desire to pursue some splendid career. What means the most to some people means least to me. I cannot in God's name value careerist ambitions. I want to live, but I don't want to go running down some career path—supposedly such a grand enterprise. What's so grand about it: people acquiring crooked backs at an early age from stooping at undersized desks, wrinkled hands, pale faces, mutilated workday trousers, trembling legs, fat bellies, sour stomachs, bald spots upon their skulls, bitter, snappish, leathery, faded, insipid eyes, ravaged brows and the consciousness of having been conscientious fools. No thank you! I prefer to remain poor but healthy and forego a stately dwelling in favor of an inexpensive room, even if the view is of the darkest of alleyways; I'd rather live with financial difficulties than be faced with the difficult decision of where to travel on summer holidays to restore my ruined health, though to be sure I currently enjoy the respect of only a single person, namely myself. But this is the one whose respect is worth the world to me; I am free and can always, when necessity commands, sell my freedom for a certain length of time so as to be free again after. It's worth remaining poor for the sake of freedom. I have enough to eat; for I possess the talent of feeling sated after eating very little. I fly into a rage whenever someone approaches me with the words 'lifetime position' and all the presumptions implied therein. I wish to remain a human being. In a word: I love what is risky, unfathomable, floating and uncontrolled!"

"I like you," the nurse said.

"I certainly had no intention of inducing you to like me, but it nonetheless pleases me if you do, as I've been speaking quite freely and frankly. Incidentally, there was no call for me to be so testy in speaking of others. That's always stupid—you have no right to disparage circumstances simply because they don't happen to be to your liking. One can always leave, I can always leave! But no, things are quite to my liking. My situation pleases me. People please me just as they are. For my part, I use all the means at my disposal to induce my fellow men to like me. I'm hardworking and industrious when I have a task to perform, but I won't sacrifice the pleasure I take in the world for anyone's sake, at most I'd sacrifice it for our sacred fatherland—the occasion for which, however, has to this day failed to present itself, a circumstance I expect to continue. Let them pursue their careers, I can understand this, they wish to live in comfort and see to it their children will also have something, they're good providers whose actions are nothing if not laudable; so let them also leave me to do as I please, to pluck life's pleasures as I see fit—this is something everyone tries to do, every one of us, just not in the same way. How wonderful it is to be mature enough to let others do as they will in their own way, as best they know how. No, if a person has faithfully discharged his duties for thirty years, he is certainly no fool when he reaches the end of his career, as I said before in my testiness; rather, he is a man of honor who has earned the wreaths that will be placed on his grave. You see, I don't want any wreaths on my grave—that's the whole difference. My end is a matter of no interest to me. They're always telling me, other people, that I shall have to pay bitterly one day for my cockiness. Well then, so I'll pay, and I'll learn then what it means to pay for something. I like to learn things and so I'm not nearly as apprehensive as people who worry about their nice smooth futures. I'm always afraid some life experience might pass me by. In this sense I'm as ambitious as ten Napoleons. But now I'm hungry, I'd like to get something to eat, would you join me? It would be a pleasure for me."

And the two of them went off together.

After his rather wild speech, Simon had suddenly grown soft and gentle. With enchanted eyes he gazed at the beautiful world, the round, opulent crowns of the tall trees and the streets where people were walking. "Dear, mysterious people!" he thought to himself and raised no objection when his new friend touched his shoulder with his hand. It pleased him that the other was becoming so chummy: This fit quite nicely, it was both a bond and a release. He saw everything with laughing, happy eyes, at the same time thinking: "How beautiful eyes are!" A child was looking up at him. To be walking along beside a companion like the nurse struck him as a great novelty, something he'd never before experienced, but agreeable in any case. On the way, the nurse purchased a portion of fresh beans from a greengrocer's and some bacon at a butcher shop, and he invited Simon to come have lunch with him, an offer that was willingly accepted.

"I always cook myself," the nurse said when the two of them had reached his apartment, "it's become a habit with me. I enjoy cooking, take my word for it. Just wait and see how tasty you'll find the beans with this lovely bacon. I also knit my own socks, for example, and do my laundry myself. You save a lot of money this way. I've learned to do all these things, and why shouldn't such tasks be suitable for a man in exceptional cases if he happens to have a taste for them? I don't see what could be shameful about activities of this sort. I also make my own house slippers, like these you see here. Such a task certainly requires a bit of care. Knitting wrist warmers for winter or making vests doesn't cause me any particular difficulty. When one is always so alone and on journeys like myself, one picks up the oddest habits. Make yourself at home, Simon! May I call you by your first name? I feel we're becoming friends—"

"Yes of course, please do!" And Simon blushed, which he found utterly incomprehensible.

"I felt fond of you right from the beginning," said the nurse, whose name was Heinrich, "one need only look at you to be convinced that you are a dear chap indeed. I should rather like to kiss you, Simon—"

Simon was finding the air in the room oppressively close, and he got up from his chair. He guessed what sort of man it was who was looking at him with such odd tenderness. But what harm could it do. "I'll go along with it," he thought. "I see no reason to be uncivil to this Heinrich, who is otherwise so nice, over such a small thing!" And he yielded up his mouth and let himself be kissed.

It was just a kiss, after all!

Besides which he found it charming—it suited the state of softness in which he found himself to allow these tender liberties. Even if this time it was only a man! He felt quite clearly that Heinrich's strange affection for him required the most delicate and provisionally indulgent consideration, and found himself incapable of dashing the man's hopes, even though these hopes happened to be unworthy ones. Had he any cause to feel indignant? "Not at all," Simon thought to himself, "for the time being I'll let him do as he pleases—it goes well with everything else taking place around me!"

The two of them spent the evening wandering from one bar to another, the nurse being a fairly passionate drinker, since he didn't know what else to do with his free time. Simon found it appropriate to follow his lead in every sense. There in the tiny, stuffy bars, he made the acquaintance of individuals who played cards with unbelievable endurance. The card game appeared to constitute a world of its own to these people, one in which they were unwilling to be disturbed. Others just sat there all evening long clenching the long pointed stalk of a cigar between their teeth without otherwise calling notice to themselves except by the fact that when the nub of their cigar got too short to be pressed between their lips, they would stick it on the tip of their pocket knives to be able to smoke it all the way down to the most miniscule brevity. An emaciated, ravaged-looking pianist told him that her sister was a bad sister but a celebrated concert singer, and that she'd long since broken off all familial ties with her. Simon found this comprehensible, but he behaved with delicacy and refrained from telling her he found it comprehensible. This person, he felt, was more unfortunate than morally corrupt, and he always honored misfortune, and corruption he saw as a consequence of misfortune, and therefore it also required at least a certain decorousness. He saw short, fat, horribly sprightly innkeepers' wives who approached their guests with untoward familiarities of all sorts while their husbands dozed on sofas and in armchairs. Often a splendid old folksong would be sung by a person who masterfully executed the modulations of key and voice that were part of these old songs. How beautiful and melancholy they sounded, you couldn't help sensing how many a rough vibrant throat must already have sung them in bygone days and long before. One man was constantly telling jokes, a short young fellow wearing an old, large, wide, tall, deep hat he must have purchased in a junk shop somewhere. His mouth was lubricious and his jokes no less so, but they forced you to laugh whether you wanted to or not. Someone said to him: "You there, I admire your wit!" But the witty man thrust aside this foolish admiration with well-feigned astonishment, and this was truly a joke that might have brought pleasure even to a learned man. The male nurse told all the people who came to sit beside him that he was basically too flawed and at the same time, when he thought it over more carefully, too good for his native country. Simon thought: "How idiotic!" But then the nurse gave a far more appealing report on the topic of Naples, saying for example that the museums there contained wonderful remnants of ancient human beings, and that one could see by looking at them that these ancestors far outstripped us in height, width and girth. These people had arms nearly the size of our legs! Now that must have been a race of women and men! What were we by comparison? Merely a degenerate, crippled, atrophied, attenuated, longitudinally and latitudinally cracked, torn and shredded, emaciated generation. He also gave a charming portrait of the Gulf of Naples. Many listened to him attentively, but many were asleep and, being asleep, didn't hear a thing.

It was very late when Simon got home, and he found the downstairs door locked from within; as he didn't have his key with him, he brazenly rang the doorbell, for he was in that condition which inevitably causes one to behave inconsiderately. A window flew open at once following the jangle of the bell, and a white figure, no doubt the woman in her nightgown, threw down the key wrapped in heavy paper.

The next morning, rather than being angry, she smiled at him with the friendliest "Good morning!" and said not a word about the disturbance in the middle of the night. Simon therefore decided it would be inappropriate to mention it, and so, half out of delicacy, half out of laziness, he offered no apology.

He left and went looking for the nurse. Monday morning was once more resplendent. People were all at work, and so the streets were empty and bright, and when he went into the nurse's room, he was still lying sleepily in bed. Today Simon noticed on the walls something he'd failed to observe the day before, a number of rather saccharine Christian wall decorations: little angels with ruddy little heads cut out of paper along with plaques containing adages framed in mysterious dried flowers. He read all the adages, some of them were profound and thought-provoking, maxims perhaps older than eight old people taken together, but there were also slick, newfangled sayings that read as if they'd been mass-produced in a factory. He thought: "How strange this is! Everywhere, in so many individual rooms and chambers, wherever you might be and regardless of your present business, you are constantly seeing these fragments of old religions hanging on the walls, fragments that in part say a great deal, in part not so much, and in part nothing at all. What does the male nurse believe? Surely nothing! Perhaps religion for many people nowadays is nothing more than a half-measure, a superficial, unconscious matter of taste, a sort of interest and habit, at least with men. Perhaps a sister of the nurse decorated the room this way. I could believe that—girls have more personal grounds for piety and religious contemplation than men do, whose lives have always been in conflict with religion, always unless they happened to be monks. But a Protestant minister with his snow-white hair, his mild patient smile and his noble gait is and remains a beautiful sight when he strides through a lonely forest clearing. In the city, religion is less beautiful than in the countryside, where peasants live whose very way of life has something deeply religious about it. In the city, religion is like a machine, which is unfortunate, whereas in the country one perceives the belief in God as being just the same as a field of blossoming grain, or like a huge lush meadow, or like the delightful swell of lightly curving hills behind which a house stands hidden, containing quiet people for whom contemplation is a sort of friend. I don't know, to me it seems as if the minister in the city lives too close beside the stock market speculator and the godless painter. In the city, the belief in God lacks the necessary distances. Religion here has too little sky, it smells too little of the soil. I'm not putting it very well, and besides, what use is any of this to me? Religion in my experience is a love of life, a heartfelt attachment to the earth, joy in the present moment, trust in beauty, belief in mankind, a feeling of carefree pleasure during revelries with friends, the desire to ponder and a sense of not being responsible for misfortune, smiling when death arrives and showing courage in every sort of undertaking life has to offer. In the end, a profound human decency has become our religion. When human beings maintain decency in their dealings with each other, they are maintaining it before God. What more could God want? The heart and all the finer sentiments can together produce a decency that might well be more pleasing to God than dark fanatical belief, which can only disconcert even the Divine One himself, so that in the end He'll no doubt wish not to hear the prayers thundering up to His clouds any longer. What can our prayers mean to Him if they come bawling up so clumsily, presumptuously, as if He were hard of hearing? Mustn't you imagine Him possessing infinitely acute ears if you can picture Him at all? I wonder whether the sermons and the peals of the organ are agreeable to Him, the Ineffable One? Well, He'll surely just smile at our efforts, dubious as they may be, and hope that it will occur to us some day to leave Him in peace a bit more often."

"You look so pensive, Simon," the nurse said.

"Shall we go?" Simon asked.

The nurse had made himself ready, and the two of them walked the steep paths together that led up the mountainside. The sun was glowing hot. They went into a small, opulently overgrown beer garden and ordered a morning pint. When they were about to leave again, the innkeeper's pretty wife encouraged them to stay, and indeed they remained until evening. "And this is how you can drink away a bright summer's day without even noticing," Simon thought with a feeling comprised of dizzy pleasure and a gentle, lovely, melodious ache. The colors of the evening amid the foliage were making him drunk. His friend gazed deeply and with desire into his eyes and wrapped one arm around his neck. "Actually this is ugly," Simon thought. On the path, the two of them addressed flamboyant words to all the women and girls they met. The workers were just coming home from work, people who still walked in a hale, spry way, their shoulders rocking strangely from side to side as though breathing sighs of relief. Simon discovered the most splendid figures among them. When they reached the forest atop the mountain, still warm though it was already tinged with darkness, the sun was just setting down below in the distant world. They lay down among the green leaves and bushes and were silent, just breathing as they lay there. And then came what Simon had been expecting, his comrade's approach, which, however, left him cold.

"There's no point," he said, "please stop," and then, "listen, cut it out!"

The nurse allowed himself to be mollified, but he was aggrieved; people came by and they had to get up and leave the place. Simon thought: "Why am I spending the day with such a person?" But immediately thereafter he confessed to himself that he took a certain pleasure in this man, despite his strange, unlovely inclinations. "Another person might despise the nurse," he thought further as they set out for home, "but I am the sort who considers each and every person, his virtues and vices notwithstanding, worthy of my interest and love. I shall never arrive at the point of despising other people, or rather, I despise only cowardice and vacuousness, but it's not hard for me to find something interesting about depravity. Indeed, it sheds light on a great many things, allows us to look more deeply into the world, it makes a person more experienced and helps him judge more leniently and rightly. One must get to know all things, and one makes a thing's acquaintance only by touching it courageously. To avoid some person out of fear—I'd consider that unworthy. Besides, having a friend is priceless! What does it matter if the friend is somewhat unusual—"

Simon asked:

"Are you angry with me, Heinrich?"

But Heinrich wasn't saying anything. His face had assumed a dour expression. Once more they arrived at the beer garden whose delicate outlines now lay in darkness. Colorful, shimmering lanterns lit up the dark foliage at several points, sounds and laughter were emanating from within, and both of them, drawn by the lusty fiery life there, went back in, where the innkeeper's wife gave them a friendly welcome.

The red dark wine was sparkling in the light glasses, the shimmering lights conjoined with the heated faces, the leaves of the bushes touched the dresses of the women, it seemed so natural to be spending the warm summer night in a susurrating garden, drinking, singing and laughing. From the railway station at the bottom of the hill, the noise of the trains rose up to the revelers' ears. A wealthy, tall, red-cheeked wine merchant's son applied himself to a bold philosophical conversation with Simon. The male nurse was constantly contradicting everyone because he was vexed and disgruntled. The waitress, a slim brunette, sat down beside Simon and allowed him to pull her close to him to kiss her. She suffered the kiss willingly, with proud curved lips that looked as if made to sip wine, laugh and kiss. The nurse's mood was becoming ever blacker, and he wanted to leave, but the others prevented him. Then someone, a young, swarthy, dark-haired lad with a green hunter's hat, sang a song while his girl, nestled close against his chest, leaned in close to sing along with him in soft happy notes. "This sounds so intoxicating, dark and Mediterranean," Simon thought: "Songs are always melancholy, at least the beautiful ones are. They remind us that it's time to go!" But he remained a long time still in the nocturnal garden.

—16—

For the entire rest of that week, Simon carried on this otiose social intercourse with the nurse, with whom he'd get into arguments and then make up again. He played cards like someone who'd been doing so for years, and rolled billiard balls around in the middle of the warm day while everyone possessed of hands was working. He saw streets filled with sunlight and alleyways in rainy weather, but always through a windowpane, with a glass of beer in his hand; made long, useless, wild speeches morning, noon and night among all manner of strangers, until finally he saw he had nothing more to live on. And one morning he didn't go to visit Heinrich but instead made his way to a room where any number of young and old men sat at desks writing. This was the Copyists Office for the Unemployed, where people came who, owing to their particular life circumstances, found themselves in such a position that securing employment in a regular place of business was out of the question. Individuals of this sort worked for meager day-wages here, copying out addresses with hasty fingers beneath the strict supervision of a supervisor or secretary—business addresses for the most part, in lots of one thousand, for which large firms contracted with the office. Writers brought in their scribbled manuscripts, and female students their all but illegible dissertations so as to have them either typed out on the typewriter or copied in a smooth clean hand. People who didn't know how to write but had something they needed written down brought their documents here, where the work was quickly seen to. Cake-counter ladies, waitresses, laundresses and chambermaids had their letters of recommendation copied out tidily before proffering them for examination. Benevolent associations turned in thousands of yearly reports that had to be addressed and disseminated. The Association for Natural Healing had multiple copies made of the invitations to their folksy lectures, and professors had no end of work for the copyists, who in turn were happy to have the work. This entire copying enterprise was supported by yearly subventions from the local government and headed by an administrator—himself formerly unemployed—for whom the post had been created to give him a suitable occupation for his old days. He was the scion, so to speak, of an old patrician family and had wealthy relatives on the city council who didn't want to sit back and watch one of their family members go to ruin under shameful circumstances. And so this man became the king and protector of all the vagabonds, lost souls and hard-luck cases, and he discharged these duties with a casual dignity, as if he'd never in all his wild days, some of which he'd spent on the road in America, tasted the bitterness of deprivation.

Simon made a bow before the administrator of the Copyists Office.

"What do you want?"

"Work!"

"Today there's nothing. Come back tomorrow morning, perhaps we'll have something suitable for you then. For now, write down your name, permanent residence, place of birth, profession and age along with your current address on this sheet of paper, and then come back tomorrow at eight on the dot, otherwise there won't be any work left," the administrator said.

He was in the habit of smiling as he spoke, and speaking through his nose. What's more, he always assumed an almost scornfully mild-mannered tone in his dealings with the unemployed—not intentionally, that's just how it happened to come out. His face, sunken and ravaged, was the color of cold white lime and terminated in a ragged gray beard with a point to it, as though the beard itself were a pointy scrap of his face hanging down. His eyes lay deep in their sockets, and the man's hands bore witness to ill health and physical ruin.

The next morning at eight, Simon was already installed at the Office, and a few days later he'd accustomed himself to his co-workers. These were all people who at some point in their lives had succumbed to some form of dissolution and lost the ground under their unsteady feet. There were people there who because of some serious offense committed years before had spent time in jail. An old, very handsome man was known to have spent years in prison because of a heinous crime against morality he'd committed against his own flesh and blood: his daughter, who denounced him to the judge. In all the time Simon observed him, his silent strange face remained free of all expression, as though silence and listening were native to that face and had become a necessity. He worked calmly, peacefully and slowly, was handsome, looked at you calmly when you looked at him, and appeared to be not in the least conscious of some tormenting memory. His heart seemed to be beating as quietly as his old hand was working. No trace of a grimace could be remarked in any of his features. He appeared to have atoned for and washed away everything that might ever have disfigured or soiled him. His clothes were tidier than those of the administrator, although he must have been poor. His teeth and hands were curiously well groomed, as were his shoes and clothes. His soul appeared to be calm and unusually pure. Simon thought of him: "Why not? Can't sins be washed away, and should a jail sentence destroy an entire life? No, one sees neither a sin once committed nor a jail term served when one looks at this man. He appears to have forgotten both of them completely. There must be goodness and love in this man, and great strength, really a huge amount of it—but all the same: how strange!"

Embezzlement, theft, fraud and vagrancy all had their representatives in the Copyists Office. Present as well were the merely unfortunate, greenhorns who'd been duped by life and foreigners from abroad who simply found themselves without a bite to eat because their hopes had been dashed. Surely there were also notorious idlers and eternal malcontents. Every combination of culpability and bad luck could be found there, along with that sort of frivolity which takes pleasure in being so out-of-pocket. Simon might have used this opportunity to make the acquaintance of man in his various guises, but he wasn't much thinking about observing other people, as he himself was kept as busy as all the others filling out forms and sinking as if in a river amid the life and bustle of the Copyists Office with all its cares, labors, little incidents and questions. Someone who's sunk beneath the surface of a thing doesn't think so much about the thing itself as about his own physical needs, just like all the others. Everyone here was copying away to earn what they would soon have to invest in food and drink if they wished to go on living. Their earnings flowed down their throats, from hand to mouth. Simon also managed to buy himself a straw hat and a pair of cheap shoes. But when he thought of the rent for his room, he had to confess to himself that he wasn't in a position to find the cash for this as well. Yet he was always tired and happy in the evenings when he'd finished writing. He'd go walking then, in the company of one of his fellow scribes, through the city streets with his head held high, absentmindedly smiling at the people walking past. He didn't even have to make an effort to achieve a beautiful proud posture; he stood up straight without even trying, his chest broadened and stretched like a tightly-drawn bow the moment he walked out the door of the Office and into the air. He suddenly felt he was the born lord and master of his limbs and consciously attended to each of his own footsteps. He now no longer kept his hands in his trouser pockets, that would have struck him as undignified. In fact, he no longer slouched at all but rather strolled with measured attentiveness, as if he were only just now, in his twenty-first year of life, beginning to cultivate a beautiful firm gait. Looking at him, a person was not to think of poverty; he was merely to sense that this was a young man who was just coming from work and now permitting himself an evening stroll. The swift, bustling world of the street enchanted his eye. When a carriage with a pair of dancing, delicate horses passed by, he fixed his gaze on the gait of the trotting animals, not deigning to cast even a brief glance at the gentlefolk sitting in the wagon, as though he were a connoisseur of horses, interested only in them. "How agreeable this is," he thought. "A person really must learn to master his gaze and send it only to places where it is seemly and manly for his eyes to rest." He cast sidelong glances at a number of women and had to laugh inside to see the sort of impression this made. And all the while he was daydreaming, as always! Except that now he gritted his teeth while dreaming, no longer allowing himself an indolent weary posture: "Even if I'm one of the poorest devils, it wouldn't occur to me to let this be evident in my person; on the contrary, financial woes practically oblige one to assume a proud comportment. If I were rich, I might possibly allow myself a certain negligence. But under these circumstances, it's out of the question, as a person must be conscious of maintaining an equilibrium. I'm dog-tired, but I cannot help thinking: Others have cause to feel weary as well. A person doesn't live merely for himself, but for others as well. You have an obligation to cut a stalwart exemplary figure as long as you're being observed, so that those of lesser courage can take you as a model. You should give the impression of carefree solidity, even if your knees are trembling and your stomach is warbling up into your throat out of emptiness. Such things are a source of pleasure to a young man who's just growing up! The clock has not yet struck twelve, not for any of us; after all, any person lying on the ground impoverished enjoys the prospect of rising up again. I've a hunch that a proud free bearing can itself draw life happiness to a person like an electrical current, and it's certainly true that you feel richer and more exalted when you walk about with dignity. Should you happen to be in the company of a second ill-dressed poor devil, as is presently the case, all the more cause to walk with head erect, thereby gently and vigorously apologizing, as it were, for the other's inferior hairstyle and posture before people who may be taken aback to see two individuals who comport themselves so differently strolling along as cozy as can be, clearly intimate friends, in this elegant street. A thing like this brings you respect, fleeting as it might be. Certainly it's charming to think you stand out agreeably from a companion who doesn't yet quite have what it takes or never will. Incidentally my companion is an older, unfortunate man, the former owner of a basket-weaving shop, who has sunk in life thanks to all sorts of adversity and now is a copyist for daily hire, just like me, except that I don't look entirely like a copyist and day laborer but rather more like a mad Englishman, whereas my comrade looks like someone painfully longing to return to former better days. His gait and the way his head is constantly, sweetly, touchingly wobbling speak of his misfortunate in quite shameless words. He's an older man and no longer wishes to impress; all he wants is to hold himself a little bit upright. Me he impresses; for I know his pain and understand what a heavy burden he carries. I feel proud to be walking beside him through an elegant part of town, and press myself impertinently close to him to demonstrate my unabashed affection for his paltry suit. I'm receiving many astonished glances, many a splendid eye is looking at me in a strangely quizzical way, which can only amuse me—to so-and-so with all that! I speak loudly, emphatically. The evening is so beautifully suited to speaking. I worked all day long. It's a splendid thing to have worked all day and then in the evening be so beautifully weary and at peace with all things. To have not a worry, scarcely even a thought. To be allowed to stroll along so frivolously, with a sense of having done no harm to any man. To look around to see if you're meeting with approval. To feel you're now a bit more deserving of love and respect than before, when you were just a malingerer whose days sank one behind the other into an abyss and drifted away on the air like smoke. To feel much, so very much, on a gift of an evening such as this! To see the evening as a gift, for this is what it is to those who sacrifice their days to work. Thus one gives and receives in turn—"

Simon was noticing more and more that the Copyists Office was a small world all its own within the larger world. Envy and ambitions, hate and love, preferential treatment and honesty, vehement and modest natures manifested themselves here in microcosm, where only the pettiest advantages were at stake, just as clearly and unmistakably as anywhere people struggled to make a living. There were no sentiments or urges that could not find themselves actualized here, if only on a paltry scale. Glorious troves of knowledge, to be sure, were of little use in the Office. A bearer of such knowledge could put it to use here at most improvisatorially, it could boost his standing, but it wouldn't help him to acquire a better suit. Several members of the copyists fraternity spoke and wrote three languages to perfection. They were put to work translating, but doing so didn't earn them any

294

more than the loutish address writers and manuscript copiers received—the Copyists Office did not allow any one individual to rise within its ranks, that would have contradicted its own goals and purpose. After all, the point of its existence was to permit the unemployed to eke out a meager existence, not to disburse high, outrageous salaries. A person had to consider himself fortunate to find work at all at eight in the morning. Often enough it happened that the administrator would say to a group of waiting men: "Terribly sorry. Unfortunately there's nothing today. Come back at ten. Perhaps some jobs will have come in by then!" and then at ten: "You'd better try again tomorrow morning. Not too likely anything else will turn up today." The ones thus rejected, a group that included Simon on more than one occasion, then walked slowly and gloomily, one after the other, back down the stairs and onto the street where they remained standing for a little while in a nice round group, as though feeling the need to reflect first for a moment, only then to disperse again in all directions, one after the other. It was no pleasure to go rambling about the city streets with no money in one's pocket, each of them knew this and each one thought: "What will it be like when winter comes?"

Sometimes elegantly dressed people with dainty manners came to the Copyists Office to ask for work. To them the administrator was in the habit of saying: "It's my impression that you'd be better suited to the hustle and bustle of worldly life than to the Copyists Office. Here a person must sit still all day long, bent over and diligently working if he wants to earn his pittance. I'm speaking to you openly in this way because I have a feeling this work would not in fact suit you. Nor do you appear to be suffering doleful, needy poverty. I, however, am charged with giving employment first and foremost to the poor, that is, to those whose clothes might well be hanging off them in tatters as proof of their squalor. You, on the other hand, look far too grand, it would be a sin to employ you here. My advice to you is to mingle with other elegant people. It seems you've failed to recognize the gloom of the Copyists Office if you come here wearing such a cheerful expression to ask for work, as though you were going to a ball. Here it is customary to make clumsy defiant bows, or, most commonly, none at all, but you bowed to me a moment ago like a perfect man of the world. That's no good, I have no use for you, I have neither employment that might satisfy you nor a world in which you might fit. You will have no difficulty finding a position as a shop or hotel clerk, should you have other intentions than just seeking adventure in this city, as I am inclined to suspect. Here a young man will experience only discouragement, but no other sorts of adventure. A person who comes here knows why he has come. You appear most assuredly not to have known this. Your entire person is an affront to my workers, you'll have to admit this if you cast so much as a single look about the room. Just look at me: I too have seen the world, I know every metropolis, and I too would not be sitting here if I were not compelled to do so. A person who comes here has already experienced misfortune and all manner of adversity. Those who come here are the good-for-nothings, beggars, rogues and shipwrecks: in a word, the unfortunate. Now I ask you: Are you such a one? No, and therefore I now ask that you depart at once from this establishment, which contains no air that you would be capable of breathing for long. I know the creatures who belong here! Know them better perhaps than suits me! And now farewell!"

And with a wave of his hand he would smilingly dismiss those people who had no business in the Copyists Office. The administrator possessed poise and education, and he enjoyed showing them off on occasion before such happenstance and maladroit visitors who came more out of curiosity than need.

Beside the Copyists Office flowed a quiet, green, deep and old canal, a former fortress moat and the connecting link between the lake and the flowing river which in this way was given lake water to take along with it on its journey to distant seas. In general this was the quietest part of town; there was something secluded and village-like about it. When the ones who were sent away now tramped back down the stairs, they liked to sit for a while upon the railing at the edge of this canal, which then looked as if a row of large, strange, foreign birds were perched there. There was something philosophical about this, and indeed, many a one gazed down into the green dead water world and pondered the unrelentingness of fate just as fruitlessly as a philosopher is wont to do sitting in his study. The canal had something about it that invited one to dream and reflect, and the unemployed had ample time for this.

At the same time, the Copyists Office was a job market for the mercantile trade. A gentleman or lady, for example, might walk into the Office, go into the administrator's office and ask to have a man, that is, a temporary worker for his or her place of business. Then the administrator would appear in the doorframe, looking over his charges, and after considering for a while would call one man by name: The person in question had then found work for a short while, perhaps eight, one, two or fourteen days. It was always an envy-arousing event when someone was called by name, for everyone was eager to work on the outside, since the pay was then higher and the work more interesting. Besides which, such a man who found work with kindhearted employers would be given a nice snack mornings and evenings, which was by no means to be despised. And so there was always a certain competition for such positions and an ogling of the one selected. Many believed they were always unjustly overlooked, while others, on the other hand, thought it advantageous to court and flatter the administrator and his under-official to attain what they so yearned for. It was approximately like a pack of trained dogs leaping up to snatch at a sausage that was constantly being jerked out of reach on a string, each dog firmly convinced that the others had no business going after the sausage, though without, of course, being able to substantiate that belief. Here too one man would growl at another who'd succeeded in snatching the prize, much as in the greater spheres of trade, scholarship, art and diplomacy, where things aren't done so very differently, just with more cunning, arrogance and culture.

Simon also worked a few times on the outside—as abbreviated in the copyists' patois—but he didn't have much luck at it. Once he was sent to the devil by his boss, a shifty, rather brutal real estate and property agent who nearly fancied himself God almighty, because he'd been reading the newspaper when he should have been writing; and another time he hurled his pen right in the face of his employer, a wholesale fruit and vegetable merchant, with the words: "Do it yourself!" The fruitseller's wife had insisted on bossing Simon around; so he simply broke things off; for, as he saw it, this female was merely trying to hurt and humiliate him, which in the end he didn't see any reason to put up with; at least that's how he felt about it.

—17—

Several weeks of marvelous summer passed in this way. Simon had never before experienced so marvelous a summer as this year, when he was spending so much of his life on the street looking for work. Nothing came of his efforts, but at least it was beautiful. When he walked in the evening through the modern, leaf-trembling, shadowy, light-flickering streets, he was always unceremoniously approaching people and saying something foolish, just to see how it would feel. But all the people just looked at him in bewilderment—they didn't say anything. Why wouldn't they speak to the one walking and standing there, why didn't they ask him, their voices low, to come with them, go into a strange house and there engage in some activity only people of leisure indulge in, people who, like himself, have no other life purpose than watching the day pass by and evening arrive, in full expectation that evening will bring miracles and fantastical deeds? "I'd be prepared to undertake any deed, provided it was bold and required some derring-do," he said to himself. For hours he sat upon a bench listening to the music that came murmuring from some regal hotel garden, as if the night had been transformed into soft notes. Nocturnal womenfolk passed by the solitary watcher, but they only needed to take a good look to know how things stood with the young man's wallet. "If only I knew a single person whom I could touch for a bit of money," he thought. "My brother Klaus? That wouldn't be honorable; I'd get the money, but accompanied with a faint, sad reproach. There are people one can't go begging to because their thoughts are too pure. If only I knew someone whose respect weren't so important to me. No, I can't think of anyone. I care about everybody's respect. I'll have to wait. You don't actually need so much in summer, but winter's on its way! I'm a bit scared of winter. I have no doubt that things will go badly with me this coming winter. Well, then I'll go running about in the snow, even if I'm barefoot. What harm can come of it. I'll keep going until my feet are on fire. In summer, it's so lovely to rest, to lie upon a bench beneath the trees. All of summer is like a warm fragrant room. Winter is a thrusting open of windows, the winds and storms come howling and blustering in and that makes you have to move about. I'll soon give up my laziness then. It'll be fine with me, come what may! How long the summer seems to me. It's only been a few weeks I've been living in summer, and it already seems so long. I think time must be sleeping and stretching out as it sleeps if you're always having to think what to do next, just to get through the day on your few coins. Besides which, I believe that time spends the summer sleeping and dreaming. The leaves on the tall trees are growing ever larger, at night they whisper, and in the daytime they doze in the warm sunshine. I, for example, what do I do? When I have no work, I spend entire days lying in bed with the shutters closed, in my room, reading by candlelight. Candles have such a delightful smell, and when you blow them out, a fine, moist smoke floats through the dark room, and then a person feels so peaceful, so new, as if resurrected. How will I manage to pay my rent? Tomorrow it's due. Nights are so long in the summer because you stroll and slumber all day long, and the moment night falls, you awaken from all sorts of confused buzzings and stirrings and begin to live. Now it would seem to me almost sinful to sleep through even a single summer night. Besides, it's too humid to sleep. In summertime your hands are moist and pale as if they sense the preciousness of the fragrant world, and in winter they're red and swollen as if angry about the cold. Yes, that's how it is. Winter makes you go stamping around in a rage, whereas in summer you wouldn't be able to find any cause for anger, except perhaps the circumstance that you're incapable of paying your rent. But this has nothing to do with the beautiful summer. And I'm not angry anymore either, I think I've lost the talent for flying into a rage. It's nighttime now, and anger is such a daylight phenomenon, as red and fiery as a thing can be. Tomorrow I'll have a talk with my landlady—"

The next morning he inserted his head into the door of the room where his landlady lived and asked with intentionally precise intonation whether he might have a word with her, should she have the time.

"Of course! What is it?"

Simon said: "I can't pay you this month's rent. I won't even try to explain how embarrassing this is to me. Anyone can say that in such a case. On the other hand, I assume it goes without saying that you consider me capable of striving to find a way and means to acquire a substantial sum of money such that I can eradicate my debt as quickly as possible. I know people who'd give me money if I so desired, but my pride forbids me to borrow money from people whom I prefer to have beholden to me. From a woman, to be sure, I'd accept a loan, in fact I'd do so willingly, for I have quite different sentiments regarding women, sentiments that must be judged by a different sort of honor. Would you, Frau Weiss, be willing to advance me the money, first of all the money to cover the rent, and then a small additional sum to cover my living expenses?—Is it now your impression that my behavior is outrageous? You shake your head. I believe you have some trust in me. You can see how I'm blushing at my own shameless request, you see me standing here not without embarrassment at this moment. But I'm in the habit of seizing resolves rather quickly and carrying them out promptly, even if this impulsiveness should take my own breath away. I'm happy to accept a loan from a woman because I'm incapable of deceit where women are concerned. With men I can lie when circumstances require, lie mercilessly, take my word for it. But with women never. Do you really wish to loan me so much? I could live on that for half a month. By then, many things will improve in my current situation. And I haven't even thanked you yet. You see, that's the sort I am. Only rarely in my life have I expressed feelings of gratitude to another person. Where gratitude is concerned, I'm a bungler. Well, I should also say, to be sure, that I've always, whenever possible, disdained acts of benevolence. A benevolent act! I truly feel at this moment what benevolence is. I really shouldn't be accepting this money."

"Just listen to you!"

"Well, I'll take it then. But don't fret about not having it returned. I'm temporarily overjoyed about this money. Money is something only a dunce could despise."

"Are you leaving already?"

Simon had already gone back out the door and returned to his room. He found it uncomfortable, or at least acted as if he found it uncomfortable, to go on speaking about this matter. Besides, he'd accomplished what he'd set out to do, and he wasn't fond of giving long apologies or making promises when he'd asked someone for a favor and had it granted. If he himself were one day to be the giver, he wouldn't demand excuses or assurances; it wouldn't occur to him to do so. You should either have trust and sympathy and therefore give, or else just turn your back coldly on the petitioner because you find him distasteful. "She found me not at all distasteful, in fact I noticed that she gave me the money with a sort of eager joy. It's all a matter of bearing when you wish to achieve an aim. It gives this woman pleasure to make me beholden to her, probably because in her eyes I'm a tolerable person. No one likes to give anything to disagreeable persons because you don't want to have them beholden to you; after all, an obligation like the repayment of a debt brings people together, it rubs shoulders, binds, shares confidences and closeness, remaining always at one's side. How utterly unenviable it is to have distasteful debtors—such people sit practically astride their creditors' necks, it makes you want to forgive their debts just to be rid of them. It's delightful when someone thoughtlessly, swiftly gives you something; what better attestation could there be to the fact that you still have people around who find you agreeable—"

304

Popping the money he'd received into his vest pocket, he walked over to the window and beheld, down below in the narrow alleyway, a woman dressed all in black who seemed to be looking for something, for she kept tilting her head to look up, and in one such moment her eyes met those of Simon. These were large, dark eyes, true female eyes, and Simon involuntarily thought of Klara, whom he hadn't seen in such a long time now; indeed he'd almost forgotten her. But it wasn't Klara. This beautiful creature in the deep alley with her elegant, opulent dress offered a strange contrast to the dismal filthy walls between which she was slowly walking. Simon would have liked to call out to her: "Is it you, Klara?" But already the figure was vanishing around a corner, and nothing of her remained in the alleyway except the faint scent of melancholy that beauty always leaves behind in dismal places. "How beautiful it would have been, and how fitting, just at the moment when she looked up, to have thrown her a large dark red rose that she would have bent down to pick up. She would have smiled at this, astonished to be met by such a friendly greeting in so squalid an alleyway. A rose would have suited her well, as a pleading, crying child suits its mother. But how would a person who's just had to avail himself of others' generosity come to be in possession of expensive roses, and how could it be foreseen that at precisely nine in the morning a beautiful female figure would pass through this alleyway—which is the darkest of all alleys—a woman who appears to be the most elegant creature I've ever set eyes on?"

He went on for quite some time daydreaming about this woman who'd reminded him so strangely of his forgotten, vanished Klara, then he left the room, raced down the stairs and through the streets, spent his day doing nothing, and then toward evening found himself in one of the outlying districts of this sprawling city. Here workers lived in relatively attractive tall apartment buildings; but when you looked at these buildings more closely, you were struck by a certain austere squalor creeping up the walls, peering out of the monotonous cold rectangles of the windows and even perching on rooftops. The landscape of woods and meadows that began here formed a strange contrast with the tall but shabby building blocks that more disfigured than graced the area. Beside them, several lovingly built, low old cottages could be seen nestled in the landscape like children in their mother's warm lap. Here the land formed a forest-topped hill beneath which the train line ran through a tunnel, having just emerged from the jumble of buildings. Evening light fell on the meadows; standing here, one felt one was already in the country, that the city and all its hubbub had been left behind. Simon was not put off by the ugliness of the workers' housing; to him the entire admixture of city and country presenting itself here in a strange, graceful tableau was beautiful. When he walked a bare stone street and felt the warm meadow close beside him, this struck him as most peculiar, and when immediately afterward he went striding between meadows upon a narrow, earthen path, what harm did it do to know this was actually municipal and not country soil? "The workers have it good here," he thought: "through every one of their windows they have a green forest view, and when they sit on their small balconies, they enjoy a good, strong, spicy breeze and an entertaining panorama featuring hills and vineyards. Even if the new tall buildings are smothering the old ones and will eventually force them out altogether, you must nonetheless consider that the earth never stands still and that people must always remain in motion, even if it's in what appears at present to be a less than charming form. An area is always beautiful because it always bears witness to the life present both in nature and architecture. To build a settlement in a pretty meadow and woodland region might seem at first somewhat barbaric, but in the end every eye will make its peace with the unification of building and world, finding all sorts of enchanting views to glimpse from between the new walls, and forget its irritably critical condemnation, which after all never gives rise to better things. We need not compare the old and new buildings like architectural scholars; we can take pleasure in both sorts, in both the modest and the vainglorious. When I see a building standing here, there's no cause to think that if I find it insufficiently attractive I can just knock it down, for it stands rather firmly on its foundations, housing a great many sentient persons, and is therefore a respectable entity whose creation was the work of many diligent hands. Those who search for beauty must oftentimes feel that the mere search for beauty in this world gets you only so far, that there are other things worth finding besides the good fortune of being able to stand before a charming antique. The struggle of the poor for a bit of peace—I'm referring to the so-called Workers' Question—is itself quite an interesting matter, so to speak, and must certainly engage a stalwart mind more than the question of whether a house is well or poorly situated in a landscape.

What smooth-tongued idlers this world contains! To be sure: Every thinking head counts, and every question is priceless, but it's surely more admirable and does more honor to our heads to address life questions first and more delicate artistic questions later. Of course questions of art are sometimes life questions as well, but life questions are questions of art in a far higher and nobler sense. Naturally I'm thinking this way now because the first question on my mind is how I shall go on existing, given that my sole employment is copying out addresses for paltry day-wages, and I cannot sympathize with the snobbery of art since at the moment it strikes me as the most irrelevant thing on earth; and indeed just consider, what is art compared with Nature, which dies and awakens over and over again? What means does art have when it wishes to portray a blossoming fragrant tree, or the face of a human being? I admit I'm musing somewhat insolently now, condescendingly—or rather furiously con-*ascendingly*, from down in the depths inhabited by people who have no money. The thing is, I'm critical but at the same time feel quite melancholy because of my lack of funds. I've got to get some money, it's quite simple. Borrowed money isn't money; money must be earned or stolen or received as a gift—and then there's one thing more: evening! In the evening I'm generally tired and dispirited."

As he was thinking in this way, he'd been walking up a short but fairly steep street and now paused before a building from which a woman's head was looking out at him through an open window. Looking into the woman's eyes, Simon thought he was gazing into a distant sunken world, but then a wonderfully familiar voice called down to him: "Oh, Simon, it's you! Do come up!"

It was Klara Agappaia.

When he'd leapt up the stairs, he beheld her sitting at the window in a heavy dark red dress. Her arms and breast were only half concealed by the luxurious fabric. Her face had grown paler since he'd seen her last. In her eyes a deep fire was burning, but her mouth was pressed closed. She smiled and held out her hand to him. In her lap lay an open book, apparently a novel she'd started reading. At first she was unable to speak. It seemed to be causing her shame and effort to ask questions and relate things. She seemed to be struggling to shake off the sense of alienation she now felt before her young former friend. Her mouth appeared to weep each time it tried to open and soften. Her beautiful, long, voluptuous hands seemed to have taken over the task of speaking, at least until her mouth was able to shake off its self-consciousness. She didn't look Simon up and down the way people examine friends they haven't seen in a long while; instead she gazed into his eyes, whose peaceful expression calmed her. Once more she seized his hand and at last said:

"Give me your hand, let me be to you what I am to my son, who understands me as soon as he hears the rustle of my garments from the next room, who grasps me with a single glance, to whom I needn't say a word, not even a whispered one, to share my secrets with him; whose sitting, coming, going, standing and lying down tell me all his feelings exist only with the goal of understanding his mother; before whom a person must bend down to the ground, to his feet, to tie his shoes better when the laces have gotten loose; to whom one gives a kiss when he's been courageous and good; for whom one keeps all secret things open; from whom one wouldn't even know how to keep a secret; to whom one gives everything even though he's a little traitor and has managed to neglect his mother for a long, long time, just like you, even though he's been able to forget her, like you. No, you never managed to forget me. No doubt you often tried to shake me off in defiance, but whenever a woman crossed your path who looked even a tiny bit like me, you imagined you were seeing me, thought you'd found me again. Didn't this make you tremble, didn't you feel, as you experienced this deceptive encounter, as if suddenly above a bright regal staircase carved in stone a pair of doors had swung open to admit you to a chamber filled with the joy of reunion? What a joyous thing it is to see someone again. When we've lost one another on the street or in the countryside and then a year or so later find each other again, quietly, without further ado, on such an evening when the bells are already tolling out a premonition of this reunion, we press each other's hands and no longer think of the separation and the cause of this long digression. Leave your hands in mine! Your eyes are still just as kind and beautiful. You remain identical to yourself. Now I can tell you:

"When all of us, Kaspar, I and you, had to leave the forest house last summer, do you remember, and your brother then disappeared, and I didn't know where to, I rented myself an elegant room down in the city, yearning for the two of you and for a long time inconsolable. Toward winter everything around me appeared suffused in a red glow, I forgot everything and hurled myself into the maelstrom of worldly pleasures, for I still possessed part of my fortune, a small part, but still a lot by local standards. I used them up, and received in exchange the realization that often one needs a bit of rapture to be able to keep oneself more or less afloat upon the waves of life. I had a box at the theater, but the theater interested me far less than the balls where I could show how beautiful and spirited I was. The young men swarmed around me and I saw nothing that might have prevented me from feeling contempt for them all or from subjecting them to my whims. I thought of you and your brother, and often wished, standing at the center of all that emasculated swarming, to see your peaceful faces and open manner. Then a dark black-haired man approached me, a student at the polytechnical university, heavy and clumsy in appearance, a Turk with large forceful eyes, and he danced with me. After this dance, he possessed me body and soul, I was his. For us women, when we are whirling about in worldly raptures, there is a particular sort of man that can vanquish us only on the dance floor. If I'd encountered him anywhere else, I might well have laughed at him. From the first moment on, he behaved towards me as though he were my master, and while I marveled at his insolence, I couldn't manage to defend myself against it. He commanded me: now like this, and now like this! And I obeyed. We women can achieve stunning feats of obedience when we feel moved. We accept everything then, and wish, perhaps out of shame and fury, for our beloved to be even more brutal than he is. No matter how brutally he treats us, it isn't enough. To this man, the last bit of money I had to my name was quite simply his property, and I agreed and gave it to him, I gave him everything. When eventually he'd had his fill of oppressing, tyrannizing, preying on and exploiting me, he went away, back to his native land, to Armenia. His slave—I—did nothing to hold him back. I found all his actions appropriate. Even if I'd loved him less than I did, I'd still have let him go, for my pride would have prevented me from trying to detain him. And so it was simply my duty to obey him when he ordered me to help him prepare his departure: The love in me was happy to obey. I wasn't mortified to be kissing him goodbye, this man who scarcely even deigned to look at me any longer. He gave voice to the hope that he would later, when his circumstances allowed, bring me to his country to make me his wife. I could tell it was a lie, but I felt no bitterness. With regard to this man, any unlovely feeling in me was utterly impossible. I have a child by him, a girl, she's sleeping there in the next room."

Klara paused for a moment, smiled at Simon, and then went on:

"I was forced to seek employment, and found a job working for a photographer as his receptionist. Coming into contact with so many people there, I was courted and even proposed to several times, but I brushed them all aside with a smile. All men thought, looking at me: 'There's something so tender about her, so domestic-motherly, she'd be a good one!' But I didn't become anyone's 'good one.' My position allowed me certain expenditures, at least I was able to keep all my lovely dresses, which has proved useful to this day. My boss was a man I was able to respect, which made my work much easier, and I performed my work as if caught up in a quiet pleasant dream. I'd accustomed myself to flashing a quite particular smile when clients came in, and this made me quite popular, everyone thought I was kind, and I attracted customers, which prompted my employer to increase my salary. At the time I was almost happy. Everything vanished before me in a haze of lovely sweet memories. I felt the approach of my labor pains, and this contributed to my melancholy-happy mood. It was snowing, the streets were completely enveloped in flakes. And when in the evening I walked through the snowy streets, I thought of you brothers, you and Kaspar and a great deal of Hedwig, to whom I paid grateful homage in my thoughts and feelings. I only allowed myself to write her a single time. She never answered. 'But that's for the best,' I thought. I found myself too for the best when I thought such things. I was becoming more and more fulfilled by everything, and I walked always with slow steps, feeling every footstep as an act of human kindness. Meanwhile I gave up my elegant room in the center of town and found lodgings here where you now see me. In the morning and evening I'd ride the electric streetcar back and forth, always attracting the attention of the other passengers. There was something odd about me, I myself could feel this. Many unconsciously starting talking to me, a few wishing just to exchange a word or two, and others to make my acquaintance. But acquaintances no longer had much appeal for me. I thought I could tell everything in advance, and this gave me such a decisive, rejecting but also gentle feeling that soothed me. Men! How often they spoke to me. They resembled curious children who wanted to know what I did, where I lived, whom I knew, where I ate lunch and how I was in the habit of spending my evenings. They appeared to me like innocent, rather importunate children; that's what I was like at the time. Never did I respond harshly to a single one of them; I had no need to, for not one man allowed himself liberties: To them I was a lady who simultaneously attracted them and left them cold. Once a small, clever-looking girl spoke to me, this was Rosa, the Rosa you know. She revealed all her sufferings to me and her life story, the two of us became friends, and now she's gone and married, though I advised her not to. She often visits me, me, the Queen of the Poor!" —

Again Klara fell silent for a moment, looking at Simon with childish amusement, and then went on speaking:

"The Queen of the Poor! Yes, that's who I am. Do you not see how regally your Klara is dressed? This is a dress left over from my ball wardrobe: with a low-cut back! After all, I do have to keep up appearances given my status as regent. My adherents like to see me dressed like this, they have a taste for majesty, the splendor of a ball gown makes quite a singular impression in this realm of stained gray female garments. One must stand out, dear Simon, if one wishes to have influence, yet please do keep listening to everything in order. What an expert, pleasant listener you are. No one listens like you! It's one of your good qualities. It feels so natural, so lovely to be telling you things: When I moved here to this remote neighborhood, I slowly but surely learned to love the poor, the ones who've been thrust to the other, darker side of the world, the masses, as this entire world of longing and hardship is dismissively called. I saw I could be needed here, and without forcing the matter or making any fuss about it, I found a place for myself here, and now in fact I am needed. If I were to leave again today, these people, these womenfolk, children and men would wail with sorrow. At the beginning I was put off, actually repulsed by their squalor, but then I saw that this squalor was not so hideous when seen from close up as from a stiff grandiose distance. I taught my hands and even my mouth how to touch these children whose faces were not the cleanest. I accustomed myself to shaking the rough hands of workers and day-laborers, and quickly noticed the gentleness with which these people took my hand. I found many things in this world that reminded me of you two, of you and Kaspar. A great many delicate and hidden things finally enticed me to become the mistress of and advocate for these people. Doing so was simultaneously easy and difficult. The womenfolk for one thing! How much effort it cost to convince them of their infirmities and horrific failings such that they gradually were seized by a desire to free themselves from their disgrace. I introduced them to the blessings and pleasures of cleanliness and I saw that after their long, distrustful hesitation they came to take great pleasure in it. The men proved easier to influence: I was beautiful, and so they obeyed me better, and were more talented in grasping my simple lessons. Simon! If you only knew how happy it makes me to have become a secret educator of these poor people! How little one needs to know to find people even more impoverished in knowledge whom one can guide. No, knowledge itself is not enough. Here one needs the courage and the desire to take a stand vigorously, to shore up one's stand with clemency and pride, and to approach others with passion. I accustomed myself to a way of speaking that explained all the learning I possessed and could impart in a readily graspable way, using the sorts of expressions loved by the humble and humiliated. And so I became their ruler by adapting myself to their thoughts and feelings, though often these were not to my taste. But with time I found them to my taste. A person who exerts influence simultaneously has a talent for being imperceptibly influenced by those he's influencing. One's heart and habits can easily bring this about. And then one day as I lay in bed, painfully awaiting the arrival of my child who is asleep there in the next room, they came to me, the women and girls, they tended and cared for me and showered me with kindnesses until I was able to get up again. During this time, their menfolk asked after me with concern, and when they saw me again, they seemed delighted to be finding me even more beautiful than before. Thus did they honor their queen. This was in the springtime. Still rather weak from giving birth, I sat in my room covered with flowers, for all of them brought me flowers, as many as they could manage. A wealthy young man from the neighborhood often visited me and I allowed him to sit at my feet; I saw this as a sort of tribute, and it was tender of him. One day he implored me to become his wife. I pointed to the child, yet this only encouraged him to repeat his proposals, which struck me as rather peculiar, over the following days. He told me the whole story of his empty restless life, and I felt pity for him and promised him my hand in marriage. A mere gesture or glance from me is enough to satisfy him, and he loves me in such a way that I am conscious of it at every moment. If I say to him: 'Artur, it's impossible,' he turns pale and I must fear some calamity. He's in a position of utter helplessness before me, and I lack the strength to make him unhappy. Besides, he's rich, and I need money for my people, and he'll give it to us. He does everything I want. He won't allow me to ask for things, instead he asks me to command him. That's how it is with him. He's about to come now, I'll introduce you to him. Or would you rather go? You look as though you're about to leave. Well, go then! Perhaps it's better this way. Yes, it's better. He would be suspicious. In this regard he's quite awful. He's perfectly capable of banging his head against the wall until it bleeds if he sees me with a young man. Besides, I don't want to have anyone else here when you're here. And when others are here, you shouldn't be. I want to have you all to myself, to myself alone. There's so much more I must say to you about how all of this came to be. We say so much, but are these the right things?—Go now. I know you'll come back again soon. Besides, I'll write to you. Leave me your address. Well then, farewell!"

On the staircase as he was going out, Simon passed a dark fleeting figure. "That must be this Artur," he thought and went on his way. Night had fallen. He set out upon a small narrow dirt path, turning around after he'd gone a few steps: The window was now closed, and dark red curtains had been drawn behind it, luminous in a curiously dismal way in the light of a lamp that had no doubt just been lit. A shadow moved behind the curtain, it was Klara's shadow. Simon walked on, slowly, deep in thought. He was in no hurry whatever to arrive back in the city. No one was waiting there for him. The next day he would be writing at the Copyists Bureau again. It was high time he at last put his shoulder to the grindstone, worked, earned some money. Perhaps he might finally find a post again somewhere. He laughed as he thought the word "post." When he arrived in town, it was already quite late. He went into a music hall that was still open, hoping to amuse himself, but there wasn't much of interest. He saw the act of a comic whom he'd have liked to see vanish as an ordinary person among the crowd watching him. In fact this comic deserved, based on his performance, to have his ears boxed. But no! Soon Simon was feeling the most emphatic pity for this poor wretch who was having to contort his legs, arms, nose, mouth, eyes and even his poor bony cheeks, only to fail after all these torments to achieve his goal of being comical. Simon would have liked to shout out "Boo!" and then again nothing more than "Alas!" One could clearly tell, just looking at the man, that he was honest, decent and not particularly cunning; but this made what he was doing on stage all the more horrid, for this was an activity suitable only for people who must be equally supple and dissolute if they wish to present a rounded, pleasing tableau. Simon had an inkling that this comic had perhaps, not long ago, still been practicing some quiet solid profession from which, no doubt because of some error or misdeed, he'd been ejected. The entire man made a profoundly shameful, repulsive impression on him. Then a petite young singer came on stage dressed in the short tight uniform of a hussar officer. This was better, for what this girl had to offer verged on the artistic. Then came a juggler who, however, would have done better extracting corks from bottles than balancing bottles on the tip of his nose, which he went about in an utterly childish, tasteless fashion. He placed a burning lamp upon his flat head and was insolent enough to expect the audience to see this as artistic. Simon stayed long enough to hear a little boy singing a song that pleased him, and then he immediately left the establishment on this good note, going back out to the street.

Hardly any people were still walking about. There appeared to be a dispute in progress in a side street, and indeed, as Simon drew closer, he witnessed a violent scene: Two girls were striking one another, one using her fists, the other a red parasol. This battle was illuminated by a lone, melancholy lantern that in part lit up the girls' faces. Of their clothing and hats only rags remained, and all the while the two of them were screaming, not so much out of fury as pain, and this pain wasn't so much on account of the blows as out of a leftover sense of shame at seeing themselves act in such a miserably bestial way. A horrific battle but only a short one, it was soon ended by a constable. He led away both girls along with an elegantly dressed gentleman who appeared to have been the cause of the dispute. A postman had played the role of snitch, and now he was putting on airs. The girls now directed the full force of their fury at the postman, who as a result beat a quick retreat.

Simon went home. But when he reached the alley where he lived, he caught sight of a group of people who were laughing and shrieking, and it turned out to be a woman who was attracting the attention of these night owls. She held a switch with which she was striking a drunkard who appeared to be her husband, whom she had just dragged out of some little bar. All this while she was shrieking, and as Simon approached, she cried out to him in loud shrieked words, lamenting what a scoundrel she had for a husband. All at once from the top of the building beneath which the group was standing, a stream of water came shooting out, maliciously wetting the heads and clothes of those standing below. It was a custom in this corner of the old part of town to pour water on nocturnal revelers who got too noisy. This custom might well have attained a venerable, hallowed age, but it was nonetheless always shockingly novel and striking for those on whom it was brought to bear. Everyone directed imprecations in the direction of the woman standing up above in a white mantilla gazing down at them like a malevolent wicked spirit. Simon more than all the others shouted up to her: "What in the world are you thinking of up there, you woman or man in the window frame? If you have too much water, pour it on your own head instead of other people's. Your head may well be in more need of it. What sort of manners is that, dousing the street in the post-midnight hour and treacherously plunging people into a bath along with their clothes. Were you not so high up, and I not so far below, I'd take a bite right out of that apple-head of yours until your mouth watered! Good Lord, if there is such a thing as justice, you should pay me a thaler for every drop that's sprinkled my shoulders, since it seems to me this would spoil your pleasure. Withdraw from sight, you ghost up there, or you'll tempt me to scale the wall of your building in order to ascertain whether you're wearing woman's or man's hair. The outrage of being sprinkled like this is enough to turn a man into a devil!"

Simon was whipping himself into a frenzy with this vulgar speech. It did him good to be able to shout and bluster. A few moments later, after all, he'd be lying in bed fast asleep. How tedious it was always to be doing exactly the same thing. Starting tomorrow, he would resolve to become a different person. The next day, sitting in the Copyists Office, filled with and distracted by his thoughts of Klara, he made many slips of the pen, causing the secretary of the Office, a former staff captain, to reproach him and threaten that he'd be given no more work if he didn't intend to go about it more conscientiously.

Autumn came. Simon had walked so many more times though the nocturnal warmth of the alley, and he walked there still, but now the season was no longer mild. You could tell the trees out in the meadows must be losing their leaves even if you didn't go there yourself to watch the leaves falling. Even in the alleyway you could feel it. One sunny autumn day Klaus had arrived, a scholarly project and plans had brought him to the region for a day. Lured by the beautiful sunshine, the two of them walked out into the high hilly fields, not saying much and carefully avoiding all-too-intimate topics of conversation. The path led them through a forest and then out again past wide expanses of meadow whose late, succulent grass Klaus admired along with the brown-spotted cows grazing there. Simon had found it lovely, a bit pensive but nonetheless lovely, to be walking there beside Klaus without much fuss or conversation through the autumnal lowlands, listening to the cowbells, speaking a few words but more often gazing off into the distance than speaking. Then they ascended a wooded hill at a comfortable, leisurely pace, for Klaus wished not to leave behind a single twig or berry without lovingly observing it; then they arrived at the top beside a lovely forest's edge where the unspeakably mild, caressing, autumnal evening sun received them, and where once more an open vista lay before them, a view down into a valley in which a glimmering white river snaked along between yellow treetops and the little woods sticking out, passing a charming red-roofed village amid the brown slopes of the vineyards that couldn't help but bring joy to all who saw them. Here they'd thrown themselves down upon the meadow and for a long time lay there quietly, without speaking, letting their eyes feast on the vast expanses of land and their ears on the sound of the bells, both of them thinking that somehow, somewhere sounds can be heard in every landscape even when no bells are ringing, and then they'd had one of those silent conversations, more felt than spoken, that cannot be written down and have no other purpose than establishing goodwill, conversations that aren't trying to say anything at all but whose scents and sounds and intentions nonetheless remain unforgettable. Klaus had said: "Certainly if I can be allowed to imagine things might still turn out well with you, I'd be of better cheer. The thought of you becoming a useful, purposeful, fulfilled human being has always filled my heart with the loveliest chiming and pealing. You're as well equipped as anyone to enjoy people's respect, and on top of this you have qualities others lack, though in you they're too ardent and avid. You've just got to dampen your avidness and stop making demands on yourself so testily. This harms a person, it wears you down and eventually turns you cold, take my word for it. If you happen not to find every last little thing in this world to your liking, this is not by a long shot grounds for feeling resentment. Others' opinions and dispositions must prevail as well, and overly good intentions are far more likely to poison a man's heart than their opposite, though that too is a malaise. You possess, it seems to me, too much desire to leap about. Running yourself breathless while chasing after some goal gives you pleasure. That won't do. Let every day take its calm, natural, rounded-off course, and be a bit more proud of having made things comfortable for yourself, as after all is fitting for a human being. It's our duty to set an example for others of how to live a life of ease with dignity and a certain gravitas, for we live surrounded by quiet pensive cultural worries that are far removed from the hot resentful breath of the scufflers and brawlers. You have—I must say this to you—something savage about you, and then, in the blink of an eye, you can change course and display a tenderness that then requires too much tenderness on the part of others to survive. Many things that should hurt you don't offend you in the least, while you allow yourself to be wounded by quite ordinary things, natural products of the world and of life. You must try to become one of a multitude, then things will surely go well for you, as you know no weariness when it comes to fulfilling demands, and once you've won people's love, you'll feel the urge to prove to them that you deserve it. The way you are now, you're just slinking around corners and expiring in sentimental longings not truly worthy of a citizen, human being and above all a man. So many things occur to me that you might undertake and do to solidify your standing, but in the end I must leave to you the labor of giving shape to your own life, for advice is rarely worth a fig."—Simon said then: "Why are you filled with worries on so beautiful a day when looking out into the distance can make a person dissolve in happiness?" —

Then the two of them chatted about nature and forgot all serious matters.

The next day Klaus departed.

Then winter arrived. How strange: Time marched right past all good intentions just as surely as past the bad qualities one hasn't yet overcome. There was something beautiful, accepting and forgiving in this passage of time. It swept past both the beggar and the president of the Republic, the strumpet and the lady of refinement. It made many things appear small and unimportant, for it alone represented the sublime and the grand. What could life's hustle and bustle signify, all those stirrings and strivings, compared to this loftiness that paid no heed to whether a person became a man or a simpleton, and found it a matter of indifference whether or not one desired what was right and good. Simon loved to hear the rustle of seasons overhead, and when one day snow flew down into the dark, black alleyway, he felt joy at seeing the progress of eternal welcoming nature. "Nature is snowing, it's winter, and, fool that I am, I believed I wouldn't experience another winter," he thought. It seemed to him like a fairy tale: "Once upon a time there were snowflakes that, not having anything better to do, flew down to earth. Many of them flew into the field and remained lying there, others fell upon rooftops and remained lying there, and yet more and different ones fell upon the hats and caps of the rapidly hurrying people and remained lying there until they were shaken off, and a few, a very few, flew into the loyal dear face of a horse that stood hitched to a cart and remained lying upon the horse's long eyelashes, one snowflake flew in through a window, but what it did there is something no one knows, in any case it remained lying there. In the alley it's snowing, and in the forest high up on the mountain—oh, how beautiful it must be now in the forest. A person could go there. With any luck it'll still be snowing in the evening when the lanterns are lit. Once there was a man who was all black, he wanted to wash, but he had no soapy water. As he now saw that it was snowing, he went out into the street and washed with snow water, which made his face as white as snow. This was something for him to boast about, which he certainly did. But he got a cough and now he was constantly running around coughing, for one entire year this poor man was forced to cough, until the next winter came. Then he ran up the mountain until he was sweating, and still he was coughing. His coughing just wouldn't stop. Then a small child came up to him, it was a beggar child with a snowflake in its hand, the flake looked like a small, delicate flower. 'Eat the snowflake,' the child said. And now this big man ate the snowflake, and his cough was gone. Then the sun went down and everything was dark. The beggar child sat in the snow and yet didn't freeze. At home it had been given a beating, it didn't know what for. It was just a little child and didn't know anything yet. Even its little feet weren't cold, and yet they were bare. In the child's eye a tear was glistening, but it wasn't yet clever enough to know it was crying. Perhaps the child froze to death during the night, but it felt nothing, felt nothing at all, it was too small to feel anything. God saw the child, but this did not move Him, He was too big to feel anything—"

These days Simon was forcing himself to leap out of bed

early despite the wintry cold that reigned in his room, even if there was nothing in particular he had to do. Then he'd simply stand there, gritting his teeth, waiting for an occasion for action to present itself. There was always something or other to do. After all, he could always while away the time by rubbing his hands or back, or else try walking across the floor on his hands. He always had to be exerting his will in some way, even in the most ridiculous fashion, as this drove away thoughts and steeled and enlivened the body. Every morning he washed in cold water from top to bottom until he was glowing, and he didn't deign to put on a coat before going out. This season he intended to teach himself to ward things off! He used his coat to wrap his feet in when he sat at the table reading. He acquired a pair of bulky, sturdy shoes such as recruits wear in the military so he could wade up the mountain in the deep snow at any time. That would teach him to so much as glance at elegant footwear. With such a solid pair of shoes, one stood twice as firmly in the world. The main thing now was to keep one's feet on the ground and stand firm. If he could just keep his head high, something was sure to turn up for him of its own accord, something proper he could grasp hold of. Starting over from the beginning, even if it was for the fiftieth time now, what did it matter. As long as his gaze and mind remained alert, the thing he needed was sure to come.

These days he resembled a person who'd lost some money and was exerting the full force of his will to get it back, but besides exerting his will was doing nothing else to this end.

Around Christmastime he went walking up the slope of the mountain. It was getting on toward evening and terribly cold. A biting wind whistled about people's noses and ears, which grew red and inflamed from the cold. Simon automatically chose the path that once had led to Klara's woodland home and now had been cleared and widened. Everywhere the trace of transforming human hands was visible. He saw a large but nonetheless charming building on the very spot where the wooden chalet used to stand that he'd gone into so often when Kaspar was still painting there, with the dear, peculiar woman living in it. Now a health resort had been established there, and it appeared to be quite popular, for any number of well-dressed people were going in and out. Simon spent a moment considering whether he too should go inside, but the bitter cold alone was enough to make the thought of a warm room filled with people agreeable. And so he went in. The warm acrid smell of fir twigs engulfed him, the entire large bright room, practically a ballroom, was trimmed and lined with fir branches, all but wallpapered with them. Only the proverbs painted on the white walls had been left exposed, and one could read them. At all the tables sat gay and solemn people, many women, but also men and children, seated singly at round little tables or else clustered in groups about a long table. The smell of the drinks and food combined with the yuletide scent of pines. Prettily dressed girls walked around, serving the guests in a friendly and at the same time utterly unhurried way that had nothing at all waitressly about it. It looked as if these enchanting girls were only waiting on table here as part of some smiling game, or as if they were merely providing this service to their parents, relatives, brothers, sisters or their children, for it all looked so parental and filial at the same time. A small stage that was also thickly framed with fir twigs stood at another end of the hall, perhaps intended for the performance of some Christmas play or a skit with some other charming content. In any case, it was a warm, friendly, hospitable-looking room, and Simon sat down alone at a round little table, waiting to see whether one of the girls would come over to him to ask what he desired. But for the time being none of them came. And so he remained sitting there quietly at the little table for quite some time, propping his chin in his hand as young men are wont to do, when suddenly a slender tall lady approached him; she gave him a friendly nod, and then, turning to one of the girls with an exclamation, asked how this young man could have been left sitting here for so long unattended. This reproach was delivered in manner more kind and laughing than serious, but in any case this lady was a sort of director or manager or whatever it was called.

"Please forgive us for leaving you alone so long," she said, turning back to Simon.

"Oh, I don't know what there is to forgive. I should be asking forgiveness instead for obliging you to reproach one of your serving girls. In fact I'm quite happy to be sitting here unnoticed, for in all honesty I can't give the serving girl much by way of an order—"

"Eat and drink as much as you like. You don't have to pay for anything," the lady said.

"Is that just for me, or for everyone here?"

"Just for you, of course, and only because I shall give orders that no one is to ask anything of you."

She sat down beside him at the small brown table:

"I've got a moment's time to chat with you and don't see why I shouldn't. You appear to be a lonely young man, your eyes are telling me so, and they're also saying quite clearly that the person to whom they belong feels a desire to come into contact with other people. I'm not sure why I can't help taking you for a well-educated person. When I saw you sitting here, I at once felt an urge to speak with you. If I'd bothered to observe you with my keen lorgnette, I'd perhaps have discovered that you look somewhat tattered, but who would wish to learn to recognize people only with the help of glasses? As the director of this establishment, I have an interest in learning as accurately as possible who my guests are. I've made it my habit to judge people not by a shabby fedora but by the way they move, which explicates their characters better than good or poor items of clothing, and in the course of time I've found this to be the right path to follow. May God preserve me, if he means at all well by me, from becoming snobby or supercilious. A businesswoman who isn't a good observer of human nature will in time come to make bad business decisions, and what does our ever-increasing knowledge of human nature teach us? The simplest thing in the world: To be kind and friendly to all! Are not all of us who live upon this lone lost planet brothers and sisters? Siblings! The brothers of sisters, sisters of sisters, and sisters of brothers? This can all be quite affectionate, and indeed it must always be so: above all in one's thoughts! But then it must also burgeon and come to fruition. If an uncouth man or a female simpleton comes before me, what can I do? Must I immediately feel deterred and put off? Oh, not at all, not at all! I then think to myself: No, this person is certainly not so agreeable to me, I find him repulsive, he's uncultured and presumptuous, but there's no cause to make either him or myself all too conscious of this fact. I must dissemble a little, and then perhaps he will do so as well, if only out of indolence or stupidity. How nice it is to be considerate. I secretly carry a sacred, ardent conviction that this is true, and that's all I can say on the subject. Or perhaps just this one thing more: A brother need not necessarily be one of the finest and most select individuals, and yet he can—perhaps, let us say, at a certain appropriate distance—be a brother. I've made this my own personal law, and it's stood me in good stead. Many people come to like me whose first glimpse of me made them shrug their shoulders and grimace. Why should I not, with regard to so charming a principle as exercising an affectionate observant patience, be a tiny bit Christian? All of us perhaps have more need of Christianity now than ever before; but I'm speaking foolishly. You smiled, and I know perfectly well what you're smiling about. You're right, why do I have to bring up Christianity when it's merely a question of simple sensible amicability? Do you know what? Sometimes I think to myself: Christian duty has in our lifetimes been quietly, almost imperceptibly giving way to human duty, which is far simpler and more easily put into practice. But now I must go. They're calling me. Stay where you are, I'll be back—"

With this, she went off.

Several minutes later she returned and, still at a distance of several paces, resumed the conversation by exclaiming: "How encompassed by novelty everything here is! Just look around: Everything is fresh, novel, newborn. Not a single memory of anything old! Usually every house, every family possesses some old piece of furniture, a whiff of olden times, a concrete souvenir that we still love and honor because we find it beautiful, just as we find a scene of parting or a melancholy sunset beautiful. Do you see anything of the sort here, even the faintest hint of memory? It seems to me like a dizzying, curved, light bridge leading into the as yet inexplicable future. Oh, to gaze into the future is more beautiful than dreaming about the past. It's also a sort of dreaming when you imagine a future. Isn't there something marvelous about this? Wouldn't it be cleverer for persons of fine sensibilities to devote their warmth and inklings to the days yet to come rather than those that lie in the past? Times yet to come are like children to us and need more attention than the graves of the departed, which we adorn perhaps with somewhat too exaggerated a love: these bygone days! A painter will do well now to sketch costumes for distant people who will possess the grace to wear them in decorum and freedom; let the poet dream up virtues for strong individuals not gnawed at by longing, and the architect design as best he can forms that will charmingly give life to the stone and to building itself, let him go to the forest and there take note of how tall and noble the firs shoot up from the ground, let him take them as a model for the buildings of the future; and let man in general, in anticipation of things to come, cast off much that is common, ignoble and unserviceable, and whisper his thoughts into the ear of his wife as clearly as he can when she offers him her lips for a kiss, and the woman will smile. We women understand how to spur you men on to perform deeds with our smiles, and we fancy we've done our duty when we've succeeded in vividly, delightfully filling your senses with your own duties, just by virtue of a smile. The things you achieve make us happier than our own accomplishments. We read the books you write and think: If only they were willing to do a bit more and write a bit less. In general we don't know what would bring much more profit than subordinating ourselves to you. What else can we do! And how willingly we do so. But now of course I've forgotten to speak of the future, this bold arch across dark waters, this forest full of trees, this child with gleaming eyes, this unspeakable entity that always tempts one to catch it in words as if in a snare. No, I believe the present is the future. Doesn't everything around us seem to radiate presentness?"

"Yes," Simon said.

"Outside the winter's so horribly severe now, and here indoors it's so warm, so perfect for having conversations and for my sitting here beside you, a quite young and apparently somewhat down-at-the-heels person, and any minute now I'll be neglecting my duties. Your comportment has something fascinating about it, do you realize this? One can't help wanting to box your ears straight off, out of a secret fury at the way you sit here so foolishly and yet have such a strange capacity to seduce a person into wasting her precious time with you, a random guest. Do you know what: Why don't you go on sitting there a while longer. Surely you're not in so much of a hurry. I'll come back later to have another crack at your ears. For the moment, duty calls—"

And she was gone.

In the lady's absence, Simon observed his surroundings. The

lamps gave off a bright warm light. People were chatting unrestrainedly with one another. A few of them, now that night had fallen, were leaving because they still had to go back down the mountain to return to town. Two old men sitting cozily at a table struck him because of the tranquil way they sat there. Both of them had white beards and rather fresh faces and were smoking pipes, which gave them a patriarchal air. They didn't speak to one another, apparently considering that superfluous. Now and then their respective pairs of eyes would meet, and then there was a shrugging of pipes and the corners of mouths, but this all occurred quite tranquilly and no doubt as a matter of habit. They appeared to be idlers, but calculating, premeditated, superior idlers—idle out of prosperity. Surely the two of them had taken up with one another only because they shared these same habits: smoking their pipes, taking little walks, a fondness for wind, weather and nature, good health, preferring silence to chatter, and finally age itself with all its special perquisites. To Simon the two of them appeared not lacking in dignity. One couldn't help smiling a little at the appealing cordoned-off spectacle they presented, but this spectacle did not exclude reverence, which age itself demands as its right. A sense of purpose was expressed in their tranquil visages; they possessed a completeness that could in no way be disputed any longer. These old men were most certainly beyond entertaining uncertainties as to the path they'd chosen, even if it had been chosen in error. But then what did it mean to be in error? If a person picked an error as his lodestar at the age of sixty or seventy, this was a sacrosanct matter to which a young man must respond with reverence. These two old codgers—for there was certainly something codger-like about them—must have had some sort of procedure or a system according to which they'd sworn to one another to go on living until the end of their days; that's how they looked, like two people who'd found something that worked and made it possible for them to await their end with equanimity. "The two of us have found it out, that secret"—this is what their expressions and bearing seemed to say. It was amusing and touching and no doubt worth pondering to observe them and attempt to guess their thoughts. Among other things, one quickly guessed that these two would always only be seen as a pair and never any other way, never singly, always together! Always! This was the main thought you felt emanating from their white heads. Side by side through life, maybe even side by side down into the abyss of death: This appeared to be their guiding principle. And indeed, they even looked like a couple of living, old, but nonetheless still jolly and good-humored principles. When summer came again, the two of them would be seen sitting outside on the shady terrace, but they'd still keep filling their pipes with a mysterious air and prefer silence to speech. When they left, it would always be the two of them leaving, not first one and then the other: This seemed unthinkable. Yes, they looked cozy, this much Simon had to give them: cozy and hardheaded, he thought, looking away from them to gaze at something else.

He cast fleeting glances at various people and discovered an English family with strange faces, men who appeared to be scholars and others to whom it would have been difficult to ascribe any sort of post or profession; he saw women with white hair and girls with their bridegrooms, observed people who—one could tell just by looking—felt somewhat ill at ease here and others who seemed just as comfortable as if they were sitting at home in the bosom of their families. But the hall was rapidly emptying. Outside winter was howling and one could hear the fir trees creaking as they knocked together. The forest lay a mere ten paces removed from the building, Simon knew well from earlier days.

While he was abandoning himself to his thoughts in this way, the proprietress reappeared.

She sat down beside him.

A silent change appeared to have taken place in her. She seized Simon's hand: This was unexpected. —Hereupon she said quietly, overheard by no one, and unobserved:

"Now it's unlikely they'll disturb me again and prevent my sitting here with you, people are starting to leave. Tell me, who are you, what's your name, where are you from? You look as if one must ask these things. You emit a certain wondering and amazement, not amazement that you yourself feel—it's rather the person sitting in front of you who feels amazed, observing you. One wonders about you, feels amazed, and then is filled with a longing to hear you talk, imagining what it must be that is speaking within you. A person involuntarily worries on your account. One goes away from you and does one's work, and then suddenly one's taking mercy on you by thinking about you. It isn't pity, for pity is something you by no means inspire, nor is it truly mercy, strictly speaking. I don't know what it could be: curiosity, perhaps? Let me reflect for a moment. Curiosity? A desire to know something about you, just one little thing, some sound or note. One has the impression one already knows you and finds you not terribly interesting but nonetheless listens and listens, just in case you say something that might be worth hearing from your lips a second time. Looking at you, a person can't help feeling sorry for you: casually, condescendingly, looking down on you from above. You must have something profound about you, but no one seems to notice because you make no effort at all to let it shine forth. I'd like to hear what you have to tell. Do you have parents still, and siblings? Just looking at you, one cannot help assuming your sisters and brothers must be important people. You yourself, however, a person cannot help considering utterly insignificant. Why is this? It's so easy to feel superior to you. But one need only speak with you a short while to realize one's succumbed to the sort of error liable to occur when speaking to so even-tempered a person, someone who'd scorn the notion of snapping to attention and who has no wish to look better or more dangerous than he is. You don't look particularly interesting, let alone dangerous—and women are what you get when you combine the need for tenderness with a lust for unadulterated danger, a constant source of peril. Of course you won't hold what I've just said against me, for you hold no grudges. One doesn't know where one stands with you. Would you tell me your story, I'm so eager to hear it! Do you know, I'd very much like to be your confidante, even if only for an hour, and perhaps even if it's just in my imagination. When I was upstairs just now I felt such an urge to hurry back to you as if you were an important personage who mustn't be kept waiting and whose good graces and even condescending respect it's crucial to enjoy. And what I found was a person whose cheeks glow more brightly when I come running up! How silly of me, but isn't this odd all the same? All right now, I shall sit quietly now and listen to you—"

Simon said to her:

"My name is Tanner, Simon Tanner, and I have four siblings, I am the youngest and the one who occasions the fewest hopes. One brother is a painter, he lives in Paris, and he lives there more quietly and reclusively than in a village, for he is painting. He must have changed a bit by now, it's been over a year since I last saw him, but I think if you were to meet him the impression you'd have is of an important and utterly autonomous person. Getting close to him is not without its perils: He captivates people in such a way that one can commit foolhardy acts for his sake. He's a consummate artist, and if I, his brother, understand something about art, it's to his credit rather than my own understanding, which only developed a little as it was drawn to him. I think he must be wearing long curls now, but on him the curls look as natural as a closely shorn head on an officer, they aren't obtrusive. He disappears in the crowd, and it's his wish to disappear so he can work in peace. Once in a letter to me he wrote something about an eagle that spreads its pinions above rocky crags and feels most at home hovering above chasms, and another time he wrote to me that a man and artist must work like a horse—collapsing from exhaustion meant nothing at all, it was necessary to collapse and get back up again at once to return to work. He was still just a boy then, and now he paints pictures. If some day he ceases to be able to paint, he'll scarcely be alive any longer. His name is Kaspar, and as a schoolboy he was always considered a lazybones both at school and in the parental home, take my word for it, and this was only because his general manner was so placid, so mild. He was taken out of school at an early age since he wasn't doing well there, and had to carry about boxes and crates, and then he escaped from his homeland, and outside it learned to compel people to give him the respect he deserved. He's one of my brothers, and another is named Klaus. Klaus is the oldest, and I consider him the best and most thoughtful person in all the world. His very gaze bespeaks his forbearance, scrupulousness and consideration. He's an able man, so very able that his modest, discreet abilities will always remain hidden. He watched us younger ones grow up and devote ourselves to our desires and passions, he observed this all in silence and waited, occasionally speaking a word of concern or advice, but always he saw that everyone must tread his own path, he merely did what he could to avert misfortune, and his uncanny acuity of vision always let him discern what was good in a person. This brother is secretly worried about me, I know this quite well, for he loves me, in fact he loves all people and has a strangely shy esteem for them that we younger ones lack. Although he holds a position of prominence in the scholarly world, I am nonetheless convinced that only his scrupulousness—which is tempered always with shyness—is to blame for his not yet occupying an even higher one, because he deserves the very highest position, the one of greatest responsibility. I have a third brother as well who is unfortunate and nothing more; all that remains of him is what memories of his earlier days can tell a person. He's in the madhouse—shouldn't I be permitted to state this candidly? Given that you're sitting here listening to me with such an attentively harkening ear, I assume you're interested in hearing all there is to tell in its most truthful form or else nothing at all, isn't that right? You nod, which says to me I already know you rather well if I make bold to assume you to be a simultaneously kind-hearted and courageous woman. Please keep listening. This unfortunate brother was surely, and I may say so without hesitation, the ideal of a young beautiful man, and he had talents that would have been better suited to the gallant, charming eighteenth century than our times, whose demands are so much harder and drier. Allow me to pass over his misfortune in silence; for in the first place talk of it might dishearten you, and secondly and thirdly, and as far as I'm concerned sixthly, it isn't proper to tug apart all the folds of misfortune and cast aside all ceremony, all lovely veiled mourning, which can exist only when one keeps silent on such matters. I've now given you a tentative, sketchy portrait of my brothers, and now a girl will appear, a lonely schoolmistress sequestered in a little village with thatched roofs, my sister Hedwig. Would you like to make her acquaintance? You and all your sensibilities would be delighted by this girl. There is no prouder creature on all the planet. I lived a full three months with her in idleness in the countryside; she wept when I arrived and laughed at me when, suitcase in hand, I tried to bid her a tender farewell. She threw me out, and at the same time gave me a kiss. She said to me that all she felt for me was a faint, insuppressible contempt, but she said that so sweetly

I couldn't help but feel it as a caress. Just imagine, she gave me shelter in her home when I came to her with more beggarly, more importunate demands than the most insolent vagabond who only remembered his sister because it occurred to him: "You can go there until you're standing on your own two feet again." —But then we lived for three entire months as if in a gay pleasure garden filled with bower-lined paths. Such a thing can never be forgotten. When I went out and took walks in the woods, finding myself too indolent to know whether to scratch my chin or behind my ears, I dreamed of her, of her alone, as if wanting to dream of what was simultaneously closest and farthest away. She was far from me out of reverence and close out of love. She was so proud, I'll have you know, that she never allowed me to feel how very shabby I must have appeared to her. She just felt glad when I made myself at home and settled in with her. This persisted until the very last hour, and then she simply cut my farewell off before it left my lips, in the presentiment that I would say only hurtful, stupid things. When I'd left, I turned to look back down the hill behind me and saw her waving at me amicably and simply, as if I were just heading off to the nearest village cobbler and would return in an hour's time. And yet she knew she was being left behind, alone with her isolation, and would be faced with the task of adjusting to the absence of a companion—and this certainly was a task, an internal labor. When we sat together in the evenings, we'd tell each other stories about our lives, and we heard the wings of childhood beating once more, just as our mother's dress would rustle on the floor of the room when she came toward her children. My mother and my sister Hedwig always comprise in my head an intimately con-joined and interwoven image. When our mother fell ill, it was Hedwig who cared for and tended her, as one must tend a little child. Just imagine: A child must watch her own mother become a child, and becomes a mother to her own mother. What a strange displacement of feelings. My mother was a highly re-spected woman, and the esteem she received from all sides was pure and heartfelt. The impression she made was always at once rural and refined. Simultaneously unassuming and dismissive, she could quickly put a damper on disobedience and unkind-ness. Her expression could ask and command at one and the same time. How the ladies in our town would cluster about her when she went for a walk, how many gentlemen's hats were doffed before her. Then, when she fell ill, she was forgotten and became an object of worry and shame. For one feels ashamed when a family member is ill and is almost enraged to remember the days when a healthy woman commanded the respect of all who knew her. Shortly before her death—I was fourteen years old at the time—she sat down at noon one day to write a letter: "My beloved son." But do you imagine her whimsically slender handwriting continued any further than this salutation? No, she just gave a weary confused smile, murmured something and was compelled to lay down the pen once more. There she sat, there lay the beginning of a letter to her son, there the pen, and the sun was shining out of doors, and I observed all these things. One night Hedwig then knocked at the door of my room, telling me to get up, Mother had died. A thin ray of light fell through the crack of the door as I leapt out of bed. As a girl, my mother had been unhappy, born into unfavorable circumstances. She left the distant mountains and came to live in town with her sister, my aunt—where she was forced to work as a maid practically. As a child she walked a long road deeply covered in snow to get to school, and she did her homework in a tiny little room by the light of a paltry candle stub that made her eyes hurt because she could scarcely read the letters in her book. Her parents were unkind to her, and so she became acquainted with melancholy at an early age, and one day, when she was a girl, she stood leaning against the railings of a bridge, wondering whether it wouldn't be better to leap down into the river. She must have been neglected, shunted back and forth and in this way maltreated. When as a boy I once heard about her wicked childhood, I trembled with indignation, rage shot into my face, and from then on I hated the unknown figures of my grandparents. For her children, our mother had, when she was still healthy, something almost majestic about her that frightened and intimidated us; when she became ill in her mind, we pitied her. It was a crazy leap to make: from fearful, mystical awe to pity. All that lay between—tenderness and trust—remained unknown to us. And so it happened that our pity was strongly intermingled with an unspeakable regret over all we'd never felt, which then caused us to pity her all the more deeply. I remembered all my boyish pranks, all my disrespectful behavior—and then the sound of our mother's voice, with which she meted out punishments even at a distance, so that the actual physical punishment that followed was sweet, laughable sugar-candy by comparison. She employed just the right tone of voice to make you instantly regret the error you'd committed and desire to see her outrage mollified as quickly as possible. There was something so wonderfully mild about her mildness, and seeing it was like receiving a present; we didn't receive it often. Oversensitive irritability was my mother's usual state. We weren't nearly as frightened of our father as of her, we feared only that he might say or do something that would cause Mother to fly into a rage. He was powerless before her—it was in his nature to prize vigor far less than relaxation. He was a boon companion, and as such well-loved, but when it came to difficult matters, he wasn't the one to take things in hand. Now he's eighty years old, and when he dies, a piece of town history will die along with him; the old people will shake their heads more pensively and wearily when they no longer see the old man going about his business, which he still does today, and on fairly spry legs. In his youth he was rather a wild fellow who was gradually polished by city life, but this life also gave him a taste for luxury. Both Mother and Father came from rugged, secluded, mountainous regions and then found themselves in a town that even at the time was known, if not notorious, for its liberal vitality. Industry was flourishing in those days like a fiery plant, permitting an easy, carefree lifestyle—much money was earned, and much spent. When five or six days a week were workdays, this was considered industriousness. Workers lay for days at a time upon the sunny riverbank, catching fish, when they weren't getting up to mischief. And whenever they needed more money to finance this life, they'd go work a few days more, earning enough to return to their leisure. The craftsmen were making money off the workers, for when even the poor have money, how much more prosperous must the well-to-do be. The city appeared to have acquired an additional ten thousand inhabitants overnight, everyone came streaming in from the surrounding countryside into buildings that were occupied and filled the moment they looked on the outside as though they might be finished, never mind how damp and dirty the inside might still be. Construction firms were having a heyday, all they had to do was keep producing buildings, which they did as shoddily as could be managed. Factory owners rode around on horseback, and their ladies traveled in barouches while the town's old nobility observed these activities and sniffed. On festival days the town went all out, surpassing all rivals, and left no stone unturned in its bid to be celebrated everywhere as the best town for revelries. The merchants had nothing to complain about under these circumstances, nor did the schoolchildren; the only ones who felt uneasy were a handful of insightful individuals who couldn't find the courage to join their neighbors on the unsteady, rose-strewn pleasure ground of superficial amusements. Into such surroundings my parents now came, Mother with her irritable sensitivities and her taste for simple refinement, and Father with his talent for assimilating everything around him. For children, every region is lovely and charming, but this particular place, thanks to its setting, was made for children who love to pursue their games amid lairs such as rocks, caves, riverbanks, meadows, hollows, gorges and wooded ravines. And so we enjoyed this entire landscape for our games and inventions until we left school. When Mother died, I was sent to a bank as an apprentice. During the first year I acquitted myself splendidly; for the novelty of what I encountered in this world filled me with timidity and fear. The second year found me a model apprentice, but in the third year of my apprenticeship the director cursed me to the devil, keeping me on only as an act of mercy, in deference to my father, whose close acquaintance he'd been for many years. I'd lost all gusto for work of any sort and spoke insolently to my superiors, whom I considered unworthy of ordering me around. There was something in me that I now find incomprehensible—I recall that everything, every piece of furniture, every object, every word caused me pain. Eventually, I became so timid that the time had come to send me away, and that's what they did. They found me a job in a far-off town just to get rid of me, as I had proved myself utterly useless. And so I left.—But now I don't want to think of the past any longer, nor speak of it. There's something wonderful about having escaped one's early youth, for youth is by no means always beautiful, lovely and easy; often it's harder and more filled with worries than the life of many an old man. The more one has lived, the more gently one lives. A person with a tempestuous youth may well in later years rarely or—preferably—never again behave in a tempestuous manner. When I think of how we children, each of us in turn, had to go through all these things, the years of error and violent emotion, and that all children on earth must do this at their own youthful peril, well then I don't wish to be overhasty in praising the sweetness of childhood, and yet I will praise it, for childhood remains a precious memory all the same. How difficult it often is for parents to be good protective parents; and as for being a well-behaved obedient child—how can this be more

346

than a cheap empty phrase for most children? As a woman, by the way, you know this better than I do. To this day I've remained the least capable of human beings. I don't even have a suit to my name that might bear witness to my having put my life more or less in order. Looking at me, you can't see anything that might point to my having made a certain choice in life. I'm still standing at the door of life, knocking and knocking, though admittedly none too forcefully, and breathlessly listening to see whether someone will decide to open the bolt and let me in. A bolt like this is rather heavy, and people don't like to come to the door if they have the feeling it's just a beggar standing outside knocking. I'm good at nothing but listening and waiting, though in these capacities I've achieved perfection, for I've learned how to dream while waiting. These two things go hand in hand, and dreaming does a person good and preserves respectability. Might I have missed the chance to find my true profession? This is a question I no longer ask myself; a youth might ask such a thing, but not a man. Any profession would have brought me exactly as far as I am now. And why should I concern myself with that! I'm quite conscious of my virtues and weaknesses, and take pains to avoid boasting about either. To every person I offer my knowledge, strength, thoughts, achievements and love if he has any use for them. Anyone who wants need only stick out a finger and beckon, and though many a one would thereupon just come hobbling up, not me—I come leaping and bounding, do you see, the way the wind whistles, and I skip over and tread heedlessly upon memories of all sorts if that lets me run unhindered. And the entire world comes rushing along with me—all of life! That's how it must be, just like that! Nothing in this world is mine, but I no longer yearn for anything. Longing has become a stranger to me. When I still felt certain longings, I found people a matter of indifference, mere hindrances, I sometimes even despised them, but now I love them because I need them and I offer myself to them to be put to use. That's what we're here for. Let's say someone appears and says to me: "Hey there, you, come here! I need you. I can give you work!" This person makes me happy. Then I know what happiness is! Happiness and pain are completely transformed, they become clearer and more comprehensible to me, they elucidate themselves to me, they permit me to woo them in love and anguish, to court them. Whenever I must submit a letter of application to someone offering my services, I always draw attention to my brothers and point out that since they have both proven to be useful productive individuals, I too might perhaps also be of use, which makes me laugh every time. I'm not at all worried that I myself might not, some day, take on some form, but I want to put off forming myself as long as possible. And then it would be best if this came about of its own accord, unintentionally. Now, for starters, I've had myself measured for a pair of sturdy broad shoes with which I shall tread more firmly and show people with my very footsteps that I am a person with a purpose and no doubt abilities as well. To be put to the test is a pleasure for me! I scarcely know any higher pleasure. That I am poor at the moment, what does that signify? It needn't mean anything at all, it's merely the tiniest slip in the overall composition that can be erased again with a few vigorous strokes. It might at most cause a healthy person a moment of embarrassment, perhaps even worry, but certainly not alarm. You're laughing. No? You're saying you weren't? What a shame that would be, for your laughter is a beautiful thing. For a time it was always my idea that I could become a soldier, but I no longer quite trust this romantic notion. Why not remain where one is? If it's my intention to perish, can it be that no suitable opportunities are available to me in this country? I should be able to find a more worthy occasion here for putting my health, strength and joie de vivre on the line. For the moment, I'm delighted about my health and the joy of being able to move my legs and arms at will, then about my mind, which I still find quite lively, and finally about the thrilling recognition that I stand here before the world as a deeply burdened debtor who has every reason to finally take a deep breath and start working himself back into the world's good graces. I adore being a debtor! If I had no choice but to tell myself that humankind had insulted me, I'd be inconsolable. Then I'd have to withdraw into apathy, antipathy and bitterness. No, things stand quite differently, they stand brilliantly, they couldn't possibly stand any more brilliantly for a person just becoming a man: It is I—I—who have insulted the world. The world stands before me like an infuriated, offended mother: that wonderful face I'm so in love with: the face of Mother Earth, demanding atonement! I tally up everything I've neglected, squandered, dreamed away, overlooked and transgressed. I shall satisfy the one I've offended, and then some day, in some beautiful, intimate evening hour, I'll tell my siblings all about how I managed to make things turn out in such a way that I can hold my head high. It might take years, but after all, I find a task all the more delightful the longer and more difficult the exertions it requires. Now you know me a little."

The lady kissed him.

"No," she said, "you won't sink. If such a thing were to happen, what a shame it would be—a shame for you. You must never again condemn yourself so criminally, so sinfully. You respect yourself too little, and others too much. I wish to shield you against judging yourself so harshly. Do you know what it is you need? You need things to go well for you again for a little while. You must learn to whisper into an ear and reciprocate expressions of tenderness. Otherwise you'll become too delicate. I shall teach you; I wish to teach you all the things you're lacking. Come with me. We shall go out into the winter night. Into the blustery forest. There's so much I must say to you. Do you know that I'm your poor, happy prisoner? Not another word, not one word more. Just come—"